Anonymous

Book of Popular Songs

Being a Compendium of the Best Sentimental, Comic, Negro, Irish...

Anonymous

Book of Popular Songs
Being a Compendium of the Best Sentimental, Comic, Negro, Irish...

ISBN/EAN: 9783744786317

Printed in Europe, USA, Canada, Australia, Japan

Cover: Foto ©Andreas Hilbeck / pixelio.de

More available books at **www.hansebooks.com**

THE

BOOK OF POPULAR SONGS,

BEING A

COMPENDIUM OF THE BEST

SENTIMENTAL, COMIC, NEGRO, **IRISH**, **SCOTCH**,
NATIONAL, PATRIOTIC, MILITARY, NAVAL,
SOCIAL, CONVIVIAL AND PATHETIC
SONGS, BALLADS AND MELODIES,

AS SUNG

BY THE MOST CELEBRATED OPERA AND BALLAD
SINGERS, NEGRO MINSTRELS AND COMIC
VOCALISTS **OF THE DAY.**

PHILADELPHIA:
G. G. EVANS, PUBLISHER,
No. 439 CHESTNUT STREET.
1861.

CONTENTS.

	PAGE
A Mother's Love	17
A Cottage by the Sea	23
A Parody on the Last Rose of Summer	26
All's for the Best	37
A Song of the Oak	61
Away, away, to the Mountain's Brow	77
Ah! Mourn Her Not	85
Across the mountains, Ho	89
Am I not fondly thine own	89
Annot Lyle	92
American Star, The	127
Age of Progress	132
American Boy, The	144
Angel's Whisper, The	170
Annie Laurie	178
Auld Lang Syne	190
All's Well	205
A Yankee ship and a Yankee crew	205
Anchor's Weighed, The	215
A Wet Sheet and a Flowing Sea	215
A Health to the Outward Bound	216
A Life on the Ocean Wave	218
Author and Cobbler	249
A Glass is good and a Lass is good	267
Aint I glad to get out of the Wilderness	287
A Few Days	300
Ahoo! Ahoo!	305

	PAGE
By the Sad Sea Waves	24
Bell Brandon	28
Batti, Batti	39
Be Mine, Dear Maid	42
Behold how Brightly Breaks the Morning	44
Bird Song	73
Beautiful Star	94
Battle Song, from Norma	112
Bosting Tea Party	139
Brother Jonathan	145
Bryan O'Linn	168
Bold Soldier Boy	174
Bonnie Jean	193
Bruce's Address	194
Banks of Allan Water	197
Ben Bolt	204
Barney, Leave the girls Alone	227
Billy Barlow	248
Bag of Nails	254
Belle of Baltimore	302
Backside of Albany	208
Bachelors' Hall	159
Canadian Boat Song	14
Come, Maiden, with Me	20
Come Brave the Sea	39
Chide Me, Chide Me!	39
Come, Oh Come With Me	45
Come, Come Away	51
Cavalier, The	57
Come, Arouse thee	70
Come, Listen to my Song	93
Cavaliers' Battle Call, The	109
Come, strike the bold Anthem	127
Columbia's our Happy Land	130
Columbia the Gem of the Ocean	138
Cross-keen Lawn	169
Capting Kydde	199
Convivial Song, Success to Toddy	262
Cove what Spouts, The	268

PAGE

Come, Darkies, Listen to my Story.. 292
Camptown Races.. 296

Drink ye to Her that each Loves Best.. 41
Do They miss me at Home... 49
Don't be Angry, Mother.. 68
Do I not Prove thee... 82
Death of Osceola.. 99
Darlin' Ould Stick.. 156
Don't be addicted to Drinking... 235
Days when I was Hard Up... 273
Dolly Day... 285
Dan Tucker.. 289
Dearest Mae... 301
Days when this Old Nigger was young, The.. 315

Ever of Thee.. 13
Ever Be Happy... 55
Ellen Bayne... 72
Erin is my Home... 151
Exile of Erin... 160
Erin Mavourneen... 171
Ethiopian Medley.. 313
Ever be Happy, Negro Chorus... 308

Farewell to the Home of my Childhood.. 63
Farm Maid and the Fop, The.. 123
Flag of our Union, The.. 128
Freedom of Elections, The... 143
Flaming O'Flanigan.. 158
Flower of Ellerslie... 189
Flow Gently, Sweet Afton.. 189
Far, far upon the Sea... 203
Far o'er the Deep Blue Sea.. 219
Few Days.. 300

Gentle Annie.. 19
Gaffer Green.. 46
Gascon Vespers.. 70
Golden Girl, The.. 78
Gentle Zitella.. 98

PAGE

God Bless the Farmer's Toil........121
Groves of Blarney, The........155
Gow's Farewell to Whiskey, O........192
Grieving's a Folly........213
Gunpowder Tea........223
Gawkey Shanks........234
Great Hen Convention........265
Gentle Jennie Gray........281
Gum Tree Canoe........293
Gal from de South........304
Good-bye, Sally, Dear........309

Home, Sweet Home........15
Here's a Health to all Good Lasses........28
Hazel Dell........30
Helen is the Fairest Flower........75
Home Again........84
He Came Not........87
Happy Birdling........95
Hard Times, Come again no More........105
Harvester's Joy........124
Hail Columbia........131
Harp that once through Tara's Halls, The........163
Hail to the Chief........196
Harry Bluff........212
Have you seen my Sister........231
Here's Success to Toddy........262
Hard Times........272
Here's to the Maiden........279
Hop De Dooden Doo........316

In Happy Moments........19
I am the Bayadere........21
Ivy Green, The........64
In this Old Chair........66
I Dreamt that I dwelt in Marble Halls........73
I Have something sweet to tell You........87
Indian Girl, The........94
Indian Warrior's Grave, The........96
Indian Hunter, The........97
Independence Day........137

PAGE

Immortal Washington... 146
Irish Wedding............... 161
Irish Love Letter, The................ 171
Irishman's Shanty, **The**................... 172
Ingle Side, The... 193
I Wish I was **in** Yankee Land....................................... 256
I Come from Old Virginny.. 311

Jinny Green.. 47
Jenny Lind's Bird Song... 73
Jeanie with the Light Brown Hair................................ 108
Jeannette and Jeannot...................................... 115
John Anderson my Joe... 195
Just So... 250

Kiss but never Tell.. 38
Kissing through the Bars... 107
Kathleen Mavourneen.. 152
Kitty Tyrrell... 153
Kiss Me Quick and Go.. 298

Love's True Elixir... 20
Let us speak of a Man as we find Him.......................... 25
Last Rose of Summer, The....................................... 26
Light of Other Days, The.. 32
Let us **all** Help One Another.................................. 34
Listen to **the** Mocking Bird.................................. 36
Lone Starry **Hours**... 37
Like the Gloom of Night Retiring............................... 40
List, and I'll Find, Love.. 44
Let the Toast be Dear Woman.................................... 52
Lulu is our Darling Pride.. 60
Little Nell.. 62
Lords of Creation, The... 65
Lucy is a Golden Girl... 78
Love's Approach... 85
Lilly Dale... 96
Life let us Cherish.. 97
Love's Ritornella.. 98
Love Not.. 104
Long Life and Success to the Farmer...................... 118

	PAGE
Little Blacksmith, The	118
Larry O'Brian	165
Light Barque, The	**217**
Larboard Watch	217
Land Ho	219
Lazy Club	251
Love Struck Quaker	255
My Boyhood's Home	**15**
My Native Highland Home	**17**
May Dew, The	**21**
Maggie by **my Side**	**27**
My Home shall **be the Waves**	32
My Barque is Bounding **near**	34
My **Pretty** Jane	35
Morning its **Sweets is** Flinging	36
Meet **me in** the Willow Glen	40
My Mother Dear	42
My Sister Dear	43
My Own Native **Land**	59
My Helen is the **Fairest Flower**	75
Minstrel's **Return from the War, The**	79
My Cot beside **the Sea**	80
My Boat **is on** the Shore	83
May **Morning**	85
My Soul **in one** Unbroken Sigh	104
March to the Battle Field	110
Mother, He's Going Away	154
Molly Bawn	**163**
My **Love** is like the Red, Red Rose	187
Macgregors' Gathering	187
Maltese **Boat Song, The**	207
My Grandfather **was a** Wonderful **Man**	240
My Grandmother was **a** Wonderful Dame	243
My **Mary** has **the Longest Nose**	254
Mighty Dollar or Two	275
Massa's in de cold, cold Ground	**284**
Merry Sleigh Bells, The	**295**
Mary Blane	301
Medley	313

	PAGE
'Neath this Leafy Shade Reclining	40
No ! No !	92
Norah M'Shane	106
Not a Drum was Heard	114
Nervous Family, The	245
Nowadays	246
Nelly Gray	283
Nelly was a Lady	297
Nancy Till	304
Negro Medley	306
Nigger's History of the World	311
On the Lake where Drooped the Willow	22
Oft in the Stilly Night	45
Old Dog Tray	59
Old Arm Chair, The	61
Oh! Share my Cottage	63
Old Play-Ground, The	68
Oh, would I were a Boy Again	81
Oh, do not Mingle	82
Old Farm House, The	117
Old Oaken Bucket, The	119
Our Union Right or Wrong	129
Oh, Why left I my Hame	177
Oh, Whistle, and I'll come to you my Lad	188
Our Mary Ann	267
"Out," John	277
Old Folks at Home	282
Oh, Susanna	290
Old Kentucky Home	308
Old Bob Ridley	314
Parody on the Last Rose of Summer	26
Prairie Lea, The	90
Parody on Whistle, and I'll Come to You	188
Plough Boy at Sea, The	202
Pilot, The	220
Popular Convivial Song	262
Philosophy	270
Quilting, The	242
Queer Sayings now are all the Go	259

	PAGE
Rosalie, the Prairie Flower	18
Rose of Allandale, The	41
Recline, Dear Boss	43
Ready Barber	43
Rock Beside the Sea, **The**	65
Rapture Dwelling, **The**	78
Reaper of the Plain, The	122
Relics of Washington, **The**	132
Red, White, **and** Blue	138
Rambler from **Clare**, The	148
Row, Row, Homeward, &c	222
Raging **Kanawl**	257
Rosa **Lee**	290
Rosa May	293
Say a Kind Word when you Can	29
Shells of the Ocean	31
See our Oars with Feathered Spray	31
Swift as the Flash	52
Some One to Love	67
Swiss Boy	70
Song of the Sexton	75
She **Wore a Wreath** of Roses	76
Silver Moon	88
Slumber's **Golden Chain**	91
Star of **the Evening**	94
Soldier's Tear, **The**	109
Soldier's Last **Sigh**, The	112
Soldier's Last Bugle, The	112
Soldier's Dream, **The**	113
Song of the Farmer, The	120
Sweet the Hour	122
Star Spangled Banner	126
Squeak the Fife, and Beat the Drum	137
Strong Lads of Labor, The	141
Since I've been in the Army	164
Savourneen Deelish	171
Scotch Lad's Song **in America**	179
Sailler Boy, The	206
Sailor's **Last Whistle**, The	209
Siege **of Plattsburgh**, The	209

CONTENTS.

PAGE

Sailor Boy's Dream, The 210
Sea, The 214
Song of the Turf 229
Silent Sam 232
Singing **Darkies** 292
Sugar Cane Green 312

The dearest spot on earth to me, is Home, **Sweet Home** 14
The Prairie Flower 18
The May Dew 21
There'll be no Sorrow There 25
The Last Rose of Summer 26
Thou art Gone from my Gaze 29
The Light of Other Days 32
The Watchman 33
The Voice of Her I Love 35
The Lone Starry Hours 37
The Rose of Allandale 41
There's Room enough for All 50
'Tis Better to Laugh than be Sighing **54**
'Tis Home where the Heart is **56**
'Twas a Beautiful Night **57**
Twinkling Stars **58**
Thou art Mine Own, Love **66**
There's a Good Time Coming **69**
Twenty Years Ago 71
The Bonny Boat 77
The Beating of my Own Heart 87
Take me Home to Die 100
They Ask me if I Ever Weep 102
The Song my Mother Loved to Sing 116
The Farmer Sat in his Easy Chair 125
The Bold Privateer 147
There's Whiskey in the Jug 152
Teddy O'Neal **172**
Terence's Farewell **175**
The Four Leaved Shamrock **176**
The Lass wi' the Bonnie Blue E'en 190
The Tempest 221
Times and Fashions of 1860 224
Trust to Luck 230

	PÃ.
Trust to Pluck	231
Things I don't Like to See	247
The Days when I was Hard Up	273
Taking Tea in the Arbor	276
Unfurl the Glorious Banner	133
Uncle Sam's Farm	136
Unlucky Fellow, The	237
Vedrai Carino	44
Vilkins and his Dinah	317
When the Golden Stars are Beaming	10
Willie's on the Dark Blue Sea	23
What Fairy Like Music	33
Woodman, Spare that Tree	48
What is Home Without a Mother	50
Willie, we have Missed You	53
We Meet by Chance	56
When Wakes the Sun	90
When Bound in Slumber's Golden Chain	91
When the Trump of Fame	111
When a Little Farm we Keep	124
Widow Machree	149
Wid a Dhudieen	150
Within a mile of Edinboro'	185
What's a' the Steer, Kimmer	195
White Squall, The	'212
What are You Going to Stand	259
When I was out a Sleighing	260
We're all Cutting	269
What is a Bachelor Like	278
Wait for the Wagon	288
Witching Dinah Crow	299
Ye Sons of Freedom	134
Young America	142
You're Going to the Wars	162
Yankee Ship, &c	205
Yankee Midshipman	221
Yankee Manufacture	256
Yaller Busha Belle	293
Yellow Rose of Texas	310

SONGS OF SENTIMENT, &c.

EVER OF THEE.

A NEW AND POPULAR BALLAD.

EVER of thee I'm fondly dreaming,
  Thy gentle voice my spirit can cheer,
Thou wert the star that mildly **beaming**,
  Shone o'er my path when all **was dark** and drear.
Still in my heart, thy form I cherish,
  Every kind thought like a bird flies **to thee ;**
Ah ! never till life and memory perish
  Can I forget how dear thou art to me,
Morn, noon, and night, where e'er I may be.
  Fondly I'm dreaming ever of thee,
  Fondly I'm dreaming **ever** of thee.

Ever of thee, when sad and **lonely**,
  Wandering afar my soul joy'd **to dwell**;
Ah ! then I felt, and I loved thee only,
  All seem'd to fade before affection's spell.
Years have not chill'd the love **I** cherish,
  True **as** the stars hath my heart been to thee ;
Ah ! never till life and memory perish,
  Can I forget how dear thou art to me.
Morn, noon, **and night**, where e'er **I may be,**
  Fondly I'm dreaming **ever** of thee,
  Fondly I'm dreaming **ever** of thee.

THE CANADIAN BOAT SONG.

FAINTLY as tolls the evening chime
Our voices keep tune and our oars keep time,
Soon as the wood on shore looks dim,
We'll sing at St. Ann's our parting hymn.
  Row, brothers row, the stream runs fast,
  The rapids are near and the daylight's past.

Why should we yet our sails unfurl?
There's not a breath the blue wave to curl,
But when the breeze blows off the shore,
Oh! sweetly we'll rest on our weary oar.
  Blow, breezes blow, the stream runs fast,
  The rapids are near, and the daylight's past.

Utawa's tide! the trembling moon
Shall see us float over thy surges soon,
Saint of the Green Isle! hear our prayers,
Grant us cool heavens and favoring airs.
  Blow, breezes blow, the stream runs fast,
  The rapids are near and the daylight's past.

MOORE.

THE DEAREST SPOT ON EARTH TO ME,
IS HOME, SWEET HOME.

Sung with great applause by Miss Adelaide Philipps.

  THE dearest spot of earth to me,
    Is home, sweet home,
  The fairy land I long to see,
    Is home, sweet home.
  There how chained the sense of hearing,
  There where hearts are so endearing,
  All the world is not so cheering,
    As home, sweet home.
  The dearest spot on earth to me
    Is home, sweet home,
  The fairy land I longed to see,
    Is home, sweet home.

I've taught my heart the way to prize
    My home, sweet home,
I've learned to look with lovers' eyes,
    On home, sweet home.
There where vows are truly plighted,
There where hearts are so united,
All the world besides I've slighted,
    For home, sweet home.
Oh! the dearest spot on earth to me,
    Is home, sweet home,
The fairy land, &c.

MY BOYHOOD'S HOME.

My boyhood's home, I see thy hills,
    I see thy valley's changeful green,
And manhood's eye a tear-drop fills
    Tho' years have rolled since thee I've seen.
I come to thee from war's dread school,
A warrior stern o'er thee to rule,
But as I gaze on each lov'd plain
I feel I am a boy again.

To the war steed adieu—
    To the trumpet farewell,
To the pomp of the palace
    The proud gilded dome,
For the green scenes of childhood I bid you farewell,
The soldier returns to his boyhood's loved home.

HOME, SWEET HOME.

Mid pleasures and palaces tho' we may roam,
Be it ever so humble there's no place like home;
A charm from the skies seems to hallow us there,
Which seek through the wide world, is ne'er met with elsewhere.
    Home, home, sweet, sweet home,
    Be it ever so humble, there's no place like home.

An exile from home, splendor dazzles in vain,
Oh! give me my lowly thatched cottage again;
With the birds singing gaily that came at my call,
Give me them with that peace of mind dearer than all.
    Home, home, sweet, sweet home, &c.
                            JOHN HOWARD PAYNE,

"WHEN THE GOLDEN STARS ARE BEAMING."

As sung by Madame **Parodi.**

WHEN **the** golden **stars are** beaming,
  On **the** heaven's dome,
Am I **still and** sadly dreaming,
  Of my distant home.

In a country, strange and **endless,**
  Have my pleasures gone,
And I wander still and friendless,
  Sadly and alone.

And affliction deep and growing,
  Goes where'er I roam,
Longing, longing, still and glowing,
  Draws the wanderer home.

Nowhere is the breeze **so** fragrant,
  And the sun so bright,
As in thee, **my** country distant,
  On the mountain height.

Here no herd is gently mounting,
  All **the** hills alone,
Nowhere is the Alp-**horn** sounding,
  Nor **the** herdsman's **song!**

Lo! if **sun or stars** are beaming,
  In the heaven's dome,
Am I still and sadly dreaming
  Of my distant home!

And so **are** afflictions going
  With me hand in hand!
Longing draws me still and glowing,
  Home to Switzerland—

PROCH.

MY NATIVE HIGHLAND HOME.

My Highland home, where tempests blow,
  And cold thy wintry looks,
Thy mountains crown'd with driven snow,
  And ice-bound are thy brooks;
But colder far the exile's heart,
  However far he'd roam,
To whom these words no joy impart,
  My native Highland home.
Then gang along with me to Scotland dear,
  We ne'er again will roam,
And with thy smile so bonny cheer,
  My native Highland home.

When summer comes, the heather bell
  Shall tempt thy feet to rove,
The cushat dove within the dell
  Invites to peace and love ;
For blithesome is the break of day
  And sweet's the bonny broom,
And pure the trickling rills that play,
  Around my Highland home
Then gang along with me to Scotland dear,
  We ne'er again will roam,
But with thy smile so bonny cheer,
  My native Highland home.

A MOTHER'S LOVE.

A MOTHER'S love, a mother's love,
  The dew that falls in opening life,
When life is most like Eden's grove,
  With pure and playful life.
Our earliest joy, our latest thought,
  Where e'er we rove—where e'er we rove,
Thou only good of earth unbought,
  We think of thee—a mother's love,
  We think of thee—a mother's love.

2

ROSALIE, THE PRAIRIE FLOWER.

On the distant prairie, where the heather wild,
In its quiet beauty lived and smiled,
Stands a little cottage, and a creeping vine,
Loves around its porch to twine.
In that peaceful dwelling was a lovely child,
With her blue eyes beaming, soft and mild,
And the wavy ringlets of her flaxen hair,
Floating in the summer air.
   Fair as a lily, joyous and free,
   Light of that prairie home was she,
   Ev'ry one who knew her felt the gentle power
   Of Rosalie, the prairie flower.

On that distant prairie, when the days were long,
Tripping like a fairy, sweet her song,
With the sunny blossoms and the birds at play,
Beautiful and bright as they.
When the twilight shadows gathered in the west,
And the voice of nature sunk to rest,
Like a cherub kneeling seem'd that lovely child,
With her gentle eyes so mild.
   Fair as a lily, &c.

But the summer faded, and the chilly blast
O'er that happy cottage swept at last,
Where the autumn song birds woke the dewy morn,
Little prairie flower was gone;
For the angels whispered softly in her ear,
" *Child, thy father calls thee, stay not here,*"
And they gently bore her, robed in spotless white,
To the blissful home of light.
   Tho' we shall never look on her more,
   Gone with the love and joy she bore,
   Far away she's blooming in a fadeless bower,
   Sweet Rosalie, the prairie flower.

GENTLE ANNIE.

Written **and** composed **by Stephen C.** Foster. Music published **by**
Firth & Pond, **547** Broadway, **N. Y.**

Thou **wilt come no** more, gentle Annie,
  Like **a** flower thy spirit **did depart,**
Thou art gone, alas ! like the **many**
  That have bloomed in the **summer of my heart.**
Shall we never more behold **thee,**
  Never hear thy winning **voice** again,
When the spring time **comes,** gentle Annie,
  And the wild flowers **are scattered** o'er the **plain ?**
Chorus—Shall we never **more behold thee,** &c.

We have roamed and loved **'mid the bowers,**   .
  When thy downy cheeks were **in the** bloom,
Now I stand alone 'mid the flowers,
  While they mingle their perfumes o'er thy tomb.
    Shall we never **more,** &c.

Ah ! the hours grow **sad while I** ponder,
  Near the silent spot where thou wast laid ;
And my heart **bows** down **when I** wander,
  By the streams and meadows where **we stray'd.**
    Shall we never more behold thee, &c.

IN HAPPY MOMENTS.

In happy moments day by **day**
  The sands **of** life may **pass,**
In swift but tranquil tide **away,**
  From Time's unerring glass ;
Yet hopes we used as bright to **deem,**
  Remembrance **will recall,**
Whose pure and whose unfading beam
  Is dearer than them all.

Though anxious eyes upon us gaze,
  And hearts with fondness beat,
Whose smile upon each feature **plays,**
  With truthfulness replete ;
Some thoughts none others can replace,
  Remembrance **will** recall,
Which in the blight of years we trace,
  Is dearer than them all.

From Maritana.

COME, MAIDEN, WITH ME.

Music published by F'rth & Pond, 547 Broadway, N. Y.

COME, maiden, with me   the silvery sea,
My bark is impatiently waiting for thee,
The bright stars are smiling to see thee appear,
And the light waves are dancing to welcome thee here;
Cool zephyrs are wooing thy ringlets to come,
And wanton with them on our own ocean home,
Where the sea-birds shall wake thee when danger is near,
And their gambols shall teach thee to laugh at thy fear.
      Come, maiden, with me, &c.

My bark is as swift as the wind, when the deep,
And wild leaping ocean waves rock them to sleep,
And stout as the billow she stems in her pride,
To bear thee afar on its bosom, my bride.
Her anchor's aweigh, for the far coral groves,
Where the mermaidens sing of their sports and their loves;
Then linger not here on this dull shore alone,
For its haunts are unfit for thee, beautiful one.

And when o'er the wave we are bounding along,
'Ere the land disappears thou shalt warble a song
Of farewell to the scenes we leave joyless behind,
Whose soft notes shall dwell on the wings of the wind,
And its burden shall be as it floats on the breeze
Of beauty and love and a life on the seas.
Then hasten, dear maiden, o'er the star lighted sea,
My proud bark shall bear thee to freedom with me.

"LOVE'S TRUE ELIXIR."

A popular Song from "The Love Spell."

WITH a tender look I'll charm him,
   With a modest smile invite him,
With a tear or sigh alarm him,
   With a fond caress excite him.
Never yet was man so mulish,
   That I could not make him yield, sir,
Nemorino's fate's decided,
   When Adina takes the field, sir.
My receipt is in my eyes,
THERE LOVE'S TRUE ELIXIR LIES.

THE MAY DEW.

Oh! come with me, love, I am seeking
  A spell in the young year' owers,
The magical May dew is w ng
  Its charm o'er the summer bowers.
Its pearls are more precious than those they find
  In jeweled India's sea,
For the dew drops might serve to bind,
  Thy heart for ever to me.
Oh! come with me, love, I am seeking
  A spell in the young year's flowers,
The magical May dew is weeping,
  Its charm o'er the summer bowers.
Then come love, &c.

Haste, or the charm will be missing,
  We seek in the May dew now,
For soon the warm sun will be kissing,
  The bright drops from blossom and bough.
And the charm is so tender the May dew sheds,
  Or the wild flowers' delicate dyes,
That e'er with the touch of the sunbeam 'tis said,
  The mystical influence flies.
Then come with me, love, I am seeking
  A spell in the young year's flowers,
The magical May dew is weeping,
  Its charm o'er the summer bowers.
Then come love, come love,
  Come love to me, &c.

I AM THE BAYADERE.

Madame **Anna** Bishop's Celebrated Song.

I AM the Bayadere,
  And the gay tamborine,
Tra la la la la!
  Drives me from all care,
Tra la la la la!
  As I dance on the green.
Born on the banks of the Ganges,
  Young pleasure is my guide,
And bless him that ranges
  The forest at my side.
Tra la la la la!

ON THE LAKE WHERE DROOPED THE WILLOW.

On the lake where drooped the willow,
    Long time ago,
Where the rock threw back the billow,
    Brighter than snow,
There dwelt a maid beloved and cherished,
    By high and low,
But with the Autumn leaf she perished,
    Long time ago.

Rock and tree and flowing water,
    Long time ago,
Bird and bee and blossom taught her,
    Love's spell to know.
While to my fond words she listened,
    Murmuring low,
Tenderly her dove eye glistened,
    Long time ago.

Mingled were our hearts for ever,
    Long time ago,
Can I now forget her never?
    No, lost one, no.
To her grave these tears are given,
    Ever to flow,
She's the star I missed from heaven,
    Long time ago.

                GEORGE P. MORRIS.

WILLIE'S ON THE DARK BLUE SEA.

Music published by Oliver Ditson, 227 Washington St., Boston.

My Willie's on the dark blue sea,
    He's gone far o'er the main,
And many a weary day will pass,
    Ere he'll come back again,
Then blow ye gentle winds o'er the dark blue sea,
    Bid the storm king stay his hand,
And bring my Willie back to me,
    'Tis his dear native land.

I love my Willie best of all,
 He e'er was true to me—
But lonesome, dreary, are the hours,
 Since he has gone to sea.
There's danger on the waters now
 I hear the bleak hills cry,
And moaning voices seem to speak
 From out the cloudy sky.

I see the vivid lightning's flash,
 And hark! the thunders roar,—
Oh! Father, save my Willie from
 The storm king's mighty power.
And as she spoke the lightning ceased,
 Hushed was the thunder's roar,
And Willie clasped her in his arms
 To roam the seas no more.
Chorus—Now gentle winds o'er the dark blue sea,
 No more we'll stay thy hand,
Since Willie's safe at home with me,
 In his own dear native land.

A COTTAGE BY THE SEA.

Music at Firth & Pond's, 547 Broadway, N. Y.

CHILDHOOD's days now pass before me,
 Forms and scenes of long ago,
Like a dream they hover o'er me,
 Calm and bright as evening glow,
Days that know no shade of sorrow,
 There my young heart pure and free,
Joyful hailed each coming morrow,
Chorus—In the cottage by the sea.
 In the cottage by the sea.

Fancy views the rose trees twining,
 Round the old and rustic door,
And below the white beach shining
 Where I gathered shells of yore,
Hears my mother's gentle warning,
 As she took me on her knee,
And I feel again life's morning,
 In the cottage by the sea,
 In the cottage by the sea.

What though years have rolled above me,
Tho' mid fairer scenes I roam,
Yet I ne'er shall cease to love thee,
Childhood's dear and happy home.
And when life's long day is closing,
Oh! how pleasant it would be,
On some faithful heart reposing,
In the cottage by the sea.
Chorus—In the cottage by the sea,
In the cottage by the sea.

BY THE SAD SEA WAVES.

As sung by Jenny Lind, Mad. Parodi, &c., &c.

By the sad sea waves,
I listen while they moan,
I lament o'er the graves
Of hope and pleasure gone.
I was young—I was fair,
I once had not a care,
From the rising of the morn
To the setting of the sun,
Yet I pine like a slave,
By the sad sea wave.
Come again bright days of hope and pleasure gone,
Come again bright days,
Come again, come again.

From my care last night,
By holy sleep beguiled,
In the fair dream light,
My home upon me smiled.
Oh! how sweet mid the dew,
Ev'ry flower that I knew,
Breathed a welcome back,
To their worn and weary child.
I awoke, in my grave,
By the sad sea wave.
Come again bright dream so peacefully that smiled,
Come again bright dream,
Come again, &c.

LET US SPEAK OF A MAN AS WE FIND HIM.

LET us speak of a man as we find him,
  And censure alone what we see,
And should a man blame, let's remind him,
  That from vice we are none of us free.
If the veil from the heart could be torn,
  And the mind could be read on the brow,
There are many we'd pass by with scorn,
  Whom we're loading with high honors now.
      Let us speak of a man,
      Let us speak of a man,
      Let us speak of a man as we find him.

Let us speak of a man as we find him,
  And heed not what others may say,
If he's frail, then a kind word may bind him,
  When coldness would turn him away;
For the heart must be barren indeed,
  Where no bud of repentance can bloom,
Then pause, ere you cause it to bleed,
  Or a smile or a frown hangs it down.
      Let us speak of a man,
      Let us speak of a man, &c.

THERE'LL BE NO SORROW THERE.

  OH! sing to me of heaven,
    When I am called to die,
  Sing holy songs of ecstasy,
    To waft my soul on high.
Chorus—There'll be no more sorrow there,
    There'll be no more sorrow there,
    In heaven above where all is love,
    There'll be no more sorrow there.

  When cold and sluggish drops
    Roll off my marble brow,
  Wake in sweet strains of joyfulness,
    And heaven begins below.
    There'll be no more sorrow there,
    There'll be no more sorrow there.

THE LAST ROSE OF SUMMER.

'Tis the last rose of summer
    Left blooming alone,
All her lovely companions
    Are faded and gone.
No flower of her kindred,
    No rosebud is nigh,
To reflect back her blushes,
    Or give sigh for sigh.

I'll not leave thee, thou lone one,
    To pine on the stem,
Since the lovely are sleeping,
    Go sleep thou with them.
Thus kindly I scatter
    Thy leaves o'er the bed,
Where thy mates of the garden
    Lie scentless and dead.

So soon may I follow
    When friendships decay,
And from love's shining circle,
    The gems drop away.
When true hearts lie withered,
    And fond ones are flown,
Oh! who would inhabit
    This bleak world alone?

A PARODY ON THE SAME.

'Tis the last piece of silver
    Left gleaming alone,
All its specie companions
    Are paid out and gone.
No cash of its kindred,
    No red cent is nigh,
To reflect back its lustre,
    Or show die for die

I'll not keep thee, thou lone one,
  Like a pipe's broken stem,
Since the rest is expended,
  I'll spend you like them.
Thus kindly I scatter
  Thee with the last "*red;*"
And my empty exchequer
  Is cent-less and dead.

MAGGIE BY MY SIDE.

THE land of home is flitting,
  Flitting from my view,
The wind in the sail is sitting,
  Toils the merry crew.
Here, let my home be,
  O'er the waters wide,
I roam with a proud heart,
  Maggie's by my side.
Chorus—My own love, Maggie dear,
  Sitting by my side,
Maggie dear, my own love,
  Sitting by my side.

The wind howls o'er the billow,
  From the distant lea,
Storms raging round my pillow
  Bring no cares to me.
Roll on, ye dark waves,
  O'er the troubled tide,
I heed not your anger,
  Maggie's by my side.
My own love, &c.

Storms can appal me never,
  While her brow is clear;
Fair weather lingers ever,
  Where her smiles appear.
When sorrow's breakers
  Round my heart shall bide,
Still may I find her,
  Sitting by my side.
My own love, Maggie dear, &c

BELL BRANDON.

NEATH a tree by the margin of the wildwood,
    Whose spreading leafy boughs swept the **ground,**
With a path leading thither o'er the prairie,
    Where silence hung her night garb around ;
Where oft I have wandered in the evening,
    When the summer winds were fragrant o'er the lea,
There I saw the little beauty, Bell Brandon,
    As we met by the old arbor tree.
There I saw, &c.

Bell Brandon was a birdling of the mountain,
    She sported on her wings wild and free, -
And they said the life current of the red man
    Tinged her veins from a far distant sea ;
And she loved her humble dwelling on the prairie,
    And her guileless, happy heart clung to me ;
And I loved the little beauty, Bell Brandon,
    And we both loved the old arbor tree.
For I loved, &c.

On the trunk of an aged tree I carved them,
    And our names on the sturdy oak remain,
But I now repair in sorrow to its shelter,
    And murmur to the wild winds my pain.
After I sat there in solitude repining,
    For the beauteous dream brought night to me,
Death has wed the little beauty, Bell Brandon,
    And she sleeps 'neath the old arbor tree.

HERE'S A HEALTH TO ALL GOOD LASSES.

A POPULAR GLEE.

HERE's a health to all good lasses,
Pledge it merrily, fill your glasses,
    Let the bumper toast go round,
    Let the bumper toast go round.
May they live a life of pleasure,
Without mixture, without measure,
    For with them true joys are found.
Fill your glasses—mine's a bumper—
All good lasses—mine's a thumper.
    Here's a health to all good lasses, &c.

THOU ART GONE FROM MY GAZE.

THOU art gone from my gaze like a beautiful dream,
And I seek thee in vain by the mountain and stream,
Oft I breathe thy dear name to the wind passing by,
But thy sweet voice is mute to my bosom's lone sigh.

In the stillness of night, when the stars mildly shine,
My heart fondly holds a communion with thine,
For I feel thou art near, and where e'er I may be,
That the spirit of love keeps a watch over me.

Of the buds in thy bower, new companions I make,
Every simple wild flower I prize for thy sake,
The deep woods and dark wilds can a pleasure impart,
For their solitude suits my sad sorrow-worn heart.

Thou art gone from my gaze, but I will not repine,
Ere long we shall meet in a home that's now thine,
For I feel thou art near, and where e'er I may be,
That the spirit of love keeps a watch over me.

SAY A KIND WORD WHEN YOU CAN.

WHAT were life without something to cheer us
   With a word or a smile on our way ?
A friend who is faithfully near us,
   Who heeds not what others may say.
The bravest of spirits have often,
   Half failed in the race they have ran,
For a kind word life's hardships to soften ;
   Then say a kind word when you can
Chorus—Say a kind word, &c.

Each one of us own to some failing,
   Tho' some may have more than the rest,
But there's no good in heedlessly railing
   'Gainst those who are striving their best.
Remember a word of complaining
   May blight every effort and plan,
Which a kind word would help in attaining,
   Then say a kind word when you can.

Oh! say a kind word then, whenever
  Twill make the heart cheerful and glad,
But chiefly, forget it oh never!
  To the one that is hopeless and sad.
For there's no word so easy in saying,
  So begin—if you have not began,
And never in life be delaying,
  To say a kind word when you can.
Then say a kind word, &c.

J. R. THOMAS.

HAZEL DELL.

IN the hazel dell my Nelly's sleeping,
  Nelly loved so long,
And my lonely, lonely watch I'm keeping,
  Nelly lost and gone.
Here in moonlight oft we've wandered,
  Through the silent shade,
Now where leafy branches drooping downward,
  Little Nelly's laid.
All alone my watch I'm keeping,
  In the hazel dell,
For my darling Nelly's near me sleeping,
  Nelly, dear, farewell.

In the hazel dell my Nelly's sleeping,
  Where the flowers wave,
And the silent stars are nightly weeping
  O'er poor Nelly's grave.
Hopes that once my bosom fondly cherished,
  Smile no more for me,
Ev'ry dream of joy, alas! has perished,
  Nelly, dear with thee.
All alone, &c.

Now I'm weary, friendless, and forsaken,
  Watching here alone,
Nelly, thou no more wilt fondly cheer me,
  With thy loving tone.
Yet for ever shall thy gentle image
  Within my memory dwell,
And my tears thy lonely grave shall moisten,
  Nelly, dear, farewell.

SHELLS OF THE OCEAN.

One summer eve, in pensive thought,
  I wandered on the sea-beat shore,
Where oft in heedless infancy,
  I gathered shells in days before,
  I gathered shells, &c.
The flashing waves like music fell,
  Responsive to my fancy wild,
A dream came o'er me like a spell,
  I thought I was again a child.
A dream came o'er me like a spell,
  I thought I was again a child.

I stooped upon the pebbly strand,
  To cull the toys that round me lay,
But as I took them in my hand,
  I threw them one by one away,
  I threw them, &c.
Oh! thus, I said, in ev'ry stage,
  By toys our fancy is beguiled,
We gather shells from youth to age,
  And then we leave them like a child.
We gather shells, &c.

SEE OUR OARS WITH FEATHERED SPRAY.

A POPULAR GLEE.

See our oars with feathered spray,
Sparkle in the beam of day,
In our little bark we glide
Swiftly o'er the silent tide.

From yonder lone and rocky shore,
The warrior hermit to restore;
And sweet the morning breezes blow,
While thus in measured time we row.
See our oars, &c.

MY HOME SHALL BE THE WAVES.

Speed on my bark, the day beam
  Is bursting on my sight,
Still o'er the rolling billows,
  Speed on thy rapid flight.
'Tis life along the waters,
  With eagle's wing to sweep,
To breathe the song of freedom,
  Upon the boundless deep.
Speed on, &c.

With thee my bark undaunted,
  Whatever chance be thine,
I'll share it gladly with thee,
  And may thy fate be mine.
I will not fix my dwelling
  Amid a world of slaves,
With thee through life for ever,
  My home shall be the waves.
I will not, &c.

THE LIGHT OF OTHER DAYS.

THE light of other days is faded,
  And all their glories past,
For grief with heavy wing hath shaded
  Those hopes too bright to last.
The world, which morning's mantle clouded,
  Shines forth with purer rays ;
But the heart ne'er feels in sorrow shrouded
  The light of other days.

The leaves which Autumn tempests wither,
  The birds which then take wing,
When winter winds are past, come hither
  To welcome back the spring.
The very ivy on the ruin
  The gloomful life displays,
But the heart alone sees no renewing
  The light of other days.

THE WATCHMAN.

Good night, good night, my dearest,
  How fast the moments fly !
'Tis time to part ; thou hearest
  That hateful watchman's cry,
" Past twelve o'clock," good night.

Yet stay a moment longer,
  Alas ! why is it so ?
The wish to stay grows stronger
  The more 'tis time to go.
" Past one o'clock," good night.

Now wrap thy cloak about thee,
  The hours must sure go wrong,
For when they are past without thee,
  They're oh ! ten times as long.
" Past two o'clock," good night.

Again that dreadful warning,
  Had ever time such flight ?
And see the sky,—'tis morning,
  So now indeed, good night.
" Past three o'clock," good night.

Thomas Moore.

WHAT FAIRY LIKE MUSIC.

What fairy like music
  Steals over the sea,
Entrancing the senses,
  With charmed melody !
'Tis the voice of the mermaid,
  That floats o'er the main,
As she mingles her song
  With the gondolier's strain.

The winds are all hushed,
  And the waters at rest,
They sleep like the passions
  In infancy's breast,
Till storms shall unchain them
  From out the dark cave,
And break the repose
  Of the soul and the wave.

MY BARQUE IS BOUNDING NEAR.

Oh! listen, dearest lady,
  It is thine own one calls,
Pale stars are o'er thee shining,
  Dim twilight round thee falls.
Come, come, this heart awaits thee,
  My lady love appear,
Come, fly with me across the lake,
  My barque is bounding near,
  My barque is bounding near, &c.

Oh! hasten, dearest lady,
  As o'er the tide we rove,
Each silvery wave shall echo
  Sweet notes of minstrel love.
And vows of truth I'll breathe to thee,
  I'll kiss away each tear,
Come, fly with me across the lake,
  My barque is bounding near,
  My barque is bounding near, &c.

LET US ALL HELP ONE ANOTHER.

Let us all help one another,
  And all heart of kindness show,
As adown time's flowing river,
  In the boat of life we row.
For though rough may be the weather,
  And the sky be overcast,
If we only pull together,
  We can brave the storm at last.

Let us all help one another,
  In misfortune's wintry day,
And be kinder still as ever ere,
  Earth's best gifts are snatched away.
When bright fortune gilds the morrow,
  Hollow hearts will fawn and cling,
But when comes the night of sorrow,
  True hearts only comfort bring.
Let us all help, &c.

MY PRETTY JANE.

My pretty Jane, my pretty Jane,
  Ah! never look so shy,
But meet me in the evening
  While the bloom is on the rye.

The Spring is waning fast, my love,
  The corn is in the ear,
The Summer nights are coming, love,
  The moon shines bright and clear.

But name the day, the wedding day,
  When I will buy the ring,
The lads and maids in favors white;
  And the village bells shall ring.
My pretty Jane, &c.

THE VOICE OF HER I LOVE.

A Celebrated Harp Song.

How sweet at close of silent eve,
  The harp's responsive sound!
How sweet the vows that ne'er deceived
  Or deeds by virtue crown'd!
How sweet to sit beneath a tree,
  In some delightful grove,
But oh! more sweet, more dear to me,
  Is the voice of her I love.

Whene'er she joins the village train,
  To hail the new born day,
Mellifluous notes compose the strain,
  Which zephyrs waft away.
The frowns of fate I'll calmly bear,
  In humble sphere to move,
Content and blest whene'er I hear
  The voice of her I love.

LISTEN TO THE MOCKING BIRD.

A Celebrated Imitation Song.

I'M dreaming now of Hally, sweet Hally, sweet Hally,
  I'm dreaming now of Hally;
  For the thought of her is one that never dies.
    She's sleeping in the valley, the valley, the valley,
  And the Mocking-bird is singing where she lies.
        Chorus.—Listen to the Mocking-bird,
             Listen to the Mocking-bird,
      The Mocking-bird still singing o'er her grave,
            Listen to the Mocking-bird,
            Listen, &c.
  Still singing where the weeping willows wave.

Ah! well I yet remember, remember, remember,
  Ah! well I yet remember,
  When we gathered in the cotton, side by side;
    'Twas in the mild September, September, September,
    'Twas in the mild September,
  And the Mocking-birds were singing far and wide.
      Chorus.—Listen to the Mocking-bird, &c.

When the charms of Spring awaken, awaken, awaken,
  When the charms of Spring awaken,
  And the Mocking-bird is singing on the bough;
    I feel like one forsaken, forsaken, forsaken,
  Since my Hally is no longer with me now.
      Chorus.—Listen to the Mocking-bird,
        Listen to the Mocking-bird, &c.

MORNING ITS SWEETS IS FLINGING.

MORNING its sweets is flinging
  Over each bower and spray,
Flowers to life are springing,
  To greet the opening day;
Zephyrs are gently winging
  Round their sportive way,
Birds on each branch are singing,
  While echo repeats the lay, ·
  While echo repeats the lay.
  'Tis an enchanted grove,
  Sacred to peace and love.
            From CINDERELLA.

THE LONE STARRY HOURS.

Music published by Ditson, 227 Washington St., Boston.

Oh ! the lone starry hours give me, love,
  When still is the beautiful night,
When the round laughing moon I see, love,
  Peeps through the clouds silver white.
When no winds sweep through the woods, love,
  And I gaze on the bright rising star,
When the world is in dream and asleep, love,
  O wake while I touch my guitar.

Till the red rosy morn grows bright, love,
  Far away o'er the distant sea,
Till the stars cease their gentle light, love,
  Will I wait for a welcome from thee.
And oh ! if that pleasure is thine, love,
  We will wander together afar,
My heart shall be thine, thine, my love,
  Then awake while I touch my guitar.

ALL'S FOR THE BEST.

Music published by Firth & Pond, 547 Broadway, N. Y.

ALL's for the best; be sanguine and cheerful,
  Trouble and sorrow are friends in disguise,
Nothing but folly goes faithless and fearful,
  Courage forever is happy and wise.
All's for the best; if a man would but know it,
  Providence wishes that all may be blest,
This is no dream of the pundit or poet,
  Fact is not fancy, and all's for the best,
  Fact is not fancy, and all's for the best.

All's for the best; set this on your standard,
  Soldier of sadness or pilgrim of love,
Who to the shores of despair may have wandered,
  A way-wearied swallow or heart-stricken dove.
All's for the best; be a man but confiding,
  Providence tenderly governs the rest,
And the frail barque of his creature is guiding,
  Wisely and warily ; all's for the best.

All's for the best; dispel idle terrors,
    Meet all your fears and your foes in the van,
And in the midst of your dangers and errors,
    Trust like a child and strive like a man.
All's for the best; unavailing, unbounded,
    Providence wishes that all may be blest,
And both by wisdom and mercy surrounded,
    Hope and be happy then, all's for the best.
    All's for the best: all's for the best;
    Hope and be happy, &c. &c.

"KISS BUT NEVER TELL."

Music by F. Buckley.   Firth & Pond, 547 Broadway, N. Y.

WHEN love grows warm there is a charm,
    And oft a sacred bliss,
When fond hearts greet, for lips to meet,
    In sweet affection's kiss;
But to reveal the secret seal,
    Which hallows it so well,
May quench love's flame, with breath of shame,
    So kiss, but never tell.
Oh, kiss, but never tell to any,
    Breathing breaks the spell,
True love's pledge to keep forever.
    Kiss, but never tell.

At night when eyes like stars beam bright,
    And kindred souls commune,
When heart to heart, love's vows impart,
    Beneath the smiling moon;
At such an hour of magic power,
    What holy raptures dwell,
In each true breast by honor blest,
    To kiss, but never tell!
Then kiss, but never tell, oh, never,
    Breathing breaks the spell,
True love's pledge to keep forever.
    Kiss, but never tell.

SILAS S. STEELE.

BATTI, BATTI—"CHIDE ME, CHIDE ME!"

Piccolomini's Celebrated Song, from Don Juan.

CHIDE me, chide me, dear Masetto,
  Chide Zerlina at your will,
Like the patient lamb I suffer,
  Meek, and mute, and loving still.

Rend those locks you praised so highly,
  From thine arms Zerlina cast,
These fond eyes in rage extinguish,
  Fondly still they'll look their last.

Ah! I see, love, you're relenting,
  Pardon, kneeling I implore,
Night and day to thee devoted,
  Here I vow to err no more.

COME BRAVE THE SEA.

Air—Liberty. Duett in Il Puritani.

COME brave the sea with me, love,
The empire of the free, love,
There shalt thou dwell with me, love,
  My blessing and my pride.
Oh! hasten with me there, love,
While yet the wind is fair, love,
While the sparkling billows foam, love,
Where e'er fate bids us roam, love
My ship shall be thy home, love,
  And thou be the sailor's bride.
Come brave the sea, &c.

Come then and with me roam, love,
From father, friends, and home, love,
Where the sparkling billows foam, love,
  So boundless and so wide.
For dangers dread thee there, love,
Where tempests rend the air, love,
Tho' fair the earth may be, love,
It is not like the sea, love,
Where soars the spirit free, love,
  While o'er its breast we ride.
Come brave the sea, &c.

"NEATH THIS LEAFY SHADE RECLINING."

A gem from the Elixir of Love.

'NEATH this leafy shade reclining,
Sweet repose with pleasure blending,
While the noontide sun is shining
    Here we pass an hour away,
Screened from heat by fragrant bowers
Cooling streams and fragrant flowers.
But when LOVE exerts, exerts his power,
Nought, oh! nought's impervious to his ray,
No, when love exerts, exerts his sway,
Tower nor bower's impervious to his ray.

MEET ME IN THE WILLOW GLEN.

As sung by Miss Sheriff.

MEET me in the willow glen,
    When the silver moon is beaming,
Songs of love I'll sing to thee,
    When all the world is dreaming.
No prying eye shall come, love,
    No stranger foot be seen,
And the distant village hum, love,
    Shall echo through the glen.
        Meet me in the willow glen
            When the silver moon is beaming,
            Songs of love I'll sing you there,
            If you'll meet me in the willow glen.

LIKE THE GLOOM OF NIGHT RETIRING.

As sung by Madame Parodi.

LIKE the gloom of night retiring,
    When in splendor beams the day,
Hope again my heart inspiring,
    Doubt and fear shall chase away.

Life shall yield its sweetest treasure,
    When our plighted faith we seal,
Care not one dear drop of pleasure
    From our cup of joy shall steal.
Like the gloom of night, &c.

DRINK YE TO HER THAT EACH LOVES BEST.

DRINK ye to her that each loves best,
  And if you nurse a flame,
Told *only* to **her** mutual breast,
  We will not ask her name.
Enough, while memory tranced and glad,
  Paints silently the fair,
That each should dream **of joys he's had,**
  Or yet may hope to share.
Yet far from hence be jest or boast,
  From hallow'd thoughts so dear,
But drink to them that we love most,
  As they would like **to** hear.
Then drink **to** her that each loves best, &c.

CAMPBELL.

THE ROSE OF ALLANDALE.

THE **morn** was fair, the skies were clear,
  No breath **came** o'er the lea,
When Mary **left her** Highland **cot,**
  And wandered forth with **me.**
Though flowers decked the **mountain side,**
  And fragrance filled the vale,
By far **the sweetest** flower there,
  Was **the** Rose **of** Allandale.

Where e'er **I** wandered, east or **west,**
  Tho' fate began to lower,
A solace still was she to me,
  In sorrow's lonely hour.
When tempests lashed our gallant bark,
  And rent our shivering sail,
One maiden form withstood the storm,
  'Twas the Rose of Allandale.

And **when** my fevered lips were parched,
  On Afric's burning sand,
She whispered hopes of happiness,
  And tales **of** distant land.
My life had been a wilderness,
  Unblest by fortune's gale,
Had fate not linked my lot with hers,
  Sweet Rose of Allandale.

MY MOTHER DEAR.

THERE was a place in childhood,
  That I remember well,
And there a voice of sweetest tone,
  Bright fairy tales did tell.
And gentle words with fond embrace
  Were given with joy to me,
When I was in that happy place,
  Upon my mother's knee.
My mother dear, my mother dear,
My gentle, gentle mother dear.

When fairy tales were ended,
  "Good night," she softly said,
And kissed, and laid me down to sleep,
  Within my tiny bed.
And holy words she taught me there,
  Methinks I yet can see
Her angel eyes as close I knelt,
  Beside my mother's knee.
Oh! mother dear, &c.

In the sickness of my childhood,
  The perils of my prime,
The sorrows of my riper years,
  The cares of ev'ry time—
When doubt, or danger, weighed me down,
  Then pleading all for me,
It was a fervent prayer to heaven,
  That bent my mother's knee.
My mother, &c.

BE MINE, DEAR MAID.

From "Guy Mannering."

BE mine, dear maid, this faithful heart
  Can never prove untrue,
'Twere easier far from life to part,
  Than cease to live for you.
Then turn thee not away, my love,
  Oh! turn thee not away,
For by the light of truth I swear,
  To love thee night and day,
  To love thee, &c.

The lark shall first forget to sing,
  When morn unfolds the east,
Ere I by change or coldness wring
  Thy fond confiding breast.
Then turn thee not away, my love,
  Oh! turn thee not away,
For by the light of truth I swear,
  To love thee night and day,
    To love thee, &c.

RECLINE, DEAR BOSS, OR THE READY BARBER.

A PARODY ON THE ABOVE.

RECLINE dear boss, my razor's sharp,
  My hand is firm and true,
'Twere easier far my blood to start,
  Than make a cut on you.
Then turn thy head this way, dear boss,
  Then turn thy head this way,
For by the Tonsor's art I swear,
  To shave thee right away, boss.
(*Repeat, strapping razor to symphony.*)
  To shave thee right to-day, boss,
    To shave thee right away,
  To shave thee, to shave thee,
    To shave thee ri-hi-ight away, boss.

MY SISTER DEAR.

From Massaniello.

MY sister dear, o'er this rude cheek,
I oft have felt the tear-drop stealing,
When those mute looks have told the feeling
  Heaven denied the tongue to speak,
And thou had'st comfort in that tear,
Shed for thee, my sister dear.

  And now, alas! I weep alone
By thee, by joy, by hope forsaken,
Midst thoughts that darkest fears awaken,
  Trembling for thy fate unknown,
And vainly flows the bitter tear,
Shed for thee, my sister dear.

"BEHOLD HOW BRIGHTLY RREAKS THE MORNING,"

Or the Fisherman's Barcarole, **from** the same.

BEHOLD how brightly breaks the morning,
  Tho' bleak our lot, our hearts are warm,
To toil inured, all danger scorning,
  We hail the breeze, aud brave the storm.
Put off, put off, our course we **know,**
  Take heed—whisper low.
Look out and spread your net **with care;**
The prey we **seek,** we'll soon, we'll **soon** ensnare.

Away, no cloud is lowering o'er us,
  Freely now we'll stem the wave,
Hoist, hoist all sail, while full before us,
  Hope's beacon shines to **cheer** the brave.
Put off, put off, &c.

VEDRAI CARINO—LIST, AND I'LL FIND, LOVE.

From Don Juan.   As sung by all vocalists of celebrity.

LIST, **and** I'll find, **love,**
If you **are** kind, love,
Balm for your mind, love,
  Patient be.

This balm so pure, love,
Simple and sure, love,
Sweet to endure, love,
  None know but me.

Thrilling and **healing,**
Over thee stealing,
Exquisite **feeling,**
  Meant **but** for thee.

To thy entreating
  I'll yield it here,
Feel how 'tis beating,
  Beating just here.

COME, OH COME WITH ME.

Come, oh come with me,
  The moon is beaming;
Come, oh come with me,
  The stars are gleaming;
All round above with beauty beaming,
    Moonlight hours are meet for love.
      Tra la la la, &c. &c.

My skiff is on the shore,
  She's light and free;
To ply the feathered oar,
  Is joy to me;
And while we glide along,
  My song shall be,
My dearest maid, I love but thee.
    My skiff is on the shore, &c. &c.

OFT IN THE STILLY NIGHT.

Oft in the stilly night,
  Ere slumber's chain has bound me,
Fond memory brings the light
  Of other days around me.
The smiles, the tears, of boyhood's years,
  The words of love then spoken,
The eyes that shone, now dimm'd and gone,
  The cheerful hearts now broken.
      Oft in the stilly night, &c.

When I remember all
  The friends thus linked together,
I've seen around me fall,
  Like leaves in wintry weather,
I feel like one who treads alone,
  Some banquet hall deserted:
Whose lights are fled, whose garlands dead,
  And all but he departed.
Thus in the stilly night,
  Ere slumber's chain has bound me,
Fond memory brings the light
  Of other days around me.

THOMAS MOORE.

GAFFER GREEN AND ROBIN RUFF,

OR A THOUSAND A YEAR.

A NEW AND POPULAR DUETT.

Copied by permission of Firth **Pond & Co.**, publishers, 547 Broadway, **N. Y**

ROBIN RUFF—
If I had but a thousand a year, Gaffer Green—
  If I had but a thousand a year,
What a man would I be, and what sights would **I** see,
  If I had but a thousand a year!

GAFFER GREEN—
The best wish you could have, take my word, Robin Ruff,
  Would scarce find you in bread or in beer;
But be honest and true, and say what would you do,
  If you had but a thousand a year?

ROBIN RUFF—
I'd do—I scarcely know what, Gaffer Green,
  I'd go—faith I scarcely know where;
I'd scatter the chink, and leave others to think,
  If I had but a thousand a year.

GAFFER GREEN—
But when you are aged and gray, Robin Ruff,
  And the day of your death it draws near,
Say, what with your pains, would you do with your gains,
  If you then had a thousand a year?

ROBIN RUFF—
I scarcely can tell what you mean, Gaffer Green,
  For your questions are always so queer;
But as other folks die, I suppose so must I,—
GAFFER GREEN—
  What! and give up your thousand a year?

There's a place that is better than this, Robin Ruff—
  And I hope in my heart you'll go there,
Where the poor man's as great, though he hath no estate,
  Ay, though he'd "*A thousand a year.*"

JINNY GREEN AND BOBBY LUSH.

A PARODY ON GAFFER GREEN.

As sung by Dick Cunningham and Miss Fanny Gilmore.

If I had but a barrel of beer, Jinny Green,
  If I had but a barrel of beer,
     How jolly I'd be,
     As I drinked it so free,
If I had but a barrel of beer, Jinny Green,
  If I had but a barrel of beer!

Now if I had a wish, take my word, Bobby Lush,
  'Tis a barrel of beef, and not beer;
     For I always shall rue,
     That the last I e'er knew,
And was too fond of drinking beer, Bobby Lush,
  And was too fond of drinking beer.

You surely don't know what is good, Jinny Green,
  Or you'd not be a teetotaler;
     Whatever you may think,
     I'll stick to my drink,
And not give up drinking beer, Jinny Green,
  And not give up drinking beer.

If you live to be aged and gray, Bobby Lush,
  Which is not very likely, I fear;
     Your aches and your pains
     Will be all your gains,
Which you'll get by drinking your beer, Bobby Lush,
  Which you'll get by drinking your beer.

It is all very true what you say, Jinny Green,
  And drunkenness I cannot bear;
     But I am sure I should die,
     If I was but to try,
To give up drinking my beer, Jinny Green,
  To give up drinking my beer.

WOODMAN, SPARE THAT TREE.

WOODMAN, spare that tree!
  Touch not a single bough,
In youth it shelter'd me,
  And I'll protect it now;
'Twas my forefather's hand,
  That placed it near his cot;
There, woodman, let it stand,
  Thy axe shall harm it not.

That old familiar tree,
  Whose glory and renown
Are spread o'er land and sea,
  And would'st thou hack it down?
Woodman, forbear thy stroke,
  Cut not its earth-bound ties;
Oh! spare that aged oak,
  Now towering to the skies!

When but an idle boy,
  I sought its grateful shade;
In all their gushing joy,
  Here too my sisters play'd.
My mother kissed me here;
  My father pressed my hand;
Forgive this foolish tear,
  But let that old oak stand!

My heart-strings round thee cling,
  Close as thy bark, old friend!
Here shall the wild birds sing,
  And still thy branches bend.
Old tree! the storm still brave!
  And, woodman, leave the spot,
While I've a hand to save,
  Thy axe shall harm it not.

GEORGE P. MORRIS.

DO THEY MISS ME AT HOME.

Do they miss me at home, do they miss me?
  'Twould be an assurance most dear,
To know that this moment some loved one,
  Were saying, I wish he were here.
To feel that the group at the fireside
  Were thinking of me as I roam,
Oh, yes, 'twould be joy beyond measure
    To know that they miss'd me at home,
    To know that they miss'd me at home.

When twilight approaches, the season
  That ever is sacred to song,
Does some one repeat my name over,
  And sigh that I tarry so long?
And is there a chord in the music
  That's miss'd when my voice is away,
And a chord in each heart that awaketh
  Regret at my wearisome stay,
  Regret at my wearisome stay?

Do they set me a chair near the table,
  When ev'ning's home pleasures are nigh,
When the candles are lit in the parlor,
  And the stars in the calm azure sky?
And when the " good nights" are repeated,
  And all lay them down to their sleep,
Do they think of the absent, and waft me
  A whispered " good night" while they weep,
  A whispered " good night" while they weep?

Do they miss me at home—do they miss me
  At morning, at noon, or at night?
And lingers one gloomy shade round them
  That only my presence can light?
Are joys less invitingly welcome,
  And pleasures less hale than before,
Because one is miss'd from the circle,
  Because I am with them no more,
  Because I am with them no more?

WHAT IS HOME WITHOUT A MOTHER.

Copied by permission of Lee & Walker, Music publishers, 722 Chestnut
street, Philadelphia.

WHAT is home without a mother?
  What are all the joys we meet,
When her loving smile no longer
  Greets the coming, coming of our feet?
The days seem long, the nights are drear,
  And time rolls slowly on :
And oh! how few are childhood's pleasures,
  When her gentle care is gone.

Things we prize are first to vanish :
  Hearts we love to pass away :
And how soon, e'en in our childhood,
  We behold her turning, turning gray !
Her eye grows dim, her step is slow,
  Her joys on earth are past :
And sometimes ere we learn to know her,
  She hath breathed on earth, on earth her last.

Older hearts may have their sorrows,
  Griefs that quickly die away,
But a mother lost in childhood,
  Grieves the heart, the heart from day to day :
We miss her kind, her willing hand,
  Her fond and earnest care,
And, oh! how dark is life around us :
  What is HOME without her there?

THERE'S ROOM ENOUGH FOR ALL.

WHAT need of all this fuss and strife,
  Each warring with his brother?
Why need we through the crowd of life,
  Keep trampling on each other?
Is there no goal that can be won,
  Without a squeeze to gain it?
No other way of getting on,
  But scrambling to obtain it?
Oh, fellow men, remember then,
  Whatever chance befall,
The world is wide in lands beside,
  There's room enough for all.

What if the swarthy peasant find
  No field for honest labour?
He need not idly stop behind,
  To thrust aside his neighbour.
There is a land with sunny skies,
  Which gold for toil is giving,
Where every brawny hand that tries
  Its strength can grasp a living.
Oh, fellow men remember, &c.

COME, COME AWAY.

Oh! come, come away, from labour now reposing,
  Let busy care awhile forbear,
    Oh come, come away:
  Come, come, our social joys renew,
  And there where trust and friendship grew,
  Let true hearts welcome you,
    Oh come, come away.

From toil and cares, on which the day is closing,
  The hour of eve, brings sweet reprieve,
    Oh come, come away:
  Oh come, where love will smile on thee,
  And round its hearth will gladness be,
  And time fly merrily,
    Oh come, come away.

While sweet Philomel, the weary trav'ller cheering,
  With evening songs, her note prolongs,
    Oh come, come away:
  In answering songs of sympathy,
  We'll sing in tuneful harmony,
  Of hope, joy, liberty,
    Oh come, come away.

The bright day is gone, the moon and stars appearing,
  With silver light, illume the night,
    Oh come, come away:
  Come join your prayers with ours; address
  Kind heaven, our peaceful home to bless,
  With health, hope, happiness,
    Oh come, come away.

LET THE TOAST BE DEAR WOMAN.

BRIGHT, bright are the beams of the morning skies,
  And sweet dew the red blossom sips,
But brighter the glances of dear woman's eyes,
  And sweet is the dew on her lips;
Her mouth is the fountain of rapture,
  A source from whence purity flows,
Oh! who would not taste of its magic,
  As the honey-bee sips of the rose?

Chorus—

  Then the toast, then the toast, be "dear woman,"
    Let each breast that is manly approve;
  Then the toast, then the toast, be "dear woman,"
    And nine cheers for the girls that we love.
      Hip! hip! hurrah! hip! hip! hurrah!
        Hurrah! hurrah! hurrah!
    And nine cheers for the girls that we love.

Come raise, raise the wine-cup to heaven high;
  Ye gods of Olympus approve,
The offering thus mellow'd by woman's bright eye,
  Out rivals the nectar of Jove.
Then drain, drain the goblet with transport;
  A spell of life's best joy impart;
The cup thus devoted to woman,
  Yields the only true balm to the heart.
    Then the toast, &c.

SWIFT AS THE FLASH.

SWIFT as the flash, that mocks the sight,
Thou seem'st a bird in airy flight,
  When home returning,
We leave these cool fountains,
In our native mountains,
  Thy praise we'll recite:
    Swift as the, &c.

Thy steps so light, our songs invite,
Come fairy sprite, our eyes delight;
  When home returning,
We leave these cool fountains,
In our native mountains,
  Thy praise we'll recite:
    Swift as the, &c.

"THE HEART BOW'D DOWN."
From the Bohemian Girl.

THE heart bow'd down by weight and woe,
  To weakest hopes will cling,
To thought and impulse while they flow,
  That can no comfort bring.
With those exciting scenes will blend
  O'er pleasure's pathway thrown,—
But misery is the only friend
  That grief can call its own.

The mind will in its worst despair,
  Still ponder o'er the past,
On moments of delight that were
  Too beautiful to last;
To long departed years extend
  Its visions with them flown,
For mem'ry is the only friend
  That grief can call its own.

WILLIE, WE HAVE MISSED YOU.

Copied by permission of Firth, Pond, & Co., publishers, 547 Broadway, N. Y.

OH ! Willie, is it you, dear, safe, safe at home ?
They did not tell me true, dear, they said you would not come.
I heard you at the gate, and it made my heart rejoice,
For I knew that welcome footstep, and that dear familiar voice,
Making music on my ear, in the lonely midnight gloom,
Oh ! Willie, we have missed you ; welcome, welcome home.

We longed to see you nightly, but this night of all ;
The fire was burning brightly, and lights were in the hall,
The little ones were up till ten o'clock and past,
Then their eyes began to twinkle, and they went to sleep at last ;
But they listened for your voice, till they thought you'd never
    come,
Oh ! Willie, we have missed you ; welcome, welcome home.

The days were sad without you, the nights long and drear,
My dreams have been about you, oh, welcome, Willie dear,
Last night I wept and watched, by the moonlight's cheerless ray,
Till I thought I heard your footstep, then I wiped my tears
    away,
But my heart grew sad again, when I found you had not come ;
Oh ! Willie, we have missed you ; welcome, welcome home.

"'TIS BETTER TO LAUGH THAN BE SIGHING."

It is better to laugh than be sighing,
When we think how life's moments are flying,
For each sorrow fate ever is bringing,
There's a pleasure in store for us springing.
Though our joys like the waves in the sunshine,
   Gleam awhile, then be lost to the sight:
Yet for each sparkling ray that so passes away,
   Comes another as brilliant and light.
      Then 'tis better, &c.

In the world, we some beings discover,
Far too frigid for friends or for lover,
Souls unblest and forever repining,
Though good fortune around them be shining.
It were well if such hearts we could banish,
   To some planet far distant from ours,
They're the dark spots we trace, on this earth's favored space,
   They're the weeds that choke up the fair flowers.
      Then 'tis better, &c.

"EVER BE HAPPY."

Words by AUGUSTINE DUGANNE.   Music by BALFE.

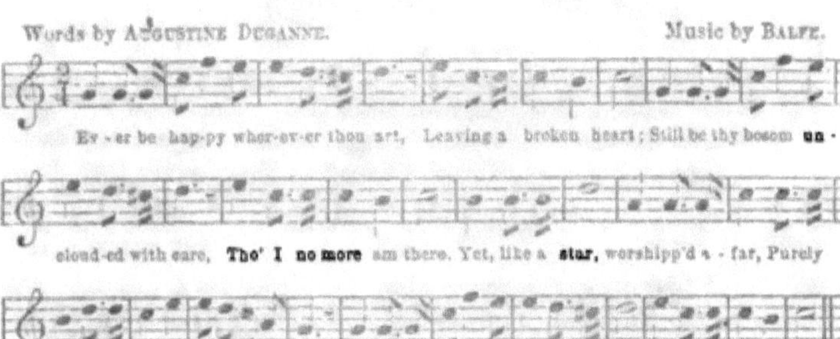

EVER be happy wherever thou art,
   Leaving a broken heart:
Still be thy bosom unclouded with care,
   Though I no more am there.
Yet, like a star, worshipp'd afar,
   Purely loved still thou art,
      Loved by a broken heart.
Ever be happy wherever thou art,
   Loved by a broken heart.

Well I remember the hours that we met;
   Oh! that I could forget!
Oh! that oblivion might haply o'ercast,
   Joys that too brightly pass'd.
Oh! that my soul thought might control,
   And forget that thou wert
   Loved by a trusting heart,
Ever be happy wherever thou art,
   Loved by a trusting heart.

I can but bless thee wherever thou art,
   Bless thee with hopeless heart!
I can but pray that no grief shall be thine,
   Grief such as now is mine.
Though in the dust lies all my trust,
   Yet beloved still thou art,
   Loved by a changeless heart.
Ever be happy wherever thou art,
   Loved by a changeless heart.

"WE MEET BY CHANCE."

When evening brings the twilight hour
    I pass a lonely spot,
Where oft she comes to cull the flower,
    We call " Forget-me-not."
She never whispers go, nor stay ;
We meet by *chance*, the usual way.

Once, how I cannot well divine,
    Unless by chance we kissed ;
I found her lips were close to mine,
    So I could not resist.
As neither whispered yea, nor nay,
They met by *chance*, the usual way.

The roses, when the zephyrs woo,
    Impart what they receive,
They sigh and sip the balmy dew,
    But never whisper give.
Our love is mutual, this we know
Though neither tells the other so.

Kucken.

'TIS HOME WHERE THE HEART IS.

Music published by Firth, Pond, & Co., 547 Broadway, N. Y.

'Tis home where e'er the heart is,
    Where e'er its loved ones dwell,
In cities, or in cottages,
    Throng'd haunts or mossy dell.
The heart's a rover ever,
    And thus on wave and wild,
The maiden with her lover walks,
    The mother with her child.

'Tis bright where e'er the heart is,
    Its fairy spell can bring
Fresh fountains to the wilderness,
    And to the desert spring.
Green isles are in the ocean,
    O'er which affection glides,
A haven on each sunny shore,
    When love's the sun that guides.

'Tis free where e'er the heart is,
  Nor chains, nor dungeons dim,
May check the mind's aspiring thought,
  The spirit's pealing hymn.
The heart gives life its beauty,
  Its glory and its powers :
'Tis sunlight to the rippling stream,
  And soft dew to its flowers.

THE CAVALIER.

'TWAS a beautiful night,
  The stars shone bright,
And the moon o'er the waters play'd,
    When a Cavalier
    To a bower drew near,
A lady to serenade.
    To tend'rest words
    He swept the chords,
And many a sigh breathed he ;
    While o'er and o'er
    He fondly swore—
" Sweet maid ! I love but thee,
    Sweet maid, sweet maid,
    Sweet maid, I love but thee."

    He rais'd his eye
    To her lattice high,
While he softly breathed his hopes,
    With amazement he sees
    Swing about in the breeze,
Already, a ladder of ropes !
    Up, up he has gone,
    The bird is flown !
" What's this on the ground ?" quoth he—
    " Oh, it's plain that she loves,
    Here's some gentleman's gloves,
She's off and it's not with me,
    For these gloves, these gloves,
    They never belong'd to me."

Of course, you'd have thought,
He'd have followed and fought,
As that was a "duelling age,"
But this gay Cavalier
He quite scorn'd the idea
Of putting himself in a rage:
More wise by far,
He put up his guitar,
And as homeward he went, sung he—
"When a lady elopes
Down a ladder of ropes—
She may go to—Hong Kong for me—
She may go, she may go,
She may go, to—Hong Kong for me."

TWINKLING STARS.

TWINKLING stars are laughing, love,
Laughing on you and me,
While your bright eyes look in mine,
Peeping stars they seem to be;
Troubles come and go, love,
Brightest scenes must leave our sight,
But the star of hope, love,
Shines with radiant beams to-night.
Chorus—Twinkling stars are laughing love,
Laughing on you and me,
While your bright eyes look in mine,
Peeping stars they seem to be.

Golden beams are shining, love,
Shining on you to bless,
Like the queen of night, you fill
Darkest space with loveliness.
Silver stars how bright, love,
Mother moon in thronely might,
Gaze on us to bless, love,
Purest vows here made to-night.
Twinkling stars, &c.

OLD DOG TRAY.

THE morn of life is past, and evening comes at last;
  It brings me a dream of a once happy day,
Of many forms I've seen, upon the village green,
  Sporting with my old Dog Tray.
Chorus—Old Dog Tray's ever faithful,
      Grief cannot drive him away.
    He's gentle, he is kind; I'll never, never find
      A better friend than old Dog Tray.

The forms I called my own, have vanished one by one,
  The loved ones, the dear ones have all passed away,
Their happy smiles have flown, their gentle voices gone;
  I have nothing left but old Dog Tray.
    Old Dog Tray's ever faithful, &c.

When thoughts recall the past, his eyes are on me cast,
  I know that he feels what my breaking heart would say,
Although he cannot speak, I'll vainly, vainly seek
  A better friend than old Dog Tray.
    Old Dog Tray's ever faithful, &c.

MY OWN NATIVE LAND.

I'VE roved over mountain, I've crossed over flood,
  I've traversed the wave-rolling sand;
Though the fields were as green, and the moon shone as bright,
  Yet it was not my own native land.
    No, no, no, no, no, no.   No, no, no, no, no, no,
Though the fields were as green, and the moon shone as bright,
  Yet it was not my own native land.

The right hand of friendship how oft I have grasped,
  And bright eyes have smiled and looked bland;
Yet happier far were the hours that I passed
  In the West—in my own native land.
    Yes, yes, yes, yes, yes, yes.   Yes, yes, yes, yes, yes, yes,
Yet happier far were the hours that I passed
  In the West—in my own native land.

Then hail dear Columbia, the land that we love,
  Where flourishes Liberty's tree;
The birth-place of Freedom, our own native home,
  'Tis the land, 'tis the land of the free!
    Yes, yes, yes, yes, yes, yes.   Yes, yes, yes, yes, yes, yes,
The birth-place of Freedom, our own native home,
  'Tis the land, 'tis the land of the free!

LULU IS OUR DARLING PRIDE.

Printed by permission of J. E. Gould, publisher, Philadelphia.

LULU is our darling pride,
　Lulu bright, Lulu gay;
Dancing lightly at our side
　All the livelong day.
Not a bird that wings the air
　Soaring to the sun,
Freer is from every care
　Than our darling one.
Chorus—Oh, Lulu is our darling pride,
　Lulu bright, Lulu gay,
Dancing lightly at our side
　All the livelong day.

As the flowers of early spring
　Seem more bright, seem more gay,
As their perfume first they fling
　Fragrant at our feet,
So tho' others lov'd there be,
　Blooming in our bower,
Lulu wins our hearts,
　For she's our loveliest flower.
Oh, Lulu is our darling pride,
　Lulu bright, Lulu gay,
Dancing lightly at our side
　All the livelong day.

When the clouds of trouble come,
　Lulu soothes all our care;
Ah, how dark would be our home
　Were not Lulu there!
Lulu with her sunny smile,
　Cheering every heart,
Till each trouble she beguiles,
　And the clouds depart.
Oh, Lulu is our darling pride,
　Lulu bright, Lulu gay,
Dancing lightly at our side
　All the livelong day.

THE OLD ARM CHAIR.

I LOVE it, I love it, and who shall dare,
To chide me for loving that Old Arm Chair?
I've treasured it long as a holy prize,
I've bedew'd it with tears and embalm'd it with sighs;
'Tis bound by a thousand bands to my heart,
Not a tie will break, not a link will start.
Would ye learn the spell, a mother sat there,
And a sacred thing is that Old Arm Chair.

I sat and watch'd her many a day,
When her eyes grew dim, and her locks grew gray;
And I almost worshipp'd her when she smil'd
And turn'd from her Bible to bless her child.
Years roll'd on, but the last one sped,
My idol was shatter'd, my earth-star fled;
I learnt how much the heart can bear,
When I saw her die in that Old Arm Chair.

'Tis past, 'tis past, but I gaze on it now,
With quivering breath, and throbbing brow,
'Twas there she nurs'd me, 'twas there she died,
And mem'ry flows with lava tide.
Say it is folly, and deem me weak,
While the scalding drops start down my cheek;
But I love it, I love it, and cannot tear
My soul from a mother's Old Arm Chair.

ELIZA COOK.

THE BRAVE OLD OAK.

Sung by Mr. Russell.

A SONG of the oak, the brave old oak,
  Who hath ruled in the greenwood long;
Here's health and renown to his broad green crown,
  And his fifty arms so strong.
There is fear in his frown, when the sun goes down,
  And the fire in the west fades out;
And he showeth his might, on a wild midnight,
  When storms through his branches shout.
Then sing to the oak, the brave old oak,
  Who hath ruled in his land so long;
And still flourish he a hale green tree,
  When a hundred years are gone.

He saw the times, when the Christmas chimes
  Were a merry sound to hear;
And the squire's wide hall, and the cottage small,
  Were full of American cheer;
And all the day, to the rebeck gay,
  They frolick'd with lovesome swains;
They are gone, they are dead, in the churchyard laid,
  But the tree, he still remains.
    Then sing to the oak, &c.

LITTLE NELL.

THEY told him, gently, she was dead,
  And spoke of heaven and smiled;
Then drew him from the lonely room,
  Where lay the lovely child.
'Twas all in vain, he heeded not
  Their pitying looks of sorrow.
"Hush! hush!" he cried, "she only sleeps,
  She'll wake again to-morrow!"
                "Hush! hush!" &c.

They laid her in a lowly grave,
  Where winds blew high and bleak;
Though the faintest summer breeze had been
  Too rough to fan her cheek.
And there the poor old man would watch,
  In strange, though childish, sorrow,
And whisper to himself the words,
  "She'll come again to-morrow!"
                And whisper, &c.

One day they missed him long, and sought
  Where most he loved to stray:
They found him dead upon the turf,
  Where little Nelly lay.
With tottering steps he'd wander'd there,
  Fresh hope and strength to borrow,
And e'en in dying breath'd this prayer,
  "Oh! let her come to-morrow!"
    The old man, dying, breath'd the prayer,
      "Oh! let her come to-morrow!"

FAREWELL TO THE HOME OF MY CHILDHOOD.

FAREWELL to the home of my childhood,
  Farewell to my cottage and vine,
I go to the land of the stranger,
  Where pleasure alone will be mine.
When life's fleeting journey is over,
  And earth again mingles with earth,
I can rest in the land of the stranger,
  As well as in that of my birth.
Yes, these were my feelings at parting,
  But absence soon alter'd their tone;
The cold hand of sickness came o'er me,
  And I wept o'er my sorrow alone.

No friend came near me to cheer me,
  No parent to soften my grief,
Nor brother, nor sister, were near me,
  And strangers could give no relief.
'Tis true that it matters but little,
  Though living, the thought makes one pine,
Whatever befalls the poor relic,
  When the spirit has flown from its shrine.
But, oh! when life's journey is over,
  And earth again mingles with earth,
Lamented or not, still my wish is,
  To rest in the land of my birth.

OH! SHARE MY COTTAGE.

By J. Shrival, formerly of the " Seguin Opera Troupe.",

OH! share my cottage, gentle maid,
  It only waits for thee,
To give a sweetness to its shade,
  And happiness, happiness to me.
Here from the splendid gay parade,
  Of noise and folly free,
No sorrows can my peace invade,
  If only bless'd with thee.
      Then share my cottage, &c.

The hawthorn with the woodbine twin'd,
  Present their sweets to thee,
And ev'ry balmy breath of wind,
  Is fill'd with harmony.
A truly fond and faithful heart,
  Is all I offer thee,
And canst thou see me thus depart,
  A prey to misery?
     Then share my cottage, &c.

THE IVY GREEN.

OH, a dainty plant is the ivy green,
  That creepeth o'er ruins old:
Of right choice food are his meals, I ween,
  In his cell, so lone and cold.
The wall must be crumbled, the stone decayed,
  To pleasure his dainty whim;
And the mouldering dust that years have made,
  Is a merry meal for him.
     Creeping where no life is seen,
     A rare old plant is the ivy green.

Fast he stealeth on, though he wears no wings,
  And a staunch old head has he;
How closely he twineth, how tight he clings,
  To his friend, the huge oak tree.
And slily he traileth along the ground,
  And his leaves he gently waves;
As he joyously hugs, and crawleth round
  The rich mould of dead men's graves.
     Creeping where grim death hath been,
     A rare old plant is the ivy green.

Whole ages have fled, and works decayed,
  And nations have scattered been!
But the stout old ivy shall never fade,
  From its hale and hearty green.
The brave old plant in its lonely days,
  Shall fatten upon the past;
For the stateliest building man can raise,
  Is the Ivy's food at last.
     Creeping on where time has been,
     A rare old plant is the ivy green.

THE LORDS OF CREATION.

THE lords of creation men we call.
  And they think they rule the whole,
But they're much mistaken after all,
  For they're under woman's control.
As ever since the world began,
  It has always been the way,
For did not Adam, the very first man,
   The very first woman obey, obey, obey?
   The very first woman obey?

Ye lords, who at present hear my song,
  I know you will quickly say;
"Our sizes more large, our nerves more strong;
  Shall the stronger the weaker obey!"
But think not though these words we hear,
  We shall e'er mind the thing you say;
For as long as a woman's possessed of a tear,
  Your power will vanish away.

THE ROCK BESIDE THE SEA!

Music published by **Lee & Walker**, 722 Chestnut street, Phila.

OH, tell me not the woods are fair,
  Now spring is on her way:
Well, well I know how brightly there,
  In joy the young leaves play:
How sweet, on winds of morn or eve,
  The violet's breath may be,
Yet ask me, woo me not to leave } *Repeat.*
  My lone rock by the sea. }

The wild waves' thunder on the shore,
  The curlews' restless cries,
Unto my watching heart are more
  Than all earth's melodies.
Come back my ocean rover, come!
  There's but one place for me,
Till I can greet thy swift sail home—
  My lone rock by the sea!

5

"IN THIS OLD CHAIR."

Music by M. W. BALFE.

And here, alas! when they were gone
  In beauty's own array,
A pitying angel on me shone,
  To chase each grief away;
But oh! it was delusive love,
  Alas! too pure, too sweet to last,
And if such dream time must remove,
  Why, mem'ry, paint the past?

"THOU ART MINE OWN, LOVE."

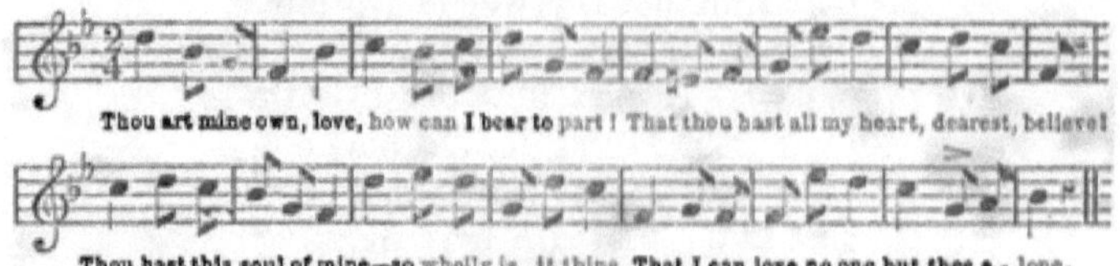

Blue is the flow'ret, called the "Forget-me-not!"
Ah! lay it on thy heart and think of me;
Should hope fade with the flowers, love's wealth shall still be ours,
That will remain with me, dearest, believe!

Were I a bird, love, soon would I fly to thee,
Falcon nor hawk to me should terror bring;
If shot by huntsman's hand, I at thy feet lay dead,
If thou one tear would'st shed, gladly I'd die.

"SOME ONE TO LOVE."

Words by JAMES SIMMONS.   J. R. THOMAS.

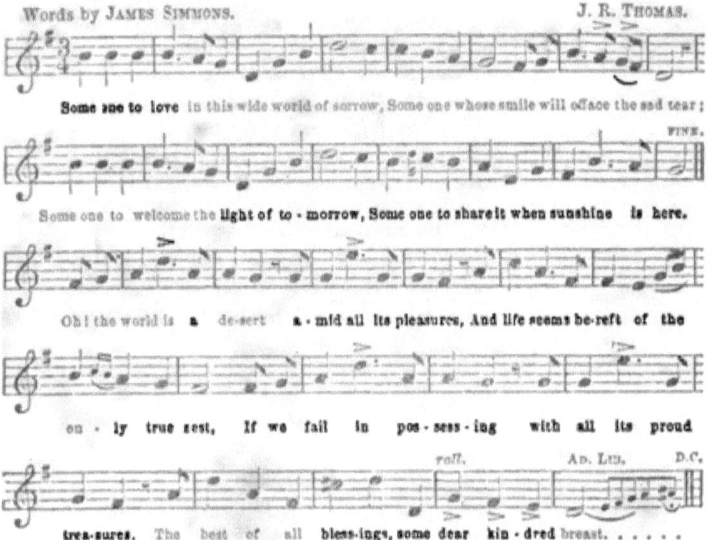

SOME one to love in this wide world of sorrow,
  Some one whose smile will efface the sad tear;
Some one to welcome the light of to-morrow,
  Some one to share it when sunshine is here.
Oh! the world is a desert amid all its pleasures,
  And life seems bereft of the only true zest,
If we fail in possessing with all its proud treasures,
  The best of all blessings, some dear kindred breast.
      Some one to love, &c.

Some one to love whose affection will cherish
  The sweet bud of hope when 'tis blighted with care;
Some faithful heart that will ne'er let it perish
  By sinking forever in depths of despair.
'Tis an angelic radiance, a beacon to guide us,
  Resembling those lamps that are shining above,
'Tis a guardian from heaven, a light to decide us,
  Teaching us lessons of wisdom and love.
      Some one to love, &c.

DON'T BE ANGRY, MOTHER!

Don't be angry, mother, mother,
  Let thy smiles be smiles of joy,
Don't be angry, mother, mother,
  Don't be angry with thy boy.
Years have flown since we have traversed
  O'er the dark and stormy sea;
Whilst your boy, quite broken-hearted,
  Ne'er has ceased to think of thee.

Don't be angry, mother, mother,
  Let the world say what it will,
Though I don't deserve thy favor,
  Yet I fondly love thee still;
We have lived and loved together,
  And our hearts ne'er knew a pain,
But forgive me, mother, mother,
  Oh, forgive thy boy again.

Pray remember, mother, mother,
  I've been kneeling at thy feet,
And I am dreaming of thee nightly,
  While reclining in my sleep;
But forgive me, mother, mother,
  It will ease thy heart of pain,
But forgive me, mother, mother,
  Oh forgive thy boy again.

THE OLD PLAY-GROUND.

I'm sitting to-day in the old play-ground,
  Where you and I have sat so oft together,
I'm thinking of the joys when you and I were boys,
  In the merry days now gone, John, forever;
'Twas here we sat in the merry olden time,
  And we dreamed of the wide world before us,
And our visions and hopes of the coming time
  Were as bright as the sun that shone o'er us.

Chorus.—I'm sitting to-day in the old play ground,
  Where you and I have sat so oft together,
I'm thinking of the joys when you and I were boys,
  In those merry days now gone, John, forever.

O'er the threshold, John, we passed forlorn,
To wander we knew not where,
The heaven we thought so bright was o'ershadowed by night,
And the pathway lay dark and drear.
But I am sitting to-day in the old play ground,
Where you and I have sat so oft together,
And these memories wild have made me a child,
As in the merry days now gone, John, forever.
Chorus.—I'm sitting to-day, &c.

THERE'S A GOOD TIME COMING.

There's a good time coming, boys,
A good time coming;
There's a good time coming, boys,
Wait a little longer;
We may not live to see the day,
But earth shall glisten in the ray
Of the good time coming;
Cannon balls may aid the truth,
But thought's a weapon stronger;
We'll win our battles by its aid,
Wait a little longer.
There's a good time coming, boys,
A good time coming,
There's a good time coming, boys,
Wait a little longer.

There's a good time coming, boys,
A good time coming;
There's a good time coming, boys,
Wait a little longer;
The pen shall supersede the sword,
And right, not might, shall be the lord,
In the good time coming;
Worth, not birth, shall rule mankind,
And be acknowledged stronger,
The proper impulse has been given,
Wait a little longer.
There's a good time coming, boys,
A good time coming;
There's a good time coming, boys,
Wait a little longer.

THE GASCON VESPERS.

HARK! the merry peal is ringing,
  List ye, how the bells around,
O'er the Garonne's banks are flinging,
  Far and near, their cheerful sound.
Hark ye! how each Gascon maiden,
  To the rising moon now sings;
While with sweets the night breeze laden,
  Wafts their voices on its wings.

Haste then, stranger, join our chorus,
  Come then with onr maidens pray,
Join the happy group before us,
  Chanting neath the moonlight ray.
Glide on, my bark! how sweet to rove,
With such a beaming sky above,
O'er the dark sea, whose murmurs seem,
Like fairy music in a dream;
No sound is heard to break the spell,
Except the water's gentle swell;
Whilst midnight, like a mimic day,
Shines on, to guide our moon-lit way.

SWISS BOY.

COME, arouse thee, arouse thee, my brave Swiss boy,
Take thy pail and to labor away!   [*Repeat.*]
The sun is up with ruddy beam,
The kine are thronging to the stream.
Come, arouse thee, arouse thee, my brave Swiss boy,
Take thy pail, and to labor away.

Am not I, am not I, say, a merry Swiss boy,
When I hie to the mountains away!
For there a shepherd maiden dear,
Awaits my song with listening ear.
      Am not I, &c.

Then at night! then at night—Oh! a gay Swiss boy,
I'm away to my comrades, away!
The cup we fill—the wine is pass'd,
In friendship round until at last,
With good night! and good night! goes the happy Swiss boy,
To his home and his slumbers, away.

TWENTY YEARS AGO.

I HAVE wandered by the village, Tom—I've sat beneath the
    tree,
Upon the school-house playing-ground which sheltered you and
    me,
But none are left to greet me, Tom, and few are left to know,
That played with us upon the green just Twenty Years Ago.

The grass is just as green, dear Tom, bare-footed boys at play
Are sporting just as we were then, with spirits just as gay,
But master sleeps upon the hill, all coated o'er with snow,
That afforded us a sliding-place just Twenty Years Ago.

The old school-house is altered some, the benches are replaced
By new ones, very like the same our penknives had defaced;
But the same old bricks are in the wall, the bell swings to and
    fro,
The music just the same, dear Tom, 'twas Twenty Years Ago.

The boys are playing some old game, beneath that same old tree,
I do forget the name just now—you have played the same with
    me;
On that same spot 'twas played with knives, by throwing so and
    so,
The leaders had a task to do there Twenty Years Ago.

The river is running just as still—the willows on its side,
Are larger than they were, dear Tom, the stream appears less
    wide;
The grape-vine swing is ruined now, where once we played the
    beau,
And swung our sweethearts, pretty girls, just Twenty Years
    Ago.

The spring that bubbled 'neath the hill, close by the spreading
    beach,
Is very high—'twas once so low that we could almost reach;
But in kneeling down to get a drink, dear Tom, I started so,
To see how sadly I am changed since Twenty Years Ago.

Down by the spring upon an elm you know I cut your name—
Your sweetheart is just beneath it, Tom—and you did mine the
    same,
Some heartless wretch has peeled the bark—'twas dying sure
    but slow,
Just as the one whose name you cut did Twenty Years Ago.

My lids have long been dry, dear Tom, but tears come in **my**
      eyes,
I thought of her I loved so well—those early broken ties ;
I visited the old church-yard, and took some flowers to strew
Upon the graves of those we loved some Twenty Years Ago.

Some are in the church-yard laid, some sleep beneath the sea,
But few are left of our old class, excepting you and me ;
But when our time shall come, dear Tom, and we are called
      to go,
I hope they'll lay us where we played just Twenty Years Ago.

ELLEN BAYNE.

SOFT be thy slumbers,
  Rude cares, depart !
Visions, in numbers,
  Cheer thy young heart.
Dream on, while bright hours
  And fond hopes remain,
Blooming, like smiling bowers,
  For thee, Ellen Bayne !
Chorus—Gentle slumbers o'er thee glide,
  Dreams of beauty round thee bide,
While I linger by thy side,
  Sweet Ellen Bayne !

Dream not in anguish,
  Dream not in fear,
Love shall not languish—
  Fond ones are near.
Sleeping or waking,
  In pleasure or pain,
Warm hearts will beat for thee,
  Sweet Ellen Bayne !
Gentle slumbers, &c.

Scenes that have vanished,
  Smile on thee now.
Pleasures once banished,
  Play round thy brow—
Forms long departed,
  Greet thee again,
Soothing thy dreaming heart,
  Sweet Ellen Bayne !
Gentle slumbers, &c.

"I DREAMT THAT I DWELT IN MARBLE HALLS."

From the Bohemian Girl.

I DREAMT that I dwelt in marble halls,
  With vassals and serfs at my side,
And of all who assembled within those walls,
  That I was the hope and pride.
I had riches too great to count—could boast
  Of a high ancestral name,
But I also dreamt, which pleased me most,
  That you loved me still the same.

I dreamt that suitors sought my hand,
  That knights upon bended knee,
And with vows no maiden heart could withstand,
  They pledged their faith to me.
And I dreamt that one of that noble host,
  Came forth my hand to claim,
But I also dreamt, which charm'd me most,
  That you loved me still the same.

JENNY LIND'S CELEBRATED BIRD SONG.

BIRDLING, why sing in the forest wide?
    Say, say! Say, say!
Callest thou thy bridegroom or thy bride?
    Oh, say! Oh, say!
I call no bridegroom nor bride,
Yet must I sing in the forest wide;
Nor know, nor know, know I,
Why thus I'm singing la, la, la, **la, la, la, la,** la, la.
  Know not why thus I'm singing.

Birdling, oh say, is thy heart so blest,
    Oh, say! Oh, say!
That song must burst from thy joyous breast?
    Oh, say! Oh, say!
Oh, yes! my heart is glad and light,
I know no sorrow, day or night;
Nor know, nor know, know I
Why thus I'm singing la, la, la, la, la, la, la, la, la.
  Know not why thus I'm singing.

Birdling, what singest thou all the day?
        Say what! Say what!
And tell me who listens to thy lay;
        Oh, tell! Oh, tell!
I sing, I sing through all day long,
Nor know I the burden of my song;
Yet must, yet must, yet must
I still be singing la, la, la, la, la, la, la, la, la.
    Must I still be singing.

OH! GIVE ME FREEDOM EVER,

OR THE INDEPENDENT MAID.

Copied by permission of Firth, Pond & Co., 547 Broadway, N. Y.

Oh, give me freedom ever!
    A chainless heart and hand,
Slave of no jealous lover,
    Nor husband's stern command;
To rove through ball and bower,
    With honest smiles for all,
Prey to no suitor's power,
    And holding none in thrall.
Chorus—Oh, give me freedom ever!
    A chainless heart and hand,
Slave of no jealous lover,
    Nor husband's stern command;
La, la, la, la, la, la,
    La, la, la, la, la, la, la,
To laugh at Cupid's archery,
    With heart for ever free.

Set maids to catch a lover,
    Their brighest smiles put on,
Too soon they may discover,
    Their prize and hopes are gone;
While wives half broken-hearted,
    To tyrant husbands cling,
Free-footed and free-hearted,
    I laugh at care and sing.—
Oh, give me freedom ever, &c.
                            SILAS S. STEELE.

MY HELEN IS THE FAIREST FLOWER.

My Helen is the fairest flower
  That ever graced the sun or shade,
Or deck'd with charms the lover's bower,
  The desert wild, or mountain glade :
Her bosom fairer than the snow,
  Or April showers, or May-morn's breath,
Than moonlight rays, or rubies' glow,
  Than weeping lily clos'd in death.
      Yes, Helen is, &c.

Her azure eyes, when cast above,
  Are brighter than yon starry sky ;
Her mellow voice in notes of love
  First rais'd my soul to bliss on high.
Her cheeks they mock the rose's bloom,
  Her dear, dear lips the coral's hue,
Her breath rich India's choice perfume,
 'Her breast is tender, kind, and true.
      Yes, Helen is, &c.

SONG OF THE SEXTON.

Oh, the sights that I see as I ply my lone trade,
In the mouldering dust that a cent'ry hath made,
  Where the coffin-worm doth creep.
I began long ago, when my life was still green,
And my mattock and spade have been active, I ween,
  To fashion the grave so deep.
Ho ! I laugh as I dig, for they all seek my aid,
To provide them a home with my mattock and spade.

The rich man hath pass'd me with towering head,
But I sang o'er his grave when the scorner was dead,
  And laugh'd as I shovel'd the mould.
The hungry and wretched ne'er enter'd his door,
His heart never bled for the wrongs of the poor,
  For the proud man loved his gold.
Ho ! I laugh'd as I dug, for they wanted my aid,
To provide him a home with my mattock and spade.

I saw a young man in the fresh bloom of life,
As he came to the church with a trembling young wife,
   Lift against me the finger of scorn.
Oh, the revel was joyous, the dance lasted long;
But the shriek of the widow soon banish'd the song—
   The young man died ere morn!
Ho! I laugh'd as I dug, when they came for my aid,
To provide him a home with my mattock and spade.

I saw a fair child bend her beautiful head,
And cull the lone flowers that bloom o'er the dead,
   To form a simple wreath.
The crimson of hectic suffused her pale face;
In her eyes fearful lustre I trembled to trace,
   The herald of early death.
But I pray that ere then, the deep home I have made,
May close over *me*, and my mattock and spade.

SHE WORE A WREATH OF ROSES.

SHE wore a wreath of roses the night when first we met,
Her lovely face was smiling beneath her curls of jet;
Her footsteps had the lightness, her voice the joyous tone,
The tokens of a youthful heart where sorrow is unknown;
I saw her but a moment, yet methinks I see her now,
With the wreath of summer flowers upon her snowy brow.

A wreath of orange flowers when next we met she wore,
The expression of her features was more thoughtful than be-
    fore,
And standing by her side was one who strove, and not in vain,
To soothe her leaving that dear home she ne'er might view
    again;
I saw her but a moment, but methinks I see her now,
With the wreath of orange blossoms upon her snowy brow.

And once again I see that brow, no bridal wreath is there,
The widow's sombre cap conceals her once luxuriant hair;
She weeps in silent solitude, and there is no one near,
To press her hand within his own, and wipe the fallen tear!
I see her broken-hearted, and methinks I see her now,
In the pride of youth and beauty, with a wreath upon her brow.

THE BONNY BOAT.

On, swiftly glides the bonny boat,
  Just parted from the shore,
And to the fishers' chorus note,
  Soft moves the dipping oar;
Their toils are borne with happy cheer,
  And ever may they speed,
That feeble age, and helpmate dear,
  And tender bairnies feed.

We cast our lines in Largo bay,
  Our nets are floating wide,
Our bonny boat with yielding sway
  Rocks lightly on the tide;
And happy prove its daily lot
  Upon the summer sea,
And blest on land our kindly cot,
  Where all our treasures be.
    We cast our lines in Largo bay, &c.

The mermaid on her rock may sing,
  The witch may weave her charm,
But water sprite nor eldrich thing
  The bonny boat can harm;
It safely bears its scaly store
  Through many a stormy gale,
While joyful shouts rise from the shore,
  Its homeward prow to hail.
    We cast our lines in Largo bay, &c.

AWAY! AWAY, TO THE MOUNTAIN'S BROW.

Away! away, to the mountain's brow,
  Where the trees are gently waving,
Away! away, to the mountain's brow,
  Where the stream is gently laving.
And beauty, my love, on thy cheek shall dwell,
  Like the rose as it opes to the day,
While the zephyr that breathes thro' the flow'ry dell
  Shakes the sparkling dew-drops away.
    Away! away, to the mountain's brow, &c.

Away! away, to the rocky glen,
  Where the deer are wildly bounding,
And the hills shall echo in gladness again
  To the hunter's bugle sounding;
While beauty, my love, on thy cheek shall dwell,
  Like the rose as it opes to the day,
While the zephyr that breathes thro' the flow'ry dell,
  Shakes the sparkling dew-drops away.
    Away! away, to the rocky glen, &c.

THE GOLDEN GIRL.

Lucy is a golden girl,
  But a man, a man should woo her;
They who seek her, shrink aback,
  When they should, like storms, pursue her:
All her smiles are hid in light,
  All her hair is lost in splendor,
But she hath the eyes of night,
  And a heart that's over tender.
      Oh! Lucy is, &c.

Yet the foolish suitors fly,
  (Is't excess of dread or duty?)
From the starlight of her eye,
  Leaving to neglect her beauty:
Men by fifty seasons taught,
  Leave her to a young beginner,
Who without a second thought
  Whispers, woos, and straight must win her.
      Oh! Lucy is, &c.

THE RAPTURE DWELLING.

The rapture dwelling within my breast,
  And fondly telling its fears to rest;
The rapture dwelling within my breast,
  And fondly telling its fears to rest;
Comes o'er me weaving its charmed chain,
  No vestige leaving of sorrow's strain,
    No vestige leaving of sorrow's strain,
    Of sorrow's, sorrow's strain.

MINSTREL'S RETURN FROM THE WAR.

THE minstrel's return'd from the war,
  With spirits as buoyant as air,
And thus on his tuneful **guitar**,
  He sung in the bower of **his fair**:
"The noise of the battle is **over**,
  The bugle no more calls to arms;
A soldier no more—but a lover,
  I bend to the power of thy charms.
    Sweet lady, fair lady, I'm thine,
      I bend to the magic of beauty,
    Tho' the banner and helmet are mine
      Yet love calls the soldier to duty."

The minstrel his suit warmly press'd,
  She blush'd, sigh'd, and hung down her **head**,
Till conquer'd she fell on his breast,
  And thus to the happy youth said:
"The bugle shall part us love, never,
  My bosom thy pillow shall be,
Till death tears thee from me, for ever,
  Still faithful, I'll perish with thee."
    Sweet lady, &c.

But fame call'd the youth to the field;
  His banner wav'd high o'er **his** head,
He gave his guitar for a shield,
  And soon he lay low with the **dead**,
While she, o'er her young hero **bending**,
  Received his expiring adieu:
"I die whilst my country defending,
  But I die to my lady love true."
    "Oh, **death**! (then she cried) I am **thine**,
      I tear **off** the roses of beauty;
    The grave of my hero is mine,
      For he died true to love and to duty!"

"MY COT BESIDE THE SEA."

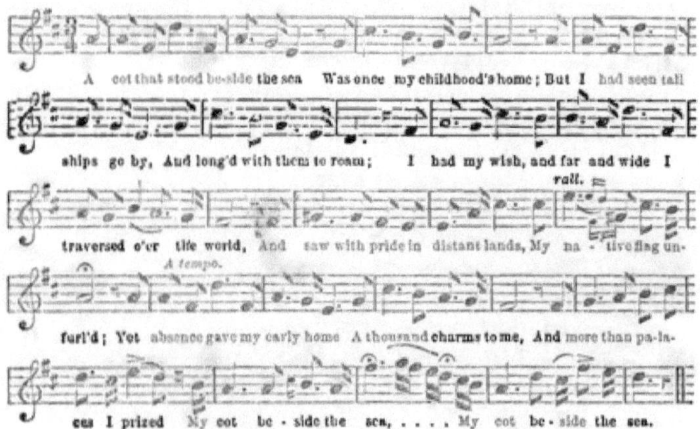

Though kind hearts beat in many lands,
   Though gentle looks were dear;
My longing hopes of home gave birth
   To many a fervent prayer.
And when I laid me down to rest,
   The sweet desire of day,
Gave place to bright and happy dreams
   Of dear ones far away.
I woke, and fondly thought their dreams,
   Perchance, had been of me :
Thus day and night I longed to greet
   My cot beside the sea.

I hailed at length the happy land,
   I pressed my native shore,
I felt my heart grow young again,
   What could I ask for more ?
But phantom-like, my visions fled,
   The friends I love are gone,
A stranger in my childhood's home,
   I stand unloved, unknown ;
Yet while one link in mem'ry's chain,
   Unbroken there shall be—
'Twill bind me to that once loved home,
   My cot beside the sea.

"OH! WOULD I WERE A BOY AGAIN."

Words by MARK LEMON.　　　Music by F. ROMER.

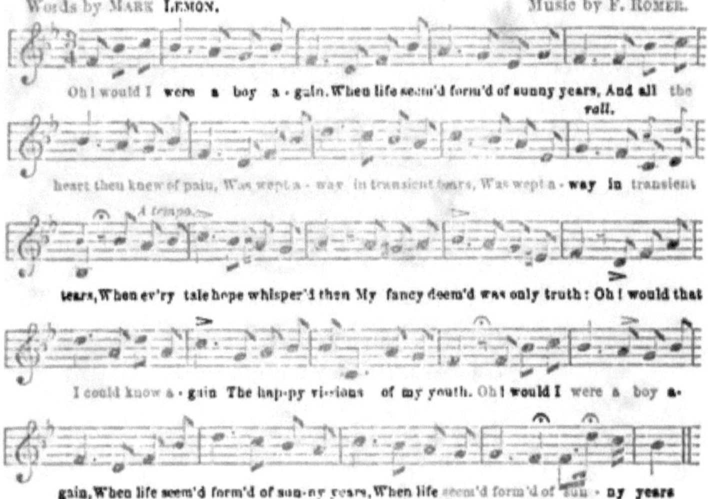

Oh! would I were a boy again,
　When life seemed formed of sunny years,
And all the heart then knew of pain,
　Was wept away in transient tears.
When every tale hope whispered then
　My fancy deemed was only truth:
Oh! would that I could know again
　The happy visions of my youth.
Oh! would I were a boy again,
　When life seemed formed of sunny years

'Tis vain to mourn that years have shown
　How false these fairy visions were,
Or murmur that mine eyes have known
　The burthen of a fleeting tear.
But still the heart will fondly cling
　To hopes no longer prized as truth;
And mem'ry still delights to bring
　The happy visions of my youth.
Oh! would I were a boy again,
　When life seemed formed of sunny years.

G

OH, DON'T MINGLE ONE HUMAN FEELING.

Oh, don't mingle one human feeling,
With these blisses o'er each sense stealing,
While these tributes to me revealing,
  Elvino faithful to his love.
Ah! embrace me; while thus forgiving,
Each a pardon thus receiving,
On the earth while we are living,
  We will to a heaven of love.
  Come then, away, lead to the temple;
None have pass'd a doom severer,
Let our greeting loudly cheer her,
Since her trials make her dearer,
  To our hearts and to our love.

DO I NOT PROVE THEE.

The celebrated parting Duett in Norma.

Norma.   Do I not prove thee,
    How I must love thee?
Thus with thee sharing a doom of terror,
    Yes! hoping brightly,
    Still beating lightly
My heart might feel not regret or fear!
    But false love swayed thee,
    And hath betrayed thee,
And, haughty Roman, quail for thy error!
    For in this hour
    Shall flames devour
Thee! faithless being still held most dear.

Claudian.   Oh, dread reflection!
    Thy true affection
Too late convinceth my frenzied reason;
    Truth flashing o'er me,
    Unveils before me
The ghastly vision of shameful death!
    I own I left thee,
    Of peace bereft thee,
Thy love repaying with heartless treason:
    Then doom me only,
    I'll perish lonely,
And bless thee, e'en with my latest breath!

MY BOAT IS ON THE SHORE.

My boat is **on** the shore,
  And my bark is on the sea;
But before I go, Tom Moore,
  Here's a double health to thee.

Here's **a** sigh for those that love,
  And a smile **for those who** hate,
And whatever sky's **above,**
  Here's a heart for **ev'ry fate.**

Though the ocean roars around me,
  Yet it still shall bear me on,
Though a desert should surround me,
  It hath springs that may be won.

Were't the last drop **in** the well,
  As I gasp upon the brink,
Ere my sinking spirits fell,
  'Tis to thee that I would **drink.**

In this water **as** this wine,
  The libations I would pour,
Should be **peace to** thee and thine,
  And **a health to** thee, Tom Moore.

I'D CHOOSE **TO BE A DAISY.**

Copied by permission of Firth, Pond & **Co.,** publishers, 547 Broadway, N. Y.

I'D choose to be a **daisy,**
  If I might be a **flower,**
My petals closing softly,
  At twilight's quiet hour
And waking **in** the morning,
  When falls the early dew,
To welcome heaven's bright sunshine,
  And heaven's bright tear-drops too.
Chorus.—I'd choose to **be a** daisy,
      If I might be a flower,
    My petals closing softly,
      At twilight's quiet hour.

I love the gentle lily,
  It looks so meek and fair,
But daisies I love better,
  For they grow everywhere.
The lilies bloom so sadly,
  In the sunshine or in shower,
But daisies still look upward,
  However dark the hour.
     I'd choose to be a daisy, &c.

HOME AGAIN.

Copied by permission of Ditson & Co., 227 Washington street, Boston.

HOME again, home again,
  From a foreign shore :
And oh ! it fills my soul with joy,
  To meet my friends once more.
Here I dropped the parting tear,
  To cross the ocean's foam :
But now I'm once again with those,
  Who kindly greet me home.
     Home again, &c.

Happy hearts, happy hearts,
  With mine have laughed in glee,
But oh ! the friends I loved in youth,
  Seem happier to me.
And if my guide should be the fate,
  Which bids me longer roam,
But death alone can break the tie,
  That binds my heart to home.
     Home again, &c.

Music sweet, music soft,
  Lingers round the place—
And oh ! I feel the childhood charm,
  That time cannot efface.
Then give me but my homestead roof,
  I'll ask no palace dome—
For I can live a happy life,
  With those I love at home.
     Home again, &c.

LOVE'S APPROACH.

If Love should dare to creep,
  Our hedge of roses through,
Disturbing hearts asleep,
  With airy fancies new,
    What shall **we** do?

We will not show amaze,
  Nor like the vanquished **sigh**,
But **on** the intruder gaze
  With mild **and** steady **eye**,
    And bid **him try.**

Then if before our feet,
  Rare treasure he display,
Pure gold and garlands sweet
  And robes of **rich array,**
    What shall **we say?**

Since these gifts are **true,**
  Thou canst not mean **us wrong,**
And we, if well thou woo,
  May give thee song for song,
    Some day ere long, &c.
Wm. Vincent Wallace.

MAY MORNING.

Duett.

"Come away from the harp! **come** away from the book,"
  Says a voice in the cottage eaves;
"**Your** music to learn from the valley-brook,
  And to read from the greenwood leaves."

There's never a cloud in the blue to-day,
  To threaten of winds or showers;
Or to ruffle the crown we will weave for May,
  While playing among the flowers.

The spring is awake with her sun-bright eyes,
  And her garlands so fresh and gay;
From the green hill-top like a bird she cries,
  "The winter hath fled away."

She gives a new tune to the harper's rhyme,
  And a hope to the sick man's hours;
Come away, come away! 'tis the one blest time
  For playing among the flowers.
WM. VINCENT WALLACE.

ADIEU; OR, AH! MOURN HER NOT.

Duett.

MOURN not our captive free,
  Our bird departed;
Too bright for earth was she,
  Too tender-hearted.
But come through meadows lone,
  When day is dying,
The grave to look upon
  Where she is lying.
      Ah! mourn her not.

One by one dropp'd away,
  Friend, parent, lover;
Why should the reft one stay
  When joy was over,
With her poor heart distressed,
  New visions trying?
Oh! better far the rest,
  Where she is lying.
      Ah! mourn her not.

Down the hill waters glide,
  Seaward before her,
Sunbeams at eventide,
  Smile gently o'er her.
Soft leaves the turf bestrew,
  Warm winds are sighing,
The clouds weep their purest dew,
  Where she is lying.
      Ah! mourn her not.
WM. VINCENT WALLACE.

I HAVE SOMETHING SWEET TO TELL YOU,

OR I'M TALKING IN MY SLEEP.

I **HAVE** something sweet to tell **you,** but the secret you must
    keep,
And remember, if it isn't right, "I'm talking in **my sleep;**"
      For I know I am but dreaming,
        When I think your love is mine;
      And I know they are but seeming,
        All the hopes that round me shine.
I have something **sweet to tell** you, **but** the **secret you must**
    keep,
And remember, if it isn't right, "I'm talking **in my sleep.**"
So remember when I tell you what I cannot longer keep,
We are none of us responsible for what we say in sleep:
      My pretty secret's coming!
       Oh, listen with **your** heart,
      And you shall hear it humming,
        Be close! 'twill make you start.
I have something sweet to tell you, but the secret you must
    keep,
And remember, if it isn't right, "I'm talking **in my sleep.**"
Oh, shut your eyes so earnest, or mine will **wildly weep,**
I love you! I adore you! **but** "I'm talking **in my sleep:**"
      For I know I am but dreaming,
        When I think your love is mine;
      And I know they are but seeming,
        All the **hopes** that round me shine.
I have something sweet to tell you, but **the** secret you must
    keep,
And remember, if it isn't right, "I'm talking in my sleep."

THE BEATING OF MY OWN HEART.

    HE came not, **no,** he came **not!**
      The moon **came** out alone;
    The little stars sat, one by **one,**
      Each **on its** golden throne.
    The evening wind **passed** by my cheek,
      The leaves above were stirred,
    But the beating of my own heart
      Was all the sound I heard.

Fast silent tears were falling,
  When something stood behind,
A hand was on my shoulder,
  I knew the touch was kind;
It drew me nearer, nearer,
  We could not speak a word,
And the beating of our own hearts
  Was all the sound we heard.

SILVER MOON.

As I strayed from my cot at the close of the day,
  About the beginning of June,
'Neath a jessamine shade I espied a fair maid,
  And she sadly complained to the moon.
Roll on silver moon, guide the traveler's way,
  When the nightingale's song is in tune,
But never, never more, with my lover I'll stray,
  By thy sweet silver light, bonny moon.
     Roll on, &c.

As the hart on the mountain my lover was brave,
  So handsome, so manly and clever;
So kind and sincere, and he loved me so dear,
  Oh! Edwin, thy equal was never.
But now he is dead, and gone to death's bed,
  He's cut down like a rose in full bloom;
He's fallen asleep, and poor Jane's left to weep, ·
  By the sweet silver light of the moon.
     Roll on, &c.

But his grave I'll seek out until morning appears,
  And weep for my lover so brave,
I'll embrace the cold turf, and wash with my tears,
  The flowers that bloom o'er his grave;
But never again shall my bosom know joy,
  With my Edwin I hope to be soon;
Lovers shall weep o'er the grave where we sleep,
  By thy sweet silver light, bonny moon.
     Roll on, &c.

ACROSS THE MOUNTAINS, HO!

When the tempests fly o'er the cloudy sky,
  And the piping blast sings merrily;
Oh, sweet the mirth of the social hearth,
  Where the flames are blazing cheerily.
    Our way across the mountains, ho!
    Ho! ho! ho! ho! ho! ho!
    Our way across the mountains, ho!
    Ho! ho! ho! ho! ho! ho!

The moon-beam bright, of a summer's night,
  Shineth but sad, and wearily;
But sweet is the glow where contentment flows,
  And the bright fire blazes cheerily.
Oh, when the tempests fly o'er the cloudy sky,
  And the piping blast sings merrily;
Oh, sweet is the mirth of the social hearth,
  Where the flames are blazing cheerily.
    Our way across the mountains, ho! &c.

Let the storm without in their midnight rout,
  Howl through the casement drearily;
We're merry within round the blazing linn,
  Where contentment flows right cheerily.
    Our way across the mountains, ho! &c.

AM I NOT FONDLY THINE OWN?

Thou, thou, reign'st in this bosom,
  Here, here, hast thou thy throne;
Thou, thou, know'st that I love thee,
  Am I not fondly thine own?
Yes, yes, yes, yes, am I not fondly thine own?
Then, then, e'en as I love thee,
  Say, say, wilt thou love me?
Thoughts, thoughts, tender and true, love,
  Say wilt thou cherish for me?
Yes, yes, yes, yes, say wilt thou cherish for me?
Speak, speak, love, I implore thee,
  Say, say, hope shall be mine,
Thou, thou, know'st that I love thee,
  Say but that thou wilt be mine?
Yes, yes, yes, yes, say but that thou wilt be mine.

THE PRAIRIE LEA.

Oh ! the prairie lea is the home for me,
  For there I'm lord of all I see ;
The chase, the chase, o'er the boundless space,
  And the grassy course for me.
I fly unseen o'er fields of green,
  Where the hoof-crush'd blossoms scent the air,
And the pheasant springs on startled wings,
  From her wild and lonely lair.
    Oh, the prairie lea, &c.

The trumpet's sound, the war steed's bound,
  The fluttering banner's starry field,
The cannon's roar, the spouting gore,
  To some a stormy joy may yield ;
But oh ! give me the prairie lea,
  Its peaceful scenes are dear to me,
The hunter's cry, the cloudless sky,
  Oh ! these are joys for me !
    Oh, the prairie lea, &c.

The wolf leaps out at the merry shout,
  The fox steals through the dewy mead,
And moor-cocks cry, as off they fly
  From the deer and panting steed.
And oh ! at night what wild delight,
  As home we fly with careless tread,
No fence to leap, no path to keep,
  On the way to our grassy bed.
    Oh, the prairie lea, &c.

WHEN WAKES THE SUN.

When wakes the sun at early dawn,
  Then from his distant cottage home,
I list to hear my lover's horn,
  Which seems to say, I come !
And as, from Alp to Alp, the sound,
  By echo wafted, steals to cheer ;
Nearer and nearer each rebound,
  I bless and joy to hear.
    When wakes the sun, &c.
      Iyo ! Iyo !

When sun tints our glaciers bright,
  With rosy hues, then forth I rove,
And whisper in the waning light,
  The name of names I love.
And still, as to the vales around,
  Farther and farther, less and less,
Echo to echo, wafts the sound,
  Then echo's aid I bless.
    When wakes the sun, &c.

SLUMBER'S GOLDEN CHAIN.

From the Opera of Norma.

WHEN bound in slumber's golden chain,
  This dream stole gently o'er me;
Methought that in a nuptial fane,
  Elberta stood before me.
As bridal songs then rose above
  Our wedded faith was plighted,
  How swelled my heart delighted
With grateful transport and with love!

But soon was hush'd the strain of mirth,
  Each eye in terror gleaming,
While rose a phantom from the earth,
  In form a priestess seeming.
Fast flashed the lightning gory red,
  Bolt echoed bolt of thunder,
  Cleaving the fane asunder,
All striking mute with dread.

No more my lovely bride was nigh,
  Sepulchral gloom prevailing
Borne from afar her suppliant cry,
  With infants' feeble wailing.
Then burst a sound more dread than all
  My inmost soul appalling;
  'Twas Norma sternly calling,
Thus, heartless traitor, fall!

ANNOT LYLE.

THE snow white plume her bonnet bore
  Wav'd not more pure and fair;
Her sparkling eye, a floating gem—
  Like gold, her auburn hair.
The rose bud slumbering on its bed,
  Ne'er wak'd a sweeter smile,
But now she's gone! and lost to me,
  My lovely Annot Lyle!

Thy fairy form I oft have seen;
  On every passing breeze
Have heard the melody of song,
  But ah! no strains like these,
The thrilling tones that from thy harp
  The feelings oft beguile;
But now thou'rt gone, and lost to me,
  My lovely Annot Lyle!

Although thy heart's another's now,
  And beats no more for me,
Yet I will teach my soul to pray,
  That it may pray for thee.
This bursting heart alone can feel
  The absence of thy smile;
Since thou art gone and lost to me,
  My lovely Annot Lyle!

NO! NO!

The celebrated duett, arranged to the tune of "Isabel."

He.—Will you not bless, with one sentence, a lover,
  Whose bosom beats only for you;
The cause of your anger, I prythee discover
  Pray tell me the reason for?
She.   No!
He.—Say, dearest, you still love me?
She.   No!
He.—Oh, how can you doom me to sorrow,
  Yet once again bless me with——
She.   No!
He.—And promise to meet me to-morrow
  Promise—

She.　　　　No!
He.—Prythee—
She.　　　　No!
He.—Don't say, no!

He.—Must we, then, dearest Maria, sever,
　And can you then part with me?
She.　　　　　　　　No!
He.—Then swear by yon sun, to be mine only ever
　You cannot refuse me, love!
She.　　　　　　No!
He.—You hate not your fond lover?
She.　　　　　　　　No!
He.—Your hand to my faithful heart pressing
　Say, does it offend you, love?
She.　　　　　　No!
He.—Then, to marry will not be distressing,
　Answer?
She.　　No!
He.—Once more.
She.　　　　No! no! no! no!

COME, LISTEN TO MY SONG.

COME listen to my song, my love,
　'Twill not offend thine ear,
The moon is beaming bright above
　Thou hast no cause of fear.
I'll sing of lovers brave and true,
　If thou wilt list to me,
I'll sing the charms of ladies fair,
　But none so fair as thee.
　　　Then listen, &c.

I'll sing of beauty, love, and fame;
　Of love in distant climes;
I'll sing of eyes so blue and bright,
　But none so bright as thine.
Then listen to my song, my love,
　For thou art dear to me,
And while there beams a light above,
　I'll sing of love and thee.
　　　Then listen, &c.

STAR OF THE EVENING,

OR BEAUTIFUL STAR.

BEAUTIFUL star in heaven so bright,
  Softly falls thy silver light,
As thou movest from earth afar,
  Star of the evening—beautiful star.
          Beautiful star—beautiful star.

In fancy's ear thou seem'st to say,
  Follow me—come from earth away,
Upward thy spirit's pinions try,
  To realms of love beyond the sky.
          Beautiful star—beautiful star.

Shine on, O star of love divine,
  And may our souls around thee twine,
As thou movest from earth afar,
  Star of the twilight—beautiful star.
          Beautiful star—beautiful star.

THE INDIAN GIRL,

OR BRIGHT ALFARATA.

WILD roved an Indian girl,
  Bright Alfarata,
Where sweep the waters
  Of the blue Juniata.
Swift as an antelope,
  Through the forest going,
Loose were her jetty locks,
  In wavy tresses flowing.

Gay was the mountain song,
  Of bright Alfarata,
Where sweep the waters
  Of the blue Juniata.
Strong and true my arrows are,
  In my painted quiver,
Swift goes my light canoe
  Down the rapid river.

Bold is the warrior good,
　The love of Alfarata,
Proud waves his snowy plume,
　Along the Juniata.
Soft and low he speaks to me,
　And then his war cry sounding,
Rings his voice in thunder loud,
　From height to height resounding.

Thus sang the Indian girl,
　Bright Alfarata,
Where sweep the waters
　Of the blue Juniata.
Fleeting years have borne away
　The voice of Alfarata,
Still rolls the river on,
　Blue Juniata.

HAPPY BIRDLING OF THE FOREST.

AS SUNG BY MISS CATHERINE HAYES.

HAPPY birdling of the forest,
Ever singing as thou soarest,
Who hath taught thee, little minion,
Bird upon thy golden pinion,
Thus to warble wild and high,
Half to earth and half to sky—half to sky?
　　Tra, la, la, la, la—tra, la, la—tra, la, la!

Happy birdling, free from sorrow,
Never dreaming of the morrow,
Hast thou ever notes of sadness,
Or dost always sing for gladness?
Tell me, birdling, is thy strain,
But a gladsome life-refrain?
Tell me, birdling, is thy strain,
But a gleesome life-refrain?
　　Tra, la, la, la, la—tra, la, la, la, la, la, la!

Happy birdling, gayly fleeting,
Evermore thy song repeating,
I would learn thy lesson surely,
Could I only learn it purely—

LILLY DALE.

'Twas a calm, clear night, and the moon's pale light
    Shone soft o'er hill and vale,
When sad-hearted friends stood around the death-bed
    Of my poor, sweet Lilly Dale!
Chorus—Oh, Lilly! sweet Lilly! dear Lilly Dale!
  Now the wild roses wave o'er her little green grave
    'Neath the trees in the blooming vale!

Like a fair flower white, on that sad, still night,
    Swept by some icy gale,
On her couch of snow, in her beauty bright,
    Lay my dear, sweet Lilly Dale!
    Oh, Lilly! sweet Lilly! dear Lilly Dale! &c.

"I go," and she smiled, as we wept o'er the child,
    "To that sinless, happy vale,
Where a kind hand shall wipe all the pain from the brow
    Of your poor, dear Lilly Dale!"
    Oh, Lilly! pale Lilly! sweet Lilly Dale! &c.

The moon went down 'neath the forest brown,
    And the stars grew dim and pale,
And the death smile wreathed the white, cold lips
    Of my poor, lost Lilly Dale!
    Oh, Lilly! sweet Lilly! dear Lilly Dale! &c.

Where the flowers bloom o'er her lonely tomb,
    'Neath the trees of the leafy vale;
Sweetly sleepeth in peace, while the bright birds sing,
    My loved, my dear Lilly Dale!
    Oh, Lilly! pale Lilly! lost Lilly Dale! &c.

INDIAN WARRIOR'S GRAVE.

Green is the grave by the wild dashing river,
Where sleeps the brave with his arrows and quiver;
Where in his pride he roved in his childhood,
Fought he, and died, in the depths of the wildwood

In the lone dell, while his wigwam defending,
Nobly he fell 'neath the hazel boughs bending,
Where the pale foe and he struggled together,
Who from his bow tore his swift-arrowed feather.

Ere the next moon the bold warrior was buried;
And ere a moon his tribe westward had hurried.
But a rude cross, with its rough-chiselled numbers,
Half hid in moss, tells the red warrior slumbers.

INDIAN HUNTER.

Oh, why does the white man follow my path, like the hound
   on the tiger's track!
Does the flush of my dark cheek waken his wrath? does he
   covet the bow at my back?
He has rivers and seas, where the billows and breeze
Bear riches for him alone—and the sons of the wood
Never plunge in the flood, which the white man calls his own.
                       Yha, yha!

Then why should he come to the streams, where none but the
   red skin dare to swim?
Why, why should he wrong the hunter? one who never did
   harm to him!
                       Yha, yha, yha!

The Father above thought fit to give to the white man corn
   and wine—
There are golden fields where he may live, but the forest
   shades are mine.
The eagle hath its place of rest, the wild horse where to dwell,
And the Spirit that gave the bird its nest, made me a home
   as well.
                       Yha, yha!

Then back! go back! from the red man's track, for the red
   man's eyes are dim,
To find that the white man wrongs the one who never did
   harm to him.
                       Yha, yha, yha!

LIFE LET US CHERISH.

Life let us cherish
   While yet the taper glows,
And the fresh flow'ret,
   Pluck ere it close.

Why are we fond of toil and care
Why choose the rankling thorn to wear,

And heedless by the lily stray,
Which blossoms in our way?
  Life let us cherish, &c.

When clouds obscure the atmosphere,
And forked lightnings rend the air,
The sun resumes his silver crest,
And smiles adorn the west.
  Life let us cherish, &c.

The genial seasons soon are o'er,
Then let us, ere we quit this shore,
Contentment seek, it is life's rest,
The sunshine of the breast.
  Life let us cherish, &c.

Away with every toil and care,
And cease the rankling thorn to wear,
With manful heart life's conflicts meet,
Till death sounds the retreat.
  Life let us cherish, &c.

LOVE'S RITORNELLA.

A Duett. From the Brigand.

He.—GENTLE Zitella, whither away?
  Love's ritornella, list while I play.
She.—No, I have lingered too long on my road,
  Night is advancing, the brigand's-abroad!
  Lonely Zitella has too much to fear;
  Love's ritornella she may not hear.

He.—Charming Zitella, why shouldst thou care,
  Night is not darker than thy raven hair!
  And those bright eyes, if the brigand should see,
  Thou art the robber, the captive is he!
    Gentle Zitella, banish thy fear,
    Love's ritornella, tarry and hear.

She.—Simple Zitella, beware, ah beware!
  List ye no ditty, grant ye no prayer.
He.—To your light footsteps let terror add wings!
  'Tis Massaroni himself who now sings!
    Gentle Zitella, banish thy fear!
    Love's ritornella, tarry and hear!

DEATH OF OSCEOLA,

THE VICTIM OF THE WHITE FLAG.

As sung by the Tremont Vocalists.   Music by B. Baker.

OH! bring me the dying raven,
  That I may send his plume,
To tell my hunted nation,
  Their fallen chieftain's doom.
The panther of the pale face
  Hath lured me to his lair,
And the heart his fangs could never grasp
  Is breaking in his snare.
Chorus—Oh! bring me the dying raven, &c.

  I led my braves to battle,
    Against the white man's power,
He heard my arrows rattle
  In conflict's gory hour;
He came with words of thunder,
  I made his sons a grave,
He came with words of FALSEHOOD,*
  And now I am his slave.
Oh! bring me the dying raven, &c.

Farewell *Emasa's*, Florida's bowers,
  And happy hunting grounds,
Your woods and golden flowers,
  Reek with the white man's hounds.
Shades of my braves and sires,
  I seek your peaceful shore,
Where white men's chains nor fires,
  Can never reach me more.
Oh! bring me the dying raven,
  That I may send his plume, &c.

SILAS S. STEELE.

---

* The commanding officer of the Americans in the Florida War, sent a *White Flag* to Osceola, requesting an interview, and on his attendance he was instantly made *prisoner*.

"TAKE ME HOME TO DIE."

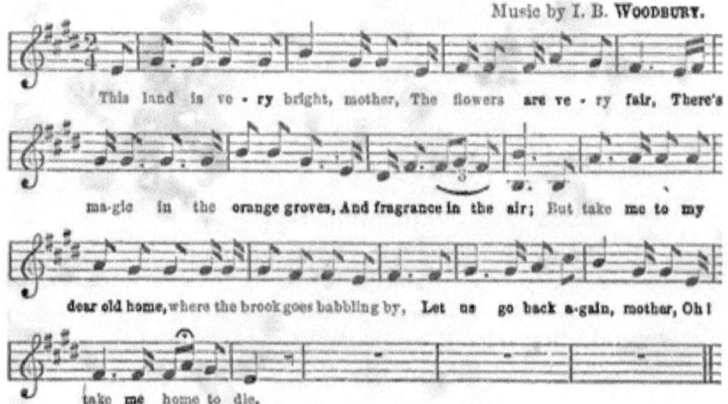

THIS land is very bright, mother,
　　The flowers are very fair,
There's magic in the orange groves,
　　And fragrance in the air;
But take me to my dear old home,
　　Where the brook goes babbling by;
Let us go back again, mother,
　　Oh! take me home to die.

Let my father's hand but rest, mother,
　　In blessing on my head,
Let my brothers and my sister dear,
　　But throng around my bed;
Oh! let me feel that loved ones near
　　Receive my parting breath,
When I bid you all good-night, mother,
　　And sleep the sleep of death.

These flowers their sweetest sweets afford,
　　I scent their fragrant breath,
But ere they bloom again, mother,
　　I shall be cold in death.
Then take me to my early home,
　　No roses are so dear
As those that bloom upon the bush,
　　To your old room so near.

It will be blooming soon, mother,
  Then come, oh, let me go!
Give me once more its **roses**,
  Before you **lay** me low:
You'll lay them **on** my grave, mother,
  Say, mother! will you not?
You'll lay me by the mossy bank,—
  I've told you oft the spot.

'Tis close beside the **church**, mother,
  And **when you kneel to pray**,
I'll listen to your words, **mother**,
  Though I am far away.
You must not weep for me, mother,
  For **I shall happy** be,
And though I cannot stay with you,
  Yet you shall **come to me.**

Dear mother, I am **weeping**,
  I cannot stop the tears,
They're swelling at the thought of home,
  And of my early years.
But I am getting faint, mother,
  Oh! take me to your breast,
And let me feel your **lip**, mother,
  But on my forehead **press.**

There's **dimness** on my sight, **mother**—
  I cannot get my breath:
Is it your sobs I hear, **mother?**
  Oh! tell me, is this **death?**
You'll tell my father how **I** yearned
  Once more to see him near:
You'll kiss my brothers **each** for me,
  They will forget, I fear.

You'll tell my sisters—brothers dear,
  I have gone up on high;
And **if** they are good children here,
  They'll see me when they die.
I feel I'm going now, mother,
  One kiss ere life is riven,
Farewell my own dear mother,
  Until we meet in heaven.

"THEY ASK ME IF I EVER WEEP."

Words by Mrs. P. E. ABEL.   Music by EUGENE THIODON.

KISSING THROUGH THE BARS.

I went again, but sought in vain
The grove my love to find;
I feared the worst, and yet I durst
Not think she was unkind.
To solve my fate I sought the gate,
And there, oh! happy stars,
I found and pressed her to my breast,
And kissed her through the bars.

I asked her why she did not fly,
Like me, on wings of love,
To where our vows beneath the boughs,
Were whispered through the grove.
She said, of late the garden gate,
Seemed nearer to the stars;
The hint was plain, and so again
I kissed her through the bars.

But kissing leads to graver deeds,
And constant visions brings,
Of golden showers and orange flowers,
White gloves and wedding rings.
And now our fate no envious gate,
With wicked wicket mars,
For wedded fast, we've learned at last,
To kiss without the bars.

"JEANIE WITH THE LIGHT BROWN HAIR."

STEPHEN C. FOSTER.

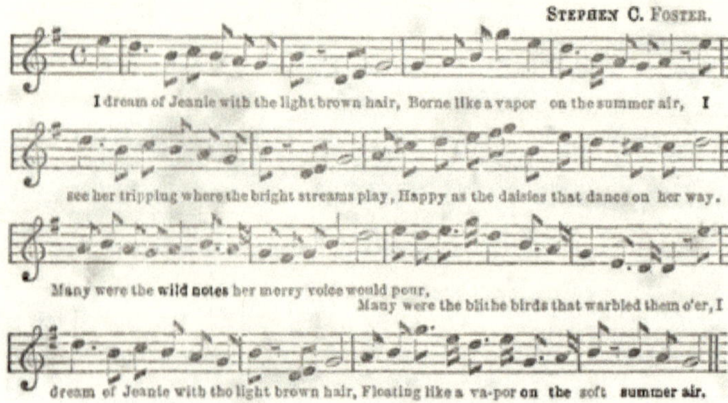

I DREAM of Jeanie with the light brown hair,
Borne like a vapor on the summer air,
I see her tripping where the bright streams play,
Happy as the daisies that dance on her way.
Many were the wild notes her merry voice would pour,
Many were the blithe birds that warbled them o'er;
I dream of Jeanie with the light brown hair,
Floating like a vapor on the soft summer air.

I long for Jeanie with the day dawn smile,
Radiant in gladness, warm with winning guile:
I heard her melodies, like joys gone by,
Sighing round my heart o'er the fond hopes that die,
Sighing like the night wind and sobbing like the rain,
Wailing for the lost one that comes not again:
Oh! I long for Jeanie, and my heart bows low,
Never more to find her where the bright waters flow.

I sigh for Jeanie, but her light form strayed
Far from the fond hearts round her native glade;
Her smiles have vanished, and her sweet songs flown,
Flitting like the dreams that have cheered us and gone;
Now the nodding wild flowers may wither on the shore,
While her gentle fingers will cull them no more;
Oh! I sigh for Jeanie with the light brown hair,
Floating like a vapor on the soft summer air.

SONGS OF THE SOLDIER.

THE CAVALIER'S BATTLE CALL.

"To sympathize with the sentiments and appreciate the real excellence of this song, we must identify ourselves in fancy with the soul of the old cavalier.—EDGAR A. POE.

COME mount, come mount, brave gallants all,
  And don your helms amain;
Death's courtiers, Fame **and Honor, call**
  Us to the field again.
No shrewish **tears** shall fill **our eye,**
  When **the sword** hilt's in **our hand,**
Heart whole **we'll** part and **no whit sigh,**
  For **the fairest in the** land.
Let piping swain and **craven** wight,
  Thus weep and puling cry,
Our business is like **men** to fight,
  And hero like to die.
          Then mount—then mount, &c. &c.
                    WILLIAM MOTHERWELL.

THE SOLDIER'S TEAR.

UPON the hill he turned to take a last fond look,
Of the valley and the village church, and the cottage **by the**
      brook;
He listened to the sound so familiar to his ear,
And the soldier leant upon his sword and wiped away a tear.

Beside that cottage porch a girl was on her knees,
She held aloft a snowy scarf which flutter'd in the breeze;
She breath'd a prayer for him, a prayer he could not
　　hear,
But he paused to bless her as she knelt, and wiped away a
　　tear.

He turn'd and left the spot; oh! do not deem him weak,
For dauntless was the soldier's heart, though tears were on
　　his cheek;
Go watch the foremost ranks in danger's dark career,
Be sure the hand most daring there has wiped away a tear.

MARCH TO THE BATTLE FIELD.

Tune.—Oft in the stilly night.

MARCH to the battle field,
　　The foe is now before us;
Each heart is freedom's shield,
　　And heav'n is smiling o'er us.
　　　The woes and pains,
　　　The galling chains,
That kept our spirits under,
　　　In proud disdain,
　　　We've brok'n again,
And tore each link asunder.
　　　　　　　March to the, &c.

Who, for his country brave,
　　Would fly from her invader?
Who, his base life to save,
　　Would, traitor-like, degrade her?
　　　Our hallow'd cause,
　　　Our home and laws,
'Gainst tyrant power sustaining,
　　　We'll gain a crown
　　　Of bright renown,
Or die—our rights maintaining!
　　　　　　　March to the, &c.

WHEN THE TRUMP OF FAME.

FROM THE OPERA OF THE MAID OF JUDAH.

Sung by Mr. Wood.

WHEN the trump of fame,
  Loud sounding freedom's call,
Bids in freedom's name,
  To fight or bravely fall—
Bold the hero goes,
  Where maddening war shouts rise,
And, midst countless foes,
  He flies, he flies.

Bright the sword now gleams,
  And banners wave on high—
Round the life-blood streams,
  'Mid cries of " Yield, or die !"
'Till victory uprears
  Her pennon, red with gore,
And shouts, to patriot ears,
  That slavery reigns no more.

When the voice of love
  To rescue calls the brave,
Who so base would prove,
  He would not fly to save ?
Love, whose torch in hall
  And bower doth brightly flame,
Champions finds in all
  Who manhood claim.

Then shame befall the knight,
  Who, false to honor's laws,
Shuns the listed fight,
  In injured woman's cause.
May he from the foe,
  In battle recreant fly,
And by some traitor blow,
  Unpitied, fall and die !

THE SOLDIER'S LAST SIGH.

THE trumpet may summon thy soldier away,
    And spur his proud spirit to arms,
Yet warm with the vigor that bids him away,
    He grieves to abandon thy charms.
        Though glory invite him and splendor abound,
            Yet mark, dearest maid, his decree,
        Subdued by defeat, or by victory crown'd,
            The soldier's last sigh is for thee.

But hark! 'tis the trumpet now speaks his adieu,
    And calls him from love to renown,
Then, oh! dearest maiden, believe his heart true,
    Though fortune may smile or may frown.
        Though glory invite him, &c.

THE SOLDIER'S LAST BUGLE.

Tune.—" The sailor's last whistle."

HARK! the muffled drum sounds the last march of the brave,
The soldier retreats to his quarters, the grave,
Under death, whom he owns his Commander-in-chief,
No more he'll turn out with the ready relief.
But in spite of death's terror's or hostile alarms,
When he hears the last bugle,
When he hears the last bugle, he'll stand to his arms.

Farewell, brother soldiers, in peace may ye rest,
And light lie the turf on each veteran breast,
Until that review when the souls of the brave,
Shall behold the chief Ensign, fair mercy's flag wave;
Then, freed from death's terrors and hostile alarms,
When we hear the last bugle,
When we hear the last bugle, we'll stand to our arms.

THE CELEBRATED BATTLE SONG.

From the Opera of Norma.

BATTLE! battle! ye heroes now calling,
    Rush like waves of the wild roaring flood;
Fierce as wolves on the sheep-fold when falling,
    Glut your deep hate in Rome's dearest blood.

Slaughter! slaughter! the cry loud and daring,
Speeds all onward vindictive, unsparing :
Cleave your foes down, when ruthless ye sally,
As the scythe mows the green waving valley !

Then will Rome's eagle stricken and gory,
  Wave no longer his pinions afar,
While the God who exults in our glory,
  Rides triumphant his storm bearing car

THE SOLDIER'S DREAM.

Our bugles sang truce—for the night-cloud had lowered,
  And the sentinel stars set their watch in the sky ;
And thousands had sunk on the ground overpowered,
  The weary to sleep, and the wounded to die.

When reposing that night on my pallet of straw,
  By the wolf-scaring fagot that guarded the slain ;
At the dead of the night a sweet vision I saw,
  And thrice ere the morning I dreamt it again.

Methought from the battle-field's dreadful array,
  Far, far I had roamed on a desolate track ;
'Twas autumn—and sunshine arose on the way
  To the home of my fathers, that welcomed me back.

I flew to the pleasant fields traversed so oft
  In life's morning march, when my bosom was young ;
I heard my own mountain-goats bleating aloft,
  And knew the sweet strain that the corn-reapers sung.

Then pledged we the wine-cup, and fondly I swore
  From my home and my weeping friends never to part ;
My little ones kissed me a thousand times o'er,
  And my wife sobbed aloud in her fulluess of heart.

Stay, stay with us—rest, thou art weary and worn ;
  And fain was their war broken soldier to stay ;
But sorrow returned with the dawning of morn,
  And the voice in my dreaming ear melted away.

Thomas Campbell.

8

NOT A DRUM WAS HEARD,

OR THE BURIAL OF SIR JOHN MOORE.

Not a drum was heard, not a funeral note,
  As his corpse to the ramparts we hurried;
Not a soldier discharged his farewell shot,
  O'er the grave where our hero we buried.
We buried him darkly at dead of night,
  The turf with our bayonets turning,
By the struggling moonbeam's misty light,
  And our lanterns dimly burning.

No useless coffin confined his breast,
  Nor in sheet nor in shroud we wound him;
But he lay like a warrior taking his rest,
  With his martial cloak around him.
Few and short were the prayers we said,
  And we spoke not a word of sorrow,
But we steadfastly gazed on the face of the dead,
  And we bitterly thought of the morrow.

We thought as we heaped his narrow bed,
  And smooth'd down his lonely pillow,
That the foe and the stranger would tread o'er his head,
  And we far away on the billow.
Lightly they'll talk of the spirit that's gone,
  And o'er his cold ashes upbraid him;
But nothing he'll reck if they let him sleep on,
  In the grave where a Briton has laid him.

But half our heavy task was done,
  When the clock told the hour for retiring,
And we heard by the distant and random gun,
  That the foe was suddenly firing.
Slowly and sadly we laid him down,
  From the field of his fame, fresh and gory,
We carv'd not a line, we rais'd not a stone,
  But we left him alone in his glory.

JEANNETTE AND JEANNOT.

You are going far away, far away from your Jeannette:
There is no oue left to love me now, and you too may forget;
But my heart will still be with you, wherever you may go,
Can you look me in the face, and say the same, Jeannot?
When you wear the jacket red, and the beautiful cockade,
I fear that you will then forget the promises you've made;
With your gun upon your shoulder, and your bayonet by your
    side,
You'll be taking some proud lady, and making her your bride.

When glory leads the way, you'll be madly rushing on,
Never thinking, if they kill you, my happiness is gone:
Should you win the day, perhaps a general you'll be,
Though I should be proud to hear it, what would become of
    me?
Oh! was I Queen of France, or, what's better, Pope of Rome,
I'd have no fighting men abroad, no weeping maids at home;
All the world should be at peace, and should kings assert their
    right,
I'd have those that make the quarrel, be the only men who
    fight.

O LET ME LIKE A SOLDIER FALL.

Oh! let me like a soldier fall
  Upon some open plain,
This breast expanding to the ball,
  To blot out ev'ry stain.
Brave, manly hearts confer my doom,
  That gentle ones may tell,
Howe'er forgot or known my tomb,
  I like a soldier fell.

I only ask of that proud race,
  Which lends its blaze to me,
To die the last, and not disgrace
  Its ancient chivalry.

Tho' o'er my clay no banner wave,
  Nor trumpet requiem swell,
Enough they murmur at my grave,
  He like a soldier fell.
Enough they murmur at my grave,
  He like a soldier fell,
  He like a soldier fell.

FROM MARITANA.

THE SONG MY MOTHER LOVED TO SING.

Music published by Lee & Walker, 732 Chestnut St., Philadelphia.

THE song my mother loved to sing
  Can ne'er forgotten be,
But ever round my heart 'twill cling
  Like heaven's melody.
'Twas first to thrill my infant breast,
  'Twas first, 'twas first to charm my ear,
And from her home among the blest,
  I think I still can hear
The song my mother loved to sing,
  In angel's accents mild;
And breathing in its hallowed tones,
  A blessing on her child.
      Chorus.—The song my mother loved to sing,
          In angel's accents mild,
            And breathing in its hallowed tones,
          A blessing on her child.

It lulled my infant brow to sleep,
  It gave me dreams of bliss,
And visions rendered heavenly
  By fond affection's kiss.
So oft I've heard its thrilling air
  With words, with words to mem'ry dear,
But next to childhood's evening prayer,
  Oh! ever let me hear
The song my mother loved to sing,
  In angel's accents mild,
And breathing in its hallowed tones,
  A blessing on her child.

S. S. STEELE.

THE OLD FARM-HOUSE.

Copied by permission of Firth, Pond & Co., 547 Broadway, N. Y.

OH! the old farm-house, down beside the valley stream,
  Where in childhood so oft I have played,
Ere sorrow had clouded my heart's early dream,
  Or life's purest joys had decayed;
How well I remember the vine-covered roof,
  And the rose bushes clustering nigh,
And the tall, stately poplar trees standing aloof,
  Whose tops seemed to reach to the sky!
    Oh! the old farm-house, my childhood's happy home.

Oh! the old farm-house, how I've sported round its hearth,
  With my sisters and brothers so dear;
How oft has it rung with our innocent mirth,
  And hallowed our soft evening prayer!
But the old farm-house now is bowing to decay,
  Its stones, like dead friends, lie apart;
But its dear cherished image shall ne'er fade away,
  From affection's domain in my heart.
    Oh! the old farm-house, my childhood's happy home.

LONG LIFE AND SUCCESS TO THE FARMER.

Tune—Tea in the Arbor, or " Over the Water to Charlie."

COME each jovial fellow, that loves to be mellow,
  Attend unto me and sit easy,
We'll rest from our labors, like friends and good neighbors,
  All toiling will make a man crazy ;
Here each is a king, let us laugh, joke, and sing,
  Let no one appear as a stranger,
But show me the ass, that hates a cup or a lass,
  And I'll order him hay in a manger.
Chorus—But show me the ass, &c.

By reaping, by sowing, by ploughing and mowing,
  Dame nature supplies me with plenty,
I've cellar well stored and a plentiful board,
  And my cupboard affords every dainty ;
I've all things in season—partake them with reason,
  I'm here as a Justice of quorum ;
At my cabin's far end, I've a bed for a friend,
  A warm fireside and some jorum.
        At my cabin's far end, &c.

Let the proud and the great, feast in splendor and state
  I envy them not, I declare it,
I eat my own lamb, my own eggs, fowl, and ham,
  I shear my own fleece and I wear it;
I've woods, and I've bowers, I've fields, and I've flowers,
  The lark is my daily alarmer.
Then my jolly friends now, here is *God speed the plough*,
  Long life and success to the Farmer.
Chorus—
    Then my jolly friends now, here's God speed the plough,
    Long life, &c.

THE LITTLE BLACKSMITH.

WE heard his hammer all day long
  On the anvil ring, and ring,
But he always came when the sun went down,
  To sit on the gate and sing ;

His little hands so hard and brown
　Cross'd idly on his knee,
And straw-hat lopping over cheeks
　As red as they could be.
Chorus—The hammer's stroke on the anvil, filled
　　His heart with a happy ring,
　And that was why, when the sun went down,
　　He came to the gate to sing.

His blue and faded jacket, trimm'd
　With signs of work, his feet
All bare and fair upon the grass,
　He made a picture sweet.
For still his shoes, with iron shod,
　On the smithy wall he hung,
As forth he came, when the sun went down,
　And sat on the gate and sung.
The hammer's stroke on the anvil, filled, &c.

The whistling rustic tending cows,
　Would keep in pastures near,
And half the busy villagers
　Lean from their doors to hear.
And from the time the robin came
　And made the hedges bright,
Until the stubble yellow grew,
　He never missed a night.
The hammer's stroke on the anvil, filled, &c.

THE OLD OAKEN BUCKET.

Tune—*Jessie the Flower of Dumblane.*

How dear to my heart are the scenes of my childhood,
　When fond recollection recalls them to view,
The orchard, the meadow, the deep tangled wildwood,
　And ev'ry loved spot that my infancy knew.
The wide-spreading pond, and the mill standing by it,
　The bridge and the rock where the cataract fell,
The cot of my father, the dairy-house nigh it,
　And e'en the rude bucket that hung in the well.
　　The old oaken bucket,
　　The moss covered bucket,
　　The iron-bound bucket,
　　That hung in the well

That moss covered vessel I hail as a treasure,
  For oft when at noon I return'd from the field,
I have found it the source of an exquisite pleasure,
  The purest, and sweetest, that nature could yield.
How ardent I seized it with hands that were glowing,
  And quick to the white-pebbled bottom it fell,
Then soon with the emblem of TRUTH overflowing,
  And dripping with coolness, it rose from the well.
      The old oaken bucket, &c.

How sweet from the green mossy brim to receive it,
  As poised on the cord it inclin'd to my lips,
Not a full blushing goblet could tempt me to leave it,
  Tho' fill'd with the nectar that Jupiter sips.
But now far removed from that loved situation
  A tear of regret will intrusively swell,
As my fancy revisits my father's plantation,
  And sighs for the bucket that hangs in the well.
      The old oaken bucket, &c.

THE SONG OF THE FARMER.

Music with Piano accompaniment, published by Winner & Shuster, Phila.

I HAVE cattle that feed in the valley,
  And herds that graze on the hill,
And I pride in the fruits of my labor,
  For I'm lord of the land that I till.
I have ploughed the rough hill and the meadow,
  'Till feeble with age and with toil,
And I know before long that another
  Shall reap the new fruits of the soil.

For the son who hath toiled for me ever,
  And faithfully stood by my side,
Hath a hand that shall gather the harvest,
  When his feeble old father hath died.
And the daughter, so kind to her mother,
  Shall share with him all I possess,
For I feel they love me as a father,
  And welcome my tender caress.

There's my faithful, my trusting companion,
　My kind-hearted, dear, loving wife,
I have toiled for her comfort with pleasure,
　For such was the pride of of my life.
And still in my manhood I love her,
　For her kind and affectionate care,
And all that the earth can afford me,
　With her I most willingly share.

GOD BLESS THE FARMER'S TOIL.

As sung at Harvest Home celebrations, Agricultural Fair **Festivals, &c.**

God bless the farmer's toil.
God crown his cultured soil,
　With bounteous hand,
Send him **a** fruitful field,
Crops that **abundance** yield,
From blight **or** flood, **oh !** shield
　His flocks and land.

Constant as earth rolls round,
He nobly tills the ground,
　From sun to sun.
Long be **his brow caress'd,**
Long may **his couch be bless'd,**
With calm and peaceful rest,
　When labor's done.

Free from the world's **turmoil,**
He by his manly toil,
　Strews ev'ry board.
Still as the seasons **come,**
May heaven's smiling **dome,**
Crown his **brow,** hearth, **and** home,
　With **blest reward.**

God bless the farmer's toil,
God crown his cultured soil,
　With bounteous hand,
Send him the fruitful field,
Crops that abundance yield,
From blight or flood, oh ! shield
　His flocks and land.

"THE REAPER ON THE PLAIN."

Words by C. G. EASTMAN.   Music by G. F. ROOT.

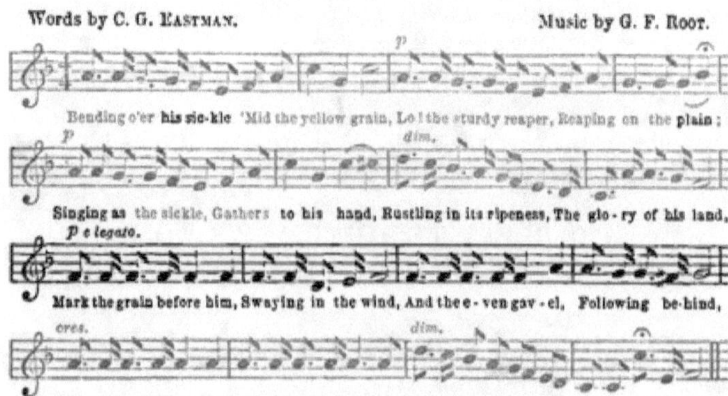

Long I've stood and pondered,
  Gazing from the hill,
While the sturdy reaper
  Sung and labored still:
Bending o'er his sickle
  'Mid the yellow grain,
Happy and contented
  Reaping on the plain.
And as upon my journey
  I leave the maple tree,
Thinking of the difference
  Between the man and me,
I turn again to see him
  Reaping on the plain,
And almost wish my labor
  Were the sickle and the grain.

SWEET THE HOUR.—A CHORUS.

SWEET the hour when freed from labor
  Lads and lasses thus convene;
To the merry pipe and tabor,
  Dancing gaily on the green.
              Sweet the hour, &c.

Nymphs with all their native graces,
   Swains with every charm to win;
Sprightly steps and smiling **faces,**
   Tell of happy hearts within.
               Sweet the hour, &c.

Blest with plenty, here the farmer,
   Toils for those he **loves alone ;**
While some pretty **smiling charmer,**
   Like the land, is all **his own.**
               Sweet the hour, &c.

Though **a** tear for prospects blighted,
   May at times unbidden flow,
Yet the heart will bound delighted,
   Where such kindred bosoms glow.
               Sweet the hour, &c.

THE FARM MAID AND THE FOP.

A Popular Character Song.

A SPRUCE **city beau** at set of sun,
Return'd from sport with game and gun,
O'ertook a blushing country maid,
And to deride her thus he essay'd.

" Where are you going my pretty maid ?"   [*Repeat.*]
" I'm *going a milking,* sir," **she** said.
" May I go with you, my pretty **maid ?**"
" It's just as you please, kind sir," **she** said.

" What is your father, **my pretty maid ?**"   [*Repeat.*]
" My father's a *farmer,* **sir,**" she said.
" Then I would marry **you,** my pretty maid,
" *That's not as you* please, kind sir," she said.

" What is your fortune, my pretty maid ?" [*Repeat.*]
" My face is my fortune, kind sir," she said.
" Then I can't marry you, my pretty maid,"
" *Nobody asked you, kind sir,*" she said,
" *Nobody asked you, kind sir,*" she said.

WHEN A LITTLE FARM WE KEEP.

A Popular Duett.

He.   WHEN a little farm we keep,
    And have little girls and boys,
  With little pigs and little sheep,
    To make a little noise.
Both.   Oh ! what happy, merry days we'll see,
  With our little lambs a sporting on our knee.

He.   Then we'll keep a little maid,
    And a little horse beside,
  A little horse and gig or sleigh,
    To take a little ride.
Both.   Oh ! how happy we will be,
  With our little children sitting on our knee.

He.   The boys I'll conduct,
She.   The girls I'll instruct,
He.   In reading I'll engage,
  Each son is not deficient.
She.   In music I'll presage,
  Each girl is a proficient.
He.   Now boy, your B. A. Ba.
She.   Now girl, your Do—re—ma.
Both   Oh ! how happy we will be,
  With our little children lisping on our knee.

THE HARVESTER'S JOYS.

THE blithe rosy summer comes laughing along,
  Beneath the sun's ripening ray,
And we hear the clear notes of the harvester's song
  Over hill and o'er meadow so gay,
How joyful to toss round the sweet-scented hay,
  Or to spread the mown grass to the sun,
While the mowers are jollily bending away,
And in merry measure their sweeping scythes play,
  And ring when the green swathe is done !

And in the green field, ere the noon-tide is near,
  What unalloy'd pleasures pervade,
When the merry farm maid with a rose in her hair,
  Spreads a rural repast in the shade !
Round the sweet milk and pie, how we make the jokes fly !
  And the heated noon hour beguiling,
We relate pleasing stories with songs of true glee,
As we sit or recline 'neath the sheltering tree,
  And heaven's blue canopy smiling

THE FARMER SAT IN HIS EASY CHAIR.

Music published by Firth, Pond, & Co., New York.

The farmer sat in his easy chair,
  Smoking his pipe of clay,
While his hale old wife with busy care,
  Was clearing the dinner away :
A sweet little girl with fine blue eyes,
On her grandfather's knee was catching flies.

The old man laid his hand on her head,
  With a tear on his wrinkled face ;
He thought how often her mother, dead,
  Had sat in the self same place :
As the tear stole down his half-shut eye—
" Don't smoke," said the child ; " how it makes you cry !"

The house-dog lay stretch'd out on the floor,
  Where the shade after noon used to steal ;
The busy old wife by the open door,
  Was turning the spinning-wheel ;
And the old brass clock on the mantle-tree,
Had plodded along till almost three :

Still the farmer sat in his easy chair,
  While close to his heaving breast,
The moisten'd brow and cheek so fair,
  Of his sweet grandchild were press'd ;
His head, bent down, on her soft hair lay—
Fast asleep were they both, that summer day.

SONGS OF AMERICA,

OR NATIONAL SONGS.

Origin of the Song—The Star Spangled Banner.

This favorite National Lyric was composed under the following circumstances :—A gentleman had left Baltimore, with a flag of truce, for the purpose of getting released from the British fleet a friend of his, who had been captured at Marlborough. He went as far as the mouth of the Patuxent, and was not permitted to return, lest the intended attack on Baltimore should be disclosed. He was therefore brought up the bay to the mouth of the Patapsco, where the flag-vessel was kept under the guns of a frigate; and he was compelled to witness the bombardment of Fort M'Henry, which the admiral had boasted he would carry in a few hours, and that the city must fall. He watched the flag at the fort through the whole day, with an anxiety that can be better felt than described, until the night prevented him from seeing it. In the night he watched the bomb-shells, and at early dawn his eye was again greeted by the proudly-waving flag of his country.

STAR-SPANGLED BANNER.

Oh, say can you see by the dawn's early light,
  What so proudly we hail'd at the twilight's last gleaming,
Whose broad stripes and bright stars thro' the perilous fight,
  O'er the ramparts we watch'd were so gallantly streaming;
And the rocket's red glare, the bombs bursting in air
  Gave proof through the night that our flag was still there?
Oh! say, does that star-spangled banner yet wave
  O'er the land of the free, and the home of the brave?

On the shore dimly seen thro' the mists of the deep,
  Where the foe's haughty host in dread silence reposes,
What is that which the breeze, o'er the tow'ring steep,
  As it fitfully blows, half conceals, half discloses?

Now it catches the gleam of the morning's first beam,
  In full glory reflected now shines on the stream :
'Tis the star-spangled banner! oh, long may it wave
  O'er the land of the free, and the home of the brave.

And where is that band who so vauntingly swore,
  That the havoc of war and the battle's confusion
A home and a country, shall leave us no more?
  Their blood has washed out their foul footsteps' pollution :
No refuge could save the hireling and slave,
  From the terror of flight, or the gloom of the grave;
And the star-spangled banner in triumph doth wave
  O'er the land of the free, and the home of the brave.

Oh! thus be it ever, when freemen shall stand
  Between their lov'd home, and the war's desolation ;
Blest with vict'ry and peace, may the heav'n rescued land
  Praise the power that hath made and preserved us a nation;
Then conquer we must, for our cause it is just,
Let this be our motto, "IN GOD IS OUR TRUST,"
And the star-spangled banner in triumph shall wave
O'er the land of the FREE and the home of the BRAVE.
FRANCIS S. KEY.

THE AMERICAN STAR.

COME, strike the bold anthem, the war-dogs are howling,
  Already they eagerly snuff up their prey ;
The red cloud of war o'er our forests is scowling,
  Soft peace spreads her wings and flies weeping away ;
The infants affrighted cling close to their mothers,
  The youths grasp their swords, for the combat prepare ;
While beauty weeps, fathers and lovers and brothers,
  All rush to display the American Star.

Come blow the shrill bugle—the loud drum awaken,
  The dread rifle seize, let the cannon deep roar ;
No heart with pale fear, or faint doubtings be shaken,
  No slave's hostile foot leave a print on our shore.
Shall mothers, wives, daughters, and sisters left weeping,
  Insulted by ruffians, be dragg'd to despair ?
Oh, no! from the hills the proud eagle comes swooping,
  And waves to the brave the American Star.

The spirits of Washington, Warren, Montgomery,
  Look down from the clouds with bright aspect serene:
Come soldiers, a tear and a toast to their memory,
  Rejoicing they'll see us as they once have been;
To us the high boon by the gods has been granted,
  To spread the glad tidings of liberty far,
Let millions invade us, we'll meet them undaunted,
  And conquer or die by the American Star.

Your hands then, dear comrades, round liberty's altar,
  United, we swear by the souls of the brave,
Not one from the strong resolution shall falter,
  To live independent, or sink in the grave.
Then freemen fill up; lo! the striped banners flying
  The high bird of liberty screams through the air,
Beneath her oppression and tyranny dying,
  Success to the beaming American Star.

THE FLAG OF OUR UNION.

A SONG for our Banner, the watchword recall,
  Which gave the Republic her station,
United we stand—Divided we fall,
  It made and preserved us a nation.
The union of lakes—the union of lands,
  The union of States ne'er can sever,
The union of hearts—the union of hands,
  And the flag of our Union for ever and ever,
  The flag of our Union for ever.

What God in his infinite wisdom designed,
  And armed with republican thunder,
Not all the earth's despots, and factions combined,
  Have the power to conquer or sunder.
The union of lakes—the union of lands,
  The union of States none can sever,
The union of hearts—the union of hands,
  And the flag of our Union for ever and ever,
  And the flag, &c.

WM. VINCENT WALLACE.

OUR UNION RIGHT OR WRONG.

As sung throughout the **States** by Miss Hiffert, &c., &c.
Music Published by Firth, **Pond** & Co., 547 Broadway, N. Y.

Rouse, hearts of Freedom's only **home**,
  Hark to disunion's cry,
Dear liberty beneath her dome,
  Proclaims that danger's nigh ;
Come let your noble **shouts** ring forth,
  In trumpet voices strong,
" We know no South, **we know** no North,
  Our Union Right or Wrong."
" We know no South, **we know** no North,
  Our Union Right or Wrong."

The temple **our brave Fathers** made,
  The **wonder of the world**,
Shall they behold their sons dismay'd,
  When treason's flag's **unfurled** ;
Oh ! never, **by** the glorious stars
  Which **on our** banner throng ;
Rouse, sons of three victorious wars,
  For Union Right **or** Wrong.

Our patriotic **Fathers' shades**,
  With Washington **on high**,
Point to **their** blood anointed **blades**
  And to their children **cry**,
Rouse, freemen by your **Fathers'** scars,
  On to the rescue throng ;
Defend our flag and sacred stars,
  The Union Right **or** Wrong.

Sons of the press, proclaim **its** worth
  In telegraphic fires,
Bid young America stand forth
  And emulate their sires ;
Wake sister States, and hand in hand,
  Round Freedom's Temple throng,
Come shout in one united Band,
  " Our Union Right or Wrong."

SILAS S. STEELE.

COLUMBIA'S OUR HAPPY LAND.

Tune—" We have come from a Happy Land."

COLUMBIA'S our happy land,
  'Neath liberty's sway,
'Tis guarded by freedom's band,
  By night and by day.
North, South, East, and West,
Hearts with peace and plenty blest,
Praise heaven's high behest,
  And sing blithe and gay.
Chorus—Columbia's our happy land,
  'Neath liberty's sway,
  Guarded by freedom's band,
    By night and by day.

Columbia's our happy home,
  Plenty's her store,
Children who from her roam,
  Still bless her the more.
Strangers who seek her lands,
Find open hearts and hands,
And in united bands,
  Sing blithe and gay.
  Columbia's our happy land, &c.

Columbia's our happy school,
  Where all can come in,
And learn wisdom's golden rule,
  To toil is to *win*.
Science and Art unite,
Shedding forth their hallow'd light,
Crowning with useful might,
  All on their way.
  Columbia's our happy land, &c.

HAIL COLUMBIA.

HAIL Columbia! happy land!
Hail ye heroes! heaven-born band!
  Who fought and bled in freedom's cause,
  Who fought and bled in freedom's **cause,**
And when the storm of war was gone,
Enjoyed **the peace your** valor won.
  Let independence be **our** boast,
  Ever mindful what it cost;
  Ever grateful for the prize,
  Let its altar reach the skies.
      Firm—united—let us be,
      Rallying round our liberty;
      As a band **of** brothers join'd,
      Peace and **safety we** shall find.

Immortal patriots! rise **once** more;
Defend your rights, defend your shore;
  Let no rude foe, with impious **hand,**
  Let no rude foe, with impious hand,
Invade the shrine where sacred lies,
Of toil and blood the well-earn'd prize.
  While **offering** peace sincere and just
  In heaven we place a manly trust,
  That **truth** and **justice** will prevail,
  And every scheme of bondage fail.
      Firm—united, &c.

Sound, sound, **the trump of fame!**
Let Washington's **great name,**
  Ring through **the world with** loud applause,
  Ring through **the world with** loud applause,
Let every clime to freedom dear,
Listen with a joyful **ear;**
  With equal skill, **and** god-like power
  He govern'd in the fearful hour
  Of **horrid war;** or guides with ease,
  The happier times of honest peace.
      Firm—united, &c.

Behold the chief who now commands,
Once more to serve his country stands—
  The rock on which the storm will beat;
  The rock on which the storm will beat;
But arm'd in virtue, firm and true,
His hopes are fix'd on heaven and you.
  When hope was sinking in dismay,
  And gloom obscur'd Columbia's day,
  His steady mind, from changes free,
  Resolv'd on death or liberty.
    Firm—united—let us be,
    Rallying round our liberty;
    As a band of brothers join'd,
    Peace and safety we shall find.

F. Hopkinson.

THE RELICS OF WASHINGTON.

Where thy bright wave, Potomac, by fair Vernon sweeps,
There, shrouded in glory, great Washington sleeps;
There the spirits of freedom exultingly roam,
Their blessings to breathe on the patriot's tomb.

No proud marble rears its high crest o'er his dust,
For honor's hand lights up the grave of the just;
And the star of his glory which brighter still glows,
Shall hallow the spot where his relics repose.

While the genius of Freedom the earth shall illume,
His deeds shall light forth her brave sons to his tomb;
And his name's hallow'd splendor a watchword shall be
For millions who yet shall resolve to be free.

Silas S. Steele.

THE AGE OF PROGRESS.

  The age of giant progress,
    Americans all hail!
The land, all interwoven
    With telegraph and rail;
No sluggish chains shall bind us,
    No tardiness delay;
The morning light is breaking (waking)
    O'er our destiny.

The age of trained lightning,
  "Despatching" human thought;
What wondrous revolution
  The scheme of Morse hath wrought!
No time, no space can hinder
  The quick, electric fire;
Intelligence is flashing (dashing)
  O'er the magic wire.

The age of grand conceptions,
  The "cable of the deep!"
It "snapped," but we will **mend it,**
  We have no time to weep.
The great Pacific Railroad!
  'Twill **not be long before**
The railroad cars are flying (hieing)
  From the golden shore.

The age of priceless knowledge,—
  The scholar's jubilee!
The land all dotted over
  With institutions free.
Our public schools! Oh, hail them!
  They offer treasures cheap:
The boys and girls are scaling (hailing)
  Science's rugged steep.

UNFURL THE GLORIOUS BANNER.

UNFURL the glorious banner,
  Let it sway upon **the breeze,**
The emblem of our **country's pride,**
  On land, **and** on **the seas—**
The emblem of our **liberty,**
  Borne proudly in the **wars,**
The **hope of** every freeman,
  The gleaming **stripes and stars.**
Chorus—Then unfurl the **glorious banner**
  Out on the welcoming **air,**
Read the record of the olden time,
  Upon its radiance **there!**

In the battle it shall lead us,
  And our banner ever be,
A beacon light to **glory**,
  And a guide to **victory**.

The glorious band of patriots
  Who gave the flag its birth,
Have writ with steel in history,
  The record of its worth;
From east to west, from sea to sea,
  From pole to tropic sun,
Will eyes grow bright, and hearts throb high
  At the name of Washington.
Then unfurl the glorious banner, &c.

Ah! proudly should we **bear it**,
  And guard this flag of ours,
Borne bravely in its infancy,
  Amidst the darker hours;
Only the brave may bear it,
  A guardian it shall be
For those who well have won the right
  To boast of liberty.
Then unfurl the glorious banner, &c.

The meteor flag of seventy-six,
  Long may it wave in pride,
To tell the world how nobly
  The patriot fathers died;
When from the shadows of their night
  Outburst the brilliant sun,
It bathed in light the stripes and stars,
  And lo! the field was won.
Then unfurl the glorious banner, &c.

YE SONS OF FREEDOM, WAKE TO GLORY.

Air—*The Marseillaise.*

YE sons of freedom, **wake to** glory!
  Hark! hark! what myriads bid you **rise**!
Your children, wives, and grandsires hoary,
  Behold their tears and hear their cries!
  Behold their tears and **hear** their **cries**!

Shall hateful tyrants, mischiefs breeding,
  With hireling hosts, a ruffian band,
  Affright and desolate the land,
While peace **and** liberty **lie** bleeding?
    To arms! to arms, **ye** brave!
        Th' avenging **sword** unsheath!
March on! march on! **all** hearts resolved
        On victory or death!

Now, now the dangerous storm is rolling,
  Which treacherous kings confederate raise;
The dogs of war, let loose, are howling—
  And lo! our walls and cities blaze!
And shall we basely view the ruin,
  While lawless force, with guilty **stride**,
  Spreads desolation far and wide,
With **crimes and** blood his hands imbruing?
        To arms, &c.

With luxury and pride surrounded,
  The vile, insatiate tyrants **dare**,
Their thirst of gold and power unbounded,
  To mete and vend the light and air.
Like beasts of burden would they load **us**—
  Like gods would bid their slaves adore—
  But man **is** man—and who is more?
Then shall they longer lash and goad **us?**
        To arms, &c

Oh, liberty! can man resign **thee,**
  Once having felt thy generous flame?
Can dungeons, bolts, and bars confine thee?
  Or whips thy noble spirit tame?
Too long the world has wept, bewailing
  That falsehood's dagger tyrants wield—
  But freedom **is our sword and** shield,
And all **their arts** are unavailing.
        To arms, &c.

UNCLE SAM'S FARM

Published by Ditson & Co., 227 Washington street, Boston.

Tune.— Walk in, walk in, &c.

OF all the mighty nations,
  In the East or in the West,
Oh! this glorious Yankee Nation
  Is the greatest and the best;
We have room for all creation,
  And our banner is unfurl'd :
Here is a general invitation,
  To the people of the world.

Chorus.—Come along, come along—
      Make no delay;
    Come from every nation;
      Come from every way;
    Our land is broad enough—
      Don't be alarmed,
    For Uncle Sam is rich enough,
      To give us all a farm.

St. Lawrence marks our northern line,
  As fast her waters flow,
And the Rio Grande our southern bound,
  'Way down to Mexico;
From the great Atlantic Ocean,
  Where the sun begins to dawn,
Leaps across the Rocky Mountains,
  Away to Oregon.
      Come along, come along, &c.

The South may raise the cotton,
  And the West the corn and pork.
New England manufactories
  Shall do up the finer work
For the deep and flowing waterfalls,
  That course along our hills,
Are just the thing for washing sheep,
  And driving cotton mills.
      Come along, come along, &c.

Our fathers gave us liberty,
   But little did I dream
The grand results that flow along
   This mighty age of steam ;
For our mountains, lakes, **and rivers,**
   Are in a blaze of fire,
And we send our news by lightning,
   On the telegraphic-wire.
       Come along, **come** along, **&c.**

INDEPENDENCE DAY.

Originally **sung** by Charley Burke.

Tune.—Bonnie Laddie, Highland Laddie.

SQUEAK **the** fife and beat **the** drum,
Independence day **is** come,
Let the roasting pig **be** bled,
Quick twist off the rooster's head,
Quickly rub the pewter-platter,
Heap the nut cakes, fried in **butter ;**
Set the cups and beaker **glass,**
The pumpkin and the apple-sass.

Send **the keg to shop for brandy,**
Maple sugar we **have handy ;**
Independent, staggering **Dick,**
A noggin mix of swingeing **thick ;**
Sal, put **on** your russet skirt,
Jonathan, get your bough**ten shirt,**
Here comes Sambo with **his** fiddle—
To-day we dance to tiddle diddle.

Sambo, take a dram of whisky,
And play us Yankee Doodle friskey,
Moll, come leave your wicked tricks,
And let **us** have a reel of six.
Father **and** mother shall make two—
Sall, Moll, and I, stand all a row :
Sambo, play and dance with quality,
This is the day of blest equality.

Father and mother are but men,
Sambo—take a sup of gin—
Come foot it, Sal—Moll, figure in,
And mother, you dance up to him.
Now saw as fast as ever you can do,
And father you cross o'er to Sambo—
Thus we dance, and thus we play,
On glorious Independence Day.

Encore Verses.

Rub more rosin on your bow,
And let us have another go—
Zounds! as sure as eggs and bacon,
Here's ensign Sneak, and uncle Deacon.
Aunt Thiah, and there's Bets behind her,
On blundering mare, than beetle blinder,
And there's the squire too, with his lady ;
Sal, hold the beast, I'll take the baby.

Moll, bring the squire our great arm chair,
Good folks we're glad to see you here—
Jonathan get the great case bottle,
Your teeth can pull its corn-cob stopple.
Ensign—Deacon, never mind,
Squire, drink until you're blind—
Thus we drink and dance away,
This glorious Independence Day.

ROYAL TYLER, 1787.

RED, WHITE, AND BLUE.

OH Columbia, the gem of the Ocean,
  The home of the brave and the free,
The shrine of each patriot's devotion,
  A world offers homage to thee.
Thy mandates make heroes assemble,
  When liberty's form stands in view,
Thy banners make tyranny tremble,
  When borne by the red, white, and blue.
    When borne by the red, white, and blue,
    When borne by the red, white, and blue,
    Thy banners make tyranny tremble,
    When borne by the red, white and blue.

When war waged its wide desolation,
    And threatened our land **to** deform,
The ark then of freedom's foundation,
    Columbia **rode** safe through the storm.
With her garland of victory o'er her,
    When so proudly she bore her bold crew,
With her flag proudly floating before her,
    The boast of the red, white, and blue.
                        The boast of, &c.

The wine cup, the wine cup **bring hither,**
    And fill you it up to the brim,
May the memory of Washington ne'er wither,
    Nor the star of his glory grow dim.
May the service united ne'er sever,
    But e'er to their colors prove true,
The army and navy **forever,**
    Three cheers for **the red, white, and blue,**
                        Three cheers for, &c.

THE BOSTING TEA PARTY OF 1773.

Tune.—Bow—wow—wow. **Sung with** immense applause.

I'M a YANKEE **lad that's jist come down,**
    An' guess I'll **sing a ditty,**
And them that doesn't **relish it,**
    I reckon **it's a** pity.
That is, I think, I should **have been**
    A plaguy sight more finish'd **man,**
If I'd been born in Boston town;
    But I warn't, 'cause I'm a countryman.
        Tol lol de **ra.**
        Ri tol de **riddle iddle, ri tol de ra.**

And t'other day the Yankee **folks,**
    Were mad about the taxes,
And so we went, like Indians dress'd,
    To split tea-chests with axes:
I mean, 'twas done in *seventy*-three,
    An' we were real gritty:
The mayor he would have led the gang,
    But Boston warn't a city.
        Tol lol de ra, &c.

Ye see we Yankees didn't care,
  A pin for wealth or booty,
And so, in State street, we agreed,
  We'd never pay the duty;
That is, in State street 'twould have been,
  But 'twas King street they call'd it then;
And the tax on tea, it was so bad,
  The women would not scald it then.
        Tol lol de ra, &c.

To Charlestown bridge we all went down,
  To see the thing corrected :
That is, we would have gone there,
  But the bridge, it warn't erected;
The tea, perhaps, was very good:
  Bohea, Souchong, or Hyson;
But drinking tea, it warn't the rage,
  The duty made it pison.
        Tol lol de ra, &c.

And then we went aboard the ships,
  Our vengeance to administer,
And didn't care a tarnal bit,
  For any king or minister;
We made a plaguy mess of tea,
  In one of the biggest dishes,
I mean, we steep'd it in the sea,
  And treated all the fishes.
        Tol lol de ra, &c.

And then, you see, we were all found out,
  A thing we hadn't dreaded;
The leaders were to London sent,
  And instantly beheaded :
That is, I mean, they would have been,
  If ever they'd been taken;
But the leaders, they were never cotch'd,
  And so they saved their bacon.
        Tol lol de ra, &c

Now heaven bless the president,
  And all **this** godly nation ;
That is, sir, if we were *not* blest,
  As **it** is, there's no occasion.
Long live them folks who threw **that** *herb*,
  In the kettle **of the sea**, sir,
That is, since they **are dead, may they**
  Drink immortali(ty) *tea*, **sir.**
      Tol lol de **ra, &c.**

THE STRONG **LADS OF LABOR.**

Tune—*" Taking **Tea** in the Arbor."*

    LET others proclaim
    The bold son of **war's** fame,
And the heroes of cannon and sabre,
    A song let me sing,
    And around let it ring,
In the praise of "the *Strong Lads of Labor.*"
    Let monarchics boast
    Of the **walls on their coast,**
To ward off **a** threatening neighbor,
    But a **nation's true power,**
    In **danger's dark hour,**
Exists in her STRONG LADS OF LABOR.
Chorus—But a **nation's true power,**
    In **danger's dark hour,**
Exists in her Strong Lads of Labor.

    Let luxury's fool,
    In his proud splendor roll,
Or dance out his life to the **tabor,**
    Could **he drink, could he eat,**
    Could he clothe head or feet,
Were it not for the Strong Lads of Labor?
    The sword, tongue, **or** pen,
    With good minds **and** good men,
May each prove **a** very **good** neighbor,
    But **in war,** plague, or panic,
    Their shield's the MECHANIC,
And the aid of the STRONG SONS OF LABOR.
    But in war, plague, or panic, &c.

From forest to city,
From cradle to coffin,
We see the great work of their hands, sir,
Each mountain's high crest,
And the ocean's broad breast,
By the might of the toiler is spanned, sir.
Then send the shout home,
To the sky's lofty dome,
Be each man to man, BROTHER and NEIGHBOR,
Sing the PLOUGH, PLANE, and PLUMB,
TROWEL, HAMMER, AND LOOM,
And reward to the " *Strong Lads of Labor.*"
Sing the plough, plane, and plumb,
Trowel, hammer, &c.

YOUNG AMERICA.

A NEW AND POPULAR SONG.

Air—Pibroch of Donald Dhu.

HEARTS that love liberty,
Hands to defend her,
Swear by your father's blood,
Nothing shall rend her.
Love for your father's gift,
Thrills your souls ever,
Firm as your mountain cliffs,
Stand ye for ever.
Freedom's young eagles each
His own brave defender,
His *home* and his fatherland,
He'll " NEVER SURRENDER."

Quick as the lightning's flash,
Free as the broad rivers
When liberty calls you,
You've a life's blood to give her.
With you there's no base heart,
There's no soul so sordid,
To give up for gold or *place*,
The glory we've hoarded.
Freedom's young eagles, &c.

THE FREEDOM OF ELECTIONS,

OR LAW AND ORDER.

Tune—*Yankee Doodle*.

WHILE some on rights and some on wrongs,
  Prefer their own reflections,
The people's RIGHT demands our song,
  The *Right of Free Elections*.
For government and order's sake,
  And law's important sections,
Let all stand by the *Ballot Box*,
  For fair and free elections.
Chorus—"Law and order" be the stake,
    With freedom and protection;
  "Let all stand by the *Ballot Box*,
    For fair and free elections.

Each town and country's wealth and peace,
  Its trade and all connections,
With science, arts must all increase,
  By fair and free Elections.
Then thwart the schemes of factious lands,
  And traitor disaffections,
Stand up with willing hearts and hands,
  For fair and free elections.
  Law and order be the stake, &c.

Should enemies beset us round,
  Of foreign, fierce complexions,
Undaunted we can stand our ground,
  Upheld by free elections.
Elections are to make us laws,
  For trade, peace, and protection,
Who fails to vote forsakes the cause
  Of freedom and elections.
Chorus—Law and order be the stake,
    With freedom and protection,
  Let all stand by the Ballot Box,
    For fair and free elections.

THE AMERICAN BOY.

"Father, look up, and see that flag!
  How gracefully it flies!
Those pretty stripes—they seem to be
  A rainbow in the skies."
"It is your country's flag, my son,
  And proudly drinks the light,
O'er ocean's wave—in foreign climes
  A symbol of our might."

"Father, what fearful noise is that,
  Like thundering in the clouds?
Why do the people wave their hats,
  And rush along in crowds?"
"It is the voice of cannonry,
  The glad shouts of the free:
This is a day to memory dear—
  'Tis Freedom's jubilee."

"I wish that I was now a man;
  I'd fire my cannon too,
And cheer as loudly as the rest:
  But, father, why don't you?"
"I'm getting old and weak; but still
  My heart is big with joy.
I've witness'd many a day like this:
  Shout you aloud, my boy."

"Hurrah, for Freedom's jubilee!
  God bless our native land,
And may I live to hold the sword
  Of freedom in my hand!"
"Well done! my boy: grow up and love
  The land that gave you birth;
A home where Freedom loves to dwell,
  A paradise on earth."

J. H. HEWETT.

BROTHER JONATHAN.

A FAVORITE COMIC SONG.

YANKEE doodle was a gentleman,
  He was true Yankee breed, sirs,
In a punkin garden he was found
  Among the scattered seed, sirs.
His father was a Johnny Bull,
  His mother Sukey Coodle;
They used to get the boy to sleep,
  By singing Yankee Doodle.
    Then success to Brother Jonathan,
      He was a lad so clever,
    He made the foes of freedom run,
      And drove them off for ever.

He raised potatoes, punkins, beans,
  And every thing in truth, sirs,
Tobacco, cotton, sugar cane,
  For the lad had a sweet tooth, sirs;
When father Bull for sugar came
  To sweeten his tea and sauces,
The boy you know was not to blame,
  For daubing Pa with lasses.
      Then success, &c.

Some thousand troops Bull then dispatch'd
  To curb this youngster's will, sirs,
But soon they all were put to flight,
  On little *Bunker Hill*, sirs.
At Princeton, and at Monmouth too,
  We shone with like resplendence,
At Yorktown victory gained the rest,
  Which gave us INDEPENDENCE
      Then success, &c.

Now Johnny thought he'd best be off,
  And leave his son be quiet,
But yet to go was rather loath,
  Unless he'd have a riot.

So he greased the pole that held the flag,
  To frighten our Yankee tars, sirs,
But soon beyond old Johnny's rag,
  Was seen the stripes and stars, sirs.
    Then success, &c.

Some thirty years had gone and past,
  And we lived snug and coodle,
John, forgetting what had passed before,
  Came back to Yankee Doodle.
Says Jonathan, if you presume,
  To touch our gals or cotton,
I guess as how I'll learn you soon,,
  A lesson you've forgotten.
    Then success, &c.

IMMORTAL WASHINGTON.

Tune—Bunch of Rushes.

COLUMBIA'S greatest glory
Was her loved chief, fair Freedom's friend;
  Whose fame, renown'd in story,
Shall last till time itself shall end.
    Ye muses, bring
    Your harps, and sing
Sweet lays that in smooth numbers run,
  In praise of our loved hero,
The great, the god-like Washington.

  His fame, through future ages,
Columbia's free-born sons shall raise;
  The theme each heart engages,
All tongues shall join to sing his praise.
    With joy sound forth
    His virtuous worth,
And tell the glorious acts he's done.
    Of all mankind, the greatest
Was our beloved Washington.

And, O ! thou great Creator,
Who form'd his youth, and watch'd his age,
  Since thou, in course of nature,
Hast call'd him from his earthly stage,
    Great power above,
    Enthroned in love,
Who was before this world began,
    Receive into thy bosom
Our virtuous hero—Washington.

BOLD PRIVATEER.

Music published by Firth, Pond & Co., NEW YORK.

IT's oh ! my dearest Polly, you and I must part,
I am going across the seas, love, I give to you my heart;
My ship she lies in waiting, so fare thee well, my dear,
I am just going on board of the Bold Privateer.

But oh, my dearest Johnny, great dangers have been crossed,
And many a sweet life by the seas has been lost;
You had better stop at home, with the girl that loves you
        dear,
Than to venture your life on the Bold Privateer.

When the wars are over—may heaven spare my life,
Then soon I will come back to my sweet, loving wife.
Then soon I will get married to charming Polly, dear,
And forever bid adieu to the Bold Privateer.

Oh ! my dearest Polly, your friends do me dislike,
Besides you have two brothers who'd quickly take my life.
Come, change your ring with me, my dear, come change your
        ring with me,
And that shall be our token when I am on the sea.

SONGS OF IRELAND.

THE RAMBLER FROM CLARE.

Oh! the first of my rambling that ever was known,
I straight steered my way to the county Tyrone,
There I fell to courting the lasses so fair,
And they knew me by the ti-tle of the Rambler from Clare.

Oh! the next of my rambling it was in June,
There I fell to courting purty Sally M'Cune,
I soon won her favor with many more there,
I could not wed them all, so played the Rambler from Clare.

Oh! whenever I'd go to a ball or a play,
Or a courting of fair girls along the highway,
They would first view my carriage, and then view my hair,
And they point with their finger at the Rambler from Clare.

The next of my rambling it was in Ardeen,
Where I fell to courting pretty Molly Moreen,
I thought to rove onward but her heart held mine there,
And a captive she made of the Rambler from Clare.

So now I'm resolved for to alter my life,
And it's take to myself, oh! a snug little wife,
And all my past rambles I mane to repair
So adieu to the t-i-i-tle of the Rambler from Clare.

WIDOW MACHREE.

Widow Machree, it's no wonder you frown,
    Och, hone! widow Machree!
Faith, it ruins your looks, that same dirty black gown,
    Och, hone! widow Machree!
How altered your hair with that close cap you wear,
'Tis destroying your hair, which should be flowing free,
Be no longer a churl with its black silken curl,
    Och, hone! widow Machree!

Widow Machree, now the summer is come,
    Och, hone! widow Machree!
When every thing smiles should a body look grim,
    Och, hone! widow Machree!
See the birds go in pairs, the rabbits and hares,
Why even the bears now in couples agree,
And the mute little fish, though they can't spake, they wish,
    Och, hone! widow Machree!

Widow Machree, and when winter comes in,
    Och, hone! widow Machree!
To be poking the fire all alone is a sin,
    Och, hone! widow Machree!
Why the shovel and tongs to each other belongs,
And the kettle sings songs full of family glee,
While alone with your cup, like a hermit you sup,
    Och, hone! widow Machree!

And how do you know, with the comforts I've told,
    Och, hone! widow Machree!
But you're keeping some poor fellow out in the cold,
    Och, hone! widow Machree!
With such sins on your head, your peace 'ud be fled,
Could you sleep in your bed without thinking to see
Some ghost or some sprite, that 'ud wake you each night,
    Crying, "Och, hone! widow Machree!"

Then take my advice, darling widow Machree,
    Och, hone! widow Machree!
And with my advice, faith, I'd wish you'd take me,
    Och, hone! widow Machree!

You'd have me desire, then stir up the fire,
And sure hope is no liar in whispering to me,
That ghost 'ud depart, when you've me near your heart,
    Och, hone! widow Machree!

Widow Machree, I don't wish to be bold,
    Och, hone! widow Machree!
But with these inducements that I have just told,
    Och, hone! widow Machree!
I give you my word, my own, my adored,
And as a reward, take this promise from me,
To atone for my sins, your first child shall be twins,
    Och, hone! widow Machree!

WID A DHUDIEEN.

A PARODY, FROM THE CELEBRATED JOHN BROUGHAM'S
PO-CA-HON-TAS.

Air—Widow Machree.

OH, wid a dhudieen I can blow away care,
    Oh, hone, wid a dhudieen!
Black thoughts and blue devils all melt into air,
    Oh, hone! wid a dhudieen!
        If you're short any day,
        Or a note have to pay,
        And you don't know the way,
        To come out of it clean,
        From your head and your heart
        You can make it depart,
    Oh, hone! wid a dhudieen!

Oh, wid a dhudieen you recline at your ease,
    Oh, hone! wid a dhudieen!
Shut your eyes and imagine what pleasures you please
    Oh, hone! wid a dhudieen!
        In dreams without sleep,
        All your senses to steep,
        While you're playing bo-peep
        Through each fairy-like scene,
        Undisturbed, I declare,
        By a single nightmare,
    Oh, hone! wid a dhudieen!

Oh, wid a dhudieen I'm as truly content,
   Oh, hone ! wid a dhudieen !
What the rest of the world does I don't care a cent,
   Oh, hone ! wid a dhudieen !
     Let some folks desire,
     To set rivers on fire,
     While some others admire,
     To run " wid de machine,"
     I've ambition enough,
     Just to sit here and puff,
Oh, hone ! wid a dhudieen !

ERIN IS MY HOME.

Oh, I have roamed o'er many lands,
   And many friends I've met !
Not one fair scene or kindly smile,
   Can this fond heart forget.
But I'll confess that I'm content,
   No more I wish to roam,
Oh, steer my bark to Erin's Isle,
   For Erin is my home.

In Erin's Isle there's manly hearts,
   And bosoms pure as snow ;
In Erin's Isle there's right good cheer,
   And hearts that ever flow.
In Erin's Isle I'd pass my time,
   No more I wish to roam,
Oh, steer my bark for Erin's Isle,
   For Erin is my home.

If England was my place of birth,
   I'd love her tranquil shore ;
If bonny Scotland was my home,
   Her mountains I'd adore ;
But pleasant days in both I've past,
   I'll dream of days to come ;
Oh, steer my bark to Erin's Isle,
   For Erin is my home.

KATHLEEN MAVOURNEEN.

KATHLEEN Mavourneen! the gray dawn is breaking,
  The horn of the hunter is heard on the hill,
The lark from her light wing the bright dew is shaking,
  Kathleen Mavourneen! what, slumbering still?
Oh, hast thou forgotten how soon we must sever?
  Oh, hast thou forgotten this day we must part?
It may be for years and it may be for ever,
  Oh, why art thou silent, thou voice of my heart?
It may be for years, and it may be for ever,
  Then why art thou silent, Kathleen Mavourneen?

Kathleen Mavourneen, awake from thy slumbers!
  The blue mountains glow in the sun's golden light;
Ah! where is the spell that once hung on my numbers?
  Arise in thy beauty, thou star of my night
Mavourneen! Mavourneen! my sad tears are falling,
  To think that from Erin and thee I must part,
It may be for years, and it may be for ever,
  Then why art thou silent, thou voice of my heart?
It may be for years, and it may be for ever,
  Then why art thou silent, Kathleen Mavourneen?

THERE'S WHISKEY IN THE JUG.

I AM a sporting fellow, I never was yet daunted,
Money in the pocket whenever it was wanted,
Robbing for gold, 'twas my own folly,
Sure I'd risk my life for you, my sporting Molly.
Chorus—Rack fal de ra, rack fal de raddy oh!
    Rack fal de raddy oh! there's Whiskey in the Jug.

As I was crossing the Mulberry mountain,
I met with Captain Kelly, his money he was counting,
At first I drew my pistol, then I drew my rapier,
Stand and deliver, for I'm your money taker.
    Rack fal de ra, rack fal de raddy oh! &c.

He handed me twenty pounds—'twas a pretty penny, oh!
I took it home to Molly, she said she'd ne'er desaive me,
I took it home to Molly, she said she'd ne'er desaive me,
But the devil's 'mongst the women, and they never can be **aisy**.
    Rack fal de ra, rack fal de raddy oh! &c.

I went into Molly's chamber for to take a slumber,
I went into Molly's chamber, not knowing of any danger,
When I was sleeping, it's well she knew the matter,
She unloaded the pistols, and filled them with water.
    Rack fal de ra, rack fal de raddy oh! &c.

Early the next morning between six and seven,
The house was surrounded—likewise with Captain Kelly;
I sprang for my pistols, being very much mistaken,
I fired off the water, and a prisoner I was taken.
    Rack fal de ra, rack fal de raddy oh! &c.

I have two little brothers enlisted in the army,
One of them's in Cork, the other's in Killarney,
If they were here to-night, I would be free and jolly,
I'd rather have them here to-night than you, deceitful Molly.
    Rack fal de ra, rack fal de raddy oh! &c.

KITTY TYRRELL.

You're looking as fresh as the morn, darling,
  You're looking as bright as the day—
But while on your charms I'm dilating,
  You're stealing my poor heart away;
But keep it and welcome, mavourneen,
  Its loss I'm not going to mourn,
Yet one heart's enough for a body,
  So pray give me yours in return.
       Mavourneen, mavourneen!
  O pray give me yours in return.

I've built me a neat little cot, darling,
  I've pigs and potatoes in store;
I've twenty good pounds in the bank, love,
  And may be a pound or two more.
It's all very well to have riches,
  But I'm such a covetous elf,
I can't help still sighing for something,
  And, darling, that something's yourself.
       Mavourneen, mavourneen!
  That something, you know, is yourself.

You're smiling, and that's a good sign, darling,
 Say " Yes," and you'll never repent ;
Or if you would rather be silent,
 Your silence I'll take for consent.
That good-natured dimple's a tell-tale,
 Now all that I have is your own ;
This week you may be Kitty Tyrrell,
 Next week you'll be Mistress Malone.
    Mavourneen, mavourneen !
  You'll be my own Mistress Malone.

CHARLES JEFFERYS.

MOTHER, HE'S GOING AWAY.

SURE, now, what are you crying for, Nelly,
 Don't be blubbering there like a fool,
With the weight of the grief, faith, I tell ye,
 You'll break down the three-legged stool.
I suppose, now, you're crying for Barney,
 But don't b'lieve a word that he'd say ;
He tells nothing but big lies and blarney,
 Sure, you know he sarved poor Kate Kearney
   " But, mother !"—" Oh, bother !"
   " But, mother, he's going away,
   And I dream'd t'other night,
   Of his ghost all in white ;
  Oh, mother, he's going away !"

If he's going away all the better,
 Blessed hour when he's out of your sight,
There's one comfort, you can't get a letter, ·
 For ye neither can read nor can write.
Why, 'twas only last week you protested,
 When he courted fat Biddy Macrae,
That the sight of the scamp you detested,
 Wid abuse, sure, your tongue never rested.
   " But, mother !"—" Oh, bother !"
   " But, mother, he's going away ;
   And I dream'd that his ghost
   Walk'd round my bed-post ;
  Oh, mother, he's going away !"

GROVES OF BLARNEY.

THE groves of Blarney, they are so charming,
　Down by the purling of sweet silent brooks;
'Tis there's the daisy spontaneous growing,
　Planted by nature all in the rocky nooks;
'Tis there's the posy, call'd the sweet carnation,
　The blushing pink, and the rose so fair,
Likewise the lily, and the daffy-dilly,
　All sweet flowers scenting the most fragrant air.

There's gravel walks there for meditation,
　And contemplation, all in sweet solitude;
'Tis there's the lovyer, may meet the plovyer,
　Or the gentle dove, by way of interlude.
And in case any young lady be so engaging,
　Just to fetch a walk, those shady bowers around,
Oh! 'tis there's her courtier, might transport her,
　Into some dark cavern, all down under the ground.

'Tis there's the cave, where no day-light enters,
　Where cats and badgers are forever bred,
Almost by nature, which makes its complature,
　Nor a coach and six, nor a downy bed.
'Tis there's the lake is well stored with fishes,
　The comely eels in the vardant mud that stray,
There's them trout and them salmon, playing together at
　　back-gammon,
　But if you try to catch hold of them, don't they all imajuntly
　　swim away?

'Tis there's the kitchen, with many a flitch in,
　And the maids a-stitchin' before the door;
There's bread and biscay, likewise the whiskey,
　Which would make you friskey, if yourself was there.
'Tis there's good Kate Whaley's daughter, Nelly,
　A-washing praters fornent the door,
Ould Roger Daly and Miss Biddy Kelly,
　All blood relations of that entirely great, noble, and
　　nowned family, my lord Donoughmore.

There's statuary gracing that noble place in,
  All heathen goddesses so fair ;
Bold Neptune, Plutarch, and sweet Nicodemus,
  All alive and naked, out in the cold frosty air.
And now to finish this brief narration,
  Which my poor genus could ne'er divine,
Oh ! was I a Homer, or even Nebuchadnezzar,
  In every feature I'd make it for to shine.

THE DARLIN' OULD STICK.

My name is bold Morgan MacCarthy from Trim
My relations all died except one brother Jim ;
He's gone a sojering out to Cabool,
I dare say he's laid low with a *nick* in his skull.
    But let him be dead or be living,
    A prayer for his corpse I'll be giving,
    To send him soon home, or to heaven,
    For he left me this darlin' ould stick.

If that stick had a tongue it could tell you some tales,
How it battered the countenances of the O'Neills ;
It made bits of skulls fly about in the air,
And it's been the promoter of fun at each fair
    For I swear by the toe-nail of Moses,
    It has often broke bridges of noses,
    Of the faction that dare to oppose us,
    It's the darlin' *kippeen* of a stick.

The last time I used it 'twas on Patrick's day,
Larry Fegan and I got into a *shilley*,
We went on a spree to the fair at Athboy,
Where I danced, and, when done, I kissed Kate McEvoy.
    Then her sweetheart went out for her cousin,
    And, be jabers ! he brought in a dozen ;
    A *doldhrum* they would have knocked us in,
    If I hadn't this *taste* of a stick.

"Ware," was the word, when the faction came in,
And to pummice us well they peeled off in their skin,
Like a Hercules there I stood for the attack,
And the first that came up I sent down on his **back**.
    Then I shoved out the eye of Pat Glancy,
      For he once humbugged my sister Nancy,
      In the meantime poor Kate took a fancy,
      To myself and my darlin' ould stick.

I *smathered* her sweetheart until he was black,
She then tipped me the wink, we were off in a crack,
We went to a house t'other end of the town,
And we cheered up our spirits by letting some down.
    When I got her snug into a corner,
      And the whiskey beginning to warm her,
      She said her sweetheart was an *informer*,
      Oh! 'twas then I said prayers for my stick.

We got *whiskificated* to such a degree,
For support my poor Kate had to lean ag'in me.
I promised to see her safe to her abode,
By the 'tarnal we fell clean in the mud on the road.
    We were roused by the magistrate's order,
      Before we could get a toe further,
      Surrounded by peelers for murther,
      Was myself and my innocent stick.

When the trial came on, Katy swore to the fact,
That before I set-too, I was dacently whack'd,
And the judge had a little more feeling than sense,
He said what I done, was in my own defence.
    But one chap swore agin me, named Carey,
      (Though that night he was in Tipperary,)
      He'd swear a coal-porter was a canary,
      To transport both myself and my stick.

When I was acquitted I leaped from the dock,
And all the gay fellows around me did flock,
I'd a pain in my shoulders, I shook hands so often,
For the boys all imagined I'd see my own coffin.
    I went and I bought a gold ring, sirs,
      And Kate to the priest I did bring, sirs,
      So next night you come, I will sing, sirs,
      The adventures of me and my stick.

FLAMING O'FLANNAGANS.

A Celebrated Comic Song, sung by M. J. Pilgrim, in the Drama of " O'Flannagan and the Fairies."

Now I'm of age I'll come into my property,
  Devil a ha'porth I'll think of but fun;
'Tis myself will be putting the ladies in papoury,
  Just to prove I'm my daddy's own son.
Och now, Mistress Honey, I'll teach ye civility,
  Judy O'Doole, escape if you can—
I'm the boy that will show ye the sweets of gentility,
  Loving most women and fearing no man.
          Horroo! wack!
For that was the way with the Flaming O'Flannagans,
  From the first illigant boys of the name.
For kissing and courting, and filling the can again,
  Drinking and fighting like cocks of the game.
          Horroo! wack!

The tazing, the cursing, the shouting, the shooting,
  The clattering of glasses, the beating of skulls,
The dancing would sure be upon the best footing,
  Wid Irish Miss Murphys, and English Miss Bulls.
The neat little party you'd like to see—
  The loves and the whisky, and the devil knows what,
And the dancers that we whacked black and blue like the
    devil,
  And the spalpeens we floored at the very first shot.
          Horroo! wack!

O'Brien he went through the world, without lying,
  And he beat the Danes, nine score of them flat,
And faix after that the Danes beat O'Brien,
  And he died victorious, mus-ha more flat was Pat.
Ever since that they've been devils for fighting,
  That ever was fought on dry land or ocean,
If blood had been spilt you'd find an O'Flannagan,
  Either beating the enemy or lying stone dead.
          Horroo! wack!

Encore Verse.

Do you see how I'm laughed at by all those queer vagabones,
  Shouting and screaming twice as loud as they can;
Paddy Flynn, I'll go bail, I give you a sore bag o' bones,
  If you'd only come here and turn out like a man.
Do ye's think I'll stop here till morning, diverting ye's,
  While my nate jug of punch is cooling outside?
Good-night boys, you know I'm sorry from parting ye's,
  But the love of the whisky was always my pride.
      Horroo! wack!

BACHELOR'S HALL.

Bachelor's hall, what a quare looking place it is,
  Kape me from sich all the days of my life,
Sure but I think what a burnin' disgrace it is,
  Niver at all to be gettin' a wife.
See the ould bachelor gloomy and sad enough,
  Placing his tay kittle over the fire;
Soon tips it over, St. Patrick, he's mad enough,
  (If he were present,) to fight with the squire.

Now like a hog in a mortar bed wallowing,
  Awkward enough see him knading his dough;
Troth! if the bread he could ate without swallowing,
  How he would favor his palate you know.
Pots, dishes, pans, and sich greasy commodities,
  Ashes and prata skins kiver the floor;
His cupboard's a storehouse of comical oddities,
  Things that had niver been neighbors before.

His meal being over, his tables left sitting so,
  Dishes take care of yourselves if you can;
But hunger returns, then he's fuming and fretting so,
  Och! let him alone for a baste of a man.
Late in the night when he goes to bed shiverin',
  Niver a bit is the bed made at all;
He crapes like a tarapin under the kiverin',
  Bad luck to the picture of bachelor's hall.

EXILE OF ERIN.

THERE came to the beach a poor Exile of Erin,
  The dew on his thin robe was heavy and chill;
For his country he sighed, when at twilight repairing,
  To wander alone by the wind beaten hill.
But the day-star attracted his eye's sad devotion,
For it rose o'er his own native isle of the ocean,
Where once, in the fire of his youthful emotion,
  He sung the bold anthem of Erin go bragh.

Sad is my fate! said the heart-broken stranger,
  The wild deer and wolf to a covert can flee;
But I have no refuge from famine and danger,
  A home and a country remain not to me.
Never again in the green sunny bowers,
Where my forefathers lived, shall I spend the sweet hours,
Or cover my harp with the wild woven flowers,
  And strike to the numbers of Erin go bragh.

Erin, my country, though sad and forsaken,
  In dreams I revisit thy sea-beaten shore;
But alas! in a far foreign land I awaken,
  And sigh for the friends who can meet me no more!
Oh cruel fate! will thou never replace me,
In a mansion of peace—where no perils can chase me?
Never again, shall my brothers embrace me?
  They died to defend me, or lived to deplore.

Where is my cabin-door, fast by the wild wood?
  Sisters and sire! did ye weep for its fall?
Where is the mother that looked on my childhood?
  And where is the bosom friend, dearer than all?
Oh! my sad heart! long abandoned by pleasure,
Why did it doat on a fast fading treasure!
Tears like the rain drop, may fall without measure;
  But rapture and beauty they cannot recall.

Yet all its sad recollection suppressing,
  One dying wish my lone bosom can draw,
Erin! an exile bequeaths thee his blessing!
  Land of my forefathers! Erin go bragh!
Buried and cold, when my heart stills her motion,
Green be thy fields—sweetest isle of the ocean!
And thy harp striking bards sing aloud with devotion—
  Erin mavourneen!—Erin go bragh!   CAMPBELL.

IRISH WEDDING.

SURE won't you hear what roaring cheer
    Was spread at Paddy's wedding, O,
And how so gay they spent the day,
    From churching to the bedding. O?
First, book in hand, came father Quipes,
    With the bride's dada, the bailie, O;
While all the way to church the pipes
    Struck up a lilt so gaily, O.
        Sing Tudewack—imitating bag-pipes.

Then there was Mat and sturdy Pat,
    And merry Morgan Murphy, O,
And Murdock Meggs, and Tirlough Sheggs,
    M'Lochlan, and Dick Durfy, O.
And then the girls dressed out in white,
    Led on by Tad O'Reilly, O,
All jigging, as the merry pipes
    Struck up a lilt so gaily, O.

When Pat was asked would his love last?
    The chancel echoed with laughter, O;
Arrah fait, cried Pat, you may say dat,
    To the end of the world and after, O.
Then tenderly her hand he gripes,
    And kisses her genteelly, O,
While, all in tune, the merry pipes
    Struck up a lilt so gaily, O.

Now a roaring set at dinner are met,
    So frolicsome and so frisky, O,
Potatoes galore, a skirraig or more,
    And a flowing madder of whiskey, O;
To the bride's dear health round went the swipes
    That her joy might be nightly and daily, O,
And as they guttled, the merry pipes
    Struck up a lilt so gaily, O.

And then at night, oh! what delight,
    To see them all footing and prancing, O,
An opera or ball was nothing at all,
    Compared to the style of their dancing, O;

And then to see old father Quipes
  Beat time with his shillelagh, O,
While the chanter with his merry pipes,
  Struck up a lilt so gaily, O.

And now the knot so tipsy got,
  They'll go to sleep without rocking, O;
So the bridemaids fair now gravely prepare
  For throwing of the stocking, O;
And round to be sure didn't go the swipes
  At the bride's expense so freely, O,
While to wish them good night the merry pipes
  Struck up a lilt so gaily, O.

YOU'RE GOING TO THE WARS.

A PARODY ON JEANNETTE AND JEANNOT.

As sung by Barney Williams with great applause.

YOU are going to the wars where the dirty fighting's done,
Wid your knapsack to your back, and your shoulder to your
        gun;
Oh, you'll dance no more at fairs, nor go out upon a spree,
What's worse than that, my Mickey, you'll be forgetting me:
Wid your *soger* coat of green, when you're thramping into
        town,
You'll break the hearts of all the gals, and turn them upside
        down;
And p'raps you'll marry some of them, and if you do, ye see,
By the powers I'll not rest in bed, but its *murthering* you I'll
        be.
          By the powers, &c.

When the drums do beat the charge, you'll be dropping on
        your back,
Like they do in Tipperary, but your skull will show no crack;
And when the *gineral* hears of it, promoted you will be,
A corporal or a body guard, what will become of me?
If I were queen of Meriky, or California's king,
I'd have no guns used in the wars, or any such *murthering*
        thing!
All the 'ventors of the pistols, I'd transport across the sea,
And I'd kill the *sogers* dacently, *Shelala's gramachree.*
          And I'd kill, &c.

MOLLY BAWN.

OH, Molly Bawn, why leave me pining,
　Or lonely waiting here for you,
While the stars above are brightly shining,
　Because they've nothing else to do?
The flowers late were open keeping,
　To try a rival blush with you,
But their mother, Nature, kept them sleeping,
　With their rosy faces washed in dew.
　　　　Oh, Molly, &c.

The pretty flowers were made to bloom, dear,
　And the pretty stars were made to shine;
The pretty girls were made for boys, dear,
　And may be you were made for mine.
The wicked watch-dog here is snarling,—
　He takes me for a thief, d'ye see?
For he knows I'd steal you, Molly, darling,
　And then transported I should be.
　　　　Oh, Molly, &c.

THE HARP THAT ONCE THRO' TARA'S HALLS.

Air—*Gramachree*.

THE harp that once thro' Tara's halls,
　The soul of music shed,
Now hangs as mute on Tara's walls
　As if that soul were fled.
So sleeps the pride of former days,
　So glory's thrill is o'er;
And hearts that once beat high for praise,
　Now feel that pulse no more.

No more to chiefs and ladies bright,
　The harp of Tara swells;
The chord alone, that breaks at night,
　Its tale of ruin tells.
Thus freedom now so seldom wakes;
　The only throb she gives,
Is when some heart indignant breaks,
　To show that still she lives.

SINCE I'VE BEEN IN THE ARMY.

A NEW AND HIGHLY POPULAR SONG.

Tune—The second part of Wha'll be King but Charlie!

I'M Paddy Whack, from Bally-na-hack, not long ago turn'd
    soldier,
In grand attack, in storm or sack, none than will I be bolder;
Wid spirits gay, I march away, I plase each fair beholder,
The ladies cry, as me they spy, Och! what a lovely soldier!
In Londonderry, or London merry, ye ladies all, I'll charm ye,
An' down ye'll come, whin I bate the drum, to see me in the
    army.
    The refrain is usually accompanied by the drum.
Chorus—
Wid my rub-a-dub dub, row dow dow, I live dear girls to
    charm ye,
An' down ye'll come, when I bate the drum, to see me in the
    army.

The lots of girls, my train unfurls, would make a dacent party,
There's Katty Lynch, a tidy wench, and Peg and Sue M'Carthy,
There's Sally Maggs, and Judy Baggs, and Martha Scraggs,
    all storm me:
And Molly Magee, she's after me, since I've been in the army.
The Kitty's, and Dolly's, the Bridget's, and Polly's, in num-
    bers would alarm ye,
Even Mrs. White, that's lost her sight, admires me in the army.

The roaring boys, that made a noise, and whack'd me like the
    divil,
Are now become, before me dumb, or else they're mighty civil,
There's Murphy Rourke, that often broke my head, now dars'nt
    dare me,
But bows an' scrapes, and off he sneaks, since I've been in the
    army,
An, if one neglect, to pay me respect, another tips the blarney,
Wid whist, my friend, and don't offend, a gintleman in the
    army

My arms are bright, my heart is light, good humour seems to
 warm me,
I'm now become, **wid every** chum, a favorite in the **army.**
If I go on, **as I've** begun, my comrades all inform **me,**
They plainly see, that I shall be **a** Gineral in the army.
Delightful notion, to get promotion, ye **ladies thin** I'll charm ye,
For its my belief, commander-in-chief **I soon shall** be in the
 army.
 With **my rub-a-dub, &c.**

LARRY O'BRIAN.

As sung by Dick Cunningham.

I'VE just newly returned from the ocean,
Where the blood **and** thunder balls were in motion,
Sure for fighting, then, I **never** had a **notion.**
 It would **never do for Larry** O'Brian.
I could box **along the shore, like a** great many more,
And **the** spalpeens, **by my soul** I'd knock down a half a score,
But I **never** thought it **clever,**
For the **balls to knock the liver,**
 Out of Larry—Larry!
Blood and thunder **to** the gabie that would **tarry,**
It would never do **for** Larry O'Brian.

I was so tight that none could come near me,
And for wit I'll engage few could scare me,
And for boxing you need **all to fear me,**
 So smart was Larry O'Brian,
So tight and so free, when I first went to sea,
Who the divil should they put into office but **me!**
And with my raker, and my scraper,
Bloody nouns they made a sweeper,
 Out of Larry—Larry, &c.

A dirty little middy of a milksop,
He ordered me **up** to the maintop,
Sure my head spun around like a whip top,
 It would never do for Larry O'Brian.
The sailors up aloft, **they** sent down a rope,
They tied it round my belly and hauled me up,
I kept bawling, I kept squawling,
But the rascals all kept hauling,
 Up young **Larry, &c.**

The next thing they all went to fightin',
That's a dirty trick I never took delight in,
And I'm sure you will all think me right in,
    Securing of Larry O'Brian.
For the powder and the shot, and the balls flew so hot,
With their hubbubaboo and dad sans culotte,
And with their funning, and their gunning,
By my soul I set off running,
    With Larry—Larry, &c.

While this hubbubaboo they were making,
In the hold I lay shivering and shaking,
Until I heard that the French ship was taken,
    Then out popped Larry O'Brian.
There I saw a man dead, lying down without his head,
By my soul, said I, my lad, you had better been in bed,
Than delighting in such fighting,
Which I thought no ways inviting,
    With your Larry—Larry, &c.

Then the captain gave orders for sailing,
But the sides of our ship wanted nailing,
Then all hands fell to pumping and bailing,
    That was labor for Larry O'Brian.
With their hammers and their knocks,
And their mighty heavy blocks,
She looked for all the world like the devil in the stocks,
Wid their oakum, devil choke'um,
And they wished for to poke'um
    On young Larry, &c.

I got rid of the captain and sailors,
Bid adieu to the caulkers and bailers,
By my soul I'll apply to the tailor's,
    To rig up young Larry O'Brian.
I've escaped free from wounds,
And now by blood an' ouns,
I'll marry some plump widow wid her twenty thousand pounds.
I'll implore her—I'll adore her,
And shall sail through life ashore, sir,
    With young Larry, &c.

LOW BACKED CAR.

WHEN first I saw sweet Peggy,
  'Twas on a market day,
On a low backed car she drove, and sat
  Upon a truss of hay.
But when that hay was blooming grass,
  And decked with flowers of spring,
No flowers were there that could compare
  With the charming girl I sing.
    As she sat in her low backed car,
    The man at the turnpike bar,
      Good natured soul!
      Never asked for his toll,
But looked after the low backed car.

In battle's wild commotion,
  The proud and mighty Mars,
With hostile scythes, demands his tythes
  Of death in warlike scars;
But Peggy, peaceful goddess,
  Has darts in her bright eye,
That knock men down, in the market town,
  As right and left they fly,
As she sits in that low back'd car,
The battle more dangerous far,
  For the Doctor's heart,
  Cannot heal the smart,
That is hit from the low back'd car.

Sweet Peggy round her car, sirs,
  Has strings of ducks and geese,
But the scores of hearts she slaughters
  By far outnumbers these—
While she among her poultry sits
  Just like a turtle dove,
Well worth a cage, I do engage,
  With the blooming God of Love.
As she sat in her low back'd car,
The lovers came near and far,
  And envy the chicken
  That Peggy is picking,
As she sits in her low back'd car.

I'd rather own that car, sirs,
  With Peggy by my side,
Than a coach and four, and gold galore,
  And a lady for my bride.
For a lady would sit forninst me
  On a cushion made with taste,
While Peggy would sit beside me,
  With my arm around her waist.
As we rode in the low back'd car,
To be married by Father Meaghar,
  Oh, my heart would beat high,
  At each glance of her eye,
As we rode in that low back'd car.

BRYAN O'LINN.

PATHETIC QUARTETTE.

MUSHA BRYAN O'LINN had no breeches to wear,
So he got him a shapeskin to make him a pair,
Wid de skinny side out an' the hairy side in,
Faix they're good for the winter, says Bryan O'Linn.
Chorus.—Patchooly alana coppeen a budhoo,
        Potien galore avick sha ma grin dhu,
        Strahawbed a oumadawn kippen traheen,
        Musha Ballysloughguttery keogh smithereen.

Oh thin Bryan O'Linn had no watch to put on,
So he got him a turnip to make him a wan,
He cotch an ould cricket an' put it therein,
Sure they'll think it's a ticking, says Bryan O'Linn.
Chorus.—Patchooly alana coppeen a budhoo,
        Potien galore avick sha ma grin dhu,
        Strahawbed a oumadawn kippen traheen,
        Musha Ballysloughguttery keogh smithereen.

Bryan O'Linn, his wife, an' his mudder,
They all crossed over the ould bridge togedder;
Troth, the bridge bruk down, an' they all tumbled in,
We'll find ground at the bottom, says Bryan O'Linn.
Chorus.—Patchooly alana coppeen a budhoo,
        Potien galore avick sha ma grin dhu,
        Strahawbed a oumadawn kippen traheen,
        Musha Ballysloughguttery keogh smithereen.

CROOS-KEEN LAWN.

LET the farmer praise his grounds,
As the huntsman does his hounds,
  And the shepherd his sweet-scented lawn ;
While I more blest than they,
Spend each happy night and day
   With my smiling little croos-keen lawn, lawn, lawn,
  Oh, my smiling little croos-keen lawn.
Leante ruma croos-keen
Sleante gar ma voor meh neen
Argus gramachree ma cooleen ban, ban, ban,
Argus gramachree ma coolen ban.

In court with manly grace,
Should Sir Toby plead his case,
  And the merits of his cause make known ;
Without his cheerful glass
He'd be stupid as an ass,
   So he takes a little croos-keen lawn.
     Leante ruma, &c.

Then fill your glasses high,
Let's not part with lips so dry,
  Though the lark should proclaim it dawn ;
But if we can't remain,
May we shortly meet again,
   To fill another croos-keen lawn.
     Leante ruma, &c.

And when grim death appears,
After few but happy years,
  And tells me my glass it is run,
I'll say, Begone you slave,
For great Bacchus gives me lave
   Just to fill another croos-keen lawn.
     Leante ruma, &c.

ANGEL'S WHISPER.

A BABY was sleeping,
Its mother was weeping,
For her husband was far on the wide raging sea,
And the tempest was swelling
'Round the fisherman's dwelling,
And she cried, " Dermont, darling, oh, come back to me !"

Her beads while she number'd,
The baby still slumber'd,
And smiled in her face as she bended her knee :
"Oh ! bless'd be that warning,
My child, thy sleep adorning,
For I know that the angels are whispering to thee."

" And while they are keeping
Bright watch o'er thy sleeping,
Oh, pray to them softly, my baby, with me ;
And say thou wouldst rather
They'd watch o'er thy father,
For I know that the angels are whispering to thee."

The dawn of the morning
Saw Dermont returning,
And the wife wept with joy her babe's father to see ;
And closely caressing,
Her babe with a blessing
Said, "I knew that the angels were whispering to thee."

SAMUEL LOVER.

THE IRISH LOVE LETTER.

OCH ! Judy, dear creature, she has won my sowl,
The thoughts of her eyes puts my heart in a filliloo ;
By the side of my donkey I lay cheek-by-jowl,
On a sheet of brown paper to write her a billy-doo.
I had no pen, so made shift with a skewer,
And thus I began all my mind to reveal :—
Och, Judy, says I, I've a mind to be sure,
That you should become lovely Mistress O'Neal.
Whack fal lal lal, fal de ral, whack fal lal.
Whack fal lal lal, &c.

My father's a seampstress, makes clothes for the army,
  My mother's a coalman on great Dublin quays,
And if you were with us I'm sure it would charm ye,
  To see all our dacent and illigant ways.
Each day for dinner we've a herring or a salmon—
  We eat our potaties without any peel!
And so you may, Judy, without any gammon,
  If you will but become lovely Mistress O'Neal.
    Whack, &c.

SAVOURNEEN DEELISH.

Sung by Miss Hughes.

OH, the moment was sad when my love and I parted,
  Savourneen deelish eileen ogg!
As I kiss'd off her tears I was nigh broken hearted,
  Savourneen declish eileen ogg!
Wan was her cheek, which hung on my shoulder,
Damp was her hand, no marble was colder,
I felt in my heart I ne'er more should behold her,
  Savourneen deelish eileen ogg!

Long I fought for my country, far, far from my true love,
  Savourneen deelish eileen ogg.
All my pay and my booty I hoarded for you, love,
  Savourneen deelish eileen ogg!
Peace was proclaim'd—escaped from the slaughter,
Landed at home, my sweet girl! I sought her,
But sorrow, alas! to the cold grave had brought her.
  Savourneen deelish eileen ogg!

ERIN MAVOURNEEN.

WHEN the pure sense of honour shall cease to inspire thee,
  And kind hospitality leaves thy gay shore;
When the nations that know thee, no longer admire thee,
  Then, Erin mavourneen, I'll love thee no more.
When the trumpet of Fame shall cease to proclaim thee,
  Of warriors the nurse, in the ages of yore;
When the muse, and the record of genius disclaim thee,
  Then, Erin mavourneen, I'll love thee no more.

When thy brave sons no longer are generous and witty,
  And cease to be lov'd by the fair they adore;
When thy daughters no longer are virtuous and pretty,
  Then, Erin mavourneen, I'll love thee no more.

TEDDY O'NEAL.

IRISH BALLAD.

I'VE come to the cabin he danced his wild jig in,
   As nate a mud palace as ever was seen,
Considering it sarved to keep poultry and pigs in,
   I'm sure it was always most iligant clane.
But now all about it seems lonely and dreary,
   Sad, and all lonely, no piper, no reel,
Not even the sun through the casement is cheery,
   Since I lost that dear darlint boy, Teddy O'Neal,
   Since I lost that dear darlint boy, Teddy O'Neal.

I dreamt but last night, an' bad luck to my dreaming,
   I'd die if I thought it was surely to pass—
I dreamt, while my tears down the pillow was streaming,
   That Teddy was courting another fair lass.
Och! didn't I wake with weeping and wailing,
   The thought of the grief was too deep to conceal,
My mother cries, Norah, child, what is your ailing?
   But all I could utter was Teddy O'Neal,
   But all I could utter was Teddy O'Neal.

I'll never forget when the big ship was ready,
   And the moment had come for my love to depart,
I cried like a spalpeen, Good bye to you, Teddy,
   With drops on my cheek, an' a stone at my heart.
Says he, 'Tis to better my fortune I'm roaming;
   But what would be gold to the joy I should feel,
If he only comes back to me honest an' loving,
   Still poor, but my own darling Teddy O'Neal,
   Still poor, but my own darling Teddy O'Neal.

THE IRISHMAN'S SHANTY.

Copied by permission of Firth, Pond & Co., publishers, 547 Broadway, N. Y.

DID ye's ever go in 'till an Irishman's shanty?
Och! b'ys that's the place where the whiskey is plenty;
With his pipe in his mouth, there sits Paddy so free,
No king in his palace is prouder than he!
   Arrah! me honey! w-h-a-c-k! Paddy's the boy

There's a three-legged stool, with a table to match,
And the door of the shanty is locked with a latch,
There's a nate feather mattrass all bustin' **with straw,**
For want **of a** bedstead, it lies on the **floor.**
  Arrah! me honey! &c.

There's a snug little **bureau** without paint or gilt,
Made of boords that was left when the shanty was built;
There's a three-cornered mirror hangs up on the wall,
The **divil a** face has been in it at all.
  Arrah! me honey! &c.

He has pigs in the sty, and a cow in **the stable,**
And he feeds them on scraps that **is left from the table;**
They'd starve if confined, so **they roam at their aise,**
And come into the shanty **whinever they plaise.**
  Arrah! me honey! &c.

He has three **rooms in** one—kitchen, **bedroom, and hall;**
And **his chist it is** three wooden pegs in the wall;
Two **suits of owld** clothes makes his wardrobe complete,
One to wear in the shanty, that same **for the street.**
  Arrah! me honey! &c.

He can relish good victuals **as ever** ye's ate,
But is always contented with praties and mate;
He prefers them when cold if he **can't** get them hot,
And makes **tea in a bowl** when he can't get a pot.
  Arrah! **me honey!** &c.

There is one who partakes of his **sorrows and joys,**
Attends to the shanty, the girls **and the boys,**
The brats he thinks more of than gold **that's refined,**
But Biddy's the jewel **that's set** in his **mind.**
  Arrah! me honey! &c.

The rich may di**vide their** enjoyment alone
With those who **have riches** as great as their own,
But Pat hangs the latch-string outside of his door,
And **will share** his last cent with the needy and poor.
  Arrah! me honey! &c.

THE BOWLD SOJER BOY.

Oh, there's not a trade that's going,
Worth showing or knowing,
Like that from glory growing,
   For a bowld sojer boy !
Where right or left we go,
Sure you know, friend or foe,
Will have the hand or toe,
   From the bowld sojer boy.
There's not a town we march thro,'
But ladies looking arch thro'
The window panes, will sarch thro'
   The ranks to find their joy.
While up the street, each girl you meet,
With look so sly, will cry " My eye,
Oh, isn't he a darling, the bowld sojer boy !"

But when we get the rout,
How they pout and they shout !
While to the right about,
   Goes the bowld sojer boy.
'Tis then that ladies fair,
In despair tear their hair,
But the divil a one I care,
   Says the bowld sojer boy.
For the world is all before us,
Where the landladies adore us,
And ne'er refuse to score us,
   But chalk us up with joy.
We taste her tap, we tear her cap,
" Oh, that's the chap for me," says she,
" Oh, isn't he a darling, the bowld sojer boy ?"

Then come along with me,
Gramachree, and you'll see,
How happy you will be,
   With your bowld sojer boy.
Faith if you're up to fun,
With me run, 'twill be done,
In the snapping of a gun,
   Says the bowld sojer boy.

And 'tis then that without scandal,
Myself would proudly dandle
The little farthing candle
Of our mutual love, my joy.
May his light shine, as bright as mine,
Till in the line he'll blaze and raise
The glory of his corps, like a bowld sojer boy.

TERENCE'S FAREWELL.

So, my Kathleen, you're going to leave me,
All alone by myself in this place;
But I'm sure you'll never deceive me,
O no, if there's truth in that face.
Though England's a beautiful city,
Full of illigant boys, O what then!
You wouldn't forget your poor Terence,
You'll come back to old Ireland again.

Och, those English deceivers by nature,
Though may be you'd think them sincere,
They'll say you're a sweet charming creature,
But don't you believe them, my dear;
No Kathleen, agra, don't be minding
The flattering speeches they'd make;
Just tell them a poor lad in Ireland
Is breaking his heart for your sake.

It's a folly to keep you from going,
Though, faith, it's a mighty hard case,
For, Kathleen, you know, there's no knowing
When next I shall see your swate face;
And when you come back to me, Kathleen,
None the better will I be off then;
You'd be spaking such beautiful English,
Sure I won't know my Kathleen again.

Aye now, where's the need of this hurry?
Don't flusther me so in this way;
I forgot, 'twixt the grief and the flurry,
Every word I was maning to say.
Now just wait a minute, I bid ye;
Can I talk if ye bother me so?
Oh, Kathleen, my blessings go wid ye,
Every inch of the way that you go.

THE FOUR LEAVED SHAMROCK,

I'LL seek a four leaved shamrock
  In all the fairy dells,
And if I find the charmed leaf,
  Oh, how I'll work my spells!
I would not waste my magic might
  On diamond, pearl, or gold,
For treasure tires the weary sense—
  Such triumph is but cold;
But I will play the enchanter's part,
  In casting bliss around;
Oh, not a tear, nor aching heart,
  Should in the world be found.

To worth I would give honor,
  I'd dry the mourner's tears,
And to the pallid lip recall
  The smile of happier years;
And hearts that had been long estranged,
  And friends that had grown cold,
Should meet again like parted streams,
  And mingle as of old.
    Oh, thus I'd play, &c.

The heart that had been mourning
  O'er vanished dreams of love,
Should see them all returning,
  Like Noah's faithful dove.
And hope should launch her blessed **bark,**
  On Sorrow's darkening sea;
And Misery's children have an ark,
  And saved from sinking be.
    Oh, thus I'd play, &c.

SONGS OF SCOTLAND.

OH! WHY LEFT I MY HAME.

AN ANCIENT SCOTCH BALLAD.

Sung by Miss Agnes Robertson, in the drama of Jessie Brown.

OH! why left I my hame?
  Why did I cross the deep?
Oh! why left I the land
  Where my forefathers sleep?
I sigh for Scotia's shore,
  And I gaze across the sea,
But I canna get a blink
  Of my ain countrie.

The palm trees waving high,
  And fair the myrtle springs,
And to the Indian maid,
  The *bulbul** sweetly sings;
But I dinna see the broom,
  Wi' its tassels on the lea,
Nor hear the lintie's sang,
  Of my ain countrie.

Oh! here, no Sabbath bell
  Awakes the Sabbath morn
Nor song of reapers heard
  Amang the yellow corn.

* The Nightingale.

For the tyrant's voice is here,
    And the wail of slavery,
But the sun of Freedom shines,
    In my ain countrie.

There's a hope for ev'ry wo,
    And a balm for ev'ry pain,
And the first joys of our heart
    Come never back again.
There's a track upon the deep,
    And a path across the sea,
But the weary ne'er return
    To their ain countrie.

ROBERT GILFILLAN.

ANNIE LAURIE.

MAXWELTON'S braes are bonnie,
    Where early falls the dew,
'Twas there that Annie Laurie
    Gave me her promise true,
    Gave me her promise true,
Which ne'er forgot can be,
But for bonnie Annie Laurie
    I'd lay me down and dee.

Her brow is like the snow-drift,
    Her throat is like the swan,
Her face it is the fairest,
    That e'er the sun shone on,
    That e'er the sun shone on,
And dark blue is her e'e,
And for bonnie Annie Laurie
    I'd lay me down and dee.

Like dew on gowans lying,
    Is the fall of her fairy feet,
And like winds in summer sighing,
    Her voice is low and sweet,
    Her voice is low and sweet,
And she's a' the world to me,
And for bonnie Annie Laurie,
    I'd lay me down and dee.
Her voice is low and sweet, &c.

ANNIE OF THE LAUNDRY.

A POPULAR PARODY ON "ANNIE LAURIE."

MAX MUTTON's beef is boney,
  Made in a fry or stew,
There Annie of the Laundry,
  Gave me an oyster stew.
She treated to a stew,
  And three cents worth of cheese,
And for Annie of the Laundry,
  I'd crawl upon my knees.

Her eye is like the snow ball,
  Her voice like " the *Black Swan*,"
Her foot it is the flattest,
  That e'er a shin stood on,
That e'er a shin stood on,
  And her hoops spread nine degrees,
And for Annie of the Laundry,
  I'd crawl upon my knees.

THE SCOTCH LAD'S SONG IN AMERICA.

SUNG AT SCOTTISH CELEBRATIONS, &c., &c.

Tune—*Wha'll be King but Charlie !*

FRAE Scotland's highland hills I came,
  My name is Donald Caird, man,
To reach this bonnie land of fame
  I mony dangers dared, man.
The stormy ocean's angry foam,
  Wi' highland pride I bore, man,
Cheer'd by the name of Freedom's home,
  The bonnie Yankee shore, man.

When first I trod her happy shore,
  How proud was I to meet, man,
The laddies wha in days of yore,
  Made freedom's foes retreat, man !
Whar welcome as their native spring
  Is ilka stranger o'er, man,
To a land whar ev'ry man's a king,
  The bonnie Yankee shore, man.

Here Plenty's overflowing horn
　Drives ilka want awa, man,
And *Equal Rights* her laws adorn,
　More dear to men than a', man.
The road is free frae sea to sea,
　To honor, wealth, and lore, man,
And who can't live, is free to die,
　Upon the Yankee shore, man.

Success to Freedom's happy land,
　May virtue rear her high, man,
And may our laddies, hand in hand,
　Wild anarchy defy, man.
In peace, and progress may they glide,
　Wi' liberty in store, man,
When nations fall, be last of all,
　The bonnie Yankee shore, man.

THE BONNET, THE FEATHER, AND CLAYMORE.

Hurrah for the lad that with heart and with hand,
Will fight for his country, his home, and his land,
And who for her freedom will gallantly stand,
　With his bonnet, and feather, and claymore!
His brows will I deck wi' the bold eagle's wing,
And the tartan around his braw shoulders I'll fling,
And the name o' my soldier in rapture I'll sing,
　With his bonnet, and feather, and claymore.
　　Hurrah for the lad, &c.

The Tradesman gives clothes, an' the Farmer gives food,
And the Statesman he toils for his country's gude,
But the Soldier defends all their rights with his blude.
　His bonnet, and feather, and claymore!
And when the war-drum of the foe rattles nigh,
His heart like his banner goes fluttering high,
For country and freedom to conquer or die,
　With his bonnet, and feather, and claymore.
　　Hurrah for the lad, &c.

SILAS S. STEELE.

ALL THE BLUE BONNETS ARE OVER THE BORDER.

March, march, Ettrick and Teviotdale!
  Why, my lads, dinna ye march forward in order?
March, march, Eskdale and Liddesdale!
  All the blue bonnets are over the border.
      Many a banner spread,
      Flutters above your head,
Many a crest that is famous in story;
      Mount, and make ready, then,
      Sons of the mountain-glen,
Fight for your king, and the old Scottish border.
          March, march, Ettrick, &c.

Come from the hills where your hirsels are grazing,
  Come from the glens of the buck and the roe,
Come to the crag where the beacon is blazing,
  Come with the buckler, the lance, and the bow.
      Trumpets are sounding,
      War steeds are bounding,
Stand to your arms and march in good order;
      England shall many a day,
      Tell of the bloody fray,
When the blue bonnets came over the border.
          March, march, Ettrick, &c.

MY BONNIE LASS, NOW TURN TO ME.

Tune.—" Wha'll be King but Charlie!"

My bonnie lass, now turn to me,
  And gie a smile to cheer me,
An honest heart I'll gie to thee,
  For in truth I love thee dearly.
    Come, o'er the heather we'll trip together,
      All in the morning early,
    With heart and hand, I'll by thee stand,
      For in truth I love thee dearly.
    Come, o'er the heather we'll trip together,
    I heed neither mother, nor father, nor brother,
    With heart and hand, I'll by thee stand,
      For in truth I love thee dearly.

There's many a lass I love full well,
And many who love me dearly,
But there's ne'er a one, except thysel',
That I e'er could love sincerely.
          Come o'er the heather, &c.

A MAN'S A MAN FOR A' THAT.

Is there for honest poverty,
  Wha hangs his head, and a' that?
The coward slave, we pass him by,
  And dare be poor for a' that.
For a' that, and a' that,
  Our toils obscure, and a' that;
The rank is but the guinea stamp,
  The man's the gowd for a' that.

What though on hamely fare we dine,
  Wear hodden grey, and a' that?
Gie fools their silk, and knaves their wine,
  A man's a man for a' that.
For a' that, and a' that,
  Their tinsel show an' a' that;
An honest man, though ne'er sae poor,
  Is chief o' men for a' that.

Ye see yon birkie ca'd a lord
  Wha struts and stares, and a' that,
Though hundreds worship at his word,
  He's but a cuif for a' that.
For a' that, and a' that,
  His riband, star, an' a' that;
A man of independent mind
  Can look, and laugh at a' that.

The king can mak' a belted knight,
  A marquis, duke, and a' that,
An honest man's aboon his might,
  Gude faith! he mauna fa' that.
For a' that, and a' that,
  His dignities an' a' that,
The pith o' sense, and pride o' worth,
  Are grander far than a' that.

MARY OF ARGYLE.

I HAVE heard the mavis singing
  Its love song to the morn;
I have seen the dew-drop clinging
  To the rose just newly born.
But a sweeter song has cheered me,
  At the evening's gentle close,
And I've seen an eye still brighter
  Than the dew-drop on the rose.
    'Twas thy voice, my gentle Mary,
      And thy artless, winning smile,
    That made this world an Eden,
      Bonny Mary of Argyle.

Though thy voice may lose its sweetness,
  And thine eye its brightness, too;
Though thy step may lack its swiftness,
  And thy hair its sunny hue.
Still to me wilt thou be dearer,
  Than all the world shall own;
I have loved thee for thy beauty,
  But not for that alone.
    I have watch'd thy heart, dear Mary,
      And its goodness was the wile,
    That has made thee mine forever,
      Bonny Mary of Argyle.

DRAW THE SWORD, SCOTLAND.

DRAW the sword, Scotland! Scotland! Scotland!
  O'er moor and o'er mountain hath pass'd the war sign;
The pibroch is pealing, pealing, pealing,
  Who heeds not the summons is nae son o' thine.
The clans they are gathering, gathering, gathering,
  The clans they are gathering, by loch and by lea;
The banners they are flying, flying, flying,
  The banners they are flying that lead to victory.
Draw the sword, Scotland! Scotland! Scotland!
  Charge as ye have charged in days lang syne!
Sound to the onset! onset! onset!
  He who but falters is nae son o' thine!

Sheathe the sword, Scotland ! Scotland ! Scotland !
  Sheathe the sword, Scotland ! for dimm'd is its shine ;
Thy foemen are flying, flying, flying,
  And who kens nae mercy is nae son o' thine.
The struggle is over, over, over,
  The struggle is over, the victory won ;
There are tears for the fallen, fallen, fallen,
  And glory for all who their duty have done.
Sheathe the sword, Scotland ! Scotland ! Scotland !
  With thy loved thistle new laurels entwine ;
Time ne'er shall part them, part them, part them,
  But hand down the garland to each son o' thine.

BONNY DOON.

YE banks and braes o' bonny Doon,
  How can ye bloom sae fresh and fair ?
How can ye chant, ye 'little birds,
  While I'm sae wae and full o' care ?
Ye'll break my heart, ye little birds,
  That wander through that flow'ring thorn ;
Ye mind me o' departed joys,
  Departed never to return.

Oft have I roam'd by bonny Doon,
  To see the rose and woodbine twine,
Where ilka bird sung o'er its note,
  And cheerfully I joined with mine.
Wi' heartsome glee I pu'd a rose,
  A rose out of yon thorny tree ;
But my false love has stown the rose ;
  And left the thorn behind to me.

Ye roses blaw your bonny blooms,
  And draw the wild birds by the burn ;
For Luman promis'd me a ring,
  And ye maun aid me should I mourn.
Ah ! na, na, na, ye need na mourn,
  My een are dim and drowsy worn ;
Ye bonny birds, ye need na sing,
  For Luman never can return.

My Luman's love, in broken sighs,
   At dawn of day by Doon ye'se hear;
And mid-day by the willow green,
   For him I'd shed a silent tear.
Sweet birds, I ken, ye'll pity me,
   And join me wi' a plaintive sang,
While echo wakes and joins the mane,
   I mak' for him I looed sae lang.

"WITHIN A MILE OF EDINBORO'."

'TWAS within a mile of Edinboro' town,
   In the rosy time of the year,
Sweet flowers bloom'd, and the grass was down,
   And each shepherd woo'd his dear.
Bonny Jocky, blithe and gay,
Kiss'd sweet Jenny making hay,
The lassie blush'd, and frowning, cry'd, "No, it will not do,
I cannot, wonnot, wonnot, buckle to."

Jocky was a wag that never would wed,
   Though long he had follow'd the lass,
Contented she earn'd and eat her brown bread,
   And merrily turn'd up the grass.
Bonny Jocky, blithe and free,
Won her heart right merrily;
Yet still she blush'd, and frowning, cried, "No, it will not do,
I cannot, wonnot, wonnot, buckle to."

But when he vow'd he would make her his bride,
   Though his flocks and herds were but few,
She gave him her hand and a kiss beside,
   And vow'd she'd forever be true.
Bonny Jocky, blithe and free,
Won her heart right merrily;
At church she no more frowning cry'd, "No, it will not do,
I cannot, wonnot, wonnot, buckle to."

DUNCAN GRAY.

Duncan fleeched, and Duncan prayed;
   Ha, ha, the wooing o't!
Meg was deaf as Ailsa Craig;
   Ha, ha, the wooing o't!
Duncan sighed, baith out and in;
   Grat his een baith bleer't and blin';
Spak' o' loupin' ower a linn;
   Ha, ha, the wooing o't!

Time and chance are but a tide;
   Ha, ha, the wooing o't!
Slichtit love is sair to bide;
   Ha, ha, the wooing o't!
"Shall I, like a fool," quoth he,
"For a haughty hizzy dee?
   She may go to—France, for me!"
   Ha, ha, the wooing o't!

How it comes, let doctors tell;
   Ha, ha, the wooing o't!
Meg grew sick, as he grew well;
   Ha, ha, the wooing o't!
Something in her bosom wrings;
For relief a sigh she brings;
And oh! her een! they spak' sic things;
   Ha, ha, the wooing o't!

Duncan was a lad o' grace;
   Ha, ha, the wooing o't!
Maggie's was a piteous case;
   Ha, ha, the wooing o't!
Duncan couldna be her death,
Swelling pity smoored his wrath;
Now they're crouse and cantie baith;
   Ha, ha, the wooing o't!

MY LOVE IS LIKE THE RED, RED, ROSE.

My love is like the red, red, rose,
  That's newly sprung in June,
My love is like the melody,
  That's sweetly play'd in tune.
So fair art thou, my bonnie lass,
  So deep in love am I;
And I will love thee still, my dear,
  Though all the seas gang dry.

Though all the seas gang dry, my dear,
  And the rocks melt with the sun,
I will love thee still, my dear,
  While the sands of life shall run.
Then fare thee well, my only love,
  And fare thee well awhile,
And I will come again, my love,
  Though it were ten thousand mile.

MAC-GREGOR'S GATHERING.

The moon's on the lake, and the mist's on the brae,
And the clan has a name that is nameless by day;
Our signal for fight which from monarchs we drew,
Must be heard but by night in our vengeful haloo;
  Then haloo, haloo, haloo, Gregalach.

If they rob us of name, and pursue us with beagles,
Give their roofs to the flame, and their flesh to the eagles;
Then gather, gather, gather. gather, gather, gather,
While there's leaves in the forest and foam on the river,
Mac-Gregor, despite them, shall flourish forever.

Glenorchy's proud mountain, Colchurn and her towers,
Glen Strae and Glenlyon, no longer are ours,
We're landless, landless, landless, Gregalach; landless, land-
    less, landless, Gregalach.
Through the depth of Loch Katrine the 'steed shall career,
O'er the peak of Benlomond the galley shall steer,
And the rocks of Craig Royston like icicles melt,
Ere our wrongs be forgot, or our vengeance unfelt;
  Then haloo, haloo, haloo, Gregalach.
    If they rob us of name, &c.

OH WHISTLE AND I'LL COME TO YOU, MY LAD.

Oh, WHISTLE and I'll come to you, my lad,
Oh, whistle and I'll come to you, my lad;
Though father and mother and a' should gae mad,
Oh, whistle and I'll come to you, my lad;
But warily tent, when ye come to court me,
And come na unless the back-gate be ajee;
Syne up the back style and let nae body see,
And come as ye were nae coming to me,
And come as ye were nae coming to me.

Oh, whistle and I'll come to you, my lad,
Oh, whistle and I'll come to you, my lad;
Though father and mother and a' should gae mad,
Jeanny will venture wi' ye, my lad.
At kirk or at market, whene'er ye meet me,
Gang by me as though that ye cared nae a flee;
But steal me a blink o' your bonnie black e'e,
Yet look as ye were nae looking at me,
Yet look as ye were nae looking at me.

Oh, whistle and I'll come to you, my lad,
Oh, whistle and I'll come to you, my lad;
Though father and mother and a' should gae mad,
Thy Jeanny will venture wi' ye, my lad.
Ay vow and protest that ye care nae for me,
And whyles ye may lightly my beauty a wee;
But court nae anither though joking ye be,
For fear that she wyle your fancy frae me,
For fear that she wyle your fancy frae me.

A PARODY ON THE ABOVE, BUT NOT *"Scotched"*

OH! *mizzle* and I will go with you, my dear,
Oh, mizzle and I will go with you, my dear,
Tho' daddy and mammy should cut short my gear,
Just mizzle and I will cut with you, my dear.
Fast youth, if you're willing to slope off with me,
I'll put up a bite and I'll *hop* like a *flea*,
A squint from your eye shall my *telegraph* be,
But squint not as tho' you were squinting at me.
Oh, mizzle, and I will slope with you, my dear,
Oh, mizzle, and I will slope with you, my dear.

THE FLOWER OF ELLERSLIE

She's sportive as the zephyr
  That sips of ev'ry sweet,
She's fairer than the fairest lily
  In nature's soft retreat;
Her eyes are like the crystal brook,
  As clear and bright to see;
Her lips outshine the scarlet flow'r
  Of bonny Ellerslie.
      Her lips, &c.

Oh! were my love a blossom,
  When summer skies depart,
I'd plant her in my bosom,
  And wear her near my heart;
And oft I'd kiss her balmy lips,
  So beautiful to see,
Which far outshine the scarlet flow'r
  Of bonny Ellerslie.
      Which far, &c.

FLOW GENTLY, SWEET AFTON.

Flow gently, sweet Afton, among thy green braes,
  Flow gently, I'll sing thee a song in thy praise;
My Mary's asleep by thy murmuring stream,
  Flow gently, sweet Afton, disturb not her dream.
Thou dove, whose soft echo resounds from the hill,
  Thou green crested lapwing, with noise loud and shrill,
Ye wild whistling warblers, your music forbear,
  I charge you disturb not my slumbering fair.

Thy crystal stream, Afton, how lovely it glides;
  And winds by the cot where my Mary resides;
There, oft as mild ev'ning weeps over the lea,
  Thy sweet scented groves shade my Mary and me.
Flow gently, sweet Afton, among thy sweet braes,
  Flow gently, sweet river, the theme of my lays,
My Mary's asleep by thy murmuring stream,
  Flow gently, sweet Afton, disturb not her dream.

Burns.

AULD LANG SYNE.

SHOULD auld acquaintance be forgot,
  And never brought to mind?
Should auld acquaintance be forgot,
  And days o' lang syne?
    For auld lang syne, my dear,
      For auld lang syne,
    We'll tak' a cup o' kindness yet,
      For auld lang syne.

We twa ha'e run about the braes,
  And pu'd the gowans fine;
But we've wander'd mony a weary foot,
  Sin' auld lang syne.
      For auld lang syne, my dear, &c.

We twa ha'e paidlet i' the burn,
  Frae morning sun till dine;
But seas between us braid ha'e roar'd,
  Sin' auld lang syne.
      For auld lang syne, &c.

And here's a hand, my trusty friend,
  And gies a haud o'thine;
And we'll tak' a right gude willie-waught,
  For auld lang syne.
      For auld lang syne, &c.

And surely you'll be your pint-stoup,
  And surely I'll be mine,
And we'll tak' a drap o' kindness yet,
  For auld lang syne, &c.
      For auld lang syne, &c.

THE LASS WI' THE BONNIE BLUE EEN

Tune—Campbells are coming.

OH, saw ye the lass wi' the bonnie blue een?
Her smile is the sweetest that ever was seen;
Her cheek's like the rose, but fresher I ween,
She's the loveliest dancer you'll see on the green.
The home of my love is down by yon stream,
Where wild flowers welcome the sun's rosy beam,
But the sweetest of flowers on that spot that is seen,
Is the lass that I love with the bonnie blue een.
    Oh! saw ye the lass, &c.

When night overshadows her cot in the glen,
She'll steal out to meet her lov'd Donald again,
And when the moon shines o'er the valleys so green,
I'll welcome the lass with the bonnie blue een ;
As the dove that has wander'd away from his mate,
He'll return on love's pinions wi' joy all elate,
And love and tranquility fall quite serene,
On the maid that I love wi' the bonnie blue een.
   Oh ! saw ye the lass, &c.

"COMIN' THRO' THE RYE."

If a body meet a body
 Comin' thro' the rye,
If a body kiss a body,
 Need a body cry ?
Ev'ry lassie has her laddie,
 Nane, they say, ha'e I,
Yet a' the lads they smile at me,
 When comin' thro' the rye.
  If a body meet a body, &c.

If a body meet a body
 Comin' frae the town,
If a body kiss a body,
 Need a body frown ?
Ev'ry lassie has her laddie,
 Nane, they say, ha'e I,
But a' the lads they smile at me,
 Comin' thro' the rye.

Amang the train there is a swain,
 I dearly love mysel',
But what's his name, or where's his hame,
 I dinna choose to tell.
Ev'ry lassie has her laddie,
 Nane, they say, ha'e I,
But there's a laddie smiles at me,
 Comin' thro' the rye.

GOW'S FAREWEEL.

You've surely heard o' famous Niel,
The man that play'd the fiddle weel,
I wat he was a canty chiel',
    And dearly lo'ed the whiskey, O !
And ay sin' he wore tartan trews,
He dearly lo'ed the Athole brose ;
And wae was he, you may suppose,
    To play fareweel to whiskey, O !

Alake, quoth Neil, I'm frail and auld,
And find my bluid grows unco cauld,
I think 'twad mak' me blythe and bauld,
    A wee drap Highland whiskey, O !
Yet the doctors they do a' agree,
That whiskey's no the drink for me :
Saul ! quoth he, 'twill spoil my glee,
    Should they part me and whiskey, O !

Tho' I can get baith wine and ale,
And find my head and fingers hale,
I'll be content, tho' legs should fail,
    To play fareweel to whiskey, O !
But still I think on auld lang syne,
When Paradise our friends did tyne,
Because something ran in their mind,
    Forbid, like Highland whiskey, O !

Come, a' ye powers of music, come !
I find my heart grows unco glum :
My fiddle-strings will no play bum,
    To say fareweel to whiskey, O !
Yet I'll tak' my fiddle in my hand,
And screw the pegs up while they'll stand,
To mak' a lamentation grand
    On gude, auld Highland whiskey, O !

THE INGLE SIDE.

It's rare to see the morning breeze,
  Like a bonfire frae the sea;
It's fair to see the burnie kiss
  The lips o' the flowery lea;
An' fine it is on the green hill side,
  Where hums the bonny bee;
But rarer, fairer, finer far,
  Is the Ingle side for me.

Glens may be gilt wi' gowans rare,
  The birds may fill the tree,
And haughs ha'e a' the scented ware,
  That simmer's growth can gie;
But the canty hearth where cronies meet,
  An' the darling o' our e'e,
That makes to us a warl' complete;
  Oh, the Ingle side for me!

BONNIE JEAN.

Of a' the airts the wind can blow,
  I dearly love the west,
For there the bonnie lassie lives,
  The lassie **I love best.**
There wild woods grow and rivers flow,
  And mony a hill between,
Both day and night my **fancy's flight**
  Is ever **with** my Jean.
    There **wild** woods **grow, &c.**

I see her in the dewy flowers,
  I see her fresh and fair;
I hear her in the tuneful birds,
  I hear her charm the air.
There's no a **bonnie** flower that springs,
  By fountain, shore, or green,
There's no a **bonnie** bird that sings,
  But minds me of my Jean.

In the correspondence between **Burns and his friend**
Thomson, is found the following additional **verse to** the above
beautiful ballad, written by the poet **when he** contemplated
leaving Scotland for the West Indies.

13

Should cruel fate cause us to part,
  Far, far from Scotia's line,
Yet her dear image round my heart,
  For ever shall entwine.
Tho' mountains frown and deserts howl,
  Or oceans roar between,
Yet dearer than my deathless soul,
  I still would love my Jean.

BURNS.

BRUCE'S ADDRESS.

SCOTS, wha ha'e wi' Wallace bled!
Scots, wham Bruce has aften led!
Welcome to your gory bed,
  Or to glorious victory!
Now's the day, and now's the hour!
See the front of battle lower!
See approach proud Edward's power!
  Edward! chains and slavery!

Wha will be a traitor knave?
Wha would fill a coward's grave?
Wha sae base as be a slave?
  Traitor! coward! turn and flee.
Wha for Scotland's king and law
Freedom's sword will strongly draw?
Freeman stand, or freeman fa'!
  Caledonians! on wi' me!

By oppression's woes and pains!
By your sons in servile chains!
We will drain our dearest veins,
  But they shall be, shall be free.
Lay the proud usurpers low!
Tyrants fall in every foe!
Liberty's in every blow!
  Forward! let us do, or die!

BURNS.

"WHAT'S A' THE STEER, KIMMER?"

What's a' the steer, Kimmer? what's a' the steer?
Jamie, he is landed, and soon he will be here.
Go lace your boddice blue, lassie, lace your boddice blue,
Put on your Sunday clothes, and trim your cap anew,
For I'm right glad at heart, Kimmer, right glad at heart,
I ha'e a bonnie breastknot, and for his sake I'll wear't,
Sin' Jamie is come hame, we ha'e nae care to fear,
Bid the neighbors a' come in and welcome Jamie here.

Where's Donald Todd, lassie? rin, fetch him here;
Bid him bring his pipes, lassie, bid him tune clear,
For we'll taste the barley mow, and foot it to and fro,
Sin' Jamie is come hame, we'll gi'e him hearty cheer.
And it's what's a' the steer, Kimmer? what's a' the steer?
Jamie, he is landed, and soon he will be here,
Bid Allan Ramsay rin, bid him kill a fatted deer,
Oh the neighbors little ken, how welcome's Jamie dear.

JOHN ANDERSON, MY JO.

John Anderson, my Jo John,
  When we were first acquent,
Your locks were like the raven, John,
  Your bonnie brow was brent.
But now your brow is bald, John,
  Your locks are like the snow;
But blessings on your frosty pow,
  John Anderson, my Jo.

John Anderson, my Jo John,
  We climb'd the hill thegither,
And mony a cantie day, John,
  We've had with ane anither.
Now we maun totter down, John,
  But hand in hand we'll go,
And we'll sleep thegither at the foot,
  John Anderson, my Jo.

Robert Burns.

THE LASS O' GOWRIE.

'Twas on a summer's afternoon,
　A wee before the sun gaed down,
A lassie with a braw silk gown,
　Came o'er the hills to Gowrie.
The rose bud tinged with morning shower,
　Bloomed fresh within the sunny bower,
But Kittie was the fairest flower,
　That ever bloomed on Gowrie.

I had nae thought to do her wrang,
　When round her waist my arms I flang,
And said, " My lassie, will ye gang
　To view the carse o' Gowrie?
I'll take ye to my father's ha'
　In yon green fields beside the shaw,
And make ye lady of them a',
　The brawest wife in Gowrie."

Saft kisses on her lips I laid,
　The blush upon her cheek soon play'd,
She whispered modestly and said,
　" I'll gang wi' ye to Gowrie."
The auld folk soon gave their consent,
　And to the kirk we quickly went,
That joined us to our hearts' content,
　And now she's " Lady Gowrie."

HAIL TO THE CHIEF.

Hail to the chief, who in triumph advances,
　Honor'd and blest be the evergreen pine;
Long may the tree in his banner that glances,
　Flourish—the shelter and grace of our line.
　　　Heaven send it happy dew,
　　　Earth lend it sap anew,
Gaily to bourgeon, and broadly to grow;
　　　While every Highland glen
　　　Sends our shout back again,
" Roderigh Vich Alpine Dhu, ho! ieroe!"

Ours is no sapling **chance-sown** by the **fountain**,
Blooming at beltane, **in winter** to fade;
When the whirlwind has stript every leaf on the mountain,
The more shall **Clan Alpine exult** in her shade.
Moor'd **in the rifted rock**,
Proof **to the tempest's shock**,
Firmer he roots him, the **ruder it blow**:
Menteith and **Breadalbane, then**,
Echo his praise again,
"**Roderigh** Vich Alpine Dhu, ho! ieroe!"

Proudly **our** pibroch has thrill'd in Glen Fruin,
And Banochar's **groans** to our slogan replied,
Glen Luss and Ross Dhu, they are smoking in ruin,
And the best of Loch Lomond lie dead on her side.
Widow and Saxon **maid**
Long shall lament our raid,
Think of Clan Alpine with fear and **with woe**:
Lenox **and** Leven **Glen**
Shake when they hear again,
"Roderigh Vich Alpine Dhu, **ho! ieroe!**"

Row, vassals, row, for the **pride of** the **Highlands!**
Stretch to your oars for the evergreen pine!
Oh! that the rose bud that graces yon islands,
Were **wreath'd** in a garland **around** him to twine.
Oh! that some seedling gem,
Worthy such noble stem,
Honor'd and blest in their shadow might grow!
Long should **Clan Alpine then**
Ring from her **deepmost glen**,
"Roderigh Vich Alpine **Dhu, ho! ieroe!**"

BANKS OF ALLAN WATER.

On **the banks of** Allan **Water**,
When the **sweet** spring **time** did fall,
Was the **miller's** lovely daughter,
The **fairest of** them all.
For his **bride** a soldier sought her,
And a winning tongue had he,
On the banks of Allan Water,
None so gay as she.

On the banks of Allan Water,
  When brown autumn spread its store,
Then I saw the miller's daughter,
  But she smiled no more:
For the summer grief had brought her,
  And the soldier false was he,
On the banks of Allan Water,
  None so sad as she.

On the banks of Allan Water,
  When the winter snow fell fast,
Still was seen the miller's daughter,
  Chilling blew the blast.
But the miller's lovely daughter
  Both from cold and care was free,
On the banks of Allan Water
  There a corpse lay she.

SEA AND NAVAL SONGS.

CAPTINGE KYDDE, YE TERRIBLE PIRATTE.

A MORANTIC SENTIMENTAL BALLADE, AS IT HATH BEEN WRITTINGE BY HIS ONLY SURVIVING DESCENDANT—"KYDD," NAMED CALABASH COD LINE, OF CAPE COD.

Oh! **my name is** Capting Kydd, **as I sailed, as I sailed,**
Oh! **my name is** Capting Kydd, **as I sailed,**
Oh! my **name is** Capting Kydd, **and so wicked-ly I did,**
That through ev'ry law I slid **(yes slantendicularly,)**
  As I sailed, as I sailed.

Oh! I sparked the **Countess Britain, ere I sailed, ere I sailed,**
Yes, I sparked the Countess Britain, **ere I sailed,**
I sparked the Countess **Britain,**
With me that gal **was smit-ten,**
But **her** folks showed me *the* mitten, **(with a feet an' a kick in**
  it,)
  Ere I sailed, **ere** I sailed.

Oh! **a witch came** riding by, ere I sailed, ere I sailed,
A **witch came riding** by, ere I sailed,
Says **she, "** Robert, don't you cry
About your gal an' folks so high,
Take revenge—in *piracy*,"
  And I sailed, and **I sailed.**

So I hoisted the *Red Flag*, and I sailed, **and** I sailed,
So I hoisted the *Red Flag*, and I sailed,
'Twas a KID upon a rag,
And I went the entire—stag (*hoy*),
        As I sailed, &c.

I seized her dad upon the sea, as I sailed, as I sailed,
I kotched my gal's dad on the sea, as I sailed,
I met him on the sea—and he tried to soft-soap *me*,
But I made him walk the plank (*partick-larly.*)
        As I sailed, &c.

I met that gal there too, as I sailed, as I sailed,
I met my gal there too, as I sailed,
Her loveyer there I slew, of his heart I made a stew,
And—I made her eat it too,
        As I sailed, &c.

Oh! I robbed the rich Duke *Grassee*, as he sailed, as he sailed,
I robbed the rich Duke Grassee, as he sailed,
I robbed the rich Duke Grassee,
He tried to come the sassy,
And I gave him peculiar "JESSE,"
        As I sailed, &c.

Four Admirals at me run, as I sailed, as I sailed,
Four Admirals at me run, as I sailed,
I cut off the head of one, an' I ramm'd it in a gun,
Sent him clear to set of sun, (and knocked spots into **it**,)
        As I sailed, &c.

But my ship got some hard knocks, as I sailed, as I sailed,
And I feared to lose my *rocks*, as I sailed,
So I kotch of whales a flock,
And they made me a *dry-dock* (on the double action lever
        principle,)
And—I repaired her on their stocks,
        Then I sailed, &c.

Oh! my crew did mutin-y, as I sailed, as I sailed,
But I hung 'em up sky high, as I sailed,
I hung forty mast head high,
Like cod fish strung up to dry,
And next time they didn't try (that speculation any more),
        While I sailed, &c.

Fifty ghosts appeared one night, as I sailed, as I **sailed,**
Fifty ghosts appeared one night, **as I sailed,**
They thought me for to fright,
But I **put** them all to flight,
By burning a blue light (made of **sea-sarpent's oil,)**
    As I sailed, &c.

My gal's ghost came and said, **as I sailed, as I sailed,**
Oh !—my gal's ghost came and said, **as I sailed,**
Oh ! quit this trade and wed,
My poor ghost without a " *red*,"
I says, Miss—enough said, (" Shake,")
    As I sailed, &c.

So I steer'd for Yankee shore, as I sailed, as I sailed,
Then I steer'd for Yankee shore, as I sailed,
There I buried all my store,
Consisting of a large majority of gold watches, brooches, dia-
    monds, plates, breastpins, &c., &c.
And some more,
And folks dived for it all o'er,
    But they failed, &c.

Oh ! they dived and dragged East River, where I sailed, where
    I sailed,
They dived and dragged East **River,**
For they kotch the *treasure fever*—
And (*thumbing his nose*) **much mud did they diskiver,**
    As they sailed, &c.

Some said 'twas on the highland, and they said, **and they said,**
Some said 'twas on **the** highland, as they said,
Some said 'twas on the highland—
But *Edgar Poe* says, *Sulliran's Island*, near Charleston, in his
    tale of the Gold Bug,
But hookey *hum-bug*,
For 'twas in a store on dry land,
    All entail'd, all entail'd, (and salted down.)

Oh! I banked it on the shore, as I sailed, as I sailed,
On the Philadelphia shore, as I sailed,
On Philadelphia shore,
At G. G. EVANS' GIFT BOOK STORE,
For him to deal out ever more,
With good books containing a warning to all young lovyers
    when they get the mitten to never turn pirates,
Or else like me, they'll mourn the day, as I do,
    THAT I SAILED, (*In a horn.*)

THE PLOUGH BOY AT SEA.

Air—Norah Creina.

IF folks who sing about the sea,
    Could half of 'em see the place they sing about,
They'd quickly change their tune with me,
    And ocean's fame would cease to ring about.
Oh! then instead of rippling waves,
    They'd tell of squalls and hurricanes thundering,
Of see-saw decks, and sea-sick heaves,
    Lurching—pitching—reeling—floundering.
Spoken—Hallo! there, Captain, stop the horses—I mean,
hitch up the boat—lift up the paddle wheel, and reef the
smoke pipe.
    For devil take the sea, say I,
    Water salt, and meat that's salterer,
Billows boiling up sky high,
    I wish that folks would yoke or halter her.

At daylight when I wakes I feels,
    Like a top with the delirium trimmins,
I find my head where I poked my heels,
    And all creation's round me swimming.
And when I goes to eat, the boat
    Jist like a wild colt, kicks and pitches
Half of my soup goes down my throat,
    And to'ther half goes down my—trowsers.
Spoken—Staggering, Hellow! wo, haw, gee, scotch the
wheel there, we're goin' down hill.
    With a devil take the sea, say I, &c.

You folks, that on the sea would roam,
  Don't trust its darn'd foundation fickle,
Before you go, pray stay at home,
  For sweets of sea-life are all "*pickles.*"
Its bracing gales, they are no good,
  Unless you splice tho *main-brace*, too sirs,
You'll think you're loose on Noah's flood,
  While no Mount *Arrow root* in view, sirs.
Devil take the sea, say I,
  Water salt, and feed that's salterer,
Seas like hay stacks, poked up high,
  I wish the folks would yoke or halter her.

SILAS S. STEELE.

FAR, FAR UPON THE SEA.

Far, far upon the sea,
The good ship speeding free,
Upon the deck we gather, young and old;
  And view the flapping sail,
  Swelling out before the gale,
Full and round without a wrinkle or a fold.
  Or watch the waves that glide,
  By the vessel's stately side,
Or the wild sea birds that follow thro' the air;
  Or gather in a ring,
  And with cheerful voices sing,
Oh! gaily goes the ship when the wind blows fair.

Far, far upon the sea,
With the sunshine on our lee,
We talk of pleasant days when we were young,
  And remember though we roam,
  The sweet melodies of home,
The happy songs of childhood which we sung;
  And though we quit her shore,
  To return to it no more,
Sound the glories that Columbia yet shall bear,
  That "Yankees rule the waves,
  And never shall be slaves,"
Oh! gaily goes the ship when the wind blows fair.

Far, far upon the sea,
Whate'er our country be,
The thought of it shall cheer us as we go,
And Scotland's sons shall join,
"In the days of auld lang syne,"
With voice by memory softened clear and low;
And the men of Erin's Isle,
Battling sorrow with a smile,
Shall sing "St. Patrick's morning" void of care,
And thus we pass the day,
And we journey on our way,
Oh! gaily goes the ship when the wind blows fair.

BEN BOLT.

Oh! don't you remember sweet Alice, Ben Bolt,
Sweet Alice with hair so brown,
She wept with delight when you gave her a smile,
And trembled with fear at your frown?
In the old church yard in the valley, Ben Bolt,
In a corner, obscure and alone,
They have fitted a slab of granite so gray,'
And sweet Alice lies under the stone.
They have fitted a slab of granite so gray,
And sweet Alice lies under the stone.

Oh! don't you remember the wood, Ben Bolt,
Near the green sunny slope of the hill;
Where oft we have sung 'neath its wide spreading shade,
And kept time to the click of the mill?
The mill has gone to decay, Ben Bolt,
And a quiet now reigns all around,   .
See, the old rustic porch with its roses so sweet,
Lies scatter'd and fallen to the ground.

Oh! don't you remember the school, Ben Bolt,
And the master so kind and so true,
And the little nook by the clear running brook,
Where we gather'd the flow'rs as they grew?
O'er the master's grave grows the grass, Ben Bolt,
And the running little brook is now dry,
And of all the friends who were schoolmates then,
There remains, Ben, but you and I.
And of all, &c.

THOMAS DUNN ENGLISH.

A YANKEE SHIP AND A YANKEE CREW.

A YANKEE ship and a Yankee crew,
  Tally hi ho! you know!
O'er the bright blue waves like a sea-bird flew,
  Singing hey! aloft and alow!
Her sails are spread to the fairy breeze,
  The spray sparkling as thrown from her prow,
Her flag is the proudest that floats on the seas,
  When homeward she's steering now.
                    A Yankee ship, &c.

A Yankee ship and a Yankee crew,
  Tally hi ho! you know!
With hearts aboard both gallant and true,
  The same aloft and alow.
The blackened sky and the whistling wind,
  Foretell the approach of a gale,
And home and its joys flit over each mind,
  Husbands, lovers, on deck there! a sail!
    A Yankee ship and a Yankee crew,
      Tally hi ho! you know!
    Distress is the word, God speed them through,
      Bear a hand aloft and alow!

A Yankee ship and a Yankee crew,
  Tally hi ho! you know!
Freedom defends the land where it grew,
  We're free aloft and alow!
Bearing down is a ship in regal pride,
  Defiance floating at each mast-head;
She's wreck'd, and the one bears that floats alongside,
  The stars and the stripes that's to victory wed.
                    A Yankee ship, &c.
                              J. S. JONES.

ALL'S WELL.

DESERTED by the waning moon,
When skies proclaim night's cheerless noon,
On tower, or fort, or tented ground,
The sentry walks his lonely round,
And should a footstep haply stray,
Where caution marks the guarded way,
  "Who goes there? Stranger, quickly tell!"
  "A friend!"—"The word?"—"Good night! All's well!"

Or sailing on the midnight deep,
While weary messmates soundly sleep,
The careful watch patrols the deck.
To **guard** the ship from fee or wreck ;
And while his thoughts oft homeward veer,
Some well known voice salutes his ear.
  " What cheer ? oh, brother ! quickly tel. !"
  " Above !" " Below !" " **Good** night ! All's well !"

THE SAILIER BOY.

A celebrated song, as sung by Miss Julia Daly.

My love is a Sailier Boy, so galorious and **so bold,**
He's as tall as a flag staff, only nineteen years **old ;**
For to cruise the wide world he left his own dear,
And my heart is a busting because he is not here.
  For his spirits was tremendious, oh, fierce to behold,
    In a young man, bred a butcher boy, only **nineteen years**
      old.

His parents they bound him to a carpenter,
But a sea-faring life he did much prefer,
His mind was a boiling but he didn't keer,
For all that he wished—was a clam boat to steer.
    For his spirits was tremendious, &c.

Oh, my bus-um is tos-sel-ed, like the deep rollin' **sea,**
For fear his affections don't still point to me ;
For a sweetheart can be had in every port, so I'm told,
More particularly for a young man, only nineteen years old.
    For his spirits are tremendious, **&c.**

My heart is a breaking with grief and repine,
For fear that fine-formed man will never be mine ;
Of all the wealth **in** the mint here, both silver and gold,
I'd give for my Sailier **Boy,** only nineteen years old.
    For his spirits was tremendious, **&c.**

If that ere young man my husband ne'er can be—
But lay a stiff corpusses in the bottom of the sea,
The weeds of a widder, so dismal to behold,
I'd wear for my Sailier Boy, only nineteen years old.
    For his spirits was tremendious, &c.

ADDITIONAL, NATIONAL, AND PATRIOTICAL VERSES.

Should enemy dare to insult our stripe or our star,
And old uncle Samuel have to go in to war;
I then would apply to galliant Stewart so bold,
For a post for my Sailier Boy, only nineteen years old.
   For his spirits are tremendious, &c.

Then should the fierce enemy come out with his host
For to stop our free trading on the ocean and coast,
They will catch Yankee thunder and find themselves sold,
By our galliant young Sailier boys, scarce nineteen years old.
   For his spirits are tremendious, &c.

THE MALTESE BOAT SONG.

SEE, brothers, see, how the night comes on,
Slowly sinks the setting sun;
Hark! how the solemn vesper's sound,
Sweetly falls upon the ear.
 Then haste, let us work till the daylight's o'er,
 And fold our nets as we row to the shore;
 Our toil of labor being o'er,
 How sweet the boatmen's welcome home,
 Home, home, home, the boatmen's welcome home,
 Sweet, oh sweet, the boatmen's welcome home.

See how the tints of daylight die,
Soon we'll hear the tender sigh;
For when the toil of labor's o'er,
We shall meet our friends on shore.
 Then haste, let us work till the daylight's o'er,
 And fold our nets as we row to the shore;
 For fame or gold howe'er we roam,
 No sound as sweet as welcome home,
 Home, home, home, the boatmen's welcome home,
 Sweet, oh sweet, the boatmen's welcome home.
   Then haste, &c.

LAND! LAND!

THE dangers of the deep are past,
We're drawing near our home at last,
We see its outline on the sky,
And join the sailor's welcome cry,
   Land! Land! Land!

Oh! joyful thought for weary men,
To tread the solid earth again;
And hark! the church bells pealing near,
From spire and turret, loud and clear,
As if they rang so loud and free,
To bid us welcome o'er the sea!
   Land! Land! Land!

The cry makes every heart rejoice,
Is this the country of our choice?
Is this the long sought happy soil,
Where plenty spreads the board of toil?
   Land! Land! Land!

How gladly through its paths we'll tread,
With bounding step, uplifted head,
And through its wilds and forest roam,
To clear our farms and build our home;
And sleep at night and never dread
That morn shall see us wanting bread.
   Land! Land! Land!

We've passed together o'er the sea,
In storm and sunshine, comrades we,
But ere we part let's gather round,
And shout with one accord the sound,
   Of—Land! Land! Land!

The land of rivers broad and deep.
The land where he who sows may reap;
The land where, if we ploughmen will,
We may possess the fields we till;
So gather all, and shout once more,
The Land! The Land! Hurrah for shore!

THE SAILOR'S LAST WHISTLE.

WHETHER sailor or not, for a moment avast,
Poor Jack's mizen-topsail is laid to the mast,
He'll never turn out, or more heave the lead,
He's now all aback, nor will sails shoot ahead ;
Yet though worms gnaw his timbers, his vessel's a wreck,
When he hears the last whistle, he'll jump upon deck !
Secur'd in his cabin, he's moor'd in his grave,
Nor hears any more the loud roar of the wave ;
Press'd by death, he is sent to the tender below,
Where seaman and lubbers must every one go.

> Yet though worms, &c.

With his frame a mere hulk, and his reckoning on board,
At length he dropp'd down to Mortality's road ;
With Eternity's ocean before him in view,
He cheerfully popt out, " My messmates adieu."

> For though worms, &c.

THE SIEGE OF PLATTSBURGH.

Tune.—Boyne Water, or Barbara Allen.

**The first of American Negro Songs, written in the year 1815, and sung for
many seasons by Mr. Tatnall, of the old circus company.**

BACKSIDE Albany stan Lake Champlain,
　Little pond half full o' water,
Plat-tes-burgh dare too stand close upon de Maine,
　Town small, but grow bigger too herearter.
　　　On Lake Champlain,
　　　Uncle Sam set he boat ;
And Massa M'Donough he sail 'em,
　　　While Gen'ral Macomb
　　　Make Plat-tes-burgh he home,
Wid de army whose courage never fail 'em.

On 'lebenth day of Sep-tem-ber,
　In eighteen hund'ed and fourteen,
Gubbener Probose, an he British sojer,
　Come to Plat-tes-burgh a tea-party courtin.
　　　An he boat come too
　　　Arter Uncle Sam boat ;
Massa M'Donough do look sharp out de winder.
　　　Den Gen'ral Macomb
　　　(Ah ! he always a-home—)
Catch fire too jiss like a tinder.
14

Bang! bang! bang den de cannons gin to roar,
  In Plat-tes-burgh, and all 'bout dat quarter;
Gubbener Probose try he hand 'pon de shore,
  While he boat take he luck 'pon de water.
        But Massa M'Donough
        Knock he boat in he head,
Break he heart, broke he shin, 'tove he caff in,
        And Gen'ral Macomb
        Start ole Probose home,
Tot me soul den, I must die a laffin.

Probose scare so, he lef all behine,
  Powder, ball, cannon, tea-pot, an kittle;
Some say he cotch a cole—trouble in he mine,
  Cause he eat so much raw and cole vittle.
        Uncle Sam berry sorry,
        To be sure, for he pain;
Wish he nuss heself up well an hearty,
        For Gen'ral Macomb
        And Massa M'Donough home,
When he notion for anudder tea-party.

THE SAILOR BOY'S DREAM.

On the midnight ocean slumbering,
  A youthful sailor lies,
While scenes of happy childhood
  In his dreaming soul arise.
Still chiming, seems the Sabbath bell,
  As sweetly as of yore;
And once again he roams the fields,
  And sees his cottage door.
In her arms his mother folds him,
  With affection's fond caress,
His gentle, bright eyed sisters, too,
  In raptures round him press.
His aged father meets him,
  And his young companions come,
To welcome him once more to share
  The dear delights of home.
              To welcome, &c.

Hark ! what wild shriek dispels his dream ?
  Whence comes that sound of woe ?
With the **storm** loud thunders mingle,
  O'er **the ship** the billows flow.
From his **hammock starts the** sailor,
  He rushes **to the deck,**
The vessel's sails with lightning **blaze !**
  She **sinks a burning** wreck.
To a mast **the winds have riven,**
  The sailor **madly** clings,
His fearful parting knell **of death,**
  The tempest loudly rings.
All is dark and drear around,
  Not a star beams **o'er the wave,**
As ocean-spirits **bear him**
  To the sailor's **shroudless grave !**
         As ocean-spirits, **&c.**

Oh, **never at the** cottage **door,**
  Shall he **again** be seen,
Nor meet his playmates **merrily,**
  To sport upon the green.
In vain for him the birds shall sing,
  The hawthorn deck the **tree,**
For, slumb'ring on the sand **he lies,**
  Beneath **the swelling sea.**
Oh, where are happy childhood's scenes ?
  Where now the passing bell ?
The fields o'er which he used to **stray ?**
  The cot he loved so well ?
Forever lost ! yet **still** he finds,
  A home of peace and joy,
Where neither stormy wind **nor wave,**
  Can wreck the sailor **boy.**
         Where neither, **&c.**

HARRY BLUFF.

WHEN a boy Harry Bluff left his friends and his home
And his dear native land o'er the ocean to roam ;
Like a sapling he sprung, he was fair to the view,
He was a true Yankee oak, boys, the older he grew.
Tho' his body was weak and his hands they were soft,
When the signal was given he the first went aloft,
The veterans all cried, " He'll one day lead the van,"
For tho' rated a boy, he'd the soul of a man,
    And the heart of a true Yankee sailor.

When to manhood promoted and burning for fame,
Still in peace or in war, Harry Bluff was the same ;
So true to his love, and in battle so brave,
The myrtle and laurel entwin'd o'er his grave.
For his country he fell, when by victory crown'd,
The flag, shot away, fell in tatters around,
The foe thought he'd struck, but he sung out, "Avast !"
And Columbia's colours he nailed to the mast,
    And he died like a true Yankee sailor.

THE WHITE SQUALL.

THE sea was bright, and the bark rode well,
The breeze bore the tone of the vesper bell ;
'Twas a gallant bark, and a crew as brave
As ever were launch'd on the heaving wave ;
She shone in the light of declining day,
And each sail was set, and each heart was gay.

They neared the land wherein beauty smiles,
The sunny shores of the Grecian Isles :
All thought of home, of that welcome dear,
Which soon should greet each wanderer's ear ;
And in fancy joined the social throng,
In the festive dance and joyous song.

A white cloud glides through the azure sky,—
What means that wild despairing cry ?
Farewell the vision'd scenes of home !—
That cry is " Help !" where no help can come ;
For the white squall rides on the surging wave,
And the bark is gulph'd in an ocean grave.

GRIEVING'S A FOLLY.

SPANKING Jack was so comely, so pleasant, so jolly,
  Though winds blew great guns, still he'd whistle and sing;
For Jack lov'd his friend, and was true to his Molly,
  And if honor gives greatness, was great as a king.
One night as we drove with two reefs in the main-sail,
  And the scud came on low'ring upon a lee shore,
Jack went up aloft for to hand the top-ga'nt sail,
  A spray washed him off, and we ne'er saw him more:
        But grieving's a folly,—
        Come, let us be jolly,
If we've troubles at sea, boys, we've pleasure ashore.

Whiffling Tom, still of mischief or fun in the middle,
  Through life, in all weathers, at random would jog;
He'd dance and he'd sing, and he'd play on the fiddle,
  And swig with an air his allowance of grog.
Longside of a Don, in the Terrible frigate,
  As yard-arm and yard-arm we lay off the shore,
In and out Whiffling Tom did so caper and jig it,
  That his head was shot off, and we ne'er saw him more.
        But grieving's a folly, &c.

Bonny Ben was to each jolly messmate, a brother,
  He was manly and honest, good natured and free;
If ever one tar was more true than another,
  To his friend and his duty, that sailor was he.
One day, with the davit, to weigh the kedge anchor,
  Ben went in the boat on a bold craggy shore,
He overboard tipp'd, when a shark, and a spanker,
  Soon nipp'd him in two, and we ne'er saw him more.
        But grieving's a folly, &c.

But what of it all, lads, shall we be down hearted
  Because that mayhap we now take our last sup,
Life's cable must one day or other be parted,
  And death in safe moorings will bring us all up:
But 'tis always the way on't; one scarce finds a brother
  Fond as pitch, honest, hearty, and true to the core,
But by battle, or storm, or some damn'd thing or other,
  He's popp'd off the hooks, and we ne'er see him more
        But grieving's a folly, &c.

THE SEA!

THE sea, the sea, the open sea!
The blue, the fresh, the ever free, the ever, ever free!
Without a mark, without a bound,
It runneth the earth's wide region round,
It plays with the clouds, it mocks the skies,
Or like a cradled creature lies.
I'm on the sea, I'm on the sea,
I am where I would ever be,
With the blue above, and the blue below,
And silence wheresoe'er I go;
If a storm should come, and awake the deep,
What matter? what matter? I shall ride and sleep.

I love, oh, how I love to ride;
On the fierce and foaming, bursting, billowy tide,
When every mad wave drowns the moon,
Or whistles aloud his tempest tune,
And tells how goeth the world below,
And why the south-west blast doth blow.
I never was on the dull tame shore,
But I loved the great sea more and more,
And back I flew to her billowy breast,
Like a bird that seeketh its mother's nest;
And a mother she was and is to me,
For I was born, was born on the open sea.

The waves were white, and red the morn,
In the noisy hour, the hour, the noisy hour when I was born:
The whale it whistled, the porpoise roll'd,
And the dolphins bared their backs of gold,
And never was heard such an outcry wild,
As welcomed to life the ocean child.
I have lived since then in calm and strife,
Full fifty summers a rover's life,
With wealth to spend and power to range,
But never have sought or sighed for change;
And death, whenever he comes to me,
Shall come, shall come on the wide, unbounded sea!

THE ANCHOR'S WEIGH'D.

THE tear fell gently from her eye,
  When last we parted on the shore;
My bosom heav'd with many a sigh,
  To think I ne'er should see her more.
"Dear youth," she cried. "and canst thou haste away?
My heart will break, a little moment stay;
Alas, I cannot, cannot part from thee!"
"The anchor's weigh'd, farewell, remember me."

  "Weep not, my love," I trembling said,
    "Doubt not a constant heart like mine,
  I ne'er shall meet another maid,
    Whose charms can fix my heart like thine"
"Go, then," she cried, "but let thy constant mind
Oft think of her, you leave in tears behind!"
"Dear maid, this last embrace my pledge shall be,
The anchor's weigh'd, farewell, remember me!"

A WET SHEET AND A FLOWING SEA.

A WET sheet! and a flowing sea,
  And a wind that follows fast,
And fills the white and rustling sail,
  And bends the gallant mast;
And bends the gallant mast, my boys,
  While like an eagle free,
Away, our good ship flies, and leaves
  Columbia on her lea.
    Oh, give me a wet sheet, a flowing sea,
      And a wind that follows fast,
    And fills the white and rustling sail,
      And bends the gallant mast.

For a soft and gentle wind,
  I heard a fair one cry,
But give to me the roaring breeze,
  And white waves heaving high,
And white waves heaving high, my boys!
  The good ship tight and free;
The world of waters is our home,
  And merry men are we.
    Oh, give me, &c.

There's tempest in yon horned moon,
And lightning in yon cloud,
And hark the music, mariners,
The wind is piping loud;
The wind is piping loud, my boys,
The lightning flashes free;
While the hollow oak our palace is,
Our heritage the sea!
Oh, give me, &c.

A HEALTH TO THE OUTWARD BOUND.

FILL! fill the sparkling brimmer,
Fill, for the moments fly,
The stars' weary light grows dimmer,
And the moon fades away from the sky.
Fill, for the signal flag is up,
And the wind is veering round;
In haste let us pledge our parting cup,
To the health of the outward bound.
In haste let us pledge our parting cup,
To the health of the outward bound.

Fill high! this hour to-morrow,
Nor toast nor jest shall be,
But a few shall meet in sorrow,
While the many plough the sea.
Then, while we're all together,
Give the toast! let it circle round:
Full sails and prosperous weather,
And a health to the outward bound.
Full sails and prosperous weather
And a health to the outward bound.

Let no adieu be spoken,
To weep is a woman's part,
Nor give we a farewell token,
But a health from our inmost heart,
And oft when the wind blows free,
And the waves below resound,
Sing in gladsome melody,
A health to the outward bound.
Full sails, &c.

THE LIGHT BARQUE.

OFF! said the stranger; off, off, and away,
And away flew the light barque o'er the silv'ry bay.
We must reach, ere to-morrow, the far distant wave,
The billows we'll laugh at, the tempest we'll brave.
The young roving lovers, their vows have been given,
Unsmil'd o'er by mortals, but hallow'd in heaven;
She was Italy's daughter, I knew by her eye,
It wore the bright beam that illumines the sky.
  Off! said the stranger, &c.

And she has forsaken her palace and halls,
For the chill breeze and the light which falls
O'er the pure wave, from the heavens above,
And their guiding star was the bright star of love.
  Off! said the stranger, &c.

LARBOARD WATCH.

Music published by Ditson, 227 Washington St., Boston.

AT dreary midnight's cheerless hour,
 Deserted e'en by Cynthia's beam,
When tempests beat and torrents pour,
 And twinkling stars no longer gleam;
The wearied sailor spent with toil
 Clings firmly to the weather shrouds;
And still the lengthen'd hour to guile,
And still the lengthen'd hour to guile,
 Sings as he views the gath'ring clouds,
 Sings as he views the gath'ring clouds,
  Larboard Watch Ahoy!
  Larboard Watch Ahoy!

But who can speak the joy he feels,
While o'er the foam his vessel reels,
And his tir'd eye-lids slumb'ring fall
He rouses at the welcome call
Of Larboard Watch Ahoy!
 Larboard Watch! Larboard Watch!
  Larboard Watch Ahoy!

With anxious care he eyes each wave,
  That swelling threatens to o'erwhelm,
And his storm beaten barque to save,
  Directs with skill the faithful helm.
With joy he drinks the cheering grog,
  'Mid storms that bellow loud and hoarse,
With joy he heaves the reeling log,
  And marks the lee-way and the course
  Marks the lee-way and the course,
    Larboard Watch Ahoy!
    Larboard Watch Ahoy!
But who can speak the joys he feels, &c.

A LIFE ON THE OCEAN WAVE.

A LIFE on the ocean wave!
  A home on the rolling deep!
Where the scattered waters rave,
  And the winds their revels keep.
Like an eagle caged I pine,
  On this dull, unchanging shore,
Oh! give me the flashing brine,
  The spray and the tempest's roar.

Once more on the deck I stand,
  Of my own swift gliding craft;
Set sail; farewell to the land,
  The gale follows far abaft.
We shoot through the sparkling foam,
  Like an ocean bird set free,
Like the ocean bird our home
  We'll find far out on the sea.

The land is no longer in view,
  The clouds have begun to frown,
But with a stout vessel and crew,
  We'll say let the storm come down.
And the song of our hearts shall be,
  While the wind and the waters rave,
A life on the heaving sea,
  A home on the bounding wave.

LAND HO!

FILL high the brimmer! the land is in sight,
We'll be happy, if never again, boys, to-night;
The cold cheerless ocean in safety we've past,
And the warm genial earth glads our vision at last:
In the land of the stranger true hearts we shall find,
To soothe us in absence of those left behind.
Then fill high the brimmer! the land is in sight,
We'll be happy, if never again, boys, to-night.

Fill high the brimmer! till morn we'll remain,
Then part in the hope to meet one day again,
Round the hearth-stone of home, in the land of our birth
The holiest spot on the face of the earth!
Dear country, our thoughts are more constant to thee,
Than the steel to the star, or the stream to the sea.
Then fill high the brimmer! the land is in sight,
We'll be happy, if never again, boys, to-night.

Fill high the brimmer! the wine sparkles rise,
Like tears from the fountain of joy, to the eyes;
May rain-drops that fall from the storm-clouds of care,
Melt away in the sun-beaming smiles of the fair.
Drink deep to the chimes of the nautical bells,
To woman, God bless her, wherever she dwells!
Then fill high the brimmer! the land is in sight,
We'll be happy, if never again, boys, to-night.

FAR O'ER THE DEEP BLUE SEA.

THE moon is beaming brightly, love,
  Upon the deep blue sea;
A trusty crew is waiting near,
  For thee, dear girl, for thee:
Then leave thy downy couch, my love,
  And with thy sailor flee,
His gallant bark shall bear thee safe,
  Far o'er the deep blue sea;
    Far o'er the deep blue sea;
      Far o'er the deep, the deep, the deep blue sea.

The storm-bird sleeps upon the rocks,
  No angry surges roar;
No sound disturbs the tranquil deep,
  Not e'en the dipping oar:

No watchful eye is on thee now,
  Come, dearest, hie with me,
And cheer a daring sailor's love,
  Far o'er the deep blue sea.
    Far o'er, &c.

She comes, she comes, with trembling steps,
  Oh! happy shall we be,
When landed safe on other shores,
  From every danger free;
Now speed ye on, my gallant bark,
  Our hopes are all in thee,
Swift, bear us to our peaceful home,
  Far o'er the deep blue sea.
    Far o'er, &c.

THE PILOT.

"Oh, pilot! 'tis a fearful night,
  There's danger on the deep,
I'll come and pace the deck with thee,
  I do not dare to sleep."
"Go down!" the sailor cried, "go down,
  This is no place for thee;
Fear not! but trust in Providence,
  Wherever thou mayst be."

"Ah! pilot, dangers often met
  We all are apt to slight,
And thou hast known these raging waves,
  But to subdue their might."
"It is not apathy," he cried,
  "That gives this strength to me:
Fear not! but trust in Providence,
  Wherever thou mayst be.

"On such a night the sea engulf'd
  My father's lifeless form;
My only brother's boat went down
  In just so wild a storm;
And such, perhaps, may be my fate,—
  But still I say to thee,
Fear not! but trust in Providence,
  Wherever thou mayst be."

THE YANKEE MIDSHIPMAN.

I'M here or there a jolly dog,
At land or sea I'm all agog
To fight, or kiss, or touch the grog,
  For I'm a jovial midshipman,
  A smart, young midshipman,
  A little, airy midshipman:
To fight, or kiss, or touch the grog,
  Oh, I'm a jovial midshipman.

My honor's free from stain or speck,
The foremast men are at my beck,
With pride I walk the quarter deck,
  For I'm a smart, young midshipman, &c.

I mix the pudding for our mess,
In uniform then neatly dress,
The captain asks, no need to press,
  " Come dine with me, young midshipman," &c.

When gallant Perry comes on board,
By all Columbia's sons adored,
From him I sometimes pass the word,
  Though I'm an humble midshipman, &c.

THE TEMPEST.

WE were crowded in the cabin,
  Not a soul would dare to sleep,
It was midnight on the waters,
  And the storm was o'er the deep;
'Tis a fearful thing in winter
  To be shattered by the blast,
And to hear the trumpet thunder,
  " Cut away the mast!"

We shuddered there in silence,
  For the stoutest held his breath,
While the hungry sea was roaring,
  And the breakers talked with death;
Sad thus we sat in silence,
  All busy with our prayers,
" We're lost!" the captain shouted,
  As he staggered down the stairs.

But his little daughter whispered,
    As she took the icy hand,
"Is not God upon the waters,
    Just the same as on the land?"
Then we kissed the little maiden,
    And we spake of better cheer,
As we anchored safe in harbor,
    When the sun was shining clear.
Chorus—And a shout rose loud and joyous,
    As we grasped the friendly hand,
God is upon the waters,
    Just the same as on the land.

ROW, ROW.

Row! row! homeward we steer
    Twilight falls o'er us,
Hark! hark! music is near,
    Friends glide before us.
Song lightens our labor,
    Sing as onward we go;
Keep each with his neighbor
    Time as we flow.
Chorus—Row! row! homeward we go,
    Twilight falls o'er us.
Row! row! sing as we flow,
    Day flies before us.

Row! row! sing as we go,
    Nature rejoices;
Hark! how the hills as we flow
    Echo our voices;
Still o'er the dark waters
    Far away we must roam,
Ere Italy's daughters
    Welcome us home.
Row, row, &c.

Row! row! see in the west
    Lights dimly burning,
Friends in yon harbor of rest
    Wait our returning;

See now they burn clearer,—
  Keep time with the oar;
Now, now we are nearer
  That happy shore.
Row, row, &c.

Home, home, daylight is o'er,
  Friends stand before us;
Yet ere our boat touch the shore
  Once more the chorus:
Row, row, &c.

GUNPOWDER TEA.

Tune—"*Molly put the kettle on.*'

JOHNNY BULL, and many more,
Soon, they say, are coming o'er—
As soon as e'er they reach our shore,
  They must have their tea.
So go and put the kettle on,
Be sure to blow the bellows strong;
Load our cannon, every one,
  With strong *gunpowder tea.*

They'll get it strong, they need not dread,
Sweetened well with *sugar* of *lead;*
Perhaps it may get in their head,
  And spoil their taste for tea.
    So go, &c.

But should they set a foot on shore,
Their cups we'd fill them o'er and o'er,
Such as John Bull drank here before—
  Nice *Saratoga tea.*
    So go, &c.

Then let them come as soon's they can;
They'll find us at our posts, each man;
Their hides we will completely tan,
  Before they get their tea.
    So go, &c.

COMIC SONGS.

THE TIMES AND FASHIONS OF 1860.

Written expressly for this work.

Tune—Bow, wow, wow.

On earth's affairs, and fashion's airs,
  Pray listen while I sing now,
For ev'ry day some new display,
  Or incident does bring now.
We've new inventions, State contentions,
  From one earth's end to the other,
And ev'ry year brings wonders near,
  More wonderful than to'ther.
Bow, wow, wow, wonders increase,
  And ne'er will cease to bow, wow, wow.

In Europe we have States contending,
  Every day and hour—
With armies, fleets, and arms to hold
  The balance of earth's power.
Each tries to terrify the rest,
  By threats, and schemes, and tricks, now;
And the more they try each strategy,
  The more they're in in a fix now.
    Bow, wow, wow, &c.

They've guns that shoot above ten miles,
  And hit a dozen marks, now,
Steam batteries with rows of guns,
  Like teeth within a shark, now.
Machines that reap a field at once,
  Or mow the largest meadow,
And sometimes too—if folks say true
  Mow off the mower's heads, now.
      Bow, wow, wow, &c.

We've telegraphs that span the earth,
  And travel under water,
And news before it happens, now,
  Is heard in ev'ry quarter.
We've ships about a mile in length,
  To navigate the seas, now,
Whole nations can live on a ship,
  And travel where they please, now.
      Bow, wow, wow, &c.

We've show bills about each
  Stretched out some hundred feet, now,
With the name of some new play or show
  Reaching from street to street, now.
Newspaper advertisements too,
  To strike all people's eyes meant,
And oft the only news we read,
  Is some shop's ADVERTISEMENT.
      Bow, wow, wow, &c.

We've patent stoves that heat themselves,
  Without the use of fuel,
They all do their own cooking, too,
  From a roast goose to a gruel.
We've famed machines for sowing grain,
  Machines for sewing breeches,
And if the world ain't well sewed up,
  It's not for want of stitches.
      Bow, wow, wow, &c.

We've patent LEVERS strong enough,
  To pull earth upside down, sir,
Steam fire-engines, that fire *up*,
  To put a fire *down*, sir.

We've patent wigs, for worn old prigs, (*imitating old men,*)
　To give youth to each feature,
And ladies with their patting hearts,
　Are PATENT RIGHTS from NATURE.
　　Bow, wow, wow, &c.

PART II.

We've patent rail cars in our streets,
　To save the people's heels, now,
They jingle up and round about,
　Like parlors upon wheels, now;
We've patent pills to cure life's ills,
　Folks now don't die, till their death, now,
We've patent tubes to help sick people
　Draw in their last breath, now.
　　　Bow, wow, wow, &c.

Our natty gents wear half Scotch caps,
　And pants like zebra's *stripe*, now,
Gold dollars in their shirt bosoms,
　And two yards of " white wipes," now,
With a Raglan coat, like shirts on poles,
　And Shanghai shawls or cloaks, sir,
And neck *ties* like a dog's collar, now,
　Squeezed round a *paper choker*.
　　　Bow, wow, wow, &c.

With hair short as a scrubbing brush,
　And long tufts on the throat, now,
They seem to wear the under jaw
　Of some dead Billy Goat, now.
With SPREAD EAGLE mustachios—
　A brass cable in their fobs, now,
And hats like churns turn'd upside down,
　Oh, don't they come the snob, now?
　　　Bow, wow, wow, &c.

Our ladies, misses, wives, and maids,
　What shall we say of them, now?
High heel'd shoes tight—their toes to bite,
　They scarcely can cry hem, now.

Umbrella *flats*, *clam shell* shaped hats,
  Hoop skirts to scare the moon, sirs,
They look like monster fairies, sirs,
  Just landed in balloons, now,
But let them all wear what they please,
  They'll please with what they wear, sirs,
And the gents will still stand close by them,
  As all creation's *Fair*, sirs.
    Bow, wow, wow.

SILAS S. STEELE.

BARNEY, LET THE GALS ALONE.

**THE GREAT JACK BARNES' CELEBRATED CHARACTER SONG,
WITH ADDITIONS.**

Tune—Polly, Put the Kettle on.

OH! Judy leads me such a life,
Oh! Judy leads me such a life,
The old boy ne'er had such a wife,
  What can the matter be?
For if I sings the funny song,
Of "Polly, put the kettle on,"
A pretty kettle of fish I'm in,
  The moment she hears me.

Spoken—Yes, she leads me the deuce of a life, that's the truth on't—she never goes to church, but what she makes me walk behind her with her parasol, smelling bottle, and hymn book, and if I happen to cast a duck's eye at the girls as they pass by, she's sure to yell out—

    Barney, let the girls alone,
    You Barney, let the girls alone,
    Why don't you let the girls alone,
      And let 'em quiet be?

Put the muffins down to roast,
Put the muffins down to roast,
Blow the fire and make the toast,
  And we'll have some tea.
Ah! Barney, you're a wicked boy,
Ah! Barney, you're a wicked boy,
And you will always kiss and toy,
  With all the girls you see.

Spoken—But if you don't want your hair pulled out by
the roots, your head pulled off your shoulders, and your
shoulders pulled off your body, why sing,

Chorus—Barney, let the girls alone,
   Oh, Barney, let the girls alone.
   Barney rock the cradle, O!
   Barney rock the cradle, O!
   Or else you'll get the ladle, O!
    When Judy harps to-day.

Spoken—Barney, rock that cradle, or I'll break your pate
with the ladle; yes, you dog, if you don't mind your P's and
Q's, I'll comb your head with a three-legged stool. You see,
the other afternoon I was ax'd out to take a comfortable dish
of *four shilling shouchong tea*, and I sat alongside of Miss
Polly Spriggins; I saw she got quite smitten with my counte-
nance—says she to me, Mr. Barney, will you have a game of
hunt the slipper? With all my heart, says I. Then my wife
bawled out, from the other end of the parlour,

   Mr. Barney, leave the girls alone,
   Mr. Barney, leave the girls alone,
   Why don't you leave the girls alone,
    And let them quiet be?
   Judy she loves whiskey, O!
   Judy she loves whiskey, O!
   She goes to uncle's shop at night,
    And spends an hour or two;
   Then, Barney, what must Barney do,
   But take a drop of whiskey, too,
   And toast the girl that's kind and true
    For that's the way with me?

Spoken—Yes, that is the way we go, to be sure, and to say
the truth on it, it is none of the pleasantest. You see I loves
a good dinner, but somehow or other we don't get much in the
week days, a pig's foot and a carrot, no great choice; but on
Sunday we always have a shoulder of mutton stuck round with
turnips. I like a piece of the brown, but my wife, she always
tucks me off with the knuckle bone, or the shoulder blade, or
a piece of the dry flap, to the tune of

   Mr. Barney leave the girls alone! (*repeat*)
   Why don't you leave the girls alone,
    And let them quiet be?

SONG OF THE TURF,

OR THE RACE COURSE.

To the course now my dear boys, if for sport you are bent,
The match soon comes off, and the morn's far spent;
Delays a dull *Trotter*, whom *Time* the fleet steed,
Will beat Flora Temple or Lantern in speed.
To the course then away, go it which ground you please,
The Suffolk, the Union, South End Park, or Point Breeze;
We're off for the sport boys, no matter who pairs,
If we match with good fellows and distance our cares.

Spoken.—Now we're off, and in for an afternoon's exhilaratory merriment? Crack go the whips, and crack go the vehicles. Look what a human race, and even a woman race, to get first to the race ground. Wheels, heads, and heels, go slambang together. Look out there, Mister, can't you keep to the right? Yes sir-ee, over the left. (*A woman's voice.*) Why goodness gracious, if yonder ain't—yes it is my husband, who promised to take me to a pic nic this afternoon, and now he's off to the races to ————; but he shan't go, I'll drag him back, neck, heels, and coach wheels. Now, my dear wife, do go along. No I won't, sir. You must *come* along, (*ad lib.* imitation of a squabble,) I say I will. The gray mare seems to be the better horse. There, woman, help, gentleman! Haven't you madam? Where on earth are you all going?

We're off for the sport no matter who pairs,
So we match with good fellows and distance our cares;
At the course now we land, all by fits and by starts,
Which groan 'neath the weight of gigs, coaches, and carts.
See in strife for the view now all parties agog,
'Till in dust all are hidden like ships in a fog,
One shouts for *Tacony*, another *Black Hawk*,
Nicodemus the Hero, or Daniel so fair,
While others crow out for Jack Rossiter's mare.

Spoken.—Now comes the lug and tug of war, confusion of tongues, and the straining of lungs. I say, Mister, can't you give me a place on your buss? No sir, got nineteen more than it will hold inside, and about as many on the wheels. Take

your foot off of my boots will you. You take your foot off
the ground then, a feller must have a footing somewhere.
(*A woman's voice.*) Oh, murder, my hoops are getting all
squashed. (in a Yankee voice,) I reckon as heow you're a
tarnal squash to wear 'em. Here, Police, take this feller's
hand out of my pocket. Beg pardon sir, but we're so jammed
up, I thought it was my own, but I pocket the insult. Look,
hurrah! there they come up to the starting post, 500 on
Flora. I'm with you ten to five on the Princess, neck or
nothing, for

We're in for the sport no matter who pairs, &c.

At the post now arrived, clear the way, pants each heart,
Hark, there goes the signal, and off they now start;
See Flora's ahead, now the betting runs high,
While the shouts ring the course, as the coursers pass by,
Now on they still fly with the speed of the wind,
One steed like an eagle leaves t'other behind,
Still along see them spring till the close of the heat,
Huzza, they rein in, and old Time's fairly beat.

Spoken.—Neck and neck, they go it tail and tail,
            Snorting like locomotives on the rail,
            See Flora comes out like a Telegraph,
            Two minutes, twenty-three seconds and a half.
Hurrah for the stakes. Let those laugh who win, for
We're off for the sport no matter who pairs,
So we match with good fellows and distance our cares.

TRUST TO LUCK.

Trust to luck, trust to luck, and stare fate in the face,
Sure the heart must be aisy if its in the right place;
Let the world wag away, and your friends turn foes—
When your pockets are dry, and thread-bare are your clothes;
Should woman deceive you, when you trusted her heart,
Ne'er a sigh will relieve you, but adds to the smart.
Trust to luck, trust to luck, stare shame in the face,
Sure the heart must be aisy, if its in the right place.

Trust to luck, trust to luck, and you'll never forget,
Bright morning will follow the darkest night yet;
Let the wealthy look grand, and the proud pass you by,
With the back of their fist and disdain in their eye;
Snap your fingers and smile, let them pass on their way,
But remember the while every dog has his day.

Trust to luck, &c.
GEORGE JAMISON.

TRUST TO PLUCK.

A PARODY ON "TRUST TO LUCK."

Sung with great applause by Bishop Buckley.

TRUST to pluck, trust to pluck, when you're in a tight place,
And the head nice and greasy will reach the right place,
When you're "hard up," and dry, and your friends thumb
      their nose,
When you hain't got a *red*, and there's holes in your toes.
Should the barber who shaved you point to the old score,
Should the landlord who trusted you show you the door,
Trust to pluck, trust to pluck, when you're in a tight place,
And your head slick and greasy will reach the right place.

Trust to pluck, trust to pluck, when you're neck deep in debt,
And the chums will fly from you when they see you're "dead
      set,"
Let the lucky pass by you, and cut you shanghai,
With a portmonkey filled and a leer in the eye,
Tuck the crown of your hat, toss your head up and sing,
And cry out that the bullfrog has never a wing.

Trust to pluck, &c.

HAVE YOU SEEN MY SISTER?

SAY, my lovely friends, have you any pity,
At your finger ends? then listen to my ditty;
Our Kate has gone away, last Thursday night we missed her,
Good people do not smile,—say, have you seen my sister?

If you have her seen, I hope you will advise her,
To return to me, or I must advertise her;
Her waist is very thick, her stays give her a twister,
Now tell me, b'hoys and g'hals, have you seen my sister?

She squints with both her eyes, in a manner very shocking,
She's got a mouth for pies, and wears no shoes or stockings;
I'm afraid she's gone astray, and some chap did enlist her,
I'm afraid she's gone astray; say, have you seen my sister?

She wants her two front teeth, you'd see it when she'd titter,
She's got such little feet, Columbia's shoes won't fit her;
She wears no cap at all, but a great big muslin whister,
Now tell me once for all, have you seen my sister?

Her figure's straight and tall, her conduct's very proper,
She's well provided for, she's eighteen pence in copper,
Now if you have her seen, I'm sure you could not have miss'd
      her,
For she's very much like me; now, have you seen my sister?

Her mouth is very small, her nose is straight and natty,
I tell you once for all, this girl is very pretty;
Now I'll sing you another song, and it shall be a twister,
If you will go with me, and help me find my sister.

SILENT SAM; OR I NEVER SAYS NOTHING TO NOBODY.

WHAT a shocking world this is for scandal,
   The people grow worse ev'ry day;
Every thing serves for a handle,
   To take people's good names away.
In backbiting and railing, each labors,
   A low fault of others to show body;
I could tell such a tale of my neighbors,
   But I never says nothing to nobody.
                    Tol de rol dol di da.

'Tis a snug house in which we reside,
   The people who live in the next door,
.Are bother'd completely with pride,
   Such as I never saw before.
Outside of doors they don't roam,
   A large sum of money they owe body;
People call, but don't find them at home,
   But I never says nothing to nobody.
                    Tol de rol dol di da.

There's the baker who lives in great style,
  Whose wife is a deuce of a fright,
Of new dresses she has a great pile,
  And they sleep out of town ev'ry night.
Country cottage complete in a state,
  Determined not to be a low body;
He's been pull'd up three times for short weight,
  But I never says nothing to nobody.
                  'Tol de rol dol di da.

There's the butcher so greasy and fat,
  When out he does nothing but boast;
He struts as he cocks on his hat,
  As if he supreme rules the roast.
Talks of himself and his riches,
  Consequence, always a show body;
His ugly old wife wears the breeches,
  But I never says nothing to nobody.
                  Tol de rol dol di da.

There's the methodist priest of great fame,
  Who I see very often go by,
His bosom is filled with love's flame,
  And he visits a girl on the sly.
All this now I daily do see,
  Of course he is but a so-so body,
But as it is nothing to me,
  Why I never says nothing to nobody.
                  Tol de rol dol di da.

There's the new married couple so happy,
  They seem quite the essence of love;
He calls her before ev'ry sappy,
  My ducky, my darling, my dove.
At home there is nothing but strife,
  Fights and quarrels enough to o'erflow body,
In fact quite a cat-and-dog life,
  But I never says nothing to nobody.
                  Tol de rol dol di da.

Oh, I could tell such a tale of my neighbors,
 All around me, both great and small,
That really without any failure,
 I'd greatly astonish you all.
But here my short ditty ends,
 I don't wish to hurt high or low body,
And I wish to keep in with my friends,
 So I never says nothing to nobody.
     Tol de rol dol di da.

GAWKEY SHANKS AND MOLLY MUMPS,

OR A GHOST WITH HIS HEAD IN HIS HAND.

A New Comic Apparition. *Tune—" Giles Scroggins."*

POOR Gawkey Shanks was born and bred,
   Ri tol de riddle lol de da.
He fell in love ears over head,
     Ri tol.

With Molly Mumps the sweetest maid,
And such coquettish tricks she playéd,
That down to his heel he went out of his head.
Spoken.—With a staring, swearing, hair-tearing, and de
spairing sort of a (*Imitating crazy*) Ri tol de riddle lol de da

Moll with another youth went to church,
   With a ri tol de riddle.
And left poor Gawkey in the lurch,
   With a ri tol.

He for a soldier straightway went,
On blood and slaughter fully bent
All for to warm " the winter of his discontent,"
With red hot shot, bombshell pots.
   Ri tol de riddle lol de da.

When to the battle he did go,
   With right—fight—de riddle.
The balls flew thick and thinn'd ranks so,
    Ri tol.

Brave Gawkey fought with might and main,
But being slewed he soon got slain,
For a bullet whipped his head off clean,
With a whizzing and bizzing sort of
   Ri tol de riddle lol de da.

One night when dreadful storms did **roar,**
          With a ri tol de riddle lol de da.
As Moll beside her **spouse did snore,**
       With (imitating snore) a ri tol de riddle.
A horse power **groan assailed her ears,**
When starting **with raised hair and** ears,
A spectre by her side appears,
With **a terrible blueful sort of**
              Ri tol de riddle lol de da.

'Twas Gawkey stood **beside her bed,**
               With ri tol.
And in his hand he held his head,
                Ri tol.
Behold ! he cried, thou **wicked one,**
See what thy *par-ju-ry* **has done,**
You're broke **my** heart, **an' my head's undone,**
With **a decapitated** and divided sort of
              Ri tol de riddle lol de da.

Now Gawkey kotched **her by the hair,**
           With a ri tol de riddle.
She screamed dismay—he grinned despair,
        With a loud fol de diddle lol de da.
He was dragging her off by the hair,
But it was a wig that she did wear,
And **down he tumbled stair by stair,**
And **broke his spine by the** great incline,
And **he gave up the ghost** with **an** expiring **sort of**
          Ri tol de riddle lol **de da.**

DON'T BE ADDICTED TO DRINKING.

As early one morning down Main street **I walked,**
  The sky being shady and clouded,
When all of a sudden **my** senses were **shocked,**
  Just to see how the rum-shops were crowded.
The folks ran out and **in, as** if running a race,
  And they poured down **the** liquor like winking ;
A glass now and then, is very well in its place,
  But don't be addicted to drinking.

Now these cold frosty mornings when raising your head,
  From your pillow you'll find it quite handy,
To knock off, as soon as you turn out of bed,
  A thumping good bumper of brandy.
A tumbler of rum in a basin of tea,
  Is a very good thing to my thinking,
Yet a pint of good liquor would better agree,
  But don't be addicted to drinking.

A glass at eleven, I've heard some folks say,
  Is a very good thing, so it is, miss,
But a man shouldn't drink every hour in the day,
  Becase it unfits him for business.
Then about one o'clock, when your dinner you get,
  Your spirits at that time are most sinking,
Take two or three glasses by way of a whet,
  But don't be addicted to drinking.

Enjoying a segar after dinner you get,
  Perhaps for an hour and a quarter,
Nothing will give such a relish to it,
  As a tumbler of brandy and water;
Then perhaps you'll feel inclined for a doze,
  You can scarce keep your eyelids from winking,
Take three or four glasses your mind to compose,
  But don't be addicted to drinking.

To think about business as soon as you wake,
  Of course you will think it will be time,
Then four or five glasses more at least you must take,
  If you wish to be sober by tea-time.
Then spending your evening at Liberty's Arms,
  Of your pretty fair maid you keep thinking,
While in hot gin and water you're toasting her charms,
  Mind you don't get addicted to drinking.

Now a bumper at parting you cannot do less
  It will just keep you from yawning,
But believe me, dear friends, if you drink to excess,
  You will have a devilish headache in the morning.
Now such, my dear friends, is my own sober plan,
  And I hope you are my way of thinking,
For I've just joined the temperance society, and am
  By no means addicted to drinking.

THE UNLUCKY FELLOW.

If there is any one here what's got a desire
　　To wed with a grumbling wife,
He had better by far poke his head into the fire
　　And at once put an end to his life.
When I courted my love, I thought her a dove,
　　But when married I wished myself dead,
For, in less than a week she got tired of love,
　　And she tore all the hair off my head.
　　　　　　Oh, crackey, oh, dear,
My heart is so full that I'm ready to cry,
Oh, dear what a poor unlucky fellow am I.

The very first mishap filled my eyes full of tears,
　　She brought me home children two,
Says she, you must father these two little dears,
　　But says I, I'll be blowed if I do.
Then she said with a sneer, how dare I presume
　　To think of my case being hard,
She knocked me down three pair of stairs with a broom,
　　Then bolted me out in the yard.
　　　　　　Oh, crackey, oh, dear,
A man who's by sorrows thus trundled about,
Is worse than a hog with a ring in his snout.

But much worse than this was the rest if you'll mark,
　　I thought I should really go wild,
I trod on our little cat's tail in the dark,
　　She moulrowed and woke the young child.
Then she up with her fist, she put me in a fright,
　　She swore she would make me rue it,
She made me go sleep in the cupboard all night,
　　Though I said I didn't go for to do it.
　　　　　　Oh, crackey, oh, dear,
A man that is married must weep and bewail,
Like a dog with a tin kettle tied to his tail.

It was one Monday morning, I swear it is true,
　　I met with a shocking bad loss,
She told me to buy some meat for a stew,
　　Says I, I will, love, don't be cross.

But what mishaps in this world we oft find!
  Before I could get it home to her,
A large Newfoundland dog came up smelling behind,
  And he stole all the meat off the skewer.
      Oh, crackey, oh, dear,
A man that is married, his pleasures are small,
Just like a poor dog what ain't got no tail at all.

THE NICE YOUNG MAN.

THERE was a nice young man, his name was Brown,
  He wore a short frock coat,
The hair on his temples was plastered down,
  And his collar on the side of his throat.
Oh, his hands they were white, his pants they were tight,
  And his hair was the color of tan;
The ladies all said, whether widow, wife, or maid,
  That he was such a *Nice Young Man!*
      Ri tol, &c.

This young man Brown spoke soft and low,
  And was civil to every body;
The temperance pledge with him was all the go,
  For he never drank a glass of toddy.
At the name of a play he would run right away,
  For the playhouse was the devil's frying pan;
He read nothing but tracts, and he stuck to them like wax,
  For he was such a *Nice Young Man!*
      Ri tol, &c.

Three times on Sunday, and once on Sunday night,
  He went to church quite regular;
He was so polite that he didn't fall asleep quite,
  But sang hymns with a fat dowager.
Oh, he turned up his eyes like a duck when he dies,
  Blowed his nose when the sermon began,
When the parson had done, to shake hands with him he'd run,
  And the parson said he was a *Nice Young Man!*
      Ri tol, &c.

To a christening party Brown invited himself,
  And offered for to stand god-pappy,
There was none so frisk as he, when he handed round the tea,
  He made them all so jovial and so happy.

Oh, he talked to the pappy, and he kissed the little baby;
   Oh, the mother admired his plan,
How beautiful he talks! But where's all my silver forks?
   They were in **the** pocket of the *Nice Young Man!*
      Ri tol, &c.

They took **him off to the** police office,
   And **the first thing** his worship said,
Was " We've been looking for you, for a year **or two,**
   And I'm glad **you** have been discovered !"
In spite **of** his good looks, **he** was upon their bad **books,**
   They **sent** him off in the police black van,
They didn't stretch his wizen, but for two years in prison,
   They locked up the *Nice Young Man!*
      Ri tol, &c.

ENCORE VERSES.

Brown served out **his** time and **came out prime,**
   And looked much nicer than **ever,**
He just changed his name to play the same **game,**
   And alter the scene of his endeavor.
Oh, he twaddled out of town before he settled down,
   And followed the self-same plan ;
He looked wise and demure, **as** stiff as any **skewer,**
   And **they** all said he was a *Nice Young Man!*
      Ri tol, &c.

He found a gold watch in his landlord's **room,**
   And he took it right away ;
For fear some one to steal **it** should **presume,**
   The landlord would be in a bad way.
The landlord discharged his maid and his clerk,
   Thinking them in the stealing plan ;
If you'd suspected Brown, he would have knocked you down,
   For suspecting such a *Nice Young Man!*
      Ri tol, &c.

In the course of his sinning, **he grew** very short of linen,
   He managed to drop into a dry good dealer's skirts,
In preaching of Parson **Sacks** over a bundle **of tracts;**
   He made *shift* to steal a dozen of *shirts!*
In spite of his looks, the shopman noticed his *hooks,*
   And straight for the police officer ran,
First of all they knocked down, then they took up Mr. Brown,
   And transported this *Nice Young Man!*

MORAL.

Now ladies all, both little and tall,
  Pray listen to what I have been describing;
This history so true that I dedicates to you,
  And a warning I hope you'll imbibe in;
When a husband you select, of course we expect,
  That you'll pick out the best you can,
But nothing can be worse, than that hollow-hearted curse
  A smooth-faced, sneaking *Nice Young Man!*

MY GRANDFATHER WAS A WONDERFUL MAN.

My grandfather was a most wonderful man,
He could do and invent, could propose and could plan.
When he was at school, a boy very small,
At reading and writing, why he beat them all;
He could dance, he could sing, he could poetry write,
He could wrestle and box, he could run, he could fight.—

(*Spoken*—Well he could fight! he once knocked a man so
deep into a snow bank, that when his friends dug him out, he
was bankrupt. Oh! he was a wonderful man, he knew every-
thing—he knew Jawology, Tautology, Conchology, Etymology,
Physiology, Noseology, Mineralogy, Phrenology, and all the
rest of the ologys. He was the boy for a song too: he once
wrote a song of a hundred and ninety-nine verses and sung it
himself; he did! it took him three hours and three quarters
to sing it, because the first verse was always repeated. He
was a wonderful smart man—but notwithstanding all that, he
couldn't fool old Death: Oh, no, old bones and scythe come
along one day, and cut the old man down very suddenly.
What a pity———)

What a pity it is this life's but a span,
For my grandfather was a most wonderful man.
He sailed 'round the world without going wrong,
He killed a large crocodile twenty feet long,
He caught a large whale and brought him ashore,
He tamed fifteen lions and killed a wild boar,
He could change brass to copper, get diamonds from coal,
He fried at the Indies, and froze at the pole.

(*Spoken*—Well he did! He once sailed 'round the north
pole, saw the pole, went up to the pole, climb'd up the pole,

look'd into the pole, cut the pole off, and brought it home
with him; used it for a fish pole for many years—finally stuck
it up for a Liberty pole; and I dare say it stands to this very
day. Oh! he was a wonderful man. Why, he once upon
one of his voyages, sailed right against the Equinoctial line,
broke it in two, caught both ends, brought them home, used
it for a fish line for a great while. My *grandmother* was a
wonderful *woman*, too, she was a washerwoman—she had no
place to dry her clothes, so my grandfather stretched the
other half of the Equinoctial line 'round the garden fence,
and she used to dry her clothes on the Equator. O! he was
a wonderful man for inventions, what a pity he died——)
What a pity it is this life's, &c.

He sailed to each part of Japan and Peru,
Could tell if a wife to her husband was true,
He swam the Nile over without any clothes,
Watch papers and miniatures cut with his toes,
He could make anything that once he had seen,
From a microscope up to a sausage machine.

(*Spoken*—Well he could! And he could make sausages
too; he once speculated in sausages; but he lost in one grand
speculation; he got to making them of bull terriers, and grey-
hounds, they got fighting, and tore the sausages all to pieces;
but then he tried another experiment—he made some of grey-
hound alone, but there came along a little boy one day, whistling Yankee Doodle, and whistled the meat all out and left
nothing but the skins lying on the stall; however, he lost nothing by the operation, for he blew up the skins and made
life preservers and bustles of them. Oh! he was a wonderful man, and had he not died, he would have lived a great
while——)

What a pity it is this life's but a span,
For my grandfather was a most wonderful man.
My grandfather was a most wonderful man.

16

THE QUILTING.

'TWAS down at Major Parsons' house,
The gals they had a quiltin'
Just for tu show their handsome looks
And have a little jiltin' !
Chorus—Yankee lasses are the U—
'niversal airth be-witchin',
They're good and true, and handsome tu
In parlor and in kitchen.

There was Deacon Jones's darter Sal,
Squire Wheeler's darter Mary,
And General Carter's youngest gal,
That looks just like a fairy !
Yankee lasses are the U, &c.

There was Lucy White and Martha Brown
And Parsons' darter Betty,
Jemima Pinkhorn, Prudence Short,
And Major Downing's Hetty.
Yankee lasses are the U, &c.

But if there was a handsome gal,
To make a fellow's heart right,
I guess it was by all accounts,
Miss Carolina Cartwright.
Yankee lasses are the U, &c.

Wal, while we were a whirlin' plate,
And playin' hunt the slipper,
Jerusha Parsons went to git
Some cider in a dipper.
Yankee lasses are the U, &c.

But just as she had left the room,
And got inter the entry,
She gave a scream, and stood stock still
Just like a frozen sentry.
Yankee lasses are the U, &c.

We all ran out, and there. I swow,
Both huggin' like creation,
Miss Cartwright and Sam Jones we saw
A kissin' like tarnation.
Yankee lasses are the U, &c.

Oh, such a laugh as we sot **up,**
  You never heerd a finer,
Says I, " I reckin kissin's cheap,
  Don't **you Miss** Carolina?"
      Yankee lasses **are** the U, &c.

I wish you'd saw Miss Cartwright blush,
  Just like as if she'd painted,
She said—she had the cholic—and—
  And in Samuel's arms had fainted.
      Yankee lasses are the U, &c.

And now, young gals, I'd say tu **you,**
  When you go to a frolic,
Don't let your fellers kiss and hug,
  Unless—you have the headache.
      Yankee lasses are the U, &c.

MY GRANDMOTHER WAS A MOST WONDERFUL DAME.

YOU'VE heard **of my** grandfather's wonderful skill,
Who such marvelous deeds could perform at his will,
But Lord bless your **soul!** they're not worthy to name,
Compared with the feats **of** my worthy granddame;
Oh, sure such a woman **can no** where be found,
If you travel a century, and search the world round.
  No wonder she gained such **a** glorious name,
  For my grandmother was a **most** wonderful dame.

(*Spoken*—There **was a** woman for you.—Talk about my grandfather; why he was **only** a patch of court plaster compared with my grandmother. Do you know that my grandmother invented the patent Elixir of Life, and lived to the good old age of two hundred and seventy? She used to take fifteen drops of the Elixir in fifteen gallons of brandy every morning before breakfast—and in less than three months, she had a new pair of eyes, a new head **of** hair, and a new sett **of** teeth. She had!)
      No wonder, &c.

She could dance, she could sing, she could fence, she could spar,
But oh, at invention, she beat others by far,
She invented—indeed of her skill I don't dream,
A patent machine *to make children by* steam;
She'd take cart loads of snuff, and still crave for more,
And drank enough tea to float a seventy-four.
  No wonder she gained such a glorious name,
  For my grandmother was a most marvelous dame.

(*Spoken*—There was a woman for you.—Do you know that my grandmother invented a steamboat to sail down the Mississippi river? Well, she started off one afternoon, about six o'clock in the morning, just before breakfast, with a whole cart load of passengers; she got as far as New Orleans, when the whirlpool took it—went round and round to the bottom —but it didn't make any difference to the steamboat, it kept going on, going on; and my grandmother believes that if it had not been for a large oyster, or the great American sea serpent, which must have swallowed it, the steamboat would have been going on to this very day—Well it would!)
  No wonder, &c.

She could cure like winkin, diasters and ills,
She beat all to nothing famed Brandreth's pills,
She knew every manual labor and art,
And she could make, from a wheelbarrow up to a cart,
She could give to old age a patent new face,
And beat every body in running a race.
  No wonder, &c.

(*Spoken*—There was a woman for you.—She invented some patent yeast, to make cakes rise—all you had to do was to take a little before going to bed, it would make you rise at any moment you wished. Grandmother put a little in the yard one night for an experiment, first thing she knew, the sun began to rise about two o'clock, it did! Do you know that my grandmother invented a steam balloon?—Well, she did—she started off one fine evening, with a new married couple, and got up so high that she couldn't get down again; balloon kept going on—grandmother lit her pipe in the moon, and snuffed out the sun—and when they did get down again (it's a fact, or grandmother wouldn't have said so), the new married couple had turned completely gray, and had a whole flock of little ones. Well they had!)
  No wonder, &c.

THE NERVOUS FAMILY.

Air.—" We're all Noddin'."

WE'RE all nervous, **shake, shake,** trembling,
We're all nervous, **at our house, at** home;
There's myself and my mother, my sister and brother,
If left all alone, are all frighten'd at each other.
Our dog runs away if a stranger's in the **house,**
And our tabby cat, too, is frightened at a mouse;
And we're all nervous, shake, shake, trembling,
We're all nervous, at our house, at home.

We all at dinner, shake, **shake, at carving;**
And as for snuffing, we oft **snuff out the** light;
Last night every one did **to** snuff the candle try,
But my wife couldn't **do it, nor** my sister, nor could I.
Come give me **the** snuffers, said mother, with **a** flout,
I'll show **you how** to do it, **and** she snuff'd the candle out.
        For she's so nervous, **shake, shake,** &c.

My nervous **wife** can't work at her needle,
And my shaking hand spills half my cup of tea;
When wine at dinner my timid sister's taking,
It's spilt on the table for so her hand is shaking,
My mother taking snuff, very carefully doth try,
To pop it up **her** nose, when **she pops** it in her eye.
        For **she's so** nervous, **shake,** shake, &c.

Our nerves foretell all the changes of the weather;
We are so nervous we're frightened at each noise;
We have got a private watchman to guard the private door,
But since we have had **him,** we are frightened more and
        more.
For he falls asleep, and we've found out too, that he,
In respect to his nerves, **oh,** he's quite as **bad as** we.
        So we're all nervous, shake, shake, &c.

NOWADAYS.

Music published by Firth, Pond, & Co., N. Y.

ALAS! how every thing is changed,
　Since I was sweet sixteen,
When all the girls wore home-spun frocks,
　And aprons nice and clean.
With bonnets made of braided straw,
　That tied beneath the chin,
The shawl laid neatly on the neck,
　And fasten'd with a pin.

I recollect the time, when I
　Rode father's horse to mill,
Across the meadow, rock, and field,
　And up and down the hill.
And when "our folks" were out at work,
　It never made me thinner,
I jumped upon a horse bare-back,
　And carried them their dinner.

Dear me! young ladies nowadays,
　Would almost faint away,
To think of riding all alone,
　In wagon, chaise, or sleigh.
And as for giving "pa" his meals,
　Or helping "ma" to bake,
Oh dear! 'would spoil their lily hands,
　Though sometimes they make cake.

When winter came, the maiden's heart
　Began to beat and flutter;
Each beau would take his sweetheart out,
　Sleigh-riding in a cutter.
Or if the storm was bleak and cold,
　The girls and beaux together,
Would meet and have the best of fun,
　And never mind the weather!

But nowadays, it grieves me **much**
   The circumstance **to** mention,
However kind the young man's heart,
   And honest his intention,
He asks no girls **to** take a drive,
   'Case he's too **much engaged.**
In shanghai clothes, races **and yacht clubs,**
   His time and tin are caged.

THINGS I DON'T LIKE TO SEE.

A VERY POPULAR COMIC SONG.

Tune.—" Irish Washerwoman."

A SONG I'll sing **now in jingling** rhymes,
About matters and things in these curious times,
A lesson to **all** I hope it will **be,**
When I sing to **you about things I don't like to see.**
Chorus.—You **may call me a quiz, you may call me a** pry,
   But **I doesn't like things that look queer to** the eye,
   And if you like them, that's nothing to me,
   So these are some things that **I don't** like to see :

I don't like **to see** little **boys just from their mammas,**
Who think they are men **and smoke** their segars,
They had better be at home a-playing with toys,
Than running the **streets** and exclaiming, "I'm one of the
   Bo'hoys."
      You may call me a quiz, &c.

I don't like to see dandies without any cash,
Promenade the Main street, and cut quite a dash,
Who stare at the ladies—look pretty and sweet,
Without a cent in their pocket and nothing **to** eat.
      You may call me a quiz, &c.

I don't like to see gals **all the** time reading sonnets,
Romances and novels, wear queer little bonnets,
Who screw up their waists and wear a tight sleeve,
And dare not, poor creatures, enjoy a good **sneeze.**
      You may **call me a** quiz, &c.

I don't like to see politicians, who take great pains,
To show their constituents they are possessed of large brains,
Who talk about this thing—and blow about that,
And all that they're after is government—pap.
   You may call me a quiz, &c.

I don't like to see ladies want satins for dress,
When their husbands are bankrupt and in great distress;
They had better be at home, washing up dishes,
Mending holes in their stockings, and their husbands' old
  pantaloons.
   You may call me a quiz, &c.

I don't like to see John Bull, " putting on airs,"
Sending troops to the Canadas, the Yankees to scare;
He'd better " dry up," or he'll git in a fix,
That will give him a specimen of " old seventy-six."
   You may call me a quiz, &c.

P. Morris.

BILLY BARLOW.

Oh ladies and gentlemen, how do you do ?
I've come out before you with one boot and shoe,
I do not know how it is, but somehow 'tis so,
Oh ! isn't it hard upon Billy Barlow ?
 Oh ! oh ! raggedy oh ! now isn't it hard upon Billy Barlow ?

As I was walking down street jist t'other day,
The people all gazed and some of 'em did say,
Why, that fellow there, why he aint so slow,
Humph ! I guess not, says a lady, that's Mr. Barlow.

I went to the races jist the other day,
The man that keeps the gate he asked me to pay,
Pay—says I, and looked at him so,
O you can pass on, I know you, you are Billy Barlow.

They say there's a wild beast show come to town,
Of lions, and monkeys, and porcupines too,
But if they start to show, I'll beat them, I know,
For they aint got a varmint like Billy Barlow.

They tried to buy me to go with that show,
But the monkeys got jealous, and the lion snapped at **me too,**
The Hyena growled, and looked at **me so;**
Thinks I, 'twill **never** do for **you, Mr. Billy Barlow.**

The tailors **in town are all running after me,**
To get the **cut of my clothes, that's plain to see,**
But before **they can get them I'll just let you know,**
They must spill out the rhino to Mr. Barlow.

Oh ladies and gentlemen, I bid you good bye,
I'll get a new **suit when** clothes aint **so high,**
My hat's shocking **bad, that** all of you know,
Yet it looks well on **the head of** this Billy Barlow.

T'other day at a free **blow of** liquor **and lunch,**
I thought to ring in **for** a good swig **of punch,**
But they elbowed me **out** with a fisty free *blow*,
And that's all the punch **they** give Billy **Barlow.**

Now ladies, long life to each sweet smiling soul,
Though my coat it is ragged, **my heart it is whole,**
If there is any in want of a genteel young beau,
Let them come to the arms of young Billy Barlow.

THE AUTHOR AND THE COBBLER,

OR LITERATURE AND COMMON SENSE.

WILLIAM and Jonathan came to town together,
William brought learning, and Jonathan some leather;
Said William to Jonathan, What d'ye mean to do?
Said Jonathan to William, I can sole a shoe,
  With my leather, **lap-stone,** hammer, nippers, pegging-awl,
    and bristles.

Said Jonathan to William, Pray, what is **your** intention?
William talk'd of things far above his comprehension,
He meant to write poetry, pamphlets, songs, and **plays,**
Epitaphs, epigrams, and puffs, the wind **to raise,**
  With **his** Latin, Greek, grammar, syntax, prosody, and
    logic.

It chanced that they lodged in the same house together,
Will stuck close to books, and Jonathan to leather;
While Johnny in the cellar as any hog grew fat,
Poor Will in the garret was as thin as a starved cat,
  With their leather, Latin, hammer, grammar, pegging-awl,
    and logic.

When they had lived in town for years nearly twenty;
Will was very poor, but Jonathan had plenty;
When meeting one day, they compar'd notes together,
And clearly proved that learning wasn't half so good as
    leather,
  Sing, leather, lap-stone, hammer, nippers, pegging-awl, and
    bristles.

"JUST SO."

Tune.—" Garryowen," or " The Campbells."

Mr. Dip—a big dealer in tallow and fat,
By love was reduced like a skeleton cat;
And the maiden he loved was as pure as the snow,
And many a sigh did he give her—just so.
           (Imitating a long sigh.)

One night when his unlucky stars did prevail,
He drank with a friend about nine pints of ale;
It got in his head—put him quite in a glow,
And made his eyes roll about him—just so.
           (Imitating.)

He then went a courting, though not very fit,
And not able to stand, why he was forced to sit;
Says he, " Oh, my love, you'll excuse me, I know,"
Says she, " Mr. Dip, you've been drinking,"—just so.
           (Imitating.)

Says he, " Oh! my angel, pray doubt not my love,
For you know I'm as faithful and true as a dove;
   feel how my heart pit-a-pats to and fro,"
   she, " Mr. Dip, you're a brute beast,"—just so.
           (Imitating.)

"My darling," says he, "only let me explain,
And I promise I never will do it again;
Come, let us be friends, kiss before I do go,"
Says she, then, to him, "Kiss the tom cat,"—just so.
(Imitating.)

"Oh! oh! then," says he, "if you're positive still,
And determined to show me you'll have your own will,
Dang me if I care for it!—I'll let you know,
I don't care a fig for your passions,"—just so.
(Imitating.)

He put on his hat, and he reeled to the door,
While the poor maiden's heart was getting quite sore;
Says he, "By your cruelty here I do go;"
Says she, "Mr. Dip, can you leave me?"—just so.
(Imitating.)

At hearing these words, Mr. Dip then turned back,
And gave her sweet lips such a good hearty smack;
Says he, "Then next Sunday to church let us go,"
Says she, "Oh, I have no objection,"—just so.
(Imitating.)

THE LAZY CLUB.

Tune.—"Green grow the rushes, oh!"

My wife is such a lazy Turk,
She will not do a bit of work,
She says she isn't such a flat,
Hard work will never make her fat.
But in the morning when she wakes,
Her breakfast up stairs then she takes,
She treats herself to toast and shrub,
And says she's joined a Lazy Club.
Chorus.—Skiddy mi dig, ri to ra lo.
Skiddy mi dig, ri to ra lo.
Skiddy mi dig, ri to ra lo.
Skiddy mi dig, ri to ra lo.

When she takes it in her head,
She makes me lift her out of bed,
To say a word, I do not dare,
But place **her** in an **easy** chair.
To stir a peg it seems a crime,
Why there she sits till supper time,
While I'm obliged to cook the grub,
Because she's joined the Lazy Club.
  Skiddy mi dig, &c.

My eldest daughter's **just as** bad,
I **really** think she's lazy mad,
She seems too lazy now to talk,
And scarce **seems** half inclined **to walk.**
Her tongue is never free **from scolds,**
Her shoes **are** always full **of holes,**
Her dress is never free **from mud,**
In honor of the Lazy Club.
  Skiddy mi dig, &c.

My doteful son shows off his airs,
He cannot sit without three chairs,
And he pretends he's got the gout,
And wants me then to carry him about.
He is too lazy to go to bed,
So snores upon the chairs instead,
Wanted me to give his boots a rub,
In honor of the Lazy Club.
  Skiddy mi dig, &c.

We keep a girl **about sixteen,**
To mind the house and keep it clean,
But lawks! she's such a lazy elf,
I'm obliged to do it all myself.
And if I ask her then to stir,
She says **I** ought **to wait on** her,
And give the yard and the kitchen a scrub,
In honor **of the** Lazy Club.
  Skiddy mi dig, &c.

We keep a very lazy dog,
Who lays about just like a log,
He seems too lazy to wag his tail,
And tries to imitate the snail.
Before the fire all in a heap,
Why there he lies, goes fast asleep,
And lawks ! he is such a lazy chub,
I think he's joined the Lazy Club.
   Skiddy mi dig, &c.

And now I'm in a pretty mess
Through their cursed laziness ;
And now my debts I cannot pay,
In prison shall be obliged to lay.
When I am there, the lazy elves,
They'll be obliged to help themselves,
And no doubt when they're in want of grub,
They must get it from the Lazy Club.
   Skiddy mi dig, &c.

A BAG OF NAILS.

My merry gentle people, pray
 Will you list a minute?
For, though my song it is not long,
 There's something comic in it.
To sing of nails, if you'll permit,
 My sportive muse intends, sirs,
A subject which I now have pat
 Just at my fingers' ends, sirs.

The world it is a bag of nails,
 And some are very queer ones,
And some are flats, and some are sharps,
 And some are very dear ones.
We've sprigs, and spikes, and sparables,
 Some little, great, and small, sirs,
Some folks have nails with monstrous heads,
 And some have none at all, sirs.

The bachelor's a hob-nail,
 He rusts for want of use, sirs.
The misers, they're no nails at all,
 They're all a pack of screws, sirs.

An enemy will get some clouts
  If here they chance to roam, sirs,
For Yankee boys, like hammers, will,
  Be sure to drive them home, sirs.

The doctor nails you with his bill,
  Which often proves a sore nail,
The undertaker wishes you
  As dead as any door-nail.
You'll often find each agent
  To be nailing his employer;
The lawyer nails his client,
  And the devil nails the lawyer.

Dame Fortune is a brad-awl,
  And often does contrive it
To make each nail go easily
  Where'er she please to drive it.
Then, if I gain your kind applause
  For what I've sung or said, sirs,
Then you'll admit that I have hit
  The right nail on the head, sirs.

MY MARY HAS THE LONGEST NOSE.

Tune—My Helen is the Fairest Flower.

My Mary has the longest nose,
  In which she greatly takes a pride,
So large the shoes her feet inclose,
  That insects strive in vain to hide.
Her hair is of the brightest red,
  Which lights her footsteps in the dark;
Her mouth is large for hiding bread,
  Her voice is sweeter than the lark.
    Yes, Mary has, &c.

In Mary there is nothing green,
  She'll let you kiss her if you can,
Her mother says she's not sixteen,
  Though twice as strong as any man.
But far ahead of these, of all,
  The charms my Mary can combine,
She's six foot six, and I can call
  This charming little creature mine.
    Yes, Mary has, &c.

THE LOVE STRUCK QUAKER.

Tune—Dost thou love, sister Ruth?

I'm a luckless mortal, veri-ly,
    Ump um! heigho! heigho!
All day long I pine and cry—
    Ump um! heigho! heigho!
Once I plump and fat was grown,
Now I'm nought but skin and bone—
Love cuts me up and cuts me down—
    Ump um! heigho! heigho!

My inward man is sore decay'd—
    Ump um! heigho! heigho!
The spirit's by the flesh betray'd—
    Ump um! heigho! heigho!
I conceive—ah, veril-y,
That I'm assailed most grievous-ly;
And us'd by Ruth most ruthless-ly—
    Ump um! heigho! heigho!

My heart by Cupid's fiercely smote—
    Ump um! heigho! heigho!
And rent in twain like Joseph's coat—
    Ump um! heigho! heigho!
Love has caught me in a snare,
Wicked Ruth scorns my despair;
Though fair herself, don't use me fair—
    Ump um! heigho! heigho!

As young lambkins frisk and play—
    Ump um! heigho! heigho!
Ruth and I have toy'd all day—
    Ump um! heigho! heigho!
She now disdains to cast one look
On me—alas! it is no joke,
My peace should be to pieces broke—
    Ump um! heigho! heigho!

To joys of earth I'll bid adieu—
    Ump um! heigho! heigho!
Leave Ruth to find a swain more true;
    Ump um! heigho! heigho!

I'll seek some shady grove straightway,
There 'neath some pine I'll pine away,
And in the ground bury my clay.
 Ump! ump! ump! heigho!

YANKEE MANUFACTURE.

Originally written and sung by Pete Morris.

Tune—*Betsy Baker.*

I WISH I was in Yankee land,
 And was a boy again, sir,
I'd suck sweet cider through a straw,
 And fish in every rain, sir.
I'd never wander from my home
 To visit other lands, sure,
But stay at home, eat pumpkin pies
 Of Yankee manufacture.

The people there all go-a-head,
 They never turn about, sir,
And when the bo'hoys go on a spree,
 "Their mothers know they're out, sir;"
The girls can read, and write, and spin,
 Are modest, chaste, and fair, sure,
No other land has got such gals
 As of Yankee manufacture.

There is a spot near Boston town,
 They call it Bunker Hill, sir,
Where Johnny Bull with Yankee lead
 Did get his stomach filled, sir;
'Twas there brave General Warren fell,
 In freedom's glorious cause, sure,
But we had left great Washington,
 Of Yankee manufacture.

I love the Yankees for their skill,
 Their perseverance too, sir,
Their telegraphs and railroads,
 And wooden nutmegs too, sir:
For onions and for enterprise
 Give me the Yankee lads, sir;
For cider, soberness, and sense,
 There is none can beat their dads, sir!

Why the Sundays there begin to dawn
On Saturday, at eve, sir,
And then all hands, in-doors and out,
Their weekly labors leave, sir;
It's wicked then for hens to lay;
And they are held as sinners,
Who work at all, except to bake
Beans for Sunday dinners.

THE RAGING KANAWL.

Tune—Enniskillen Dragoon.

COME listen to my story, ye landsmen, one and all,
And I'll sing to you the dangers of the raging Canal:
For I am one of many who expects a watery grave,
For I've been at the mercies of the winds and the waves.

We left Albany harbour about the break of day;
If rightly I remember 'twas the second day of May;
We trusted to our driver, altho' he was but small,
Yet he knew all the windings of that raging Canal.

It seemed as if the Devil had work in hand that night,
For our oil it was all gone, and our lamps they gave no light,
The clouds began to gather, and the rain began to fall,
And I wished myself far away from that raging Canal.

The Captain told the driver to hurry with all speed—
And his orders were obeyed, for he soon cracked up his lead;
With the fastest kind of towing we allowed by twelve o'clock,
We should be in old Schnectady right bang against the dock.

But sad was the fate of our poor devoted barque,
For the rain kept pouring faster, and the night it grew more
        dark;
The horses gave a stumble, and the driver gave a squall,
And they tumbled head and heels into that raging Canal.

The Captain came on deck, with a voice so clear and sound,
Crying, Cut the horses loose, my boys, or I swear we'll all be
        drowned;
The driver paddled to the shore, altho' he was but small,
While the horses sank to rise no more in that raging Canal.

17

The **Cook** she rung her hands, and she came upon the deck,
Saying, Alas! what will become of us, our boat it is a wreck!
The steersman laid her over, for he was a man of sense,
When the bowsman jumped ashore, he lashed her to the fence.

We had a load of Dutch, and we stowed them in the Hole;
They were not the least concerned about the welfare of their
      Soul;
The Captain went below, and implored them for to pray,
But the only answer he could get was, *Nix kom Raus, nix fis
      staa!*

The **Captain** came on deck with a spy glass in his hand,
But the night it was so dark he could not *diskiver* land;
He said to us, with a faltering voice, while tears began to fall,
Prepare to meet your death, my boys, this night on the Canal!

The **Cook** she being kind-hearted, she loaned us an old dress,
Which we raised upon a setting-pole as a signal of distress;
We agreed with Restoration aboard the Boat to bide,
And never quit her deck whilst a plank hung to her side.

It was our good fortune, about the break of day,
The storm it did abate, and a boat came by that way,
Our signal was discovered, and they hove along side,
And we all jumped aboard and for Buffalo did ride.

I landed in Buffalo about twelve o'clock;
The first place I went to was down upon the dock;
I wanted to go up the lake, but it looked rather squally,
When along came *Fred Emmons* and his friend *Billy Bally*.

Says *Fred*, How do you do, and whar have you been so long?
Says I, For the last fortnight I've been on the Canal,
For it stormed all the time, and thar was the devil to pay,
When we got in Tonawandy Creek, we thar was cast away.

Now, says *Fred*, let me tell you how to manage wind and
      weather;
In a storm hug to the tow-path, and then lay feather to feather,
And when the weather is bad, and the wind it blows a gale,
Just jump ashore, knock down a horse—that's taking in the
      sail.

And if you wish to see both sides of the Canal,
To steer your course to Buffalo, and that right true and well,
And should it be so foggy that you cannot see the track,
Just call the driver aboard and hitch a lantern on his back.

WHAT ARE YOU GOING TO STAND?

Tune—Nice Young Man.

QUEER sayings are now all the go,
  You cannot say I'm wrong;
But here is one I'd have you know,
  I've worked up in a song.
Where'er I go, in every street,
  I'm shook, sirs, by the hand,
No matter who it is I meet,
  It's Come, what are you going to stand?

This morn I went to get some cash,
  To swell at the west end,
Resolved I was to cut a dash,
  I met with an old friend:
I told him of the errand I'd been,
  He shook me by the hand,
I'm glad to hear it, old boy, says he,
  Come, what are you going to stand?

Says I, I doesn't mind a drop,
  My spirits it will rouse,
So off we toddled to a shop,
  Quite near to ——r's house.
Inside a lot began to shout,
  As if it had been planned:
But it is not oft we catch you out,
  Come, what are you going to stand?

My expenses amounted to a dollar,
  My cash was growing shorter,
The liquor now down they did swallow
  As though it had been water.
Just then a gal my arm did pinch,
  Her hide I could have tanned,
Says she, For old acquaintance sake,
  Come, what are you going to stand?

Egad, thinks I, this will not do,
  So I bolted from the lot,
But run against a man I knew,
  Ere a hundred yards I got.
I told him of the set I left,
  Says he, I understand,
Now since you've escaped from such a crew,
  Come, what are you going to stand?

My song I will conclude with this,
  You'll all agree I think,
That this, my friends, is quite the age
  Of intellect for drink.
So, when the boys put out the lights,
  I'll take the manager by the hand,
There's been a devilish good house to-night,
  Old boy, come, what are you going to stand?

WHEN I WAS OUT A SLEIGHING.

It snowed so hard the other day,
I could not work, I could not play,
And so I hired a horse and sleigh,
        Resolved to go a-sleighing.

I soon put on my Sunday clothes,
And round to Sally Russell's goes,
And to her I did propose,
That she would ride while yet it snows.
She very soon gave her consent,
But as my money was most spent,
Tim Bobbin to me three dollars lent,
        All for to go a-sleighing.

With bells a-ringing all the way,
Money spent and thrown away,
Oh, there is the devil to pay,
        When a man goes out a-sleighing.

As up the Main Street I did glide,
With Sally Russell by my side,
To cut a dash both of us tried,
        When we went out a-sleighing.

But some naughty boys to raise a din,
To snowball us they did begin,
One mashed my hat down o'er my chin,
Then stove Miss Russell's bonnet in.
Miss Russell she began to cry,
I turned around to say, oh, fie,
When a snow ball banged me in the eye,
    When I was out a-sleighing.
    Bells a-ringing all the way, &c.

I'd been very glad to turn back,
Because one of my eyes were black.
But we followed up the railroad track,
    Resolved to finish sleighing.

At something next our horse took fright,
And started off with all his might,
He banged the sleigh both left and right,
And sent Miss Russell in a snow bank tight.
The horse with me away he sped,
And left Miss Russell nearly dead,
And the wind blew the false curls all off her head,
    When we went out a-sleighing.
    Bells a-ringing all the way, &c.

For assistance Sally she did shout,
While I managed to turn the horse about,
But cursed the hour that I came out,
    To go with her a-sleighing.

To get her out, Sal did me tease,
And soon I went to her release,
But it is a wonder she didn't freeze,
For she stuck fast in snow up to her knees.
But what was worse for poor Miss Russell,
In the snow amid the tussle,
The strings they broke, and she lost her bustle,
    When I was out a-sleighing,
    Bells a-ringing all the way, &c.

We started home with heavy hearts,
When there came along two butchers' carts,
And smashed our sleigh in twenty parts,
    When I was out a-sleighing.

So since our horse and sleigh was gone,
Poor Sal and I had to walk home,
And for the damages we done,
I had to pay a pretty sum.
But my bills are paid and all is right,
And folks, when you go home to-night,
Oh, think upon my doleful plight,
      But don't go out a-sleighing.
      Bells a-ringing all the way, &c.

HERE'S SUCCESS TO TODDY.

A POPULAR CONVIVIAL SONG.

HERE'S success to Toddy,
  Drink it down, drink it down,
Here's success to Toddy,
  Drink it down, drink it down,
Oh, here's success to Toddy,
For it cheers both soul and body.
Then here's success to Toddy,
  Drink it down, drink it down.

Here's success to Wine,
  Drink it down, drink it down,
Here's success to Wine,
  Drink it down, drink it down,
Oh, here's success to Wine,
For it makes you feel so fine,
Then here's success to Wine,
  Drink it down, drink it down.

Here's success to Sherry,
  Drink it down, drink it down,
Here's success to Sherry,
  Drink it down, drink it down,
Oh, here's success to Sherry,
For it makes the heart so merry,
Then here's success to Sherry,
  Drink it down, drink it down.

Here's success to Whiskey,
  Drink it down, drink it down,
Here's success to Whiskey,
  Drink it down, drink it down,
Oh, here's success to Whiskey,
For it makes you feel so frisky,
Then here's success to Whiskey,
  Drink it down, drink it down.

Here's success to Punch,
  Drink it down, drink it down,
Here's success to Punch,
  Drink it down, drink it down,
Oh, here's success to Punch,
With some good friends in a bunch,
Then here's success to Punch,
  Drink it down, drink it down.

Here's success to Gin,
  Drink it down, drink it down,
Here's success to Gin,
  Drink it down, drink it down,
Oh, here's success to Gin,
For it makes the heart to grin,
Then here's success to Gin,
  Drink it down, drink it down.

Here's success to Brandy,
  Drink it down, drink it down,
Here's success to Brandy,
  Drink it down, drink it down,
Oh, here's success to Brandy,
For it makes you feel so handy,
Then here's success to Brandy,
  Drink it down, drink it down.

Here's success to Port,
  Drink it down, drink it down,
Here's success to Port,
  Drink it down, drink it down,
Oh, here's success to Port,
But let it be of the right sort,
Then here's success to Port,
  Drink it down, drink it down.

Here's success to Beer,
  Drink it down, drink it down,
Here's success to Beer,
  Drink it down, drink it down,
Oh, here's success to Beer,
The thirsty soul to cheer,
Then here's success to Beer,
  Drink it down, drink it down.

Here's success to Ale,
  Drink it down, drink it down,
Here's success to Ale,
  Drink it down, drink it down,
Oh, here's success to Ale,
That will make you strong and hale,
Then here's success to Ale,
  Drink it down, drink it down.

Here's success to Porter,
  Drink it down, drink it down,
Here's success to Porter,
  Drink it down, drink it down,
Oh, here's success to Porter,
Of strength a true supporter,
Then here's success to Porter,
  Drink it down, drink it down.

Here's success to Lager,
  Drink it down, drink it down,
Here's success to Lager,
  Drink it down, drink it down,
Oh, here's success to Lager,
For it does not make you stagger,
Then here's success to Lager,
  Drink it down, drink it down.

Here's success to Cider,
  Drink it down, drink it down,
Here's success to Cider,
  Drink it down, drink it down,
Oh, here's success to Cider,
For it makes the mirth flow wider,
Then here's success to Cider,
  Drink it down, drink it down.

Here's success to Water,
  Drink it down, drink it down.
Here's success to Water,
  Drink it down, drink it down,
Oh, here's success to Water,
On the earth's remotest quarter,
Then here's success to Water,
  Drink it down, drink it down.

Here's success to Water,
That brings no care or slaughter,
Here's success to Water,
  Drink it down, drink it down,
Oh, here's success to Water,
'Tis the noblest drink in nature,
Then here's success to Water,
  Drink it down, drink it down.

GREAT HEN CONVENTION.

A FAMOUS Hen convention was held at Humbug green,
And such a show of fuss and feathers ne'er before was seen,
With Malays, Bantams, Chittys, and Game fowls fine and tall,
But Mister Rooster Shanghai cut the biggest swell of all.
Chorus—
It was cackle, cackle, cackle, cackle, flap your wings and crow,
Shanghai crowed the highest at the great convention show,
Tuck, tuck, tuck, tuck, tuck, tuck, tuck, tuck,
Ti taa, tuck, tuck, ti taa, tuck, tuck,
Tuck, tuck, tuck, tuck, tuck, tuck, tuck, tuck.
Spoken—Shanghai's crow, all crow.

Says Malay, pulling out his gills, " I am the fairest fowl,"
Says Bantam, " You're a hen pecked race, hen hearted with no
        soul,"
Says Shanghai, " You poor Bantams are a race of chicken toys,"
Says Bantam, "If you peck at me you'll find I'm one of the
        b'hoys."
Chorus—
A poultry duel came on straight, 'twas Banty and Shanghai,
A crow at first, and then a clip, and then the feathers fly,
Young Banty spurr'd him flat amid a loud convention crow,
But Shanghai crowed the lowest at the great convention show.

NOTHING AT ALL.

In Derry down dale when I wanted a mate,
I went with my daddy, a courting of Kate,
With my nosegay so fine, in my holy-day clothes,
My hands in my pocket, a courting I goes.
The weather was cold, and my bosom was hot,
My heart in a gallop—my mare in a trot;
Now I was so bashful, so loving withal,
My tongue stuck to my mouth, and I said
                              Nothing at all.

When I came to the house, I look'd bashful and grum,
The knocker I held 'twixt my finger and thumb,
Rap went the knocker, Kate show'd her chin,
She chuckled and buckled, I bow'd and went in.
Now I was as bashful as bashful could be,
And Kitty, poor soul, was as bashful as me;
So I laugh'd, and I grinn'd, and I let my hat fall,
Giggled, scratched my head, and said
                              Nothing at all.

If bashful was I, the more bashful the maid,
She simper'd and sigh'd, with her apron strings play'd;
The old folks impatient to have the thing done,
Agreed that my Kitty and I should be one.
So, then we young ones both nodded consent,
Then hand in hand to get married we went,
When we answered the parson, in voices so small,
You scarce could have heard us say
                              Nothing at all.

But mark what a change in the course of a week,
My Kate left off blushing, I boldly could speak;
Could play with my Kitty, and laugh at a jest,
And Kate could talk, ay too, as well as the best.
And talk'd of past follies, we oft have declar'd,
To encourage young folks, who at wedlock are scar'd;
For if to your aid some assurance you call,
You may kiss and get married, and it's
                              Nothing at all.

OUR MARY ANN.

Oh, fare you well, my own Mary Ann,
  Fare you well for a while,
The ship is ready, and the wind is fair,
  And I am bound for the sea, Mary Ann.

Oh, didn't you see your *turtile* dove,
  A sittin' on yonder pile,
Lamenting the loss of his own true love,
  And so am I for my Mary Ann.
            Oh, fare you well, &c.

A lobster in a lobster pot,
  A blue fish on a hook,
May suffer some—but you know not,
  What I do feel for my Mary Ann.
            Oh, fare you well, &c.

The pride of all the produce ground,
  The dinner kitchen-garden fruit,
Is *pumpkins* some, but can't compare
  The love I bear for my Mary Ann.
        Oh, fare you well, &c.
                    BARNEY WILLIAMS.

A CHAPTER OF GOOD THINGS.

A GLASS is good and a lass is good,
  And a pipe to smoke in cold weather ;
The world it is good, and the people are good,
  And we're all good fellows together.
A bottle it is a very good thing,
  With a good deal of very good wine in it;
A song is good, when a body can sing,
  And to finish we must begin it.
A table is good, when spread with good cheer,
  And good company sitting round it ;
When a good way off, we are not very near,
  And for sorrow the devil confound it.
            A glass is good, &c.

A friend is good, when you're out of good luck,
    For that's a good time to try him;
For a justice good, the haunch of a buck,
    With such a good present you buy him.
A wife is good when she's good to her man,
    If not she's good for nothing;
A home is good if its only a pen,
    Where good content comes soothing.
                A glass is good, &c.

THE COVE WHAT SPOUTS.

I WILL tell you in my song what happened the other night,
Not detain you long, and in that you will say I am right;
My name is—no matter what, and I don't live here abouts,
But I am welcome everywhere, for I am the cove what spouts.
                Ri tol de, &c.

At the theatre the other night Booth did Richard play,
" Down, down to hell," he cried; poor Harry soon gave way,
That night I got so drunk, in a tavern I let out,
" Give me another horse, bind—" like Richard I did spout.
                Ri tol de, &c.

A watchman took me up, to the station-house he led,
And in a dirty cell, made me sleep without a bed;
In a phrenzy I arose, seized another by the snout,
" Give me my pound of flesh," like Shylock I did spout.
                Ri tol de, &c.

" Oh, murder! help!" he cried; the people flocked around,
But I was remorseless, and stuck up for my pound;
The policemen they run in, while the blood from his snout
    run out,
" Blood, blood, Iago," like Othello I did spout.
                Ri tol de, &c.

A policeman collar'd me, the nose I had to quit,
But soon I turned on him, and between the eyes I hit,
With such a murderous whack, it made him roar and shout,
" Come on, come on, Macduff," like Macbeth I did spout.
                Ri tol de, &c.

“Oh, murder! help!” he cried; the policemen in did **pour,**
And in a combined attack **got me** down upon the floor;
Said they, “We’ve .got **you now,** you shall suffer **too,** no
    doubt.”
“Lay me in the grave **with Juliet,”** like **Romeo I did spout.**
    Ri tol de, &c.

Next morning before the Mayor, they took me to be tried,
And there, with looks severe, me his honor quickly eyed;
Said he, “Pray who are you that dare kick up such a rout?”
“I am thy father’s ghost,” from Hamlet I did spout.
    Ri tol de, &c.

The people laughed at me, his honor looked amazed,
“My father’s ghost!” said he; why the man is surely crazed;
“For three months **lock him up, it’s not safe to let him out,”**
They gave me thirty days below, **for showing them how to**
    spout.

    Ri tol de, &c.

WE’RE ALL CUTTING;

OR THE WAY THROUGH LIFE.

Air.—“Nervous Family.”

WE’RE all cutting—cut, **cut, cutting,**
We are all cutting our **way through** life;
Dame nature cuts **out man, to cut his way** through life,
So being termed a cutter, **we’ll compare him** to a knife;
The little baby blade has scarce begun **to** breathe,
When a cutting it begins, you know, **by** cutting of its teeth.
Chorus.—So we’re all cutting—cut, **cut, cutting,**
    So **we’re** all cutting **our** way through life.

Childhood’s a doll’s knife, quite delicate and pretty,
And parents love their little ones **to** be consider’d smart;
To learn their A. B. C.—the first book the parent puts
Into the hands of a child, is **a** book quite full of *cuts;*
Then follows cutting horses, cutting hoops, and cutting tops—
Its cutting once begun, you know, its cutting never stops.
    So we’re all cutting, &c.

Boyhood is a cheese-knife, only fit for minor uses,
Requiring some management to bend it to your will;
He follows running coaches, to show the cutting times,
And if you sing out, Cut before, he sings out, Cut behind;
And as the youth grows older, the girls begin to bother,
He falls in love with one girl, and he cuts her for another.
      So we're all cutting, &c.

The beau is a blade set in a buckhorn handle,
Who soon will cut his tailor, if he does not cut out smart;
His only endeavor is, through life to cut a figure,
Behold now on horseback, how he cuts along with vigor;
And as he walks the streets, he seems to ask each belle,
Oh, hang it, charming creature, don't you think I cut a
    swell?
      So we're all cutting, &c.

Ladies they are fruit knives, set in pearl and ivory,
Cutting up the hearts of men according to deserts;
At opera or playhouse, at a ball or at a rout,
Their only endeavor is, to cut each other out;
The coquette she cuts many hearts to the core,
And the widow is for cutting out one loving husband more.
      So we're all cutting, &c.

PHILOSOPHY.

OR TWO SIDES OF THE WAY.

Air.—" Judy's Black Eyes."

'Tis a folly to think of life's troubles,
  There's always two sides of the way;
If one be in the shade the chance doubles,
  The other looks cheerful and gay.
We know it looks sad to be sighing,
  Yet there's good in it, wisdom decides;
For the man who with grief thinks he's dying,
  With laughter will ne'er crack his sides.
    'Tis a folly, &c.

If a man all his teeth chance to lack,
  He's sure they won't give him no pain;
If a man has no coat to his back,
  He's sure it won't spoil with the rain.
If a man has no money to mind,
  He may save the expense of a purse;
And if a man's perfectly blind,
  He's sure that his sight won't grow worse.
      'Tis a folly, &c.

If a man has but one shirt at most,
  There's no trouble to think which he'll use;
And the man who's as deaf as a post,
  Will never hear unwelcome news.
If light-headed, why still we are right,
  For there's comfort to think it not madness;
And the man who gets drunk day and night,
  He never will feel sober sadness.
      'Tis a folly, &c.

To be without hands, though no blessing,
  Thus some good economy proves;
Though awkward we find it when dressing,
  We ne'er can be in want of new gloves.
To be without legs, though queer talking,
  We can ne'er break our shins, it is plain;
For the man who's no feet to go walking,
  Won't be troubled with chilblains again.
      'Tis a folly, &c.

If but little your own you can call,
  'Tis quite certain but little you'll pay;
And if you've got nothing at all,
  You're sure they won't take it away.
Strange stories may find new upholders,
  But one thing you'll grant, which is that,
If a man has no head on his shoulders,
  He won't care a d——n for a hat.
      'Tis a folly, &c.

HARD TIMES.

As sung by Dan. Gardiner, the Clown.

COME listen awhile and give ear to my song,
Concerning these hard times, it will not take you long,
How every one is trying each other to bite,
And in cheating each other they swear they do right.
      In these very hard times,
         And it is nothing but hard times wherever we go.

The baker will cheat you in the bread that you eat,
And so will the butcher in the weight of his meat,
He will tip up the steelyards to make them go down,
And swear it is weight when it lacks half a pound.
                    In these very, &c.

The ladies must all have their silks and their laces,
And things they call bonnets to show off their faces,
Their figure however, can never be seen,
For they are hooped like a barrel with French crinoline.
                    In these very, &c.

There is the tinker, he will mend all your ware,
For little or nothing, some ale, or some beer,
But before he begins he will get half drunk or more,
And in stopping one hole he will punch twenty more.
                    In these very, &c.

Oh, there is the barber who lathers for pelf,
He will shave every blockhead that can't shave himself,
A dime he will have from his friends or his foes,
Or else he will never let go of your nose.
                    In these very, &c.

There is the doctor, he will cure all your ills,
With his puffs, and his powders, his syrup of squills,
He will give you a dose that will make you grow fat,
Or some pills that will leave but your boots and your hat.
                    In these very, &c.

The judge on his bench so honest and true,
He will stare at a man as though he would look him through,
He will send you a year or six months to the jail,
And for five dollars more, why he will go your bail.
                    In these very, &c.

Oh, there are the ladies, the sweet little dears,
At the balls and the parties how nice they appear,
With whalebones and corsets themselves they will squeeze,
And you have to unlace them before they can sneeze.

In these very, &c.

There are the lawyers, I had almost forgot,
They are the very worst ones that we have in the lot,
They will cheat, lie, and swindle. and say they do right,
And for one dime apiece they will steal sheep in the night.

In these very, &c.

The last is the sheriff, who thinks himself wise,
He will come to your house with a big pack of lies,
He will take all your property that he can sell,
Get drunk on the money, or cut a great swell.

In these very, &c.

THE DAYS WHEN I WAS HARD UP.

In the days when I was hard up,
  Not many months ago,
I suffered that which only can
  The sons of misery know.
Relations, friends, companions,
  They all turned up their nose,
And rated me a vagabond,
  For want of better clothes.

Chorus.

In the days when I was hard up,
  In want of food and fire,
I used to tie my shoes up
  With little bits of wire.
When hungry, cold, cast on a rock,
  And could not get a meal,
Oh! how I beat the devil down,
  For tempting me to steal!

18

In the days when I was **hard up**
  For furniture and drugs,
Many a summer's eve I've held
  Communion with the bugs;
I never faced them with a pike,
  Or mashed them on the wall,
I said the world was wide enough—
  Here's room enough for all.

In the days when I was hard up,
  I used to lock my door,
For fear my landlady would say
  You can lodge here no more.
But from out my own back drawing room,
  That is ten feet by six,
In the work house wall just opposite,
  I've counted all the bricks.

In the days when I was hard up,
  I felt my spirits lower,
And often have I sought a friend
  To borrow half a dollar.
How many are there in this world
  Whose evils I can scan,
The fancy suits that they do wear,
  But cannot see the man !

In the days when I was hard up,
  I had a blissful hope,
'Tis all a poor man's heritage,
  To save him from the rope;
But I found this good old maxim,
  And this shall be my plan,
If I should wear a ragged coat,
  I'll wear it like a man.

THE MIGHTY DOLLAR OR TWO.

WITH cautious steps, as we tread our way through
This intricate world, as other folks do,
May we still on our journey be able to view
The benevolent face of a "Dollar or Two."
For an excellent thing is a "Dollar or Two;"
No friend is so true as a "Dollar or Two."
Through country or town, as we pass up and down,
No passport so good as a "Dollar or Two."

Would you read yourself out of the bachelor crew,
And the hand of a female divinity sue,
You must always be ready the handsome to do,
Although it should cost you a "Dollar or Two."
Love's arrows are tipped with a "Dollar or Two;"
And affection is gained by a "Dollar or Two;"
The best aid you can meet in advancing your suit,
Is the eloquent chink of a "Dollar or Two."

Would you wish your existence with faith to imbue,
And enrolled in the ranks of the sanctified few,
To earn a good name and a well-cushioned pew,
You must freely come down with a "Dollar or Two."
A lawsuit is gained by a "Dollar or Two;"
And rogues are oft cleared by a "Dollar or Two;"
You may sin some at times, but the worst of all crimes
Is to find yourself short of a "Dollar or Two."

If you wish a fat post that will *pay* pretty true,
Or a lever to put a new *dodge* neatly through,
To bring legislative folks down to your view,
'Tis but to come down with a "Dollar or Two."
For an office is bought by a "Dollar or Two,"
A battle's oft won by a "Dollar or Two,"
Few people will care how you live—what you do,
Whilst you show them "the almighty DOLLAR OR Two."

TEA IN THE ARBOR.

WHAT pleasure folks feel when they live out of town,
 In the culture of turnips and flowers,
And getting a friend now and then to come down,
 To look at their walks and their bowers;
And such is the taste of some dear friends of mine,
 Mister, Mistress, and Miss Mary Barbor,
Who will oft have me come to their villa to dine,
 And then to take tea in the arbor;
  Where there are sweet lilies and daffydowndillies,
   Perfume like the shop of a barber;
  And roses and posies to scent up your noses,
   Then come and take tea in the arbor.

As oft as I can I decline their invite,
 For of rural delights I'm no lover;
Of insects and reptiles I can't bear the sight,
 Oh! they e'er make me shudder all over:
And when I went there a great frog made me **jump,**
 Which was excellent fun to Miss Barbor,
Then there was a long caterpillar fell plump
 In my first cup of tea in the arbor.

Of little green flies on my dress came a host,
 And a bee put me all in a flutter;
A great daddy-long-legs stuck fast on my toast
 And left one of his limbs in the butter:
On the sugar six blue-bottles sat hob-a-nob,
 And while I discoursed with old Barbor,
From above a black spider swung bibbity-bob
 In my chops, as I sat in the arbor.

In the fields at our back, boys were shooting at crows,
 And a shot coming through, I was wounded;
To expostulate with them of course I arose,
 And I climb'd up the pailings that bounded:
When behold my nankeens were bedaub'd and crossbarr'd;
 "Oh, I ought to be flogg'd," said old Barbor,
"I neglected to tell you the pailings were tarr'd,
 When I asked you to tea in the arbor."

Then I happened to tread where a man trap was set,
  Which snapping, my leg held fast in, sir,
And ere I got out, it came on heavy wet,
  And I was soaked through to the skin, sir:
In a very bad temper I homeward did jog,
  Next morning I wrote to Miss Barbor,
That smashed in my pocket I found the big frog,
  That frightened me first in the arbor.
      And tho' there be lilies and daffydowndillies,
        Said I, in my note to Miss Barbor,
      And roses perfuming, excuse me from coming,
        Again to take tea in the arbor.

"OUT," OR HOW TO DO THE DUNS.

Out John, out John, what are you about, John?
If you don't say *out* at once, you make the fellow doubt, John.
Say I'm out whoever calls, and hide my hat and cane, John;
Say you've not the *least* idea when I shall come again, John,
Let the people leave their bills, but tell them not to call, John,
Say I'm courting Miss Rupee, and mean to pay them all, John.
  Out John, run John, what are you about, John?
  If you don't say *out* at once, you make the fellow doubt, John.

Run John, run John, there's another dun, John,
If it's Podger bid him call to-morrow week at one, John,
If he says he saw me at the window as he knock'd, John,
Make a face and shake your head and tell him you are shock'd,
    John;
Take your pocket handkerchief, and put it your eye, John,
Say your master's not the man to bid you tell a lie, John.
  Out John, out John, &c.

Oh, John, go John, there's Noodle's knock I know, John;
Tell him that all yesterday you sought him high and low, John;
Tell him just before he came you saw me mount the hill, John:
Say you think I'm *only* gone to pay his little bill, John;
Then I think you'd better add that *if* I miss to-day, John,
You're *sure* I mean to call when next I pass his way, John
  Out John, out John, &c.

Hie John, fly John, I will tell you why, John,
If there is not Grimshaw at the corner, may I die, John,
He will hear of no excuse, I'm sure he'll search the house, John,
Peeping into corners hardly fit to hold a mouse, John.
Beg he'll take a chair and wait, I know he won't refuse, John,
I'll pop through the little door that opens to the mews, John.
 Out John, out John, &c.

WHAT IS A BACHELOR LIKE?

WHY, a pump without a handle,
A mouldy tallow candle!
A goose that's lost his fellows,
A noseless pair of bellows,
A horse without a saddle,
A boat without a paddle;
  A mule—a fool,
  A two-legged stool!
  A pest—a jest!
  Dreary—weary—
  Contrary—unchary—
A fish without a tail,
A ship without a sail,
A legless pair of tongs,
A fork without its prongs,
A clock without a face—
A pig that's out of place!
A bootless leg—an addled egg!
A stupid flat—a crownless hat;
A pair of breeches, wanting stitches!
A chattering ape—coat minus cape!
A quacking duck, wanting pluck!
A gabbling goose—mad dog let loose!
  A boot without a sole,
  Or a cracked and leaky bowl,
  Or a fiddle without a string,
  Or a bee without its sting,
  Or a bat—or a sprat,
  Or a cat—or a hen,
  Or a rat—or a wren,
  Or a gnat—or a pig in a pen!

Or a thrush that will not sing!
Or a bell that will not ring!
Or a penny that "won't go!"
Or a herring without roe!
Or a line without a lead!
Or a drum without a head!
Or a monkey—or a donkey!
Or a surley dog, tied to a log!
Or a frog in a bog!
Or a fly in a mug!
Or a bug in a rug!
Or a bee—or a flea—
Or a last year's pea,
Or a figure 3!
Like a bell without a tongue—
Like a barrel without a bung—
Like a whale—like a snail—
Like an owl—like a fowl—
Like a priest without his cowl!
Like a midnight ghoul—
Like a gnome in his cell—
Like a clapperless bell—
Like a man down in a well,
He's a poor forsaken gander,
Choosing lonely thus to wander!
He's like a walking stick, or satchel, or——
But to be plain,
And end my strain,
He's like nought but—a BACHELOR!

HERE'S TO THE MAIDEN.

HERE'S to the maiden of bashful fifteen,
Likewise, to the widow of fifty;
Here's to the bold and extravagant quean,
And here's to the housewife that's thrifty.
Let the toast pass,
Drink to the lass,
I warrant she'll prove an excuse for the glass.
Let the toast pass, &c.

Here's to the maiden whose dimples we **prize**,
    Likewise to her that has none, sir,
Here's to the maid with a pair of black eyes,
    And here's to her that's but one, sir.
        Let the toast pass, &c.

Here's to the maid with a bosom of snow,
    And to her that's as brown as a berry;
Here's to the wife with a face full of woe,
    And here's to the girl that is merry.
        Let the toast pass, &c.

Let her be clumsy, or let her be slim
    Young or ancient, I care not a feather;
So fill a pint bumper quite up to the **brim,**
    And e'en let us toast them together.
        Let the toast pass, &c.

R. B. SHERIDAN.

ETHIOPIAN SONGS.

GENTLE JENNIE GRAY.

My heart is sad, I'll tell you why,
  If you'll listen to my lay,
Which makes me weep, when **e'er I sing,**
  Of my gentle Jennie Gray;
But I never can forget the days,
  When with Jennie by my side,
We talked **of love** and happiness,
  When she should **be my** bride.
Chorus.—Hush the banjo, **toll the** bell,
    I'm very sad to-day,
    I cannot work, so let me weep,
    For my gentle Jennie Gray.

My Jennie **had** the sweetest face,
  And eyes of sparkling jet,
With lips like new-born roses,
  She was **my darling pet**;
But Death, he called one morning,
  And took **my** love away,
And **left me** lonely weeping,
  For my gentle Jennie Gray.
    Hush the banjo, **&c.**

And in the ground they laid her,
    Close by my cabin door ;
A rude stone marks the spot,
    Where she sleeps to wake no more ;
While at her grave I'm weeping,
    At every close of day,
I fancy then, she's sleeping,
    And not dead ! my Jennie Gray.
        Hush the banjo, &c.

OLD FOLKS AT HOME.

WAY down upon the Swanee ribber,
    Far, far away ;
Dere's wha my heart is turning ebber,
    Dere's wha de old folks stay.
All up and down the whole creation,
    Sadly I roam ;
Still longing for de old plantation,
    And for de old folks at home.
Chorus.—All de world am sad and dreary,
        Ebery where I roam ;
        Oh ! darkies, how my heart grows weary,
        Far from de old folks at home.

All round de little farm I wandered,
    When I was young ;
Den many happy days I squandered,
    Many de songs I sung.
When I was playing wid my brudder,
    Happy was I ;
Oh ! take me to my kind old mudder,
    Dere let me live and die.
        All de world am sad and dreary, &c.

One little hut among de bushes,
    One dat I love ;
Still sadly to my memory rushes,
    No matter where I rove.
When will I see the bees a humming,
    All round de comb ?
When will I hear the banjo tumming,
    Down in my good old home ?
        All de world am sad and dreary, &c.

NELLY GRAY.

There's a low green valley on the old Kentucky shore,
  There I've whiled many happy hours away,
A sitting and a singing by the little cottage door,
  Where lived my darling Nelly Gray.
Chorus.—
      Oh, my poor Nelly Gray, they have taken you away,
        And I'll never see my darling any more,
      I'm sitting by the river, and I'm weeping all the day,
        For you've gone from old Kentucky shore.

When the moon had climb'd the mountain, and the stars were
        shining too,
    Then I'd take my darling Nelly Gray,
And we'd float down the river in my little canoe—
    While my banjo sweetly I would play.
        Oh, my poor Nelly Gray, &c.

One night I went to see her, but the neighbors bid me stay,
    An' that I should never see her more;
That they had taken her far, far away,
    Far from de old Kentucky shore.
        Oh, my poor Nelly Gray, &c.

My canoe is under water, and my banjo is unstrung,
    I'm tired of living any more;
My eyes shall look downward, and my songs shall be unsung,
    While I stay on old Kentucky shore.
        Oh, my poor Nelly Gray, &c.

My eyes are getting blinded, and I cannot see my way,
    Hark! there's somebody knocking at the door;
Oh, I hear the angels calling, and I see my Nelly Gray;
    Farewell to the old Kentucky shore.
Chorus.—
    Oh, my Nelly Gray, up in heaven there they say,
      That they will never take you from me any more;
    I'm a coming, coming, coming, as the angels clear the way,
      Farewell to the old Kentucky shore.

MASSA'S IN THE COLD, COLD GROUND.

ROUND the meadows am a ringing,
  The darkies' mournful song,
While the mocking-bird is singing,
  Happy as the day is long.
Where the ivy is a creeping,
  O'er the grassy mound,
There old massa is a sleeping,
  Sleeping in the cold, cold ground.
Chorus.—Down in the corn-field,
      Hear that mournful sound ;
    All the darkies are a weeping—
      Massa's in the cold, cold ground.

When the autumn leaves were falling,
  When the days were cold,
'Twas hard to hear old massa calling,
  'Cause he was so weak and old.
Now the orange tree is blooming
  On the sandy shore,
Now the summer days are coming,
  Massa never calls no more.
      Down in the corn-field, &c.

Massa made the darkies love him,
  He always was so kind,
Now they sadly weep above him,
  Mourning, for he leave them behind.
I cannot work before to-morrow,
  So many tear-drops flow,
I try to drive away my sorrow,
  Picking on the old banjo.
      Down in the corn-field, &c.

DOLLY DAY.

I've told you 'bout de banjo,
 De fiddle and de bow,
Likewise about the cotton field,
 De shubble and de hoe;
I've sung about the bulgine,
 Dat blow the folks away,
An' now I'll sing a little song,
 About my Dolly Day.
Oh, Dolly Day looks so gay,
 I run all round and round,
To hear her fairy footsteps play,
 As she comes o'er de ground.

I like to see de clober
 Dat grows about de lane,
I like to see de 'bacco plant,
 I like de sugar cane;
But on de ole plantation
 Dar's nothing half so gay,
Dar's nothing dat I love so much
 As my sweet Dolly Day.
 Oh, Dolly Day, &c.

When de work is ober,
 I make de banjo play,
An' while I strike the dulcem notes,
 I tink ob Dolly Day.
Her form am like a posy—
 De lily of the vale,
Her voice am far de sweetest sound
 Dat floats upon de gale.
 Oh, Dolly Day, &c.

Massa gib me money
 To buy a peck of corn,
I'se gwine to marry Dolly Day,
 And build myself a barn;
Den when I'm old an' feeble,
 An' when my head am gray,
I'll trabble down de hill ob life,
 Along wid Dolly Day.
 Oh, Dolly Day, &c.

FAREWELL, MY LILLY DEAR.

Oh! Lilly, dear, it grieves me,
  The tale I have to tell;
Old Massa sent me roaming,
  So Lilly, fare you well!
Oh! fare you well my true love,
  Farewell old Tennessee,
Then let me weep for you, love,
  But do not weep for me.
Chorus—Farewell for ever to old Tennessee,
      Farewell, my Lilly dear, don't weep for me.

I's going to roam the wide world
  In lands I've never hoed,
With nothing but my banjo
  To cheer me on the road;
And when I'm sad and weary
  I'll make the banjo play,
To 'mind me of my true love
  When I am far away.
      Farewell for ever, &c.

I wake up in the morning,
  And walk out on the farm,
Oh! Lilly am a darling—
  She takes me by the arm.
We wander through the clover
  Down by the river side,
I tell her that I love her,
  And she must be my bride
      Farewell for ever, &c.

Oh! Lilly, dear, 'tis mournful
  To leave you here alone;
You'll smile before I leave you,
  And weep when I am gone.
The sun can never shine, love,
  So bright for you and me,
As when I worked beside you
  In good old Tennessee.
      Farewell for ever, &c.

AINT I GLAD TO GET OUT OF THE WILDER-NESS?

Music— **Tum, Tum,** Tum, Tum,
Chorus— Ahaa—Ahaa—Ahaa—Ahaa.
Solo— Way down south in **Beaver Creek,**
In Beaver **Creek,** in Beaver Creek,
De niggers—dey grow about ten **feet,**
  Way **down in** Alabam.
Chorus— Oh, aint I glad **we** get **out of the wilderness,**
Out of **the** wilderness?
Oh, aint **we glad we got out** of the wilderness,
  And left **old Alabam?**
    [Symphony **with** Dance as above.]

Solo— **Dey wet de** ground **wid** bacca smoke,
Wid bacca smoke, wid bacca and smoke,
When out of de ground dar **heads do poke,**
  Way down in Alabam.
    Dance & Chorus—Oh, aint **I** glad, &c.

Solo— My **wife's dead, an' I'll** get anuder one,
I'll **get** anuder one, I'll **get anuder one,**
My **wife's dead, an' I'll** get **anuder one,**
  Way **down** in Alabam.
    Oh, aint **I** glad, &c.

Solo— I met a catfish **in de ribber,**
In de ribber, in de **ribber.**
I golly, it made dis **nigger** shiver,
  Way down in Alabam.
    Oh, **aint I** glad, &c.

Solo— I steered right **straight for de** critter's snout,
De critter's snout, de critter's snout,
Turned the catfish inside **out,**
  Way down in Alabam.
    Oh, aint I glad, &c.

Solo— Oh, here we go now altogether,
All together, all together,
Nebber mind de wind or wedder,
  Way down in Alabam.
    Oh, aint I glad, &c.

WAIT FOR THE WAGON.

WILL you come with me my Phillis, dear, to yon blue moun-
    tain free,
Where the blossoms smell the sweetest, come rove along with
    me ?
It's ev'ry Sunday morning, when I am by your side,
We'll jump into the wagon, and all take a ride.
       Chorus.—Wait for the wagon,
           Wait for the wagon,
           Wait for the wagon,
             And we'll all take a ride.

Where the river runs like silver, and the birds they sing so
    sweet,
I have a cabin, Phillis, and something good to eat.
Come listen to my story, it will relieve my heart,
So jump into the wagon, and off we will start.
          Wait for the wagon, &c.

Do you believe, my Phillis, dear, old Mike with all his
    wealth,
Can make you half so happy, as I with youth and health ?
We'll have a little farm, a horse, a pig, and cow,
And you will mind the dairy, while I do guide the plough.
          Wait for the wagon, &c.

Your lips are red as poppies, your hair so slick and neat,
All braided up with dahlias, and hollyhocks so sweet.
It's ev'ry Sunday morning, when I am by your side,
We'll jump into the wagon, and all take a ride.
          Wait for the wagon, &c.

Together on life's journey, we'll travel till we stop,
And if we have no trouble, we'll reach the happy top.
Then come with me, sweet Phillis, my dear, my lovely bride,
We'll jump into the wagon, and all take a ride.
          Wait for the wagon, &c.

DAN TUCKER, IN FIVE DIALECTS.

Bones.—

 YOUNG DAN TUCKER came to this Metropolis,
 He got a little **tight, an' quite** obstropulous ;
 De Police **caught him by de** shin,
 His **shin slipt off, an' he cut** with a grin.
(*Singing.*)—Get **out de way, old** Dan Tucker,
   Get out de **way, old Dan Tucker,**
   Get out de way, old **Dan** Tucker,
   You're too late to **come to** supper.

Pompey.—

 Young Daniel **Tucker came to** Manhattan,
 In **a** shanghai **shawl, an' a cane** of rattan ;
 His shirt collar saw'd his ears in **two,**
 And he looked like a black sheep's **head in a stew**
   Get out de way, &c.

Dutch.—

 Mynheer **Von** Tucker, shuste come **apout,**
 For **to** sell some **cheese** unde sour **krout** ;
 He trank so much ob de schnapps **und lager peer,**
 Dat he schlipt all apout and hesh **no more here.**
   Kit off de vay Mynheer **Von Tucker.**

French.—

 Monsieur Dan Tuckare **came** down haire,
 To eat some soup an' **ze** *pomme de terre ;*
 Ze soup vas so hot dat **it** freeze his mouse,
 And he kicked ze roof from ze floor of **ze** house.
   Git out ze vay, **Monsieur Tuckare.**

Irish.—

 Misther Daniel Tuckerr came to York,
 To ate roasted pratees boiled on a fork ;
 He swallered the fork and a pratee too,
 And och ! bothern, but it made him cry hubbaboo.
   Get out de **way,** &c.

OH SUSANNA.

I COME from Alabama with my banjo on my knee,
Ise gwine to Lousiana dar my true love for to see.
It rain'd all night de day I left, the weather it was dry,
It snowed so hard I froze to death, Susanna, don't you cry.
Chorus.—

   Oh, Susanna, don't you cry for me,
   Ise come from Alabama, wid my banjo on my knee.
   Oh, Susanna, don't you cry for me,
   For Ise come from Alabama, with the banjo on my knee.

I jump'd aboard de telegraph, and trabelled down de ribber,
De 'lectric fluid magnified, and killed five hundred nigga.
De bulgine bust, de horse run off, I really thought to die,
I shut my eyes to hold my breath, Susanna, don't you cry.
      Oh, Susanna, &c.

I had a dream de oder night, when ebery ting was still,
I thought I saw Susanna, dear, a coming down de hill.
De buckwheat cake was in her mouf, de tear was in her eye,
Says I, "I'm comin' from de Souf, Susanna, don't you cry."
      Oh, Susanna, &c.

I'll soon be down in New Orleans, and den I'll run around,
And if I see Susanua, I'll fall upon de ground.
But if I do not see her, this darkey 'll surely die,
And when I'm dead and buried, Susanna, don't you cry.
      Oh, Susanna, &c.

ROSA LEE.

WHEN I lib'd in Tennessee,
   U li a li o la e,
I went courtin' Rosa Lee,
   U li a li o la e,
Eyes as dark as winter night,
Lips as red as berry bright,
When first I did her wooing go,
She said. "Now don't be foolish, Joe!"
   U li a li o la e,
Courtin' down in Tennessee,
   U li a li o la e,
Beneath the wild Banana tree.

I said you lubly gal, dat's plain,
   U li a li o la e,
Breff as sweet as sugar cane,
   U li a li o la e,
Feet so large and comely too
Might make a cradle of each shoe,
Rosa take me for your beau,
She said, "Now don't be foolish, Joe!"
   U li a li o la e,
Courtin' down in Tennessee, &c.

My story is yet to be told,
   U li a li o la e,
Rosa catch'd a shocking cold,
   U li a li o la e,
Send for doctor, fetch de nurse,
Doctor came, but made her worse,
I tried to make her laugh, but no,
She said, "Now don't be foolish, Joe!"
   U li a li o la e,
Courtin' down in Tennessee, &c.

Dey gib her up, no power could save,
   U li a li o la e,
She ax me follow to her grave,
   U li a li o la e,
I take her hand, 'twas cold as death.
So cold I hardly draw my breff,
She saw my tears in sorrow flow,
And said, "Farewell, my dearest Joe!"
   U li a li o la e,
Rosa sleeps in Tennessee,
   U li a li o la e,
Beneath the wild Banana tree.

SINGING DARKIES ON THE OHIO.

A POPULAR WESTERN CHANT.

Solo.—　Come, darkies, listen to my story,
　　　Ob a nigger gay and young,
　　Well known to all for fame and glory—
　　　Throughout de land it has been sung.
　　As he passed through town and village,
　　　Each little darkie sang with joy,
　　" You're too late to come to supper,
　　　Old Dan Tucker," he would cry.
　　" Oh! oh! oh!
　　　Oh! oh! oh! Tra la la la la!"
　　Sang dis little darkey on de Ohio—
　　Sang dis little darkey on de Ohio!
Chorus.—　Oh, what a beau! what a beau! what a beau!
　　　Was dis young nigger ob de Ohio!
　　Oh, what a beau! what a beau! what a beau!
　　　Was dis singing nigger ob de Ohio!

(*Change melody, and sing the Boatman Dance, as follows:*)

　　The boatman he's a lucky man—
　　Dar's none can do as de boatman can:
　　I neber see'd a pretty gal in all my life,
　　But what she was some boatman's wife.

Chorus.— Dance, de Boatman Dance!
　　Oh, dance, de Boatman Dance!
　　We'll dance all night till broad day light,
　　An' go home with the gals in the morning.

　　When you go to de boatman's ball,
　　Dance wid my wife, or don't dance at all:
　　Sky-blue jacket, an' a tarpolin' hat—
　　Look out, boys, for de nine-tail cat!
　　　Dance, de Boatman Dance, &c.

　　I went to de hen house on my knees,
　　Dar I heard a chicken sneeze,
　　He sneeze so hard wid de chicken cough,
　　Dat he sneeze his head an' tail right off.
　　　Dance, de Boatman Dance, &c.

ROSA MAY.

I REMEMBER well, sweet Rosa,
　　Though 'tis many years ago,
When de harbest moon was shinin',
　　And we stood beneaf its glow;
When I felt your hand's soft pressure
　　And I heard you sweetly say,
"Forget me not in absence—
　　Tink sometimes ob Rosa May."

Oder eyes hab looked upon me,
　　Oder songs hab filled my ear;
But dey lacked the simple freshness
　　Ob de ones I used to hear.
My heart beats not as lightly,
　　And my hair is tinged with gray,
Yet I hear no song to charm me
　　Like yours, sweet Rosa May.

I am older, and some sorrows
　　May have chilled me, but I feel
Your gentle spirit's presence,
　　And all it would reveal.
De world seems still as beautiful,
　　As volatile and gay;
But dar are no such days as those
　　Of old dear Rosa May!

YALLER BUSHA BELLE.

Published by permission of **Firth, Pond** & Co., N. Y.

As I walked out one moonlight,
I met a fair maid—her eyes shone bright;
Her face was so black, you couldn't see it well;
And she was called de Yaller Busha Belle.
Says I, "Young lady, may I walk wid ye?"
What do ye tink was the answer she gib me?
She says—
"Go away, black man, don't you come a'nigh me!
Burn you wid a chunk! if I don't, blue dye me!"
Radink-a-day, Ra, di, ink a day.

Nigger seed her eat a pumpkin all the day,
Dat she should be too dignified, I didn't care to see,
'Case I'm de hansom nigger from de elbow to de knee.
I never see a yaller gal I could like so well,
So I splash my 'fections on you, my
                    Yaller Busha Belle.

So cum, Miss Dinah, may I walk wid ye?
Still de same answer de lady she gib me.

 Spoken—She says to me, in 'zackly *de same* tone of voice
as before, *only different,*
                    " Go away, black man," &c.

We didn't walk much furder, 'case down de rain fell,
So in a minute I put up my cotton umberell.
" Miss Dinah, now I axes you to lean upon dis arm,
An' I pledge my solemn appetite, I don't mean you no harm;
So cum, young lady, may I walk wid ye?"
Dis time, a different answer she gib me.

 Spoken—You see, de rain was coming down tolerably slick,
and she says,
" Come away, black man, I'll go away wid you now!"
We walked along togeder; I don't know what I said,
But de subject ob de matrimony cum into my head.
All dat passed between, I'm not a going to tell,
But de next day I got married to my
                    Yaller Busha Belle.

Went to a nigger parson on purpose to be wed;
When he ask'd de lady's name, what do you tink she said?
                    " Go away, black man!" &c.

About twelve months after dat, I t'ought to go wild,
When my yaller gal she gabe to me a little male child,
He was black as any crow, perhaps a trifle bigger;
I 'clare, I neber saw sich a 'ansum little nigger!
But my Yaller Busha Belle—my young and lubly bride—
She didn't live much longer, cause—de next day she died '

 Spoken—She says to me, in a werry lemoncholy voice—
" Good bye, black man, I'm going away from you, now!
Mind the piccaninny, if you lub me true, now!"
Ra, di, ink a day, Ra, di, ink a day!
I 'clare, it nearly broke my heart to put her in de clay!

THE MERRY SLEIGH BELLS.

FROM THE POSTHEELONG OF LONG JAWBONE.

JINGLE, jingle, clar de way,
'Tis de merry, merry sleigh—
Joyfully we glide along,
Only listen to our song.
Ober de bridge, down by the mill,
Den upset upon de hill,
Set 'em up, de sleigh bells ring,
While we darkies laugh an' sing.

Chorus and Repeat :

Jingle, jingle, jingle, jingle, jingle, clar de way,
'Tis de merry, merry, merry, merry, merry sleigh.

Symphony.   Chorus—

Oh, shall we go a sleighing, a sleighing, a sleighing?
De white horse shall pull us o'er de snow-covered plain :
On good whiskey punch, cakes an' sassengers regaling,
Oh, den we will slope to our homes back again.

Solo—

De trees ob de forest, sleigh-runners shall lend us,
   Wid an acorn cap, an' an oak bark shell,
Wid coon skins to warm us, an' bells to attend us,
   Oh, merrily we glide to de sound ob de bell.
Jingle, jingle, jingle, jingle, jingle, clar, &c.

Jingle, jingle, on we go,
Capes an' bonnets in a row,
De ole whip snaps, de gals all funny,
Hurry up dat peach an' honey.
See de ole horse how he blows
Like a steam pipe from his nose,
An' de boys dar snow balls fling,
As de merry sleigh bells ring.
Jingle, jingle, jingle, jingle, jingle, clar, &c.

B. S. STEELE.

CAMP TOWN RACES,

OR GWINE TO RUN ALL NIGHT.

CAMPTOWN ladies, sing dis song,
Du da, du da.
Camptown race-track five miles long,
Du da, du da da.
Go down dar wid my hat caved in,
Du da, du da.
Come back home wid pocket full of tin,
Du da, du da da.
Chorus—Gwine to run all night,
Gwine to run all day,
I'll bet my money on de bob-tail hoss,
Somebody bet on de bay.

Woolley Moon came on de track,
Du da, du da.
Bob, he fling him ober his back,
Du da, du da da.
Runnin' along like a shootin' star,
Du da, du da,
Runnin' a race wid de rail-road car,
Du da, du da da.
Gwine to run all night, &c.

De bob-tail hoss he can't be beat,
Du da, du da.
Runnin' around in a two mile heat,
Du da, du da da.
I win my money on the bob-tail nag,
Du da, du da.
An' carry it home in de ole tow bag,
Du da, du da da.
Gwine to run all night, &c.

Dar's fourteen horses in dis race,
Du da, du da.
I'm snug in saddle, an' got good brace,
Du da, du da da.

De sorrel horse he's got a cough,
Du da, du da.
An' his rider's drunk in the ole hay-loft,
Du da, du da da.
Gwine to run all night,
We're gwine to run all day,
I bet my money, &c.

S. C. FOSTER.

NELLY WAS A LADY.

Composed and arranged by STEPHEN C. FOSTER. Music published by
Firth, Pond & Co., No. 1 Franklin Square, N. Y.

DOWN on de Mississippi floating,
Long time I trabble on de way,
All night de cotton wood a toting,
Sing for my true lub all de day.
Chorus and Repeat :—Nelly was a lady,
Last night she died,
Toll de bell for lubly Nell,
My dark Virginny bride.

Now I'm unhappy and I'm weeping,
Can't tote de cotton wood no more ;
Last night while Nelly was a sleeping,
Death came a knocking at de door.
Nelly was a lady, &c.

When I saw my Nelly in de morning,
Smile till she opened up her eyes,
Seem'd like de light ob day a dawning,
Jist 'fore de sun begin to rise.
Nelly was a lady, &c.

Close by de margin ob de water,
Whar de lone weeping willow grows,
Dar lib'd Virginny's lubly daughter,
Dar she in death may find repose.
Nelly was a lady, &c.

Down in de meadow 'mong de clober,
Walk wid my Nelly by my side ;
Now all dem happy days am ober,
Farewell my dark Virginny bride.
Nelly was a lady, &c.

KISS ME QUICK AND GO.

The other night while I was sparking
  Sweet Turlina Spray,
The more we whispered our love talking,
  The more we had to say;
The old folks and the little folks
  We thought were fast in bed,—
We heard a footstep on the stairs,
  And what d'ye think she said?
Chorus—Oh! kiss me quick and go, my honey,
    Kiss me quick and go!
    To cheat surprise and prying eyes,
    Why kiss me quick and go!

Soon after that I gave my love
  A moonlight promenade,
At last we fetched up to the door,
  Just where the old folks stayed;
The clock struck twelve, her heart struck two (too),
  And peeping over head
We saw a night-cap raise the blind,
  And what d'ye think she said?
    Oh! kiss me quick and go, my honey, &c.

One Sunday night we sat together,
  Sighing side by side,
Just like two wilted leaves of cabbage
  In the sunshine fried;
My heart with love was nigh to split
  To ask her for to wed,
Said I: Shall I go for the parson?
  And what d'ye think she said?
    Oh! kiss me quick and go, my honey, &c.

GUM TREE CANOE.

On Tombigbee river, so bright I was born,
In a hut made ob husks ob de tall yellow corn,
An' dare I fust meet wid my Jula so true,
An' I row'd her about, in my Gum Tree Canoe.
  Singing row away row, o'er the waters so blue,
  Like a feather we'll float, in my Gum Tree Canoe.

All de day in de field de soft cotton I hoe,
I think of my Jula an' sing as I go,
Oh, I catch her a bird, wid a wing ob true blue,
And at night sail her round in my Gum Tree Canoe.
 Singing row away, &c.

Wid my hand on de banjo and toe on de oar,
I sing to de sound ob de river's soft roar;
While de stars dey look down at my Jula so true,
An' dance in her eye in my Gum Tree Canoe.
 Singing row away, &c.

But one night de stream bore us so far away,
Dat we couldn't cum back, so we thought we'd better stay;
Oh, we spied a tall ship wid a flag ob true blue,
And it took us in tow wid my Gum Tree Canoe.
 Singing row away, &c.

WITCHING DINAH CROW.

Now, darkies, I will tell you
 Ob a most unlucky fate,
Dat happen'd to a color'd gal
 From ole Kentucky State:
De subject ob my story
 Is about one Dinah Crow,
Who was drown'd, and den found dead,
 In de ribber O-hi-o!
 Oh, witching Dinah Crow!
 Oh, witching Dinah Crow!
Who was drown'd, and den found dead,
 In de ribber O-hi-o!

On a bery cloudy morning,
 When de wind war radder high,
Oh, stormy war de wedder,
 And rainy war de sky!
She got aboard de horse boat,
 To cross de O-hi-o,
But fell into the ribber!—
 Poor, unlucky Dinah Crow!
Oh, witching Dinah Crow, &c.

De darkies all did mourn her loss—
    "They'd neber see her more !"
They got a cotton handkerchief
    Dat floated on de shore !
They held an inquest on the body,
    About the poor gal's death :
The verdict of the jury war,
    She drown'd—for want of breath !
Oh, witching Dinah Crow, &c.

A FEW DAYS.

OH ! the world is coming to an end :
        Chorus—Few days ! Few days !
I'll kick my shins, my jacket rend ;
        I am going home.
I'm gwan to run clear out of sight ;
        Few days ! Few days !
And leave these ugly diggins quite.
        I am going home.

Chorus—

  For I've a home out yonder : few days ! few days !
  For I've a home out yonder ; I am going home.
  For I can't stay in the wilderness ; few days ! few days !
  For I can't stay in the wilderness ; I am going home.
        Repeat Chorus to quick time.

Oh ! every thing is made by steam ;
        Few days ! Few days !
Leather taffy, chalk ice cream ;
        I am going home.
The boys wear beards, the women too ;
        Few days ! Few days !
Tho' all things change there's noffin new.
        I am going home.

The Shanghai grows so very tall,
        Few days ! Few days !
You cannot hear him crow at all.
        I am going home.
I'll sing my parting song once more,
        Few days ! Few days !
And then I'll pass to Jersey shore.
        I am going home.

DEAREST MAE.

Oh, niggers, come and listen, a story I'll relate,
It happened in a valley in de ole Carolina state,
It was down in de meadow I used to make de hay,
I always work de harder when I tink on you, dear Mae.
Chorus.—Oh, dearest Mae, you're lovelier dan de day,
  Your eyes so bright dey shine at night,
  When de moon am gone away.

My massa gib me holiday, I wish he'd gib me more,
I thank'd him very kindly as I shoved my boat from shore,
And down de ribber paddled, wid a heart so light and free,
To de cottage ob my lovely Mae, I longed so much to see.
  Oh, dearest Mae, &c.

On de bank ob de ribber where de trees dey hang so low,
Where de coon among de branches play, and de mink he keeps
  below,
Oh, dar is de spot, and Mae she looks so sweet,
Her eyes dey sparkle like de stars, and her lips am red as beet.
  Oh, dearest Mae, &c.

Beneath de shady oak tree, I've sot for many hours,
As happy as de buzzard bird dat sports among de flowers;
But dearest Mae, I left her, and she cried when both we
  parted,
I gib her a long and farewell kiss, and back to massa started.
  Oh, dearest Mae, &c.

MARY BLANE.

Once on a time I lov'd a gal,
  I'll tell you all her name;
She came from Old Virginia,
  And dey called her Mary Blane.
We lived happy together;
  She never caused me pain;
But on one dark and stormy night,
  I lost my Mary Blane.
Chorus.—Farewell, farewell, poor Mary Blane,
  One faithful heart still beats for you.
  Farewell, farewell, poor Mary Blane,
  If we ne'er meet again.

I took my gun—de night was dark,
  My dog went with me too;
I saw a coon, and heard a bark !
  De dog he swiftly flew.
I thought he run down by dat spot,
  And kindled quick a flame.
Pine not to hear of my sad lot;
  I shot poor Mary Blane.
Chorus.—Farewell, farewell, poor Mary Blane,
    One faithful heart still beats for you.
  Farewell, farewell, poor Mary Blane,
    If we ne'er meet again.

I toted her down by de stream,
  To bathe de wound I'd made.
De dog's death howl, it was de theme;
  We both knelt down and pray'd.
But through the dark daylight there came—
  All hope for her was vain.
Her last low sigh was Jem, farewell;
  Good-bye, poor Mary Blane.
Chorus.—Farewell, farewell, poor Mary Blane,
    One faithful heart still beats for you.
  Farewell, farewell, poor Mary Blane,
    If we ne'er meet again.

BELLE OF BALTIMORE.

I've been to Carolina,
  I've been to Tennessee,
I've trabelled Mississippi,
  For massa set me free.
I've kissed the lovely Creole,
  On Louisiana shore,
But I never found a gal to match,
  De blooming Belle of Baltimore.
Chorus.—Oh, boys, Belle's a beauty,
    Eyes so bright and cheeks so sooty,
    No gal I ever seen before,
    So sweet as Belle of Baltimore.

My Belle is tall and slender,
  And sings so very clear,
You'd think she was an owlingale,
  If once her voice you'd hear.
I walked down to her cabin,
  And I rapped agin de door;
I want to gib my dogatype
  To my sweet Belle of Baltimore.
    Oh, boys, Belle's a beauty, &c.

I found her by the riber,
  My errant I did tell,
Says she, You gay deceiber,
  Your tricks I know too well,
I seen you kiss another gal,
  De werry night before—
Wid dat she turned upon her heel,
  And off went Belle of Baltimore.
    Oh, boys, Belle's a beauty, &c.

I wrote my lub a letter,
  And scented it so sweet,
De musk, de clobes, de peppermint,
  Stuck out about a feet.
But all my trouble was no use,
  I neber seen her more—
For I squashed de tender 'fections ob
  My blooming Belle of Baltimore.
    Oh, boys, Belle's a beauty, &c.
                          S. C. FOSTER.

NANCY TILL.

As sung by E. Horn.

DOWN in de cane break, close by de mill,
Dar libed a gal, and her name was Nancy Till;
She knowed dat I lubed her—she knowed it bery long;
I'm gwan to serenade her, and I'll sing dis song :—
Chorus.—Come, love, come !—de boat lies low ;
      She lies high and dry on de Ohio !
      Come, love, come !—won't you go along wid me ?
      I'll take you down to Tennessee !

Open de window, love—oh, do!
And listen to de music Ise playing for you;
De whispering ob love, so soft and so low,
Harmonize my voice wid de old banjo.
> Come, **love**, &c.

Softly de casement began **for to** rise;
De stars am a-shining above **in** de skies;
De moon am declining behind yonder hill,
Reflecting **its rays on you**, my Nancy Till.
> Come, love, **&c.**

Farewell, love! I must now away;
I've a long way to trabel before de **brake** of day;
But de next time I come, be ready **for to go**
A-sailing on de banks ob de Ohio!
> Come, love, &c.

G. HOLMAN.

GAL FROM **DE** SOUTH.

Music published by C. Holt, Jr., 260 Broadway, **N. Y.**

OLE massa bought a colored **gal,**
 He bought her **at de South;**
Her hair it **curled so bery** tight,
 She could **not shut her** mouth.
Her **eyes dey were so bery** small,
 They **both ran into one;**
And when a **fly light in her eye,**
 Like **a June bug in the sun.**
Chorus.—**Yah yah** yah, yah yah yah,
 De gal from de South,
 Her hair it curled **so bery** tight,
 She could **not shut her** mouth.

Her nose it was so bery long,
 It turned up like a squash;
And **when** she got her dander up,
 She made me laugh, **by** gosh.
Old massa had no hooks **or** nails,
 Or nothin' else like that;
So on this darkey's nose, he used
 To hang his coat and hat.
> **Yah** yah yah, &c.

One morning massa goin' **away**,
    He went to get his coat;
But neither hat **or coat was there**,
    For she had **swallowed both.**
He took her **to a tailor shop**,
    To have her mouth **made small;**
The lady took in one long breath,
    And swallowed tailor and all.
        Yah yah **yah, &c.**

AHOO! AHOO!

A PLANTATION DANCE.

Music published by C. Holt, Jr., 260 Broadway, N. Y.

Ise **come from Tennessee** all over,
    Ahoo, **ahoo, oo, oo!**
Whar de niggars live in clover,
    Ahoo, ahoo, oo, oo!

While we watch de feedin' cattle,
    Ahoo, ahoo, oo, oo!
We make de 'lodious sheep-bone rattle,
    Ahoo, ahoo, oo, oo!

Jim Carron kotch a turkey-buzzard,
    Ahoo, ahoo, oo, oo!
Black Betsey **charm dis nigger's gizzard,**
    Ahoo, ahoo, **oo, oo!**

Her figure **set dis heart a** trottin',
    Ahoo, ahoo, oo, oo!
Her shape is like a bale **o' cotton.**
    Ahoo, ahoo, **oo, oo!**

Crow come to New Orleans to live, sir,
    Ahoo, ahoo, oo, oo!
He broke his wing 'gainst de yaller fever,
    Ahoo, ahoo, oo, oo!

> New York's got de Croaken water,
> 　Ahoo, ahoo, oo, oo !
> And now dey'll all de fire slaughter,
> 　Ahoo, ahoo, oo, oo !
>
> Old fat Sam died ob decline,
> 　Ahoo, ahoo, oo, oo !
> And dey dried him for a 'bacco sign,
> 　Ahoo, ahoo, oo, oo !

S. S. Steele.

NEW MEDLEY.

Air.—" Let's be Gay."

Chorus.—Let's be gay, and banish sorrow,
　All our work is done to-day ;
　Laugh and sing until to-morrow——

Air.—" Black Smoke am Rising."

Oh, de black smoke am rising, and de wheels goin' round,
　Daddy a do du dadda,
Dey're blowing off steam, I know it by de sound,
　Daddy a do du da do de da do daddy ah do da da da,
　He ah ahu ah, he ah ahoo ah, he ah ahoo ah.
　Chorus.—He ah ahu ah, he ah hoo ah, he ah hoo ah,
　　He ah ahu ah, he ah hoo ah, hoo,
　　He ah hoo ah, he ah hoo ah, he ah hoo ah.
　　He ah hoo ah, he ahoo ah,
　　He ah ahoo ah, hoo.
　Solo.—Look out, boys, for——

Air.—"Jenny with the Light-Brown Hair."

I dream of Jenny with the light-brown hair,
Borne like a vapor on the summer air ;
I hear her tripping where the wild streams play,
Happy as the daisies that bloom on her way ;
Many were the wild notes her merry voice would pour,
Many were the blackbirds that——

Air.—"Kiss Me Quick."

Chorus.—Kiss me quick and go, my honey,
  Kiss me quick and go;
To cheat surprise and prying eyes,
  Oh, kiss me quick and go.

The other night as I was sparking
  Sweet Melinda Pray,
The more we talked of our love at parting—

Air.—"Bell Brandon."

'Neath the trees by the margin of the woodland,
  Whose spreading leafy boughs sweep the ground,
By a path leading thither from the prairie,
  When silence hung her night garb around;
There often I have wandered in the evening,
  When the summer breeze was fragrant on the sea,
There I saw——

Air.—"Betsey Gay."

Betsey Gay, Betsey Gay, charming Betsey Gay,
She was de lubliest yaller gal——

Air.—"Rosalie, the Prairie Flower."

On a distant prairie, where the heather wild,
In its quiet beauty, lived and smiled,
Stands a little cottage, and the creeping vine
Loved around its porch to twine.
In that peaceful dwelling, lived a lovely child,
With her——

Air.—"Wait for the Wagon."

Chorus.—Oh, wait for de wagon, wait for de wagon,
      Wait for de wagon, an' we'll all take a ride.
    Oh, wait for de wagon, wait for de wagon,
      Wait for de wagon, an' we'll all take a ride.

EVER BE HAPPY.

Tune—Pirates' Chorus.

Published by Firth, Pond, & Co., N. Y

Ever be happy, darkies so gay;
  Sing for de white folks, sing—
We've all assembled here to-night,
  An' we'll make the welkin ring.

Solo—

Strike de banjo an' de bones,
Oh, such dulcimer tones
Were nebber heard since we left our darkie homes.

Chorus—

Ever be happy, darkies so gay;
  Sing for de white folks, sing,
Sing, sing, for de white folks, sing,
  Sing, sing, for de white folks, sing.

Ever be happy, black as we are;
  We've hither come to-night—
To please you all we'll do our best,
  We'll strive wid all our might.

Solo—

Long may we live to hab such fun,
As we do when our day's work am done.

Chorus—

Ever be happy, darkies so gay;
  Sing for de white folks, sing—
We've all assembled here to-night,
  To make de welkin ring.

F. LESLIE.

MY OLD KENTUCKY HOME, GOOD NIGHT.

Music published by Firth, Pond, & Co., 547 Broadway, N. Y.

The sun shines bright in the old Kentucky home,
  'Tis summer, the darkies are gay,
The corn top's ripe, and the meadows in the bloom,
  While the birds make music all the day.
The young folks roll on the little cabin floor,
  All merry, all happy and bright;
By-'n by hard times comes a-knocking at the door ·
  Then my old Kentucky home, good night!

Chorus—
Weep no more, my lady,
  Oh! weep no more to-day,
We will sing one song for the old Kentucky home,
  For my old Kentucky home, far away.

They hunt no more for the possum and the coon,
  On the meadow, the hill, and the shore;
They sing no more by the glimmer of the moon,
  On the beach by the old cabin door.
The day goes by like a shadow o'er the heart,
  With sorrow where all was delight—
The time has come when the darkies have to part,
  Then my old Kentucky home, good night!
    Weep no more, my lady, &c.

The head must bow and the back will have to bend,
  Wherever the darkey may go;
A few more days, and the trouble all will end,
  In the field where the sugar canes grow.
A few more days for to tote the weary load—
  No matter 'twill never be light;
A few more days till we totter on the road,
  Then my old Kentucky home, good night!
    Weep no more, my lady, &c.

GOOD-BYE, SALLY DEAR!

Music published by Oliver Ditson, Boston.

  My Sally dear, I'm gwan to leave you—
Full Chorus—Good-bye, Sally dear!
  Do not let my parting grieve you—
Full Chorus—Good-bye, Sally dear!
  For since, dear Sally, we must part,
  Do not let it break your heart;
  Although I'm going far away,
  I'll return anudder day.

Chorus—Den, cheer up, my Sally, do!
    Though I'm far off, my heart is true,
    And I must bid you now adieu—
    Good-bye, Sally dear!

To de cotton fields we must away—
  Good-bye, Sally dear!
Our massa's call we must obey—
  Good-bye, Sally dear!
We go to pick de corn so nice,
And gedder in de crops ob rice,
Whar all de darkies am a-hoeing,
And de cotton pods are growing.
Chorus—Den cheer up, my Sally do!
      Though I'm far off, my heart is true,
      And I must bid you now adieu—
        Good-bye, Sally dear!

I lub you more dan all my life—
  Good-bye, Sally dear!
When I return, you'll be my wife—
  Good-bye, Sally dear!
Before I go I'll take one kiss—
I don't tink dat will be amiss;
You are my charming little Sal,
My pretty little color'd gal.
      Den, cheer up, my Sally do! &c.

THE YELLOW ROSE OF TEXAS.

Music published by Firth, Pond & Co., 547 Broadway, N. Y.

THERE'S a yellow rose in Texas that I am going to see,
No other darkey knows her, no darkey only me;
She cried so when I left her, it like to broke my heart,
And if I ever find her, we never more will part.

Chorus—
She's the sweetest rose of color this darkey ever knew,
Her eyes are bright as diamonds, they sparkle like the dew,
You may talk about your Dearest Mae, and sing of Rosa Lee,
But the yellow rose of Texas beats the belles of Tennessee.

Where the Rio Grande is flowing, and the starry skies are
      bright,
She walks along the river in the quiet summer night;
She thinks if I remember, when we parted long ago,
I promis'd to come back again, and not to leave her so.

Oh! now I'm going to find her, for my heart is full of woe,
And we'll sing the song together, that we sung so long ago;
We'll play the banjo gaily, and we'll sing the songs of yore,
And the yellow rose of Texas shall be mine for ever more.

A NIGGER'S HISTORY OF THE WORLD.

A NEW VERSION.

I COME from old Virginny on a bery fine day;
De riber it was froze, and I skated all de way;
Wid my banjo in my hand, to play de folks a tune,
(What de niggers use to dance by de light ob de moon.)

Chorus—
Walk in—walk in—walk in, I say;
Walk into de parlor, and hear de banjo play;
Walk into de parlor, and hear de banjo ring,
And watch de nigger's fingers while he picks upon de strings.

De world was made in six days, and finish'd on the sebenth;
('Cording to de contrak, it should a bin de 'lebenth!
But de carpenters got fatigued, de masons couldn't work,
So de cheapest way to do it was to fill it up wid dirt!)

Adam was de fust man—Ebe was de tudder;
Cain was de wicked man, 'case he killed his brudder;
Jonah was de fisherman dat swallowed down de shark;
Noah was de last man dat went into de ark.

Now dey got rail roads all ober de land;
Dey shoot through de mountains, and dey cut through de sand;
You can get de news from war de planets was a fighting,
By a little piece ob wire dat am greased up wid de lightning!
Walk in—walk in, &c.

Oh! Samson was a strong man, his strong was in his wool,
Delilah kotch him fast asleep, and hooked it by a pull,
Goliah was a giant, tall as an oak in spring,
Little David got him half slewed, and slewed him with a sling.
Walk in—walk in, &c.

SUGAR CANE GREEN.

PARODY ON THE IVY GREEN.

Now listen awhile to dis darkey child;
  I was born on de Ohio ribber;
My mother could cook, could bake, and could boil,
  And she taught me to be a good libber.
For hoe-cake and gumbo, she had not her match;
  And for hominy no one could touch her;
Ob broders and sisters I had quite a batch;
  And she fell in love wid a butcher!

Chorus—
  Den I used to creep where no darkey was seen,
  To suck de juice ob de sugar cane green.

My fader-in-law thought well ob his bride,
  But he hated de sight ob dis nigger!
So he wallop'd me well wid a big cowhide,
  'Case he said, 'twould make me grow bigger!
He said, I was fat—my skin fitted tight—
  Like a barrel ob grease was my figure;
And all de day long he would strike away strong,
  On de carcase of dis poor nigger!

Den I used to creep where no darkey was seen, &c.

I grinn'd and I bore it for two or three years;
  Tinks I to myself, " Dis won't do!
On some of dese mighty ole darkies I'll rise,
  And, golly! I'll beat 'em all blue!"
So I catch him asleep, one night, by de fire,
  As blue as a darkey could be,
So I tied and lamm'd him to my heart's desire;
  Den I sloped—'for he'd cotch'd hold ob me!

And since dat time, I neber hab been, &c.

ETHIOPIAN MEDLEY.

Arranged by L. M. Reese.

Air.—"Lucy Long."

I'VE jist come out before you,
　To sing you a little song—
Dey plays it on de music,
　And calls it——

Air.—"Bowery Gals."

Bowery gals, won't **you come out to-night,**
Come out to-night, come out to-night?
Bowery gals, won't **you come out to-night,**
And—

Air.—"Uncle Ned."

Dar was an old nigger,
　And his name was Uncle Ned,
And he died long ago, long ago,
He had no wool on——

Air.—"Camptown Races."

De bob-tailed nag,
And who's dat bettin' on de bay?
　I'se gwine to **run all night,**
　　I'se **gwine to run all** day,
If somebody will——

Air.—"Virginny Shore."

Carry me back to ole Virginny,
　To ole Virginny shore,
Den **carry me** back to——

Air.—"Lucy Neal."

My poor Lucy Neal,
Oh, my poor Lucy Neal,
And if I had you down——

Air.—"King Crow."

Fotch on de hoe-cake,
　Go way, don't **boder me,**
Fotch on de hoe-cake,
　I tell you 'taint done.
Fotch on——

Air.—"Aunt Sally."

Sally, Sally——
My old aunt Sally, Sally, Sally,
Ra re ri ro round de corner, Sally,

Air.—"Belle of Baltimore."

Ho, boys! Belle's a beauty,
Eyes so bright, cheeks so sooty,
No gal I eber saw before,
So sweet as——

Air.—"Black Shakers."

Fi hi hi ump ti deedle deedle dum,
Fi hi hi ump ti deedle deedle dum,
Possum up a gum stump, cooney in a hollerum,
Show me de man dat stole my half a dollarum.
Fi hi hi, &c.   [*Dances off stage, a la Shaker.*]

OLD BOB RIDLEY.

Music published by Firth, **Pond, & Co., 547 Broadway, N. Y.**

Now white folks I'll sing you a ditty,
I'se from home, but dat's no pity,
Oh! to praise myself it am a shame,
But Robert Ridley is my name.
Chorus.—Oh! Bob Ridley ho,
          Oh! Bob Ridley ho,
          Oh! Bob Ridley oh! oh!! oh!!!
          Robert Ridley ho.

Oh! white folks, I have cross'd de mountains,
How many miles I didn't count 'em,
Oh! I'se left de folks at de old plantation,
And come down here for my education.
     Oh! Bob Ridley ho, &c.

De first time dat I ever got a lickin',
'Twas down at de forks at de cotton pickin',
Oh! it made me dance, it made me tremble
I golly it made my eye-balls jingle,
     Oh! Bob Ridley ho, &c.

Oh! dis yar city am a mighty fine one,
For beauty and location it aint behind none,
Oh! de ladies all **look so** sweet and gidley,
Wonder dey don't **fall in** love wid old Bob **Ridley.**
    Oh! Bob Ridley **ho, &c.**

THE DAYS WHEN THIS OLD NIGGER WAS YOUNG.

*Air.— The good **old days** of Adam and Eve.*

I'LL sing you a song **that** never has been **sung,**
'Bout de good ole days when dis nigger was young;
And when you hears **it,** you'll say " dat's so."
For I know what I **tells** you, an' tells what I know.
Chorus.——

    Singing, Oh! dear, what queer things have sprung,
    Since de safe ole times when dis nigger was young.

In de days I was young, niggers wool didn't bang high.
Poultry sold cheap and chickens wasn't shanghi;
Young folks went to meetin' an' didn't go to musses,
And **folks** went into hominy instead of homnybuses.
    Singing, Oh! dear, &c.

In dem ole **times, why a church wasn't a** pay **house,**
An' de pulpit **didn't wear clothes** like a play-house;
Den de folks sung together **by** de sigh of dar voices,
An' dey didn't pay de choir for makin' **all de noises.**
    Singing, Oh! dear, &c.

On de ole turnpike dar was **no** railway crashes,
Den de liquor still didn't make the brandy smashes;
Folks didn't get frightened **at** too many **news,**
Den cobblers didn't burn soles, but **dey** mended shoes.
    Singing, Oh! dear, &c.

Den **folks went** to bed and dey got wide awake, sir,
Den **bread was** cheap for each **house** had a baker;
Den **big** fish folks didn't **dine after** dark, sir,
An' lovers, slow and sure, took a year or two **to spark, sir.**
    Singing, Oh! dear, &c.

We'd no fast wagons like spiders on wheels, sir,
Nor shanghai coats reaching to de heels, sir;
We had no quack physic to make folks sicker,
An' every t'oder house wasn't a place for " to liquor."
    Singing, Oh ! dear, &c.

Den gals **wore** bonnets their faces to protect, sir,
An' didn't **keep** 'em fast to de back of de neck, sir;
Den darkies staid at home 'stead of fugitive slaven,
An' mad politicians didn't go about ravin'.
    Singing, Oh ! dear, &c.

Den wenches cooked **de** victuals an' kep' **in dar** places,
An' niggers didn't wear all dar wool on **dar faces;**
We swallowed down de hoe-cake hot **from de** griddle,
An' we lightened our labor wid de banjo and fiddle.
    Singing, Oh ! **dear,** &c.

HOP DE DOODEN DOO.

Music published by Wiuner & Shuster, Philadelphia.

Susy in the kitchen, Hop de dooden doo,
Susy in the kitchen, Hop de dooden doo;
Susy in the kitchen shelling out the peas,
Master in the parlor tasting of the cheese.
What's the matter, Susy, what's the matter my **dear,**
What's the matter, Susy, O I'm going to leave you **now;**
Play upon the fiddle, come play upon the drum,
Play upon the banjo, Susy can't you come.

The big dog he **bow-wow,** Hop de dooden doo,
The big dog he **bow-wow,** Hop de dooden doo ;
The big dog he **bow-wow,** watching at the gate,
He smell the meat a frying, and then he couldn't wait.
Then what's the matter, Susy, what's the matter my dear,
What's the matter, Susy, O I'm going to leave you now ;
Come play upon the fiddle, play upon the drum,
Play upon the banjo, Susy can't you come.

The old horse he kick high, Hop de dooden **doo,**
The old horse he kick high, Hop de dooden **doo** ;
The old horse he kick high, standing in the **stable,**
Old master tried to ketch him, but found he **wasn't** able.
Then what's the **matter, Susy, what's the matter my** dear ?
What's the matter, Susy ? O I'm going **to leave you** now ;
Come play **upon the fiddle,** play upon the **drum,**
Play upon **the banjo,** Susy can't you come.

The **hen flew in de** garden, Hop de dooden doo,
The **hen flew in de** garden, Hop de dooden doo ;
The hen flew in de garden, Master try to ketch him,
He **fell** against the lamp-post, and then he did **not fetch him.**
Then what's the matter, Susy, what's the matter my dear ?
What's the matter, Susy ? O I'm going to leave you now ;
Come play upon the fiddle, play upon the drum,
Play upon the banjo, **Susy** can't **you** come.

VILKINS AND HIS DINAH.

As sung by W. E. Burton, Esq., with unbounded applause.

It's **of a rich merchant I am going for to** tell,
Who had **for a daughter an unkimwin fine** young gal ;
Her name **it was Dinah, just sixteen** years old,
With **a very large fortin of silver** and gold.
(*Spoken.*)—Two shares in the Railroad to the moon.
Too ral li, too ral li da.

Chorius.—Which I sing by myself, **in consequence of the**
exorbitant price **of** Italian singers.
Too ral li, too **ral li da.**

Now as Dinah was walking in the garden one day,
[The front garding.]
Her papa came up to her **and to** her did say :
" Go **dress** yourself, Dinah, **in** gorgeous **array,**

[Take your hair out **of** paper, and **put on a** clean pair of stockings.]

And I'll **bring you** a husbiand **both galliant and** gay !"
[A nice young man sixty **years old, worth seven million—**dollars.]
Too ral li, too ral li da.

Chorius.—In favor of the parient's desire, and the wedding breakfast he had ordered for forty-two bridesmaids and their beaux.

Too ral li, too ral li da.

[Now this is what the infant progeny said in reply to the horthur of her being.]

"Oh, papa, oh, papa," [Papa is the French for **Father.**]
"Oh, papa, oh, papa, I've not made up my mind,
To marry just now, why I don't feel inclined;
 [She wanted to go to a fashionable watering place first.]
And all my large fortin I'll gladly give o'er,
If you'll let me live single a year or two more."

Too ral li, too ral li da.

Wheedling and persuasive Chorius—on behalf of the offspring's remonstrance to the horthur of her being.

Too ral li, too ral li da.

[Now this is the way the parricidal papa spoke, parenthetically and paregorically, to his daughter.]

"Go, go! boldest daughter," the parient he cried;
"If you won't consent to be this here young man's bride,
I'll give your large fortin to nearest of kin,
And you shan't reap the benefit of one single nickel."

Too ral li, too ral li da.

Chorius of the enraged parient against the progeny.

Too ral li, too ral li da.

[Now this is the most melancholy part of it, and shows what the progeny was druv to in consequence of the mingled ferocity of the inconsiderable parient.]

As Vilikins was a walking the garding around,
[This was the back garding vere the cabbiges growed.]
He saw his dear Dinah lying dead on the ground,
With a cup of cold pison lying down by her side.
With a billet dux which said as how 'twas by pison she died.
 [Genuine, original Schiedam Schnapps.]

Too ral li, too ral li da.

Chorius.—Expressive of the genuine original Schiedam.

Too ral li, too ral li da.

[This here is what the lovyer did on the diskivery.]
He kissed her cold corpus a thousand times o'er,
And called her his Dinah though she was no more;
Then swallowed the pison [the Schnapps, without the least
        bit of bitters in it,] like a lovyer so brave,
And Vilikins and his Dinah are both laid in one grave.

[The reverend parient struck with remorse had them both
planted together.]
            Too ral li, too ral li da.

Dismal, duplicate, defunct Chorius—in consequence of the
double event.
            Too ral li, too ral li da.

MORIALE.

Now all you young men, don't you thus fall in love, nor
Do not by no means, disobey your guv'nor;
And all you young maidens, mind who you clap eyes on—
Think of Vilikins and his Dinah, not forgetting the pison.

[Excepting a drop now and then as a setter up.]
            Too ral li, too ral li da.

Moriale Chorius—fearfully impressive.
            Too ral li, too ral li da.

[Now this is the superlativelely supernatural visitation
which appeared to the parient at midnight, after the disease
of his only progeny.]

At twelve the next night, by a tall popular tree,
The ghost of Miss Dinah the parient did see,

[The old gentleman was on the lookout for the comet.]

Arm in arm with her Villikins, and both looking blue,
Saying, " We wouldn't have been pisoned if it hadn't been for
        you."
            Too ral li, too ral li da.

Sepulchural Chorius—to astonish the weak nerves of the
        parient.
            Too ral li, too ral li da.

[The parient's fate, and what he thought he would do, but he didn't.]

Now the parient was struck with horror of home,
So he seized his carpet bag, [and crammed in an old pair of
　　　suspenders and a bootjack,] around the wide world to
　　　roam ;
But as he was starting he was seized with a shiver,
Which shook him to pieces and ended him foriver.
　　[And those who came to pick up the bits could only sing,]
　　　　　Too ral li, too ral li da.

Sympathetic Chorius—for the parient's fragments, though
the verdict of the jury what sot on him was "Sarved him
right."

　　　　　Too ral li, too ral li da.

ANOTHER MORIALE, NO. 2.

Now the Moriale is this—No. 1 is not reckoned ;
So this is the first Moriale though it comes the second ;
You may learn from my story which is true every word,
All this wouldn't have happened if it hadn't have occurred.
　　[And there wouldn't have been no occasion for singing,]
　　　　　Too ral li, too ral li da.

Conclusive Chorius of everybody,
　　　　　Too ral li, too ral li da.

BOOKS

PUBLISHED BY G. G. EVANS,

439 Chestnut St., Philadelphia.

————•••————

T. S. ARTHUR'S WORKS.

The following Books are by T. S. ARTHUR, the well-known author, of whom it has been said, "that dying, he has not written a word he would wish to erase." They are worthy of a place in every household.

ARTHUR'S SKETCHES OF LIFE AND CHARACTER

An octavo volume of over 400 pages, beautifully Illustrated, and bound in the best English muslin, gilt. Price $2.00.

LIGHTS AND SHADOWS OF REAL LIFE.

With an Autobiography and Portrait of the Author. Over 500 pages, octavo, with fine tinted Engravings. Price $2.00.

TEN NIGHTS IN A BAR-ROOM, AND WHAT I SAW THERE.

This powerfully-written work, one of the BEST by its POPULAR AUTHOR, has met with an immense sale. It is a large 12mo., illustrated with a beautiful Mezzotint Engraving, by Sartain; printed on fine white paper, and bound in the best English muslin, gilt back. Price, $1.00.

GOLDEN GRAINS FROM LIFE'S HARVEST-FIELD.

Bound in gilt back and sides, cloth, with a beautiful Mezzotint engraving. 12mo. Price $1.00.

WHAT CAN WOMAN DO.

12mo., with Mezzotint engraving. Price $1.00.

"Our purpose is to show, in a series of Life Pictures, what woman can do, as well for good as for evil."

ANGEL OF THE HOUSEHOLD, AND OTHER TALES.

Cloth, 12mo., with Mezzotint engraving. Price $1.00.

ARTHUR'S HOME LIBRARY.

[The following four volumes contain nearly 500 pages each, and are illustrated with fine Mezzotint engravings. Bound in the best manner, and sold separately or in sets. They have been introduced into the District, Sabbath School, and other Libraries, and are considered one of the best series of the Author.]

THREE ERAS IN WOMAN'S LIFE.

Containing Maiden, Wife and Mother. Cloth, 12mo., with Mezzotint engraving. Price, $1.00.

"This, by many, is considered Mr. Arthur's best work."

TALES OF MARRIED LIFE.

Containing Lovers and Husbands, Sweethearts and Wives, and Married and Single. Cloth, 12mo., with Mezzotint engraving. Price $1.00.

"In this volume may be found some valuable hints for wives and husbands, as well as for the young."

TALES OF REAL LIFE.

Containing Bell Martin, Pride and Principle, Mary Ellis, Family Pride and Alice Melville. Cloth, 12mo., with Mezzotint engraving. Price $1,00.

"This volume gives the experience of real life by many who found not their ideal."

THE MARTYR WIFE.

Containing Madeline, the Heiress, The Martyr Wife and Ruined Gamester. Cloth, 12mo., with Mezzotint engraving. $1.00.

"Contains several sketches of thrilling interest."

THE ANGEL AND THE DEMON.

A Book of Startling Interest. A handsome 12mo volume, $1.00.

"In this exciting story, Mr. Arthur has taken hold of the reader's attention with a more than usually vigorous grasp, and keeps him absorbed to the end of the volume."

.THE WAY TO PROSPER,

AND OTHER TALES. Cloth, 12mo., with engraving. Price $1.00

TRUE RICHES; OR WEALTH WITHOUT WINGS,

AND OTHER TALES. Cloth, 12mo., with Mezzotint engraving Price, $1.00.

THE YOUNG LADY AT HOME.

A Series of Home Stories for American Women.   12mo. $1.00

TRIALS AND CONFESSIONS OF A HOUSEKEEPER.

With 14 Spirited Illustrations.   12mo., cloth.   Price $1.00.

The range of subjects in this book embrace the grave and instructive, as well as the agreeable and amusing. No Lady reader familiar with the trials and perplexities incident to Housekeeping, can fail to recognize many of her own experiences, for every picture here presented has been drawn from life.

THE WITHERED HEART.

With fine Mezzotint Frontispiece.   12mo., Cloth.   Price $1.00.

This work has gone through several editions in England, although published but a short time, and has had the most flattering notices from the English Press.

STEPS TOWARD HEAVEN.

A Series of Lay Sermons for Converts in the Great Awakening.   12mo., cloth.   Price $1.00.

THE HAND BUT NOT THE HEART;

Or, Life Trials of Jessie Loring.   12mo., cloth.   Price, $1.00.

THE GOOD TIME COMING.

Large 12mo., with fine Mezzotint Frontispiece.   Price, $1.00.

LEAVES FROM THE BOOK OF HUMAN LIFE.

Large 12mo.   With 30 illustrations and steel plate.   Price $1.00.

"It includes some of the best humorous sketches of the author."

HEART HISTORIES AND LIFE PICTURES.

12mo   Cloth.   Price $1.00.

" In the preparation of this volume, we have endeavored to show, that whatever tends to awaken our sympathies towards others, is an individual benefit as well as a common good."

SPARING TO SPEND; or, the Loftons and Pinkertons

12mo., cloth.   Price $1.00.

The purpose of this volume is to exhibit the evils that flow from the too common lack of prudence.

HOME SCENES.

12mo.   Cloth.   Price $1.00.

This Book is designed to aid in the work of overcoming what is evil and selfish, that home lights may dispel home shadows.

THE OLD MAN'S BRIDE.

12mo.   Cloth.   Price $1.00.

This is a powerfully written Book, showing the folly of unequal marriages.

ADVICE TO YOUNG LADIES ON THEIR DUTIES AND CONDUCT IN LIFE.

By T. S. Arthur.   A new and greatly enlarged edition.   12mo., cloth.   Steel plate.   Price $1.00.

ADVICE TO YOUNG MEN ON VARIOUS IMPORTANT SUBJECTS.

By T. S. Arthur.   A new and greatly enlarged edition.   12mo., cloth.   Steel plate.   Price $1.00.

TWENTY YEARS AGO AND NOW.

By T. S. Arthur.   12mo., cloth, mezzotint engraving.   Price $1.00.

BIOGRAPHIES.

LIFE AND EXPLORATIONS OF DR. E. K. KANE,

And other Distinguished American Explorers.   Including Ledyard, Wilkes, Perry, &c.   Containing narratives of their researches and adventures in remote and interesting portions of the Globe. By Samuel M. Smucker, LL.D.   With a fine Mezzotint Portrait of Dr. Kane, in his Arctic costume.   Price $1.00.

THE LIFE AND REIGN OF NICHOLAS I.,

Emperor of Russia.   With descriptions of Russian Society and Government, and a full and complete History of the War in the East.   Also, Sketches of Schamyl, the Circassian, an' other Distinguished Characters. By S. M. Smucker, LL.D. Beautifully Illustrated.   Over 400 pages, large 12mo.   Price $1.25.

THE PUBLIC AND PRIVATE LIFE OF DAN'L WEBSTER.

By Gen. S. P. Lyman.   12mo., cloth.   Price $1.00.

THE MASTER SPIRIT OF THE AGE.

THE PUBLIC AND PRIVATE HISTORY OF NAPOLEON THE THIRD.

With Biographical Notices of his most Distinguished Ministers, Generals and Favorites. By S. M. SMUCKER, LL.D. This interesting and valuable work is embellished with splendid steel plates, done by Sartain in his best style, including the Emperor, the Empress, Queen Hortense, and the Countess Castiglione. 400 pages, 12mo. Price $1.25.

MEMOIRS OF ROBERT HOUDIN,

The celebrated French Conjuror. Translated from the French. With a copious Index. By DR. R. SHELTON MACKENZIE. This book is full of interesting and entertaining anecdotes of the great Wizard, and gives descriptions of the manner of performing many of his most curious tricks and transformations. 12mo., cloth. Price $1.00.

LIFE AND ADVENTURES OF DAVID CROCKETT.

Written by himself, with Notes and Additions. Splendidly illustrated with engravings, from original designs. By GEORGE G. WHITE. 12mo., cloth. Price $1.00.

LIFE AND TIMES OF DANIEL BOONE.

Including an account of the Early Settlements of Kentucky. By CECIL B. HARTLEY. With splendid illustrations, from original drawings by George G. White. 12mo., cloth. Price $1.00.

LIFE AND ADVENTURES OF LEWIS WETZEL.

Together with Biographical Sketches of Simon Kenton, Benjamin Logan, Samuel Brady, Isaac Shelby, and other distinguished Warriors and Hunters of the West. By CECIL B. HARTLEY. With splendid illustrations, from original drawings by George G. White. 12mo., cloth. Price $1.00.

LIFE AND TIMES OF GENERAL FRANCIS MARION,

The Hero of the American Revolution; giving full accounts of his many perilous adventures and hair-breadth escapes amongst the British and Tories in the Southern States, during the struggle for liberty. By W. GILMORE SIMMS. 12mo., cloth. $1.00.

LIFE OF GENERAL SAMUEL HOUSTON,

The Hunter, Patriot, and Statesman of Texas. With nine illu-
trations. 12mo., cloth. Price $1.00.

LIVES OF GENERAL HENRY LEE AND GENERAL THOMAS SUMPTER.

Comprising a History of the War in the Southern Department of
the United States. Illustrated, 12mo, cloth. $1.00.

DARING & HEROIC DEEDS OF AMERICAN WOMEN.

Comprising Thrilling Examples of Courage, Fortitude, Devoted-
ness, and Self-Sacrifice, among the Pioneer Mothers of the
Western Country. By JOHN FROST, LL.D. Price $1.00.

LIVES OF FEMALE MORMONS.

A Narrative of facts Stranger than Fiction. By METTA VICTORIA
FULLER. 12mo., cloth. Price $1.00.

LIVES OF ILLUSTRIOUS WOMEN OF ALL AGES.

Containing the Empress Josephine, Lady Jane Gray, Beatrice
Cenci, Joan of Arc, Anne Boleyn, Charlotte Corday, Zenobia,
&c., &c. Embellished with Fine Steel Portraits. 12mo., cloth.
Price $1.00.

THE LIVES AND EXPLOITS OF THE MOST NOTED BUCCANEERS & PIRATES OF ALL COUNTRIES.

Handsomely illustrated. 1 vol. Cloth. Price $1.00.

HIGHWAYMEN, ROBBERS AND BANDITTI OF ALL COUNTRIES.

With Colored and other Engravings. Handsomely bound in one
volume. 12mo., cloth. Price $1.00.

HEROES AND PATRIOTS OF THE SOUTH;

Comprising Lives of General Francis Marion, General William
Moultrie, General Andrew Pickens, and Governor John
Rutledge. By CECIL B. HARTLEY. Illustrated, 12mo., cloth.
Price $1.00.

KIT CARSON.

LIFE OF CHRISTOPHER CARSON, the celebrated Rocky Mountain Hunter, Trapper and Guide, with a full description of his Hunting Exploits, Hair-breadth Escapes, and adventures with the Indians; together with his services rendered the United States Government, as Guide to the various Exploring Expeditions under John C. Fremont and others. By CHARLES BURDETT. With six illustrations. 12mo., cloth. Price $1.00.

THE LIFE AND TIMES OF GEORGE WASHINGTON.

By S. M. SMUCKER, LL.D., author of "The Life of Thomas Jefferson," "Life of Alexander Hamilton," etc., etc. 12mo., cloth, with Steel Portrait. Price $1.00.

THE LIFE AND TIMES OF HENRY CLAY.

By S. M. SMUCKER, LL.D., author of the "Lives of Washington," "Jefferson," etc. 12mo., cloth, Steel Portrait. Price $1.00.

LIFE OF ANDREW JACKSON.

Containing an Authentic History of the Memorable Achievements of the American Army under General Jackson, before New Orleans. By ALEXANDER WALKER. 12mo., cloth. Price $1.00.

LIFE OF BENJAMIN FRANKLIN.

By O. L. HOLLEY. With Steel Portrait and six Illustrations. 12mo., cloth. Price $1.00.

LIVES OF THE SIGNERS OF THE DECLARATION OF AMERICAN INDEPENDENCE.

By B. J. LOSSING. Steel Frontispiece, and fifty portraits. 12mo., cloth. Price $1.00.

LIFE OF CAPT. JOHN SMITH OF VIRGINIA.

By W. GILLMORE SIMMS. Illustrated, 12mo., cloth, Price, $1 00.

THE THREE MRS. JUDSONS,

The Female Missionaries. By CECIL B. HARTLEY. A new and carefully revised edition, with steel portraits. 12mo. Price, $1 00.

INGRAHAM'S THREE GREAT WORKS.

THE
Prince of the House of David;

Or, Three Years in the Holy City. Being a series of the letters of Adina, a Jewess of Alexandria, supposed to be sojourning in Jerusalem in the days of Herod, addressed to her Father a wealthy Jew in Egypt, and relating, as if by an eye-witness, all the scenes and wonderful incidents in the life of Jesus of Nazareth, from his Baptism in Jordan to his Crucifixion on Calvary. New edition, carefully revised and corrected by the author, Rev. J. H. Ingraham, LL.D., Rector of Christ Church, and St. Thomas' Hall, Holly Springs, Miss. With five splendid illustrations, one large 12mo., volume, cloth. Price, $1 25. Full Gilt sides and edges. Price $2.00.

The same work in German. 12mo., cloth. Price, $1.25.

THE PILLAR OF FIRE;

Or, Israel in Bondage. Being an account of the Wonderful Scenes in the Life of the Son of Pharaoh's Daughter, (Moses). Together with Picturesque Sketches of the Hebrews under their Task-masters. By Rev. J. H. Ingraham, LL D., author of the "Prince of the House of David." With steel Frontispiece. Large 12mo., cloth. Price, $1 25; the same work, full gilt sides and edges. Price, $2 00.

THE THRONE OF DAVID;

From the Consecration of the Shepherd of Bethlehem, to the Rebellion of Prince Absalom. Being an illustration of the Splendor, Power and Dominion of the Reign of the Shepherd, Poet, Warrior, King and Prophet, Ancestor and type of Jesus, addressed by an Assyrian Ambassador, resident at the Court of Jerusalem, to his Lord and King on the Throne of Nineveh; wherein the magnificence of Assyria, as well as the magnificence of Judea, is presented to the reader as by an eye-witness. By the Rev. J. H. Ingraham, LL.D., Rector of Christ Church and St. Thomas' Hall, Holly Springs, Miss., author of the "Prince of the House of David" and the "Pillar of Fire." With five splendid illustrations. Large 12mo., cloth. Price $1 25; the same work, full gilt sides and edges. Price, $2 00.

The Sunny South;

OR,

THE SOUTHERNER AT HOME.

EMBRACING

Five years' experience of a Northern Governess in the Land of the Sugar and the Cotton. Edited by PROFESSOR J. H. INGRAHAM, of Miss. Large 12mo., cloth. Price, $1 25.

A BUDGET OF

HUMOROUS POETRY,

COMPRISING

Specimens of the best and most Humorous Productions of the popular American and Foreign Poetical Writers of the day. By the author of the "BOOK OF ANECDOTES AND BUDGET OF FUN." One volume, 12mo., cloth. Price $1 00.

The World in a Pocket Book.

BY

WILLIAM H. CRUMP.

NEW AND REVISED EDITION, BROUGHT DOWN TO

1860.

This work is a Compendium of Useful Knowledge and General Reference, dedicated to the Manufacturers, Farmers, Merchants, and Mechanics of the United States—to all, in short, with whom time is money—and whose business avocations render the acquisition of extensive and diversified information desirable, by the shortest possible road. This volume, it is hoped, will be found worthy of a place in every household—in every family. It may indeed be termed a library in itself. Large 12mo. Price, $1 25.

THE SPIRIT LAND.

12mo., cloth, with Mezzotint Engraving.   Price $1.00.

"These pages are submitted to the public with the counsel of the wisest and best of all ages, that amid the wiley arts of the Adversary, we should cling to the word of God, the Bible, as the only safe and infallible guide of Faith and Practice."

THE MORNING STAR; OR, SYMBOLS OF CHRIST.

By REV WM. M. THAYER, author of "Hints for the Household," "Pastor's Holiday Gift," &c., &c.   12mo., cloth.   Price $1.00

"The symbolical parts of Scriptures are invested with peculiar attractions. A familiar acquaintance with them can scarcely fail to increase respect and love for the Bible."

SWEET HOME; OR, FRIENDSHIP'S GOLDEN ALTAR.

By FRANCES C. PERCIVAL.   Mezzotint Frontispiece, 12mo., cloth, gilt back and centre.   Price $1.00.

"The object of this book is to awaken the Memories of Home—to remind us of the old Scenes and old Times."

THE DESERTED FAMILY;

OR, THE WANDERINGS OF AN OUTCAST.   By PAUL CREYTON.   12mo., cloth.   Price $1.00.

"An interesting story, which might exert a good influence in softening the heart, warming the affections, and elevating the soul."

ANNA CLAYTON; OR, THE MOTHER'S TRIAL

A Tale of Real Life.   12mo., cloth.   Price $1.00.

"The principal characters in this tale are drawn from real life—imagination cannot picture deeper shades of sadness, higher or more exquisite joys, than Truth has woven for us, in the Mother's Trial."

"FASHIONABLE DISSIPATION."

By METTA V. FULLER.   Mezzotint Frontispiece, 12mo., bound in cloth,   Price $1.00.

THE OLD FARM HOUSE.

By MRS. CAROLINE H. BUTLER LAING, with six splendid Illustrations.   12mo., cloth, Price $1.00.

WOMAN AND HER DISEASES.

From the Cradle to the Grave ; adapted exclusively to her instruction in the Physiology of her system, and all the Diseases of her Critical Periods. By EDWARD H. DIXON, M.D. 12mo. Price $1.00.

DR. LIVINGSTONE'S TRAVELS AND RESEARCHES OF SIXTEEN YEARS IN THE WILDS OF SOUTH AFRICA.

One volume, 12mo., cloth, fine edition, printed upon superior paper, with numerous illustrations. Price $1.25. Cheap edition, price $1.00.

This is a work of thrilling adventures and hair-breadth escapes among savage beasts, and more savage men. Dr. Livingstone was alone, and unaided by any white man, traveling only with African attendants, among different tribes and nations, all strange to him, and many of them hostile, and altogether forming the most astonishing book of travels the world has ever seen. All acknowledge it is the most readable book published.

ANDERSSON'S EXPLORATIONS AND DISCOVERIES.

Giving accounts of many Perilous Adventures, and Thrilling Incidents, during Four Years' Wanderings in the Wilds of South Western Africa. By C. J. ANDERSSON, LL.D., F.R.S. With an Introductory Letter, by J. C. FREMONT. One volume, 12mo., cloth. With Numerous Illustrations, representing Sporting Adventures, Subjects of Natural History, Devices for Destroying Wild Animals, etc. Price $1.25.

INDIA AND THE INDIAN MUTINY.

Comprising a Complete History of Hindoostan, from the earliest times to the present day, with full particulars of the Recent Mutiny in India. Illustrated with numerous engravings. By HENRY FREDERICK MALCOM. This work has been gotten up with great care, and may be relied on as Complete and Accurate ; making one of the most Thrillingly Interesting books published. It contains illustrations of all the great Battles and Sieges, making a large 12mo., volume of about 450 pages. Price $1.25.

SEVEN YEARS IN THE WILDS OF SIBERIA,

A Narrative of Seven Years' Explorations and Adventures in
Oriental and Western Siberia, Mongolia, the Kir his Steppes,
Chinese Tartary, and Part of Central Asia. By THOMAS
WILLIAM ATKINSON. With numerous Illustrations. 12mo., cloth,
price $1.25.

SIX YEARS IN NORTHERN AND CENTRAL AFRICA.

Travels and Discoveries in North and Central Africa, being a
Journal of an Expedition undertaken under the auspices of
H. B. M.'s Government, in the years 1849-1855. By HENRY
BARTH, Ph. D., D.C.L., Fellow of the Royal Geographical and
Asiatic Societies, &c., &c.   12mo.; cloth, price $1.25.

THREE VISITS TO MADAGASCAR

During the years 1853, 1854, 1856, including a journey to the
Capital; with notices of the Natural History of the Country
and of the present Civilization of the People, by the Rev. WM.
ELLIS, F.H.S., author of "Polynesian Researches." Illustrated
by engravings from photographs, &c.   12mo., cloth. $1.25.

CAPT. COOK'S VOYAGES ROUND THE WORLD.

One volume, 12mo., cloth.   Price $1.00.

BOOK OF ANECDOTES AND BUDGET OF FUN.

Containing a collection of over One Thousand Laughable Sayings,
Rich Jokes, etc.   12mo., cloth, extra gilt back, $1.00.

  "Nothing is so well calculated to preserve the healthful action of the
human system as a good hearty laugh."

BOOK OF PLAYS FOR HOME AMUSEMENT.

Being a collection of Original, Altered and well-selected Tragedies,
Comedies, Dramas, Farces, Burlesques, Charades, Comic Lec-
tures, etc.   Carefully arranged and specially adapted for PRIVATE
REPRESENTATION, with full directions for Performance.   By SILAS
S. STEELE, Dramatist.   One volume, 12mo., cloth.   Price $1.00.

A HISTORY OF ITALY,

AND THE WAR OF 1859.

Giving the causes of the War, with Biographical Sketches of Sovereigns, Statesmen and Military Commanders; Descriptions and Statistics of the Country; with finely engraved Portraits of Louis Napoleon, Emperor of France Frances Joseph, Emperor of Austria; Victor Emanuel, King of Sardinia, and Garribaldi, the Champion of Italian Freedom.   Together with the official accounts of the Battles of Montebello, Palestro, Magenta, Malegnano, Solferino, etc., etc., and Maps of Italy, Austria, and all the adjacent Countries, by

MADAME JULIE DE MARGUERITTES.

With an introduction by Dr. R. SHELTON MACKENZIE, one volume, 12mo., cloth, price $1.25.

From the New York Courier and Enquirer.

" This is an able, interesting and lively account of the War and the circumstances connected with it.   The author's residence in Europe has given her facilities for preparing the volume which add much to its value.

" Not only does she give a description of Italy in general, but of each Sovereignty, and State, showing the Extent, Resources, Power and Political situation of each.   Throughout the volume are found Anecdotes, Recollections, and even *Ondits*, which contribute to its interest."

THE BOOK OF POPULAR SONGS.

Being a compendium of the best Sentimental, Comic, Negro, National, Patriotic, Military, Naval, Social, Convivial, and Pathetic Ballads and Melodies, as sung by the most celebrated Opera Singers, Negro Minstrels, and Comic Vocalists of the day.
One volume, 12mo., cloth.   Price $1.00.

THE AMERICAN PRACTICAL COOKERY BOOK;

Or Housekeeping made easy, pleasant, and econmical in all its departments. To which are added directions for setting out Tables, and giving Entertainments. Directions for Jointing, Trussing, and Carving, and many hundred new Receipts in Cookery and Housekeeping. With 50 engravings. 12mo., cloth. Price $1.00.

RECORDS OF THE REVOLUTIONARY WAR.

Containing the Military and Financial Correspondence of distinguished officers; names of the officers and privates of regiments, companies and corps, with the dates of their commissions and enlistments. General orders of Washington, Lee, and Green; with a list of distinguished prisoners of war; the time of their capture, exchange, etc.; to which is added the half-pay acts of the Continental Congress; the Revolutionary pension laws; and a list of the officers of the Continental army who acquired the right to half-pay, commutation, and lands, &c. By T. W. SAFFELL. Large 12mo., $1.25.

THE ROMANCE OF THE REVOLUTION.

Being a history of the personal adventures, romantic incidents and exploits incidental to the War of Independence—with tinted illustrations. Large 12mo., $1.25.

THE QUEEN'S FATE.

A tale of the days of Herod. 12mo., cloth, with Steel Illustrations. $1.00.

"A recital of events, of an awe-arousing period, in a familiar and interesting manner."

"LIVING AND LOVING."

A collection of Sketches. By Miss VIRGINIA F. TOWNSEND.— Large 12mo., with fine steel portrait of the author. Bound in cloth. Price $1.00.

We might say many things in favor of this delightful publication, but we deem it unnecessary. Husbands should buy it for their wives: lovers should buy it for their sweet-hearts: friends should buy it for their friends.—*Godey's Lady's Book.*

WHILE IT WAS MORNING.

By VIRGINIA F. TOWNSEND, author of "Living and Loving." 12mo., cloth. Price $1.00.

THE ANGEL VISITOR; OR, VOICES OF THE HEART.

12mo., cloth, with Mezzotint Engraving. Price $1.00.

"The mission of this volume is to aid in doing good to those in affliction."

THE LADIES' HAND BOOK

OF

FANCY AND ORNAMENTAL NEEDLE-WORK.

COMPRISING

Full directions with patterns for working in Embroidery, Applique, Braiding, Crochet, Knitting, Netting, Tatting, Quilting, Tambour aud Gobelin Tapestry, Broderie Anglaise, Guipure Work, Canvass Work, Worsted Work, Lace Work, Bead Work, Stitching, Patch Work, Frivolite, &c. Illustrated with 262 Engraved Patterns, taken from original designs. By Miss FLORENCE HARTLEY. One volume, Quarto Cloth. Price, $1 25.

The Ladies' Book of Etiquette,

AND

MANUAL OF POLITENESS.

A Hand Book for the use of Ladies in Polite Society. By FLORENCE HARTLEY. 12mo., cloth. Price, $1 00.

The Gentlemen's Book of Etiquette,

AND

MANUAL OF POLITENESS.

Being a Complete Guide for a Gentleman's Conduct in all his relations toward Society. By CECIL B. HARTLEY. 12mo. Price, $1 00.

LECTURES FOR THE PEOPLE:

BY THE

Rev. H. STOWELL BROWN,

Of the Myrtle Street Baptist Chapel, Liverpool, England.

First Series, published under a special arrangement with the author. With a Biographical introduction by Dr. R. Shelton Mackenzie. With a splendidly engraved Steel Portrait. One vol., 414 pages. 12mo., cloth. Price $1.00.

Mr. Brown's lectures fill an important place, for which we have no other book. The style is clear, the spirit is kind, the reasoning careful, and the argument conclusive. We are persuaded that this book will render more good than any book of sermons or lectures that have been published in this 19th century.—*Liverpool Mercury.*

THE HOME BOOK OF HEALTH AND MEDICINE;

Or, The Laws and Means of Physical Culture, adapted to practical use. Embracing a treatise on Dyspepsia, Digestion, Breathing, Ventilation, Laws of the Skin, Consumption, how prevented; Clothing, Food, Exercise, Rest, &c. By W. A. Alcott, M. D. With 31 illustrations, Large 12mo. Price, $1.25.

LIFE OF THE EMPRESS JOSEPHINE,

First Wife of Napoleon I. Illustrated with Steel Portraits. •By J. T. Laurens, author of "Heroes and Patriots of the South." 12mo. cloth. Price, $1.00.

LIVES OF THE HEROES OF THE AMERICAN REVOLUTION.

Comprising the Lives of Washington and his Generals. The Declaration of Independence. The Constitution of the United States. The Inaugural, First Annual and Farewell Addresses of Washington. With Portraits. 12mo., cloth. Price $1.00

COLUMBA; A Tale of Corsica.

By Prosper Merimee. As a picture of Corsican life and manners, Columba is unequalled. In one handsome volume. Price $1.00

LIGHTS AND SHADOWS OF A PASTOR'S LIFE.

By S. H. ELLIOTT.   One volume, 12mo., cloth.   Price $1.00

"This is a well-written, highly instructive book.   It is a story of the life-teachings, and life-trials of a good man, whose great aim was to elevate, morally and intellectually, his fellow-men.   Like many of his nature and temperament, some of his views were Utopian.   But his successes and failures, with the causes of these, are painted with a masterly hand.   There is unusual strength and vitality in this volume."

THREE PER CENT. A MONTH;

OR, THE PERILS OF FAST LIVING.   A Warning to Young Men. By CHAS. BURDETT.   One volume, 12mo., cloth.   Price $1.00.

"The style of this book is direct and effective, particularly fitting the impression which such a story should make.   It is a very spirited and instructive tale, leaving a good impression both upon the reader's sensibilities and morals."

EVENINGS AT HOME;

OR, TALES FOR THE FIRESIDE.   By JANE C. CAMPBELL.   One volume, 12mo., cloth.   Price $1.00.

"We know of no book in the whole range of modern fictitious literature we would sooner select for a delightful and instructive companion."

RURAL LIFE;

OR, PROSE AND POETRY OF THE WOODS AND FIELDS.   By HARRY PENCILLER.   One volume, cloth, 12mo.   Price $1.00.

"Beautiful landscapes, family scenes and conversations, rural sketches of woods and vales, of the beauties of verdant fields and fragrant flowers, of the music of birds and running brooks, all described in an original and unstudied manner, which cannot fail to delight every one whose character is imbued with a love of nature."

JOYS AND SORROWS OF HOME;

AN AUTOBIOGRAPHY.   By ANNA LELAND.   One volume, 12mo., cloth.   Price $1.00

"This is one of the most beautiful domestic stories we have ever read, intensely interesting, with a natural flow and easiness which leads the reader imperceptibly on to the close, and then leaves a regret that the tale is done."

BEAUTY OF WOMAN'S FAITH;

A TALE OF SOUTHERN LIFE. One volume, 12mo., cloth. Price $1 00.

"This volume contains the story of a French Emigrant, who first escaped to England, and afterward settled on a plantation in Louisiana. It is charmingly told, and the strength and endurance of woman's faith well illustrated."

THE ORPHAN BOY;

OR, LIGHTS AND SHADOWS OF NORTHERN LIFE. By JEREMY LOUD. One volume, 12mo., cloth. Price $1.00.

"This is a work illustrating the passions and pleasures, the trials and triumphs of common life; it is well written and the interest is admirably sustained."

THE ORPHAN GIRLS;

A TALE OF LIFE IN THE SOUTH. By JAMES S. PEACOCK, M.D., of Mississippi. One volume, 12mo., cloth. Price $1.00.

"The style is fluent and unforced, the description of character well limned, and the pictures of scenery forcible and felicitous. There is a natural conveyance of incidents to the *dénouement*, and the reader closes the volume with an increased regard for the talent and spirit of the author."

NEW ENGLAND BOYS;

OR, THE THREE APPRENTICES. By A. L. STIMSON. One volume, 12mo., Cloth. Price $1 00.

"This is a very agreeable book, written in a dashing independent style. The incidents are numerous and striking, the characters life-like, and the plot sufficiently captivating to enchain the reader's attention to the end of the volume."

THE KING'S ADVOCATE;

OR, THE ADVENTURES OF A WITCH FINDER. One volume, 12mo., cloth. Price $1.00.

"This is a book so thoroughly excellent, so exalted in its character, so full of exquisite pictures of society, and manifesting so much genius, skill, and knowledge of human nature, that no one can possibly read it without admitting it to be, in every way, a noble book. The story, too, is one of stirring interest; and it either sweeps you along with its powerful spell, or beguiles you with its tenderness, pathos and geniality."

SIBYL MONROE; or, THE FORGER'S DAUGHTER.

By MARTHA RUSSELL.   One volume, 12mo., cloth.   Price $1.00.

"It is a spirited, charming story, full of adventure, friendship and love, with characters nicely drawn and carefully discriminated. The clear style and spirit with which the story is presented and the characters developed, will attract a large constituency to the perusal."

THE OPEN BIBLE;

As shown in the History of Christianity, from the time of our Saviour to the Present Day. By VINCENT W. MILLNER. With a view of the latest developments of Rome's hostility to the Bible, as exhibited in the Sandwich Islands, in Tuscany, in Ireland, France, &c., and an expose of the absurdities of the Immaculate Conception, and the Idolatrous Veneration of the Virgin Mary. By REV. JOSEPH F. BERG, D.D., author of "The Jesuits," "Church and State," &c., &c. Illustrated with numerous Engravings. 12mo., cloth, gilt back. Price $1.00.

LIFE OF CHRIST AND HIS APOSTLES.

By the REV. JOHN FLEETWOOD. With a History of the Jews, from the Earliest Period to the Present Time. Large 12mo., bound in Cloth. Illustrated. Price $1.00.
Octavo edition, with steel engravings. Turkey Antique, $3.50.

BUNYAN'S PILGRIM'S PROGRESS.

Including, "Grace abounding to the Chief of Sinners." Large 12mo., 500 pages. Cloth. Beautifully Illustrated. Price $1.00.
Octavo edition, with steel engravings. Turkey Antique, $3.50.

SCRIPTURE EMBLEMS AND ALLEGORIES.

Being a series of Emblematic Engravings, with explanations and religious reflections, designed to illustrate Divine Truth. By REV W. HOLMES. 12mo., cloth. Price $1.25.

EVANS' POPULAR SPEAKER,

LYCEUM AND SCHOOL EXHIBITION DECLAIMER.

Comprising a Treatise on Elocution and Gesture, with Illustrations, and a choice collection of pieces in Prose and Verse, and selec Dialogues, specially adapted for School and Lyceum Exhibitions, and Private Representations.   12mo., cloth.   Price $1.00.

PANORAMA OF THE OLD WORLD AND THE NEW;

Comprising a view of the present state of the Nations of the World, their Names, Customs and Peculiarities, and their Political, Moral, Social and Industrial Condition.   Interspersed with Historical Sketches and Anecdotes.   By WILLIAM PINNOCK, author of the Histories of England, Greece and Rome.   Enlarged, revised and embellished with several hundred Engravings, including twenty-four finely colored Plates, from designs by Croome, Devereux, and other distinguished artists.   In one vol. Octavo, over 600 pages, bound in embossed morocco, gilt back. Price $2.75.

THRILLING INCIDENTS IN AMERICAN HISTORY.

Being a selection of the most important and interesting events which have transpired since the discovery of America to the present time.   Compiled from the most approved authorities, new edition enlarged.   Splendidly illustrated, 12mo., cloth.   Price $1.00.

THE HOLY LAND, AND EGYPT, ARABIA PETRÆA, &c.

Travels in Egypt, Arabia Petræa, and the Holy Land.   By D. Millard.   A new and improved edition.   Illustrated. 12mo., cloth,   Price $1.00.

HUNTING SCENES IN THE WILDS OF AFRICA.

Comprising the Thrilling Adventures of Cumming, Harris, and other daring Hunters of Lions, Elephants, Giraffes, Buffaloes, and other Animals.   With Illustrations.   12mo., cloth.   Gilt back.   Price $1.00.

THE BATTLE FIELDS OF THE REVOLUTION.

Comprising descriptions of the Different Battles, Sieges, and other Events of the War of Independence. Interspersed with Characteristic Anecdotes. Illustrated with numerous Engravings, and a fine Mezzotint Frontispiece. By THOMAS Y. RHOADS. Large 12mo., cloth. Price $1.25.

PERILS AND PLEASURES OF A HUNTER'S LIFE.

With fine colored plates. Large 12mo., cloth. Price $1.25. From the table of contents we take the following as samples of the style and interest of the work :

Baiting for an Alligator—Morning among the Rocky Mountains—Encounter with Shoshonees—A Grizzly Bear—Fight and terrible result—Fire on the Mountains—Narrow Escape —The Beaver Region—Trapping Beaver—A Journey and Hunt through New Mexico—Start for South America—Hunting in the Forests of Brazil—Hunting on the Pampas—A Hunting Expedition into the interior of Africa—Chase of the Rhinoceros—Chase of an Elephant—The Roar of the Lion—Herds of Wild Elephants—Lions attacked by Bechuanas—Arrival in the Region of the Tiger and the Elephant—Our first Elephant Hunt in India—A Boa Con-trictor—A Tiger—A Lion—Terrible Conflict—Elephant Catching—Hunting the Tiger with Elephants—Crossing the Pyrenees—Encounter with a Bear—A Pigeon Hunt on the Ohio—A Wild Hog Hunt in Texas—Hunting the Black-tailed Deer.

THRILLING ADVENTURES AMONG THE INDIANS.

By JOHN FROST, LL.D. Comprising the most remarkable Personal Narratives of Events in the Early Indian Wars, as well as of Incidents in the recent Indian Hostilities in Mexico and Texas. Illustrated with over 300 engravings, from designs by W. Croome, and other distinguished artists. It contains over 500 pages. 12mo., cloth. Gilt back, $1.25.

PIONEER LIFE IN THE WEST.

Comprising the Adventures of Boone, Kenton, Brady, Clarke, the Whetzels, and others, in their Fierce Encounters with the Indians. With Illustrations, 12mo., cloth. Gilt back. Price $1.00.

McCULLOUGH'S TEXAN RANGERS.

The Scouting Expedition of McCullough's Texan Rangers, including Skirmishes with the Mexicans, and an accurate detail of the Storming of Monterey, &c., with Anecdotes, Incidents and Description of the Country, and Sketches of the lives of Hays, McCullough and Walker. By S. C. REID, JR., of Louisiana, late of the Texan Rangers. 12mo., cloth. Price $1.00.

THE DOOMED CHIEF.

OR, TWO HUNDRED YEARS AGO. A Narrative of the Earliest Border Warfare. By D. B. THOMPSON, author of "Gaut Gurley," &c. 12mo., cloth. $1.00.

HUNTING SPORTS IN THE WEST.

Containing Adventures of the most celebrated Hunters and Trappers of the West. Illustrated with new designs. 12mo., cloth. $1.00.

GAUT GURLEY;

OR, THE TRAPPERS OF UMBAGOG. A Tale of Border Life. By D. B. THOMPSON, author of "The Rangers; or, the Tory's Daughter," "Green Mountain Boys," &c. 12mo., cloth. Price $1 00.

THE RECOLLECTIONS OF A SOUTHERN MATRON.

By MRS. CAROLINE GILMAN, of South Carolina. 12mo., cloth. Price $1.00.

"This volume is one of those books which are read by all classes at all stages of life, with an interest which looses nothing by change or circumstances."

THE ENCHANTED BEAUTY.

AND OTHER TALES AND ESSAYS. By DR. WM. ELDER. 12mo., cloth. Price $1.00.

"This is a volume of beautiful and cogent essays, virtuous in motive, simple in expression, pertinent and admirable in logic, and glorious in conclusion and climax."

THE CHILD'S FAIRY BOOK.

By SPENCER W. CONE. Containing a choice collection of beautiful Fairy Tales. Illustrated with Ten Beautiful Engravings, Splendidly Colored. 12mo., cloth. Price $1 00.